SONG OF THE DEPTHS

SONG OF THE DEPTHS BOOK ONE
BONNIE L. PRICE

Editing

K.T. Hanna & Ivy Sherrard

First Edition
ISBNs

E-Book: 978-1-951235-03-1

Paperback: 978-1-951235-02-4

Hardback: 978-1-951235-04-8

TABLE OF CONTENTS

For my Alpha Floofs, *for kicking my ass into gear and putting up with all my ridiculous brain farts and phone typos.*

MORE BOOKS

CYCLES OF IMBALANCE UNIVERSE

SONG OF THE DEPTHS

A Why Choose Science Fantasy Adventure Series

Book 1 (Audio): Coming Soon

TBD: Book 2—Patreon for updates & AARCs.

OF ASTRAL AND UMBRAL

A Romantic Demon Fantasy Series

Book 1: Beneath the Mists

Book 2: Courting Balance

Book 3: Dancing with Darkness

TBD: Book 4 & 5—Patreon for updates & AARCs.

DECK OF SOULS

A Demon Fantasy GameLit Series

Book 1: Fateseal

Book 1 (Audio): Fateseal on Audible

TBD: Book 2—in editing stages as of September 2020.

FOREWORD

These images indicate a chapter's point of view.
Left: Main Character | Right: Third Person

Song of the Depths is a slow burn crossbreed of cyberpunk, science fantasy with elements of reverse harem & closed polyamorous fiction.

This series includes dark content, such as violence, interspecies slavery, and assault—none of which the main characters support.

Song of the Depths is an alien-centric series, meaning you may encounter culture and physiological quirks from some of the aliens which may make you uncomfortable. *They are not humans.*

Later installments will involve graphic, *consensual*, love scenes and other intimate acts. There may be LGBTQ+ pairings within the relationship group later in the series, such as MM or intersex individuals.

If you would like to know the definitions and meanings of the original language found in this series, you can follow along with the glossary found here:

https://bonnielprice.com/the-books/cycles-of-imbalance/song-of-the-depths/syldran-glossary/

Please e-mail me if you find any errors that managed to slip through the editing process. I will fix them immediately. You can contact me at:

bonnielprice.author@gmail.com

Alternatively, you can contact me on Discord:

https://discord.gg/5UwSSc2

CHAPTER ONE

Five years of living in isolation has a way of taking its toll on you. There's all the damn white everywhere, for one. But there's also the understanding that you're watched. Always. Make a wrong move? Become a tranquilizer pin cushion. System malfunctions? Tranquilizer. New recruits need to learn the buttons in the control center? More tranqs.

That was the only life I knew, aside from flashes and snippets of the event that had resulted in the Imperial military isolating me for study. The Resonance Incident, they called it. An alien species had fired a harmonic weapon at the city I lived in, reducing buildings to ash and the people to goo.

Except for me, and a few other survivors the researchers mentioned on occasion. Something about us was *different*. I wasn't sure what the others had gained from the experience, but I'd received elemental abilities; I could create and control both lightning and water. Doctor Abel had told me there were other, classified, abilities I'd shown during the Incident, but I hadn't consciously used them since then.

In surviving the Resonance Incident, we were reduced to a feral state. We attacked and killed the invading aliens, as well as any human responders.

People who could kill the aliens were valuable, valuable creatures; thus, we were pumped with sedatives and brought into isolation rooms to be studied.

There were just two little problems.

First, I had no memory from before the Incident. According to Doctor Abel's study, the same resonance that 'gifted' me with superhuman abilities had also stolen my past. He was hopeful that I would recover, but I didn't believe I would.

To combat the amnesia, I'd been permitted to have reading material, so I studied anything and everything they'd let me. Which, for the most part, constituted only ancient history from fallen human planets throughout the universe; I wasn't afforded much modern or present information. They had also allowed me some equipment in my cell to train both my body and my powers, but they were hesitant to allow me to spar with any of the guards.

The second problem was the issue of us 'going feral,' so to speak. Apparently the other survivors were struggling to remain themselves. Some remained stuck in their feral states, while others were all too easy to trigger.

In that state, we acted like wounded, cornered animals—hence the moniker. We lashed out with inhuman physical strength and speed, our powers, anything to destroy whatever threatened us or our territory. It was something I could *feel* within me when it wanted to surface. But by now, I was in control of my feral side. Mostly.

And so, I was up for review.

I ran my fingers over the printed piece of paper I'd been given, eyeing the instructions for conduct. Meeting military officials wasn't exactly on any list of activities I wanted to participate in, but I *did* want out of my damn cell.

"Subject Zero, place your hands on the table," a male voice ordered over the comm system. Once I had done so, he stated, "We're going to check you for weapons. Stay still."

Once the scans were complete, the doors hissed open and Doctor Abel strutted in with his hands linked behind his back, an apologetic smile on his face. "I apologize, Subject Zero. They do love their protocols. Are you ready to meet with Gideon and Zeke?"

"Ready enough." I stood when he motioned me to. "I think I've seen enough salutes to get it right."

"Good, good." Abel rubbed his hands together, his gaze flickering around the room as he led me into the hallway outside. "This way, this way. We will be meeting in the conference room near the mess hall."

The mess hall, at least, was a place I knew. As they'd begun loosening my leash, they'd started allowing me to eat some of my meals with the soldiers—most were scared of me, but there were a few who didn't care what I could do. So long as I, to use their words, 'remained on their side.'

The conference room was a little too large, in my opinion, and still just as white as the rest of the damned place. Inside, half a dozen guards awaited with two formally dressed men.

"Generals, this is Subject Zero." Abel introduced me and stepped aside. "She has yet to be briefed on the Resonance Project. If I may—"

"I don't recall giving you permission to remove her from her cell, Abel." The burlier of the two men furrowed his brow.

Sensing tensions rising, I spoke up. "Sir, if you would prefer to have this discussion in my cell, we can certainly return there."

They agreed, and with that, I was marched all the way back and locked inside the tiny room once more, with General Gideon, Abel, and the guards standing on the other side of the clear sliding doors. I had no idea where General Zeke had wandered off to—he'd received a call and stepped away to take it, telling us to go on without him.

"The Resonance Project focuses on utilizing survivors like you, people with inhuman power. We want to replicate it in our soldiers." Gideon's tone gave me the impression he thought he was wasting his time. "More importantly, we want you to kill more Syldrari. Any and every one you find. Those evil bastards must be destroyed for the good of the Empire."

"I'm supposed to just…what, take you at your word that the Syldrari are evil and it's fine for me to kill any and every one I see?" I scoffed at the man standing outside my cell. "You think the promise of freedom – if you can even call it that – is enough to make me another of the government's mindless pawns? I don't even know what a Syldrari *is*!"

"Asking the right questions." Doctor Abel nodded in approval before turning to look at the now-rather agitated general. "She doesn't remember anything from before the Incident, sir, and information has been kept sparse—as per your orders…"

I decided to keep my mouth shut and observe. Abel's 'I'm smarter than you all' attitude rubbed me the wrong way, but somehow Gideon irked me even more.

"Then let her go see the Syldrari sector herself." Gideon crossed his arms. "Once she understands the horrors of their kind, she'll be on our side."

"And if she isn't willing to kill every Syldrari she sees?"

Gideon frowned, then referenced his data pad. "You may negotiate her terms of service. If she remains unreasonable, we can always retire her. She's got an alright face, I'm sure you could find a buyer."

With that, the bastard walked off and I turned a glower on Doctor Abel, who raised his hands to placate me.

"They know they need you if they want to deal with the Syldrari.

He won't give up that easily." He slowly shook his head. "I'll be brief. There are two factions of Syldrari we are aware of: Those who live among us, and those who are responsible for the Resonance Incident that destroyed your home city of Grand Anldu and awakened your abilities.

"The higher-ups want all Syldrari off Creshe, as their factions are at war with one another. Our people often end up dragged into their conflicts, and even augmented humans don't stand a chance against Syldrari—trained or otherwise. The Syldrari are also suspected to be the cause of the increased crime rates throughout the Empire. You can't do anything about the other planets in this system, let alone the other systems under our control, but there are many Syldrari here on Creshe."

I crossed my arms. "And since I can do more than hold my own, these bastards want to use me to take care of their problems? That the gist of it?"

"Until we can discover a way to awaken more humans with abilities such as your own? Yes." The doctor released a heavy sigh. "And even then, they will insist that you train the new recruits. However, they're offering you more freedom if you cooperate. I know you don't want to spend your life in a cell or as some rich politician's pet, so what's holding you back?"

"I don't like the idea of mindlessly agreeing to serve as a weapon against the Syldrari. I'm hesitant to believe they are *all* criminals." I shrugged, shaking my head faintly. "Executing criminals, I can get behind. But I've read enough history while stuck in here to know that it's never a good thing when a government starts trying to purge an entire race or species."

Abel frowned. "Then your potential terms are…?"

"I'll only kill proven criminals—ones we have footage of, or ones I catch in the act. If they're merely suspects, I'll capture them alive or the military can send a different dog after them." I motioned loosely with one hand, smirking. "And if the government really wants me to hunt Syldrari, they can give me a good reason to believe they're all scum."

An unfamiliar man walked into view, escorted by the wayward General Zeke. Rather than a military or research uniform, he wore a sharp suit and looked clean-cut, with brunette hair combed straight back and piercing grey eyes framed by gold-rimmed glasses. Abel promptly bowed and moved out of the man's way.

"If it's proof you need, a visit to the Syldrari sector should suffice. However, you can't go looking like that. Abel, procure proper clothing for Subject Zero and arrange for her to visit the Syldrari sector. She should understand their villainy after that."

Who the hell…? I wondered, watching the new man. He had a particular presence to him, and every worker in the area bowed to him in greeting or before passing to continue their work.

"Y-yes sir." Abel bowed more deeply, wringing his shaking hands as the man strode past him and down another hall. He remained that way for a while before turning to check if the man was gone.

"Explain?" I sighed in exasperation.

"The Syldrari sector is where all the V'shir Syldrari in the Empire reside. The Empire makes certain their kind are segregated from the human population," Abel replied, his expression unreadable. "It will be a few weeks before everything is ready for you to visit there. Continue your training while I make arrangements. With any luck, some of the other Resonance victims will stabilize soon, too."

With that, he was off, muttering to himself.

A visit to the Syldrari sector so they can prove to me how terrible these aliens are? I wandered over to my bed and flopped down. *Right. So, they're expecting the Syldrari to try to do awful things to me on sight. Are these fears grounded in reason, or…? Well. I suppose it wouldn't hurt to work harder on my training, just in case.*

Several weeks passed before the Creshe Imperial Military and Doctor Abel got everything together for me to visit the capital city and the Syldrari sector. The capital, they told me, was named Lucdra for a previous imperator's consort. That seemed like a horrible way to name a city to me, right up there with getting the name of your lover tattooed somewhere on your body.

The Creshians, unfortunately, didn't find that particular observation amusing.

Pairs of monorail lines extended outward from the city in various directions, suspended hundreds of feet above the ground. The interplanetary shuttle tasked with transporting me to the Syldrari sector traveled along one of these sky roads, tracing high enough above it to avoid collision with the materials transports below.

Lucdra itself was an imposing and busy city, built from matte black and grey metals. Even from a distance, bright signs and holo-displays assaulted my vision, making it difficult to get a proper look at the city's architecture. From what little I could gather, the sectors were of various shapes and sizes, with large, cavernous gaps between them.

Upon reaching the city, my pilot followed an unseen road into a bustling, colorful sector filled with people of all kinds. In a way, humans seemed to be the least common species there—and the only one I could name on sight. Before I could linger further on the strange appearances of the general populace, the ship shot over one of the sector gaps. It had to be dozens of yards wide and only a few bridges spanned its vast width.

"We're here, miss." The pilot glanced over his shoulder. He had set the shuttle down on the very edge of the crevice, the craft turned in such a way that I could disembark facing the adjacent roads. "I'll hold position here until it's time for you to leave."

"Thanks," I offered, even if thankful wasn't exactly how I felt.

Stepping off the craft, the wind in the fissure-like sector gaps caught hold of me. I grimaced and hastily tucked my blue hair to one side, then double-checked my loose cargo pants for my wallet and communicator. With everything in order, I took off at a light jog to get out of the wind.

Once I'd reached one of the roads and found myself between buildings, I slowed to a walk and took in my surroundings.

Unlike the other sector we'd flown over, the Syldrari sector was not constructed of humanity's apparent staple of blocky, rectangular buildings. The architecture varied between spire and geometric buildings and was comprised of a type of dark, opalescent black and blue-green metals I had no name for. At least, I was fairly sure they were metal. Some of the buildings almost appeared to *breathe*—though I may have been imagining it.

Toward the center of the sector, towering above all other buildings in Lucdra, a winding spire with tiers of metal and glass twined high into the air: the Syldrari sector's crowning jewel. I couldn't determine the purpose of the building. If I wasn't mistaken, several of the large glass 'bubbles' were filled with water…and creatures. But from this distance, I couldn't be sure.

The Syldrari sector, from what Abel had told me these past few weeks, was generally treated like a slum by the humans despite its much cleaner, more vibrant appearance. The military didn't even bother patrolling since they couldn't do anything about Syldrari. For a so-called 'lawless zone,' it looked tidier than what I'd seen of the rest of the city, and there were civilians walking about.

Unless…those *were* the Syldrari?

Abel *had* warned me that they were shapeshifters, but…well, whatever.

The Creshe Empire was so confident in their plan that they hadn't even rigged me with any explosives or listening devices, although I was under the impression they could track me by my neurochip.

All I had was a wallet in one pocket and a communicator in the other. Plus, around my wrist was a band with a button I could push in case of emergency—and Abel'd had to argue pretty aggressively to make sure I'd gotten even that.

I strode into the sector, hands in my pockets and my ears trained for the faintest hint of trouble. The odd looks I received gave me the impression that, indeed, these weren't humans around me. It wasn't long before someone stopped me…but it didn't appear to be out of aggression.

"We don't get many humans in here." A slender woman with bright pink hair frowned at me. "You clearly not lost, and you dropped off by military. What can…we do for you?"

"I'm looking for a place to eat breakfast," I answered simply. When her confusion seemed to worsen, I smiled. "Where I come from, I've never heard of Syldrari. I wished to learn more, especially with what the Creshe military claims…"

"Bah! I see." The woman flapped a hand in annoyance. "Always speaking ill of Syldrari. Yes, yes, I seen before. But never with human of open mind. Why breakfast?"

I gave her a faint shrug. "Food is a good way to learn and share culture. I figured that since I don't believe the military about what will happen to me here, I'd see about getting some food since I haven't eaten today."

A man nearby interjected skeptically, a dangerous gleam in his eyes. "Honest human, huh? I suggest you keep that honesty going. The consequences for lying to a Syldrari are worse than if you leak information your masters don't want you to share."

"Oh? So that part of my briefing was true?"

"Breakfast, uh… This way!" The woman motioned me down a wider street.

The restaurant the woman led me to looked more like a cozy café or bar, but inside, a very different sight awaited me. None of the people there were in human disguise.

Each Syldrari had a different skin color—blues, pinks, reds, yellows, even the colors of stones. Just about every shade of every color humans couldn't be—and some they could. Their skin also appeared to have more depth of color than human skin, with much stronger hue gradation. Most striking, however, were the variegated bioluminescent patterns covering their bodies. While most of them glowed a steady cyan, some of the conversing men and women were shifting between various other colors while they spoke or argued.

The lambent sections in their hair matched whatever color their skin was glowing, and some of them had horns of varying lengths – or no horns at all. The horns ranged from mere stubs to a few inches in length—some glowing, some not. Most of those present, whether they were standing or sitting in the open-backed chairs, had tails. Their ears were pointed too, though some were longer than others, and rather than a smooth curve a few of them had a more fin-like appearance to their ear ridges. Yet, just as with the horns and tails, there appeared to be a wide variety.

Stranger still were their eyes. Where humans had just one round pupil, the Syldrari had either a slit or diamond-shaped pupil surrounded by multiple smaller triangular pupils.

"A human?" The blue-black-haired man behind the counter narrowed his eyes at me, then looked to the woman who had led me here.

His skin was slate blue, which was quite the complement to his eerie eyes. They were a sort of hazel, yet the colors were a faintly luminescent burgundy mixed with several shades of blue. The lightest blue seemed to have the most glow and reflected strangely when he turned his head. The luminescent patterns on what I could see of his skin reminded me of the mixture of stripes and spots I'd seen in illustrations of tiger sharks.

"I'll be blunt—the military wants to convince me that hunting and killing Syldrari is the righteous path. When I objected, they decided to send me here so that you could prove to me yourselves that I should hunt you." I crossed my arms. Several Syldrari growled, but none made a move toward me. "Since I think they're fucking idiots, I'm playing along before I go back to living out my life in my cell."

"Your cell?" The woman turned to look at me, wide-eyed. "You criminal?"

"No. I'm a survivor of the Resonance Incident. They're studying me to figure out how I lived." I turned to look at the man behind the counter—presumably the owner. He'd looked utterly disinterested right up until I'd mentioned my cell—now, he appeared contemplative. "I'll understand if you don't want to serve a human in your establishment."

"I can hear your stomach growling from here. Come here and sit down." He pointed at the empty stool across from him, his deep, commanding tone throwing me off guard. He was so…well, *pretty*; I hadn't quite expected that. Sassing him didn't seem like a smart idea with so many agitated Syldrari around, especially when I'd already chosen to be overly blunt, so I decided to obey. As I situated myself, he spoke again. "From what I've heard, most Resonance survivors don't require much convincing to hunt us. Though I've never heard of one being locked up in a cell, either."

"*Pfft*. Then they're traumatized, brainwashed imbeciles who think everyone is out to get them." I rolled my eyes. "If they spent more time reading and less time kissing ass, they'd realize it's only ever a group—not an entire species—who is 'bad.' As for why I live in a cage and they don't, it's simple. They were either further from the blast than I was or lost loved ones to it."

"What was this about returning to your cell?" the man asked as he placed a menu and a cup of steaming pink liquid in front of me.

I studied his expression for a moment, getting the feeling that the passerby's warning had been correct—honesty was the safer path when dealing with the Syldrari. Especially if I took into account the fact that I hadn't been attacked outright for my unorthodox introduction.

Sighing, I leaned back a bit in my seat. "Ah, that? I have two choices. Well, three if you stretch it. One, submit to their ridiculous demands and hunt-slash-kill every Syldrari and criminal I see. Two, live the rest of my life isolated in my cell, just like I have since the Incident. Three, the military says *fuck it* and either reprograms me to do as they want or sells me off to be some fat bastard's sex slave. I hear they've been going the latter route with survivors who aren't suitable for military work."

"...What? And you would choose the second of those options?" the woman who had escorted me exclaimed as she sat down beside me. She whacked me upside the head with her menu, then looked to the café owner. "Dumb! Stubborn-dumb!"

The man pressed his fingers to his temples. "*Honestly.* Just agree to hunt us. It's not as if humans have the means to kill us anyway."

I raised an eyebrow. "That's not quite the reaction I was expecting."

"One more human hunting us won't change anything." He shrugged and pointed to my cup. "It's a bit bitter for humans, usually. Let me know if you need sugar."

With that, he turned to speak in some other language with another customer. The woman beside me—whose glowing patterns were now a deep red-orange color—leaned over my arm to point at something on the menu.

"This very good. Hearty, traditional Syldrari breakfast. All nutrients needed for a day of hunting, and taste good too." She pointed to a massive picture of what looked like a main dish surrounded by at least thirteen side dishes, though her tone implied she was still fuming about my 'stubborn-dumb' approach. "Syldrari traditionally hunters and gatherers. Home planet have many, many dangerous beasts. Rulers and nobles only ever *iri*—er… woman—who good warriors. *Iri* is Syldran word for woman."

I nodded faintly, listening as she continued to make suggestions from the menu. While she did, I picked up my cup and gave it a tentative sniff, then a sip. "Oh, it's sweet."

That caused the owner to abruptly stop his conversation to give me an incredulous look.

"Ah! She have Syldrari tastes!" The woman giggled, nodding approvingly as her glow shifted from red-orange to a brighter green. She gave the owner a smug look. "See? Not all humans taste the same."

He pinched the bridge of his nose. "We need to work on your grammar."

"Hmmm, can I get an order of these two?" I pointed to the large meal, and then to a smaller one that appeared to consist of some manner of soup and more side dishes.

"...Do you *eat* like a Syldrari, too?" He eyed me disbelievingly. "You're a bit small to pack away that much food."

I pointed to his own sign behind him and gave him a smug grin. "I can take home what I can't eat."

"And our little jailbird has money?" he countered, just as smugly.

"Mmhmm, that I do." I reached for my wallet and pulled out the requisite amount of cash—and then some, placing it on the counter. "For the meal, for tolerating my presence, and for not having me shanked the moment you heard I have ties to the Creshe military."

Another customer laughed. "Heh. Not scared of us at all, is she?"

"The human military is way scarier than we are," another snorted.

"What sort of criminals does the military want you to pursue?" The owner took my money with a nod and then made a gesture toward the stove, which immediately fired to life. I leaned to my right to peer around his back, eyeing the stove—was that an ability of his, or did stoves have motion sensors?

"They were rather vague about that." I shrugged. "The gist was just…any, plus Syldrari. I'm under the impression they're looking for more manpower to patrol the city. They mentioned something about one in five citizens being victimized."

"You survived the Resonance, you said?" he murmured as he prepared ingredients. "That was an atrocity committed by Clan R'selkti, yes?"

"Mmhmm. They employed some kind of sound weapon. It leveled my home city—Grand Anldu—and turned most people into goo in an instant." I stretched back in my seat, crossing my legs at the ankles.

"And you…survived?" His tone belied his skepticism, for which I couldn't blame him. That part was still unclear to me, too. At least, to an extent.

I shrugged. "Not unscathed, mind you. I don't remember anything from before that day, and anyone who knew me is gone. We don't even know what my name was. Most of what I know is from being told—though I was shown some rather gruesome body-cam footage."

"Then…what do they call you?" The woman frowned.

"I'm just a number," I answered dryly.

"A number you can't divulge, I imagine." The man shook his head, then glanced over. "Finished your drink already? I'll get you another."

"Number? Numbers are not name." The woman clapped her hands together and smiled brightly. "Hmmm, call you Huntress!"

"I never agreed to—"

"You should. Sacrificing a chance at freedom—or a shard of it— would be foolish. I don't think there's any among us who would begrudge you for that choice." The man poured me a new cup of…tea? Whatever it was. "These are hard times for most people. Unless you're born into wealth, you will struggle in the Empire. If hunting Syldrari will grant you freedoms and comforts that would otherwise be denied you, then you should take your chance. Human lives are short. Ours are not. We will manage."

I raised an eyebrow. "Humans are that piddling of a threat, huh? So inconsequential a danger that you can afford to show compassion to a potential enemy?"

"Quite." A chilling smile spread across his face as he met my gaze. "Do you fear the dust under your bed?"

I let out a short laugh. "I get the point. Even so, morally—"

"Morals get you killed in this day and age—at least in the Creshe Empire. You might not know it yet, but you're in a fight for your own survival." The man made a dismissive motion. "If you cooperate with the military, at least you can hold on to part of yourself. If you disobey them, they'll turn you into someone else. We've seen what they do to enslave their own kind."

The military sends me here to get hurt, but instead I'm getting life advice. Oookay, then. I let out a small sigh and gave him a tired smile. "So, that blue stuff—it's some type of meat?"

"You can tell? Full of surprises, aren't you?" he remarked dryly. "You're an odd human. If you find some manner of middle ground with your superiors, you're welcome back anytime."

I'm…what? I blinked at his now-turned back in surprise.

"Well?" Abel asked as I disembarked from the shuttle a few hours later. "You don't look as though you've been harmed."

"The terms of my service are as follows: I will only kill criminals I catch in the act—Syldrari or otherwise. I will execute criminals if you can provide me with proof of their crimes, I'll hunt monsters, but I will not kill Syldrari just because they're Syldrari."

"Wha—" Abel looked nervously over at his superiors.

"Will you fight in a war if one breaks out?" General Gideon asked.

I nodded. "I was already assuming I'd be treated as a soldier, so yes."

"We will accept your terms," General Zeke stated. "You will be relocating to the Resonance Project Headquarters. Abel has assigned a specialized team there, and any others who join our cause will be resettled there as well. You will continue your training there—and begin training the new recruits to tame their feral states."

With that, the two generals headed deeper into the facility, muttering something about having other facets of the project to check up on.

Abel let out a relieved sigh and turned to look at me. "I'll introduce you to the head of the program when we arrive. Headquarters is in the city itself, to ensure the fastest response possible when threats are detected. The building is disguised as a civilian business, but the facilities we need are all there."

"Abel, the Syldrari…" I started.

"I would suggest keeping your opinions to yourself, Subject Zero." Abel raised his hands to stop me. "The last thing you want to do is give your superiors a reason to dispose of you."

I grimaced. "…Understood."

CHAPTER TWO

I carried a bag over one shoulder as I headed into the base of an imposing skyscraper. The building, constructed of dark metal and with no clear outer signs indicating its purpose, sat near the heart of Lucdra. From it, we could deploy to any assigned sector within minutes—or so they told me. I wasn't exactly clear on how that was possible, but I'd been assured that our transportation was easily capable of such a 'trivial task.'

Inside, Abel and our escort led me to an elevator which took us down some number of floors. When the doors opened, I was greeted by a sterile-looking entryway complete with a lounge and a single receptionist.

The receptionist looked up with a smile, pushing a lock of dirty blonde hair behind her ear. "Ah, Doctor Abel. Will you be staying to meet with the professor?"

"No, no. I'm afraid I must be leaving for other appointments.

See to it that Subject Zero finds her room and meets with him, though, will you?" Abel quickly dismissed the notion of staying as he backed toward the elevator.

"Subject Zero, is it?" The receptionist sighed and rose to her feet, shrugging as the elevator doors closed and carried Abel away. "Abel gets fidgety when he's around survivors like us. I may not have awakened to powers like you did, but he seems to think everyone who survived could go feral at any moment. With you being the only one we know of to have *truly* tamed that power…"

"The others are still being held in isolation?" I asked, following when she motioned for me to do so.

"Yep. All of them are being moved here, though. The bosses are confident that we can't get out even if we rampage." She shrugged again. "The professor is meeting with some of the other survivors right now. I'll introduce you."

She started to lead me toward a hallway, but before we could turn the corner, a handsome man with pewter hair rounded the corner. He wore a lab coat and stylish glasses, a distracted look in his vibrant blue eyes. With him were two other men, both wearing sweatpants and t-shirts.

"Ah, Sarah—" His gaze drifted past her to settle on me. "Oh? A new addition? Did I let time run away with me again?"

"Subject Zero, at your service," I stated dryly. *Really? Professor? Isn't he a bit young? He's gotta be just a few years older than me, at most. Maybe he just finished his degree in the last few years…?*

"That's a designation, not a name." The man sighed heavily, then turned to look at the two men he'd been chatting with. "'Subject Zero' is the woman I was telling you about. She will hopefully be able to teach you all to control your feral sides."

One of them glanced my way. "What should we call you?"

"I dunno. I'll come up with something eventually." I shrugged, turning my attention to the professor. "And what is your 'designation,' I wonder?"

"Zafir," he answered with an amused smile, offering me his hand. I decided to humor him and shook it. "We can dispense with the titles here, though either Doctor or Professor will suffice if you insist.

"My role isn't to study you under a microscope like Abel does. You can think of me more as your leader and counselor. As you are the only truly stable Resonance victim, you and I will be working closely with the others so they don't harm themselves or lash out. We can discuss your other purpose in my office. Sarah, if you would escort…" Zafir paused, clearly struggling with what to call me. "If you would escort her to my office after showing her to her room, it would be appreciated."

With that, we were off again, and Sarah led me through a maze of white hallways to a more posh, lived-in area of the underground complex. This room had a few sofas and chairs, a bookcase, and some scattered magazines. It looked more like a waiting room, but at least it wasn't all white walls and stainless steel.

"The professor is much nicer than Abel," Sarah informed me cheerfully, linking her hands behind her back. "He genuinely cares about our physical and mental well-being, beyond just keeping us alive for study. I heard this relocation effort is because he's in charge of the program now, and Abel was 'encouraged' to retire."

I raised an eyebrow, finding that a little strange. Following her over to a door, I spoke up. "Abel always seemed nice enough to me, so if this Zafir guy is even nicer, I'm not gonna complain."

"Abel? Nice? Good one." Sarah snorted as she unlocked the door. "Didn't take you for the humorous type… Or are you serious?"

"I'm serious."

"…Maybe you got preferential treatment?" she muttered mostly to herself, then shook her head. "Here, the keycard for your room. You should have time to change if you want before we go meet—"

I tossed my bag haphazardly into the room, closed the door, pocketed the keycard and looked at Sarah expectantly. "I don't have any clothes other than a nightgown and what I'm wearing. Personal belongings were against regulations. Apparently quite a few subjects used them as weapons against the guards, Abel, or to off themselves."

"Uh…right." Sarah made a face. "How was Abel *nice,* again?"

I decided to leave that one alone—she had a point. Instead, I followed her out of my room and down the hallway to a door at the end.

"Professor," Sarah called, knocking a rapid tattoo on the wood. "Are you in—"

"Excellent timing!" Zafir pulled the door open and gave us a bright, welcoming grin. "Sarah, I'm afraid you'll have to return to your post this time. We've sensitive matters to discuss."

"Oh…alright." She deflated a little. "I'll see you two at dinner!"

"Please tell me you're not going to be so unbearably cheerful all the time?" I sighed and looked in Zafir's direction as he perched in a comfortable-looking chair.

"Hardly. The project the government has assigned us to is a rather serious one. However, *they,*" he paused to motion to the door, "haven't been notified or briefed on the specifics due to their instability. As of this moment, you are the only functioning member of the team. It was extremely difficult to get everyone transferred here, let alone assigned to your team. Hopefully you'll be able to work with them."

I crossed my arms. "And you're aware of my terms?"

"Of course. I was happy to hear you questioned the offer instead of jumping at the opportunity. I don't have much faith that the others will do the same." He leaned back in his seat and removed his glasses, rubbing lightly at his temples, then motioned for me to sit across from him. "There is every possibility you will be deployed on solo missions now that you're here. Since you were smart enough to question why our government wishes to eradicate the Syldrari, I feel I should brief you on what has caused them to begin pushing."

I sat across from him, crossing one leg over the other. "I'm listening."

"We believe a Syldrari queen has emerged somewhere on this planet. There aren't many other explanations for the rise in conflict between the V'shir and the R'selkti." Zafir put his glasses back on and laced his fingers over his stomach. He tilted his head, his lips pursing as he thought, then a look of recognition spread across his face. "Ah—the R'selkti and the V'shir are different Syldrari clans. Their governmental structure is…much different than ours.

"The R'selkti have always been problematic, but the V'shir were always amiable toward humans. In fact, I heard that the Syldrari sector was originally funded and built by the Empire as a symbol of our alliance and trade agreement with them, so they would have a comfortable place to make use of for shore leave. Of course, that was centuries ago. As part of our arrangement, their Elders keep the other clans in order during their visits."

"A queen?" I stared at him blankly. "I didn't know what Syldrari even were until a few weeks ago. I'm afraid you're going to have to be more descriptive."

He gave me an unreadable look. "When we refer to Syldrari queens, we are not talking about a ruler—we are speaking of women born of prestigious bloodlines or who have immense amounts of power. Syldrari don't have royalty. 'Queen' is simply the closest translation.

"A queen's presence on a planet is said to cause all available…ah…breeding-capable individuals of the species to become more agitated and combative. It isn't dissimilar to how animals will react to pheromones during mating season, attempting to drive off other males.

"Without even recognizing what's happening, they will begin competing and fighting with each other to prove their worth—while those who are already of high status will begin scheming or sending their subordinates in search of the queen to find her first. From what I understand, a queen has never surfaced on our planet before. Only ever on their home world. Their casual competitions are like wars to us."

I raised an eyebrow at him. "So, if a queen really has emerged, the conflicts are going to keep getting worse. What makes you think one is here?"

"We interrogated a R'selkti deserter recently. She claimed that the males' behavior indicates as much and said the R'selkti leader has begun sending out scouts to scour the planet for information— something she has never done before." Zafir grimaced. "I won't ask you to kill misbehaving Syldrari on sight, but if you can break up their fights…"

"Keeping the peace and all that?" I shrugged, giving him a lopsided smile. "Yeah, I can do that."

"Good. Now, regarding your duties… Your file states that you have a battle suit already?" He rubbed his chin. "It also mentioned that you seem to be having rejection issues with your neurochip. We'll look into that."

I nodded. "Mmhmm. I uh…'conjured' it, for lack of a better term, when I first went feral. Now I can use it at will."

"Good. That will serve as better protection than anything the military could give you." He smiled, looking relieved. "You know how, once, diamond could only be cut by other diamonds? The material of your suit is much like that—it is the same as what the Syldrari soldiers wear. Though our understanding is limited, we have gleaned that it is tied to the abilities awakened by the Resonance. Abel hypothesized that the Syldrari use the resonance weapon on their own people to create soldiers, though I am inclined to disagree with his theory. Ah…though I suppose you aren't here for the science of it all.

"I would like to examine your suit and visor. If you don't mind, would you please 'conjure' them?"

"Sure." I concentrated briefly, summoning the lightweight bodysuit around myself.

The black material of the suit was patterned with tessellated triangles, with glowing cyan piping along certain sections. It was flexible like fabric, yet over years of testing we'd discovered that it could absorb the shock of both blunt and bladed weapons. Even the Creshe military's firearms hadn't managed to punch through it—though they'd given me some damn nasty bruises.

Across my eyes and nose sat a mask that looked opaque from the outside, constructed from black and dark grey metal. Along the center ran more of the cyan piping, following the contours of the mask. Inside was a screen with an overlay in some alien language—presumably Syldran.

"We'll need to modify your visor for communications before your first mission," Zafir remarked, rubbing his chin as he circled me. He took my arm gently in one hand, eyeing some of the connecting grooves running up my forearm. "Is it comfortable?"

"More comfortable than most clothes I've worn in the past five years, yes," I answered, receiving a blank stare in response. He looked like he was expecting me to say I was joking, but I wasn't.

"Right... Ahem. You can unsummon it for now. I'll mod your visor for you later." Zafir dropped my arm. He hesitated, seeming to search for words. "I would rather not refer to you as Subject Zero. Shall we work out your code name so that we have something to call you?"

"Code name?" I asked, taken aback by the sudden change in subject. Learning more wouldn't have bothered me at all, and I doubted I'd been making a sour face while he spoke.

Why stop? I was getting into it! Give me more information—about everything. I want to learn, damn it!

"Yes, on duty you will be using your code name." He nodded and took a step back before returning to his seat. "Ah! I almost forgot to tell you why I mentioned the queen. If we can find her and relocate her, we can avoid unnecessary bloodshed. As she is most likely in the Syldrari sector, I've secured clearance for you to continue your visits there so you can search. You will not want to use your code name there. Thankfully, you as you are now and you in your battle suit should be difficult to draw a connection between."

"Right..." I murmured, wracking my mind for interesting names. I'd come across more than a few while reading mythology from dead planets in my cell over the past several years. "Gehenna, Veles... Lethe? I don't know. The nature of my abilities hasn't been explored much."

"Lethe... Well, it's better than Subject Zero." He nodded, smiling. "We can go over your schedule after dinner. Tomorrow you'll have an opportunity to go into the city—if you need anything, I'll pay for it. The rest you can use your allowance for."

"Need? Well, about that..."

I explained to him how barebones my belongings were as we made our way to the mess hall.

"Honestly! It's no wonder most of the survivors loathe him!" Zafir exclaimed. "To be treated like samples on a petri dish, it's horrible... And you were threatened with becoming someone's toy as well? I've heard much the same from the other men and women in my care. I see it as my duty to make certain it doesn't come to that."

While Zafir continued to grumble on, I took a moment to collect my thoughts, reminding myself that, nice as he was, he was still involved with the Creshe Imperial Military.

Mmm…he's too easy to talk to. I should be careful.

I tugged at my new coat's sleeves absentmindedly as I made my way to the Syldrari sector. Shopping was exhausting and boring. Lunch sounded much more interesting, especially since I had a valid excuse to be there—one that wouldn't get me in trouble with the boss.

"Huh. Found a middle ground, did you?" The café owner didn't look terribly surprised to see me, unlike his customers. Today, however, I noticed they were all in human form. The owner himself was only recognizable by his voice.

"Mmhmm…" I glanced around again, then back at the owner. "Would it be rude of me to ask why you're all wearing human skin this time?"

"Not one for watching the news?" He scoffed and beckoned me over. "A new law was passed—all Syldrari must wear 'human skin,' as you put it, when outside our homes. As failing to do so is considered a crime, I imagine you'll be briefed on it soon enough."

"That is a stupid law." I rolled my eyes, taking a seat at the counter.

"It is supposedly to keep us from frightening you humans and damaging your poor, fragile sensibilities," he remarked dryly as he set a menu in front of me. "What would you like to drink?"

"*Frightening*? Huh, I thought you were rather pretty, myself," I muttered, scratching my head. "Drink? Mmm, surprise me? Let's see if you can find one I actually won't like."

"Pretty?" He laughed in disbelief.

I shrugged. "Maybe that's not the right word, but the point is, *frightening* isn't on my list of descriptors. Also, it occurs to me I didn't ask your name when I was here last."

"Call me Rel. You won't be able to pronounce my full name." 'Rel' gave me a smug smile, as if challenging me to go ahead and ask what his full name actually was.

"Well then, nice to officially meet you, Rel." I paused, tugging at my earlobe, and considered my options for introduction. "I guess I can't exactly tell you to call me Subject Number String or anything of the sort. Hmmm…"

"The humans didn't see fit to name you even after you agreed to work for them?" He shook his head in disbelief and set a glass filled with ice and neon green liquid in front of me. "Am I going to have to start suggesting names myself?"

"Can't find a name I like, either," I offered. "You're welcome to spit out suggestions. If you find one I like, I may just use it."

"Is that so? You're stuck?" He raised an eyebrow. "How about Elara?"

"Huh…that actually has a nice ring to it," I murmured, surprised by how swiftly he'd come up with the suggestion. "Sure, why not? Elara it is."

"Just like that? No arguments?" He stared at me.

"Nah, it's a pretty name. I like it." I paused, tilting my head. "I suppose I should ask what it means before I hop fully on board."

"The full word means *song of the depths* – or at least, that is the closest translation," he answered, looking pleased with himself. "Do you know what you want to order?"

"Mmm…" I glanced over the dishes I was struggling to decide between, then looked back to Rel with a small pout, half-expecting him to tease me again. "These five, please."

"Right. And carryout boxes again." He nodded, turning to work his magic—quite literally—at the stove. His human disguise wavered for a split second, showing a flash of his true skin color, but he regained control so quickly I wondered if I'd imagined it.

"So, am I right to think you wouldn't mind if I was able to do something about the criminals in this sector?" I inquired, earning a brief, piercing glance.

"There are…I believe you humans call them bad apples? Among any species. Here, we deal with human, Syldrari, and various other races causing trouble." Rel glanced over at a muscular man sitting off to my left, further down the counter. "Last night it was, what, Forseyl brawling in the streets?"

"And humans trying to sell both drugs and women the night before that," the big man answered with a grimace. Seeing my confusion, he added, "Without Imperial patrols, it falls to us to protect our own. With all the rumors the Empire spreads, all the city's trash is trying to move into our territory. But we have to be careful how we handle matters, too."

"Huh. I'll keep that in mind. I'd rather go after actual criminals, not people who are only protecting themselves and their loved ones." I stirred my drink briefly before taking a sip. Though I'd expected it to be sour due to the color, instead it was rather bitter. "Okay, *this* one is bitter, kind of like how tea is bitter. I'll take sugar for this—unless you have another suggestion?"

"The tea observation is quite accurate. Sugar and cream do nicely." Rel placed a creamer in front of me and gave me an odd look. "You know, most humans can't stand the smell here, let alone the taste of our fare."

"Huh. They're missing out." I shrugged dismissively. "How much cream?"

"Go a little at a time, everyone is different...*clearly*." He indicated me with a graceful motion and an amused smile. "Will we be seeing more of you?"

"Only when I'm off duty, most likely. I'm assigned to a different part of the city, though they said I may get sent near here sometimes depending on manpower limitations." It was half true, at least.

"Feel free to seek my counsel should you need it. If you are working outside the sector, you may meet Syldrari clans other than the V'shir. While most keep their heads down, Clans R'selkti and Gur'dral can be quite combative."

I hesitated, taking another sip of my drink before answering. "I appreciate it, but I have to admit I don't have the first idea how to tell the clans apart, and I get the feeling I won't be getting a briefing on it."

"Are you saying we all look alike?" a bulky man at a nearby table snarled.

"Hardly. Even if I were colorblind, I'd still be able to discern the tone variance in your skin colors," I answered dismissively. "My point was more that there appears to be even more variety within Syldrari than there is with humans. That, coupled with Resonance-induced memory loss… Well, we're lucky I'm even aware that spoken species other than humans exist."

"I'm afraid that, for a human, it will be difficult to discern by visual clues alone." Rel motioned to his eyes and their seven pupils. "While the different regions of our planet—and the clans within them—each have varying styles of dress, such things can be copied with ease. It is our binding pledges to our clan that you would need to look for, but human eyes cannot see such things. I mean no offense, but human eyes are much too...simple, in their construction."

"Even AR lenses or augmented eyes can't see them?" I asked, my curiosity piqued.

"No. It is not something humans seem to care about, and therefore they haven't bothered to create any technology that might allow them to see the appropriate spectrum." He gave me an apologetic look. "I likely shouldn't overload you with information when you're still suffering the aftereffects of a Resonance weapon. Your amnesia sounds rather extreme."

"Mmm, you're fine. I sort and process information fairly quickly." I took another sip of my drink before continuing. "So, basically, beyond knowing what the different clans' uniforms look like, it will have to be a guessing game because I have no way to verify which clan someone belongs to. And due to existing tensions, it's entirely possible that a R'selkti could pretend to be V'shir in order to redirect the government's attention."

"It is possible, but they are usually more direct. R'selkti like to show off their strength and prowess to...well, anyone who appears to know how to fight or hunt." He motioned at me briefly. "You carry yourself like someone with combat training, and I imagine you will be armed when on patrol. R'selkti *iri*—women—especially, rarely manage to find other females to challenge...and my, do they love to assert their superiority."

As I sipped my tea, I leaned forward against the counter, hoping to convey my genuine interest. "Speaking of, I've noticed there aren't many females in the sector. Is that due to them remaining on your home world, or is there yet another reason for me to loathe the Creshe Empire?"

Another man nearby snorted. He was sitting at the same table as the snappy man, but he wore what looked to be some manner of uniform. "Blunt, ain't she?"

"Men are much more common in our species than women," Rel offered with a brief shake of his head. "While it's true that the Empire enjoys taking slaves from all races, including your own, that is not why you see so few women among us."

"Most women are elevated in status and kept safe on our home planet. The more adventurous join our military or mercantile ventures," the big man added.

"Huh. Your home world sounds like an interesting place." I shifted in my seat, trying to get more comfortable. "See, this is the kind of stuff I wanted to learn. Culture. Not the 'boo hoo it's our planet and only we can be here' bullshit the higher-ups spew."

"Humans are selfish creatures." Rel paused, giving me that apologetic look again. "That is—"

"Rel. I ordered five meals and don't plan to share with anyone when I get back. I think selfish is an accurate word," I interrupted, glancing past him to the food in question. "Speaking of which, it looks like some of it is trying to run away."

Rel...flushed? blue and promptly turned his attention back to the stove to grab the runaway lobster-turtle-fish-kraken-thing.

"When do you have to leave? It may be best if I package these for you as soon as I finish them."

"Mmm, good question. Let's see..." I pulled out my communicator, finding that Zafir had indeed sent a message summoning me back. "Yeah, looks like that'd be best, if you don't mind. Apparently they need me to come back earlier than expected."

Rel levitated something over with his left hand, then poured it into a to-go cup. "A third drink for you to try, for the journey. Humans have only ever described it as tasting like shit, but to Syldrari...well, it is quite like how one might describe a milkshake."

I peered at the bright, multicolored liquid in suspicion. "Are human and Syldrari senses really so polarized?"

"I would have said unequivocally yes, before meeting you," he answered dryly, dropping a box of packets into the quickly filling bag of bundles. "Some Syldrari tea for you as well—on the house. The instructions are in our native tongue—but, essentially, prepare it as you would black tea."

"Well! Now you're just spoiling me!" I took the rather sizeable bag from him.

"I'll consider your continued patronage and understanding

payment enough," he informed me with a dismissive wave. "Off with you now, before you get yourself into trouble."

CHAPTER THREE

I gazed down at the repetitive, blocky buildings that made up Lucdra from high atop Resonance Project HQ, my body and eyes protected by my battle suit. Beneath my toes was open air, as I'd crept far enough up to the edge that I could look straight down the façade of the building.

While the blinking signs and advertisements all over the city afforded it color and life, the buildings themselves were disappointingly plain after the first few glances. It was as if someone had taken the same architecture and simply replicated it in different sizes everywhere but the Syldrari sector.

<Come back inside, please. We have much to discuss and I would really prefer if we didn't do it several hundred feet off the ground.> Zafir's voice came over the communicator inside my mask-visor-thing. His concerned face briefly appeared in my peripheral vision before he seemed to think twice about blocking my

line of sight.

Reluctantly, I made my way back inside and let the suit disappear. Zafir sighed in relief and ran his hand through his hair. "We need to discuss the status of the others, and how best to study your abilities. The reports are decidedly odd. Where would you like me to start?"

"What is it about my abilities that perplexes you?" I asked as we headed to the elevator.

Frowning, he elaborated. "The others have all exhibited elemental abilities thus far, but some of yours remain classified. One of the men emitted a cloud of what we thought was simply darkness, but we later realized it was more like plague or necrosis. From what I understand, you have multiple elemental capabilities, and…something else. I am wondering if it is also a more nuanced concept…"

He paused awkwardly as if he'd wanted to address me by name. Once we were in the elevator and heading down, I side-eyed him briefly before stating, "Elara. You can call me Elara."

"What—? You decided on a name already?" He turned toward me with wide eyes.

"Mmm, the Syldrari don't want to call me by a number either, and I wasn't planning to divulge my designation. They offered me a suggestion, and I liked it." I linked my hands behind my back as I carefully gauged Zafir's reaction.

He latched onto the topic with intense curiosity. "Elara…

I'm afraid my knowledge of the Syldran language systems isn't good. Did you find out what it means?"

"Mm. It's part of a word that means 'song of the depths.' The full word would be too difficult for humans to say, apparently." I eyed him as he started typing rapidly on his data pad. "What are you doing?"

"Inputting your name so our systems can update accordingly." He glanced over at me. "Did they say why they gave you that particular name?"

"Oh…no, I suppose I should have asked." I frowned. That was certainly a lapse in judgment. 'Elara' and its meaning had sounded so pretty that I hadn't stopped long enough to question it. For all I knew, it could have been an insult. "Maybe next time I'm in the area…"

"And you actually enjoy their food? I hear it's an acquired taste." Zafir grimaced.

"They're more surprised than you are," I mused. "I don't like *everything*. There were these vegetable things with one of the dishes that were too bitter, juicy, and slimy for me, but the rest of it is interesting in a good way. Unique, but balanced flavors. Helluvalot of seafood, I noticed."

"I hear they come from a planet which is nearly all ocean. No human has ever been to it, however, as it's quite far away and the atmosphere is toxic to us." He sighed wistfully. I tilted my head and listened, judging his tone. He didn't sound like he was lying, but it seemed odd that humans had apparently never visited the Syldran home world—or at least flown past or scanned it with long-range instruments. "I'd love to visit someday, but I can't swim. Our own oceans terrify me enough as it is, and if I can't breathe the air there… What are you snickering about?"

"You can handle mutated humans who might go berserk and kill everyone in the complex at any moment—yet you can't deal with the ocean?" I laughed in disbelief. Everything I'd read about Creshe's oceans implied they were peaceful, serene places. "I think your priorities may be a little broken."

He opened his mouth to say something but was promptly cut off as an alarm blared and the lights inside the elevator turned red, a synthetic voice echoing over the speakers.

<Alert: An unknown threat has appeared in Cascade Park. Requesting immediate combat and medical response teams.>

Zafir tapped away at his data pad, his expression growing more and more serious. When he found whatever he was looking for, mild surprise spread across his face. He recovered and turned to me, showing me the camera image on the data pad.

"Put your battle suit on—you're up. This isn't something our soldiers can handle. I'll connect to your visor and brief you on your way to Cascade Park—it's in the Syldrari sector. This monster shouldn't be on this planet."

A literal monster? I eyed the image. "That *thing* looks a lot bigger than me. What is it? Some sort of aetheromechanical chimeric monstrosity?"

"That is an apt description, yes." He pressed his fingers across a pattern of buttons. "Law-abiding Syldrari are unarmed civilians—otherwise they could take care of it on their own. That *thing* could decimate most of the sector if left unchecked, not to mention there's no telling how many of our people it will kill in the process."

"And since you think this suit is Syldrari war technology… I get it, I get it. Fine." I adjusted my gauntlets and stretched my fingers a few times. "Am I really *running* there?"

"There's a vehicle for you in the garage. It exits from a civilian docking center, so you can leave without raising suspicions about your military connections." Zafir resumed typing. "Our soldiers have instructions to wait until you've dealt with the beast before trying to 'arrest' you for illegal weaponry. They'll fail, and you'll hop on your skybike and return to headquarters. Since you haven't learned to drive yet, I've loaded the path into its programming. You just have to hold on."

"…Right." I sighed heavily and followed Zafir out of the elevator, struggling a little to keep up with his brisk pace. The vehicle he'd mentioned suited my tastes nicely, at least. On the ground, it was a sleek black motorcycle--though since he'd called it a *sky*bike, I assumed it could convert between the two. Either way, it looked appropriately badass. I straddled it and looked over at Zafir. "Recommendations on how to conduct myself?"

"Give no name other than your code name. You may speak, since the visor modulates your voice. If you recognize anyone, don't let it show. You need to keep your identity a secret if we're to follow our superiors' plans." He tapped a few buttons and the vehicle whirred to life, its wheels retracting as it began to float. "I'll brief you on the creature's weaknesses over the comms while you're in transit. Now, hold on and lean low."

Once I'd adjusted, he pressed a button and the skybike sped out of the garage and through a complex system of tunnels before exiting into the city. The contrasting dark metals and neon signs at night made visibility…well, shit, honestly.

Zafir spoke over the comms inside my mask as he fed an image into half the interior screen, allowing me to see the part-beast, part-machine creature I was supposed to fight. <The beast's spines and claws are an alien metal alloy. As far as our weaponry is concerned, it is indestructible. Its weaknesses are the parts which are still flesh and blood, as well as the tubing connecting its mechanical parts. The mechanical portions require aether, coolant, and lubricant to function properly, as the creature isn't smart enough to manage its own aether.>

Neither are humans, though… I decided to keep that thought to myself. He probably wouldn't appreciate it if I rubbed his lack of aetheric abilities in his face.

As he continued, various parts of the image lit up to indicate what he was referring to. <I can't tell if this one has a reinforced

skull, but a strike through the brain is usually the best way to stop them. If not the brain, its heart is here. You can only access it from between its ribs here and here. The brain is a safer bet. If you can destroy its cooling systems and make it angry, however…>

"I get the idea." I referenced the map. "Almost there."

<Good luck. Try to come back in one piece, alright?>

"Mmhmm," I muttered as the skybike came to a stop on one of the few flat rooftops in the Syldrari sector, just a few blocks away from the park. My best guess was that I was in part of the residential area, given the lack of shop signs and géneral activity.

Even from several blocks away, I immediately spotted the monstrosity prowling around. It was easily a full story in height. Not cool.

…Well, *kind of* cool.

Its fur, where it still had any, was a mottled grey with obsidian-colored skin beneath. The silvery mechanical parts looked shoddy, with rust around the edges in places. Glowing canisters – generators, perhaps – piped aetheric energy from its lower back to the other mechanical portions of its body.

Overall, it looked like a cross between a horse and an ape, but with teeth like a baboon. All but one of its legs had been replaced with mechanical versions.

I hopped off the bike and darted over the rooftops toward my destination, noting that there were quite a few Syldrari peering out at the monster from inside their homes. Some were even watching from the street.

There was blood all over the ground near the beast, as well as a lesser quantity of bright blue liquid. I dropped behind a cluster of nearby bushes while the creature's back was turned and waited for my instructions.

<Oh no…it killed a Syldrari, too?> Zafir's dismayed words caught me off guard. Was that the source of the blue liquid? <Kill it quickly, Lethe. It's already looking for more prey.>

Prey…that's a good word. I crept closer to the park, stalking the monster as it paced. Something stirred in me when I spotted a gash on its chest. It was already wounded. Someone had made my hunt *easier? How dare they.*

I shot out of the bushes at top speed and pulled a fist back, punching the gargantuan creature hard on the side of its jaw. It staggered, caught off guard, before roaring and swiping at me with its claws. I wove out of reach, calling aetheric lightning around my gauntlets and striking one of its flanks in the place where metal met flesh.

Nothing. The monster didn't appear to absorb the charge, but it certainly hadn't been enough to faze the damned thing.

Giddy at the prospect of a challenge, I continued pelting the monstrosity from different angles, testing each of the supposed weak points Zafir had suggested. It, in turn, grew angrier and angrier as it discovered its claws couldn't pierce my suit. The impacts hurt, of course, but its special alien alloy was no match for whatever my suit was made from.

"*Is that human using magic? It must be stolen magitech, right?*" I heard whispers nearby. Lovely. Spectators.

"Just *die* already!" I snarled, engulfing the entire beast in a sphere of water. It flailed, struggling to get to the surface.

Then a mildly sadistic idea ran through my mind. I didn't have a blade to pierce its brain with...but water was an *excellent* conductor. With a quick motion of my hand, I called a bolt of lightning down into the sphere, electrocuting the drowning monstrosity.

When its death throes were over, I let the sphere of water pop, drenching the immediate area and dropping the dead creature to the ground.

"Who—*what* are you?" a familiar voice demanded. I shifted to see the group of Syldrari onlookers, who, to their credit, were all maintaining their human disguises. At the forefront was Rel the café owner, who appeared to be struggling between gratitude, confusion, and fury. "That was—"

"—So cool!" A young woman pushed him out of her way. "Nasty thing came out of nowhere! A city is no place for monsters, no, no, no! Without weapons, we didn't know how we would hunt it... Mmm, mmm... Rel? Do you think this is R'selkti trickery?"

"It is possible." He glanced at her briefly before narrowing his eyes at me. "I believe I asked who you are."

"Lethe," I stated.

Rel's eyes unfocused slightly and his head tilted, as if processing what he'd just heard. I kept my expression passive, but internally I was wondering if the Syldrari were capable of hearing through the filters masking my voice.

"There she is! Capture her, use force if you have to!" a soldier's voice barked. I pivoted to see a squad of Creshe soldiers raising their rifles.

No thanks. I shifted my stance slightly. "I'll be going now."

"Wait—" Rel started, but I had no intention of staying and getting caught. I leapt into the air and landed on a balcony, quickly scaling my way up onto the roofs before making my way back to my skybike.

<Status report?> Zafir's face appeared in my peripheral vision as the bike shot off.

I grimaced when I realized I could taste blood in my mouth. "*Ngh.* Bruising. I either cracked something, or I bit my tongue or cheek during guarding. The suit is protected against rips and tears, but not blunt force."

<You were reckless!> he exclaimed in exasperation.

"Hunting is fun. I got carried away. It should be easier to manage as I adjust to the fact that I'm no longer caged." I winced, feeling an unfamiliar shooting pain through my temples.

<Report to the medical bay immediately when you get back.> Zafir tried to give me a warning glare, but it looked more

akin to concern.

"You said that thing killed a Syldrari?" I asked, feeling my head swim briefly.

He thankfully seemed to get the hint that conversation was needed to keep me awake and on the bike. <Ah, I see. Yes. The blue liquid around the site was Syldrari blood. The color of their bodily fluids is but one of many reasons so many humans find them disturbing. Their eyes, of course, are another.>

I groaned. "Did you have to say 'bodily fluids' like *that*?"

<Like what? It's common knowledge that all their— Ah.> He rubbed his chin. <Well, now you're aware. While yes, they are expert shapeshifters, their bodily fluids and their eyes are two things they can't disguise. As such, if you see a flustered or embarrassed Syldrari in human form, they will blush blue. They turn blue in the face when angry, as well, much like how we turn red. As for their eyes, their evolution is really quite extraordinary. The central pupil functions similarly to that of a human's, but the others capture different spectrums which are relayed to separate retinas within the eye. As such, they can see many more spectrums than us. I hear they can filter what they wish to see at will.>

"Kind of like selective hearing, but instead with sight?" I asked dryly.

<Yes! Something like that.> He laughed.

"What do you think about the woman who suggested that the monster was a R'selkti tactic?" I narrowed my eyes.

<…Hmmm. It makes me suspect her of having connections to the R'selkti. While they've been known to drop monsters into cities on other planets, they've never done so here, and no ship was sighted.> He shifted his attention to something I couldn't see, skimming it as he continued speaking. <Once you're well enough to go out without raising suspicions, I want you to go to the Syldrari sector to determine what the public opinion is. I'll arrange for you to go there on 'lunch break' from one of your 'patrols' so they don't grow suspicious of you.>

The skybike parked itself in the garage as a small team of medics, accompanied by Zafir, carefully approached me. I staggered off the bike, wincing as my muscles and bruises pulled.

"Ugh, that damn thing played *rough*… You know, no one told me I'd be fighting literal monsters."

"I wasn't aware either." Zafir motioned to the gurney. "Cooperate. I'd rather you not keel over and split your skull open out of some misplaced desire to maintain your pride."

"Blegh." I stuck my tongue out at him but did as he suggested. "I'm starving after all that."

He laughed and patted my head. "You did well, Elara. I'll have food sent to your rooms while the medics take care of you."

I blinked after him as he walked away, more than a little startled by the praise. So much so that I didn't even argue when the medics asked me to lay back on the gurney. I honestly wasn't sure what had thrown me off more—the praise, or him calling me by my new name.

CHAPTER FOUR

Fuck, my everything hurts. I rubbed the back of my neck as I made my way to the mess hall. Zafir had left a message for me the previous night, reminding me that he wanted me to be a 'role model' for the other survivors. Apparently, that meant being social and joining them for breakfast instead of hiding away in my room. Yaaay. I would have preferred to stay in and read.

"Morning, Elara." Zafir greeted me with a smile when he spotted me. "I must say, I expected you to look like you'd been in a train wreck."

"Close enough." I shrugged, walking over to his table when he beckoned me. Sarah, another woman I didn't recognize, and three groggy-looking men were already there.

"You made the news already." Zafir motioned to a nearby screen. The news channel in question was playing clips of me fighting the monster, as well as my escape up the side of the building. "The military will continue pretending they want to arrest you for a while longer, while we expect media outlets and the public to lean on them to allow you to keep doing what you do."

"No word on where the monster came from?" I frowned, turning fully to watch the clips.

"The surveillance footage has been tampered with. It's merely an empty park, then suddenly the monster is there," he answered. "From all angles. We tried to question the Syldrari, but they're being understandably stubborn. They are quite angry about the military pointing guns at you and are therefore refusing to cooperate."

"Mm..." I half-mumbled to myself, examining the footage as it panned over the crowd of Syldrari onlookers.

"What is it?"

I glanced back at Zafir. "They're all out of human disguise. Didn't they get into trouble?"

"Ah, no. I advised the higher-ups to make an exception, as this was clearly a shocking and traumatizing experience for all involved." He adopted an obnoxiously formal tone. "It would behoove us to appear lenient, lest our citizens think us merciless monsters. If we show pity to the Syldrari, it will make them look all the worse when they inevitably turn on us."

"Speak like that again and I'll do to you what I did to the beast." I shot him a cold smile before taking a seat across from him at the table.

"It may be disgusting, but it works wonders with our bosses," he countered with a charming smile. "If I spoke without a filter the way you do, *I* would be shipped off to the nearest brothel and all of you would be stressing over who your new caretaker might be."

"...Yeah, let him keep the filter." Sarah grimaced.

"Zafir in a brothel?" I murmured thoughtfully. "Huh. Can't say I can picture that..."

"One of life's small mercies," he groaned, pinching the bridge of his nose. "Let's *not* contemplate how they would have me reprogrammed, please?"

That wasn't exactly what I was thinking...but that's interesting too... I kept the thought to myself, for his sake.

"He might look cute in a dress, though," the girl I didn't know said in a surprisingly soft voice.

"*Anyway.*" Zafir shot her an unamused look. "Formal introductions are in order. Diana, Calder, Nikolai, Maelor, this is Elara—code name Lethe. She will be giving you your combat training, as well as teaching you how to control your ferals."

"Because the government wants us to be able to do...that?" Diana glanced at the TV, then at Zafir. "There must be more to it."

"That information is classified." Zafir raised a hand to ward off further questions. "Your options will be presented to you once you complete your training and can control the feral. It is my duty to give you a safe place to work on both."

Is it now? I wondered, eyeing him briefly before I turned my attention back to the TV. "When am I going on patrol?"

"After breakfast. The uniform will cover your bruises." Zafir handed me a plate. "There were things I wanted to discuss, but it can wait until our briefing tonight."

I half-smiled. "Assuming there are no more interruptions?"

"A *briefing*, huh?" Sarah raised an eyebrow.

"What about our training?" Calder interjected, a fierce look in his eyes. "You can't just introduce her as this badass and then not give us any time with her!"

"Your training begins tomorrow," Zafir answered in a placating tone. "Ideally, she needs more time to heal after the beating she took last night. The damage reports were rather concerning It is a good thing we acquired healing technology from some of the more friendly alien species."

I snorted. "'Friendly' or 'susceptible to manipulation'?"

"Both." He shook his head, then gave me an amused smile. "I'm not your enemy, you know."

"For now." I crossed my arms. "It's not anything personal. I'm just naturally cautious, and I think you already know what's put me further on edge."

"Indeed." He relaxed back in his seat, smiling. "I take no offense. I appreciate your questioning nature. It's refreshing after coming from a workplace where everyone mindlessly obeys their superiors."

Maelor shot to his feet and slammed his hands onto the

table. "Are you saying you're superior to us?!"

"He's our *boss*. Synonym: superior." I gave the fiery man an agitated look. "Flip the waffles onto the floor and I'll strangle you with your own intestines."

"Y-yes ma'am, sorry ma'am." He promptly sat back down, turning red to the tips of his ears.

"Now then, the rest of you will spend the day—" Zafir was cut off as the door to the mess hall slammed open and a woman rushed in, looking panicked.

"Sir! We have a problem related to last night's incident! A big one!" She frantically waved him over, then spotted me. "You! You should come too, it's seriously bad, bad, bad! Oh, uh, name's Amara, by the way. *Come on!*"

The spastic woman bounced impatiently on the balls of her feet as she looked between us.

"You may bring your waffles." Zafir shot me a smile and patted my head as he walked past me.

...That obvious, huh? I scooped up my plate and a drink, then followed Zafir and Amara through several corridors and into a room full of security screens and numerous other computers.

"What's the problem, Amara?" Zafir's voice took on a surprisingly smooth, soothing quality. In an instant, the woman calmed down, if only a little. If she'd been running at a ten before, she was now a six.

"Right. So, not all the cameras in Cascade Park were tampered with." Amara sat down and swiveled her chair to begin navigating through the menus on the screen. "There were hidden cameras scattered around by someone not affiliated with either the military or the media, and they're selling the footage of how the monster got there. I snatched it up before anyone else could, since they were selling it on a supposedly exclusive license. You guys need to see this. Seriously. I don't know what we should do about it."

Zafir released a faint sigh when Amara handed him what I assumed to be a receipt. I doubted the footage had come cheap.

Amara hit a button on her keyboard and a video feed of three Imperial soldiers walking into the park sprung to life on the screen. After scouring the area and picking a clearing, the man who appeared to be in the lead pulled out a device and pressed a button. Over the next several seconds, the monster I'd fought materialized fully, clearly having been transported from elsewhere.

The creature showed no reaction at first, but then the soldiers began antagonizing it, prodding it into a rampage. It chased them throughout the park and eventually off-camera. The screaming and crunching a short while later made it clear what had happened, and then the beast shambled back to its summoning area.

"What..." Zafir grasped the back of Amara's chair to steady himself. "The military? But...if they were planning such an operation, I should have been informed."

"Go back to the beast chasing them. One of the men slid close to the camera. Freeze with his face in frame, if you can," I ordered, and Amara swiftly did as she was told. I'd thought something was off about their body language; it hadn't seemed quite right.

A freeze-frame of one of their terrified faces showed me why. Those eyes didn't lie.

"A Syldrari...?" Zafir breathed. "Syldrari dressing up as Imperial soldiers and attacking their own kind? Are they attempting to start a war? The R'selkti have never gone this far..."

The R'selkti, huh... I frowned, thinking back on what I'd learned of the Syldrari thus far. "We can't be sure it's the R'selkti unless we have a Syldrari confirm which tribe those men are aligned with. From what I understand, they have some form of official bond to their clan that is invisible to the human eye."

"Then go see if your friends at the café can identify them." Zafir turned to narrow his eyes at me. "Amara may have broken the budget acquiring this footage, but the Syldrari need to know it was their own who attacked them. We can't guarantee this footage won't be sold to other buyers.

"Worst case, the Syldrari give us no helpful information or can't help. Best case, they may handle the problem for us."

"M'kay, I'll make a copy real quick that she can take to have analyzed," Amara declared as she began typing.

"Really? You're going to let me show them this?" I raised an eyebrow at Zafir. "What happened to the whole 'Syldrari are our enemies' thing?"

"I have my own thoughts on the matter." He gave me a mysterious smile. "*My* priority is reducing the overall number of crimes for citizens to fall victim to, and the people in the Syldrari sector are still citizens."

"Uh huh…" I gave him an unimpressed look. "What am I supposed to use as a cover story, exactly? If I'm skipping patrol and going straight to asking a Syldrari for help…"

Zafir stroked his chin. "Avoid questions regarding 'Lethe.' You can vaguely suggest she might be an unknown Resonance Incident survivor, if you must. Say that your bosses picked you because you already have connections in the sector. That we felt it would be ill-advised to send an unfamiliar soldier when tensions are already high."

With that, Amara handed me a copy of the footage, I got dressed in a uniform suitable for a patrolling soldier, and Zafir called a craft to take me to the Syldrari sector.

I kept my helmet off so people could recognize me, and the lack of a weapon seemed to put them further at ease. Most of them were still fairly standoffish, but they seemed less likely to confront me thanks to my prior visits.

"Well, if it isn't my favorite human—and this time in uniform." Rel cocked his head. "A bit early for lunch, isn't it?"

"I was hoping to have a word with you, privately, but I can wait for you to finish those orders." I glanced at the stove, then back to him. "Might be lunchtime by the time we're done."

Someone cleared their throat, and I looked over to see a heavily bruised man. He sighed deeply before speaking up. "This have something to do with that weird human who killed that damned monster last night? It's been rough. I'm a R'selkti deserter, you see. Some folks in the sector have the idea that it's the R'selkti's fault, the beast showin' up like that..."

"A deserter, huh?" I crossed my arms defensively. "I'm afraid I may not be the most open when it comes to accepting R'selkti, former or otherwise, but...I'll make an attempt."

"Ah, you're the Resonance survivor Rel was talking about?" The man wilted, his gaze downcast. "It was after the attack that I left. The young master killed his father, took over the clan, and had the weapon destroyed, but—"

"Wait, what?" I demanded, turning to face him fully. "There's been seven other incidents since the first! Are you saying—"

"What? We've only ever heard of the one." His attention snapped upward, eyes widening, then he shook his head. "Clan R'selkti abandoned that project when the young master took over! His focus has been on finding the queen, not—"

The entire café went silent as the man clamped both hands over his mouth. I raised an eyebrow—they really hadn't been aware? *Well, they sure are now. My job just got more difficult, didn't it?*

"The what? I wasn't aware Syldrari had royalty…" I did my best to play dumb without telling an outright lie.

"*A queen?*" The whispers started.

"*Here?*"

"*On this planet? She'll need to be found quickly…*"

"Dyorsol, I suggest reporting to the Elders with what you know. They will be able to offer you protection as well," Rel stated calmly, turning to glance in my direction. "'Queen' is the closest translation into your tongue, but it is not an indication of royalty. It is a personal matter for the Syldrari, so I hope you can forgive me if I don't elaborate."

"Of course." I nodded. "My job is to keep the peace, not pry."

"You said you wished to talk privately?" He took off his apron and hung it up, then motioned for me to follow him. "I live upstairs. We can speak there."

"Mhm." I followed him up three flights of steps, keeping my mouth firmly shut. I'd never noticed since he was always behind the counter, but he had a *really* nice ass and legs.

"Do you mind if I shift back?" He paused at a door, his skin and hair already halfway between human and his natural Syldrari coloration.

"Not at all. I'm actually more comfortable when you're *not* using a human disguise." I shook my head, closing the door behind us as we walked into his living room. "Now, as for—"

I fell silent as he disappeared, reappearing behind me with a dagger to my throat. Despite the weapon, I didn't sense any malicious intent from him. Briefly, I wondered if I should act more panicked, but it was a little late for that.

"You expect me to believe you're not here for some nefarious reason?" he asked quietly, the eerie calm of his voice making my skin prickle into goosebumps.

"I don't expect you to trust me, but my superiors and I are trusting *you* with black market footage we acquired of the events in Cascade Park last night." I reached into my pocket and pulled out the disc.

"What..." The dagger disappeared and he snatched the disc from my hand, giving me a brief, apologetic look. "Is that Lethe woman tied to the military?"

"We think she might be a Resonance survivor, but after what that man downstairs said..." I crossed my arms. "All patrols have been told to keep an eye out for her and arrest her on sight for illegal weapons usage. I told them they're crazy if they think we'll be able to arrest someone capable of what she did."

Rel frowned more deeply. "You said this is black market footage? What happened to the military cameras?"

I grimaced. "All military cameras in the vicinity were tampered with. On our official footage, the beast just appears out of thin air, as does the blood in the area. We're estimating three humans and a single Syldrari based on the amount of blood, but not enough was left in the beast's stomach to be sure. It converted most of what it ate into energy before it died."

"*Tch*, as they do..." he muttered with distaste. "Some species can't help but tamper with the natural order..."

"Indeed. Why wait for evolution when we can turn to experimentation and augmentation?" I let out a heavy sigh, then decided to continue on to the topic that really needed to be discussed. "If you don't have a secure computer, I brought—"

"Sit. I'll get you a drink." He made a dismissive motion in the direction of the sofa and headed into some other part of his abode.

With no other viable option other than to obey, I perched on the sofa and crossed my legs. When Rel returned, he was carrying not only the promised drink, but also a jar of what looked like rock candy in the shape of stars.

He handed me the refreshments, then sat down at a nearby desk. "What am I meant to look for in this footage? It's rather odd for the military to seek Syldrari assistance."

"Well...we're hoping you can identify their clan bonds via the camera footage."

"Clan bonds..." He looked back at me, his eyes widening. "That would depend on the cameras used."

"Well, this footage is suspiciously clear for supposed 'hidden cameras,' so I'm hopeful." I twisted the top off the candy jar.

"Regardless of which clan did this, it's bad news."

Rel fell silent, aside from an occasional hiss and what I guessed to be a few Syldran curses. He watched the footage several times before retrieving the disc and plopping down next to me on the sofa. He held it out to me, and when I shook my head, he placed it on the table in front of us.

"'Bad news' is an understatement." Rel slumped back in his seat. "They were from lesser clans, but all were former R'selkti—the shadow of their old allegiance still hangs over them, so they would have only recently changed affiliation. It is difficult to say whether it *isn't* the R'selkti pulling the strings, especially if they are searching for a queen, but it is impossible to say for certain."

"Why would a queen make it more reasonable to assume they're behind it?" I asked with a frown. "Is a queen not something to protect?"

"Clan R'selkti believes that bloodshed will please a queen and earn them her favor. As there is nothing appropriate on this planet to hunt, they seek to incite conflict." He rubbed the back of his neck, his expression unreadable. "Every queen is different. Some demand blood, some pleasure, but others wish for more simple things—such as a haven or protectors. They are almost divine in their whims."

"I see. So, the R'selkti are dangerous in their devotion."

"We all are. No matter the clan, queens are sacred. With all the stories and legends...every Syldrari grows up dreaming of being the one to discover a queen and become her friend and/or consort. It is the one consistent thing between all bloodlines and ranks."

"Hmmm... I see how that could be problematic." I frowned, considering. "Countless clans will be scouring the planet in search of one woman who, if they find and ally with her, will bring them instant fame, power, and honor. Right?"

"Yes. And the smaller clans may be especially desperate." He nodded. "The issue is that there are only so many places on your planet where a queen could be hiding. The Syldrari sector, a handful of research outposts... If she isn't in any of those places, she will already be on one of the docked or orbiting ships."

"Mmm...and with Resonance Incidents continuing to happen..." I muttered.

"You said there have been seven others?" he asked gently.

"Mhm. Most of the survivors come from those, from what I understand." I nodded and took a sip of my rather too-sweet drink. "If that deserter is telling the truth and the R'selkti destroyed their resonance weapon, then either someone is attempting to frame them...or the Imperial military is further along in their technological development than any of us were aware of. Or both?"

"Tell me...do you know this Lethe person?" Rel inquired, shifting in his seat so he was partially turned toward me.

"I'm under orders to neither confirm nor deny such queries." I glanced at him sideways, watching his lips pull into an amused smile.

He motioned toward me with one hand. "A strange, magic-wielding human appears out of nowhere to save the poor, poor Syldrari from a monster attack—suspiciously soon after an odd human begins befriending the Syldrari. The Imperial military attempts to chase and capture the woman for illegal weapon usage.

"Now, with slight modification, that black market footage could show mere human soldiers transporting the monster—thereby framing that same military and likely starting a war.

"But the most suspicious part of it all remains the *magic-wielding human*. Your kind has no natural magical ability, and even with magitech, feats like what I witnessed last night are simply unheard of from humans."

"That's why we think she must be a Resonance survivor, because some of the quarantined survivors exhibited elemental abilities," I pointed out as he continued to peer at me intently. "Some of us seem to be lucky to have survived at all, but—"

"If you run into Lethe, you can relay my appreciation to her," he interrupted pointedly, rising to his feet. "For now, I'm afraid I should be getting back to work. Intriguing as your company is, I do have customers waiting for me."

I eyed him with suspicion as I also stood. "What makes you think I'll run into her?"

"I think you know why." He chuckled and stopped me from placing the jar of candy back down. "Keep it. Perhaps some of your colleagues will find it to be an interesting treat as well."

"Uh…thanks? But who says I'm going to share?" I peered up at him, clutching the jar. *I know why he thinks I'll run into Lethe? What?*

"If you eat them all yourself, you're liable to get sick," he warned.

"Not if I spread it out over time," I countered as we left his apartment. Then a problem occurred to me and I sighed. "You should probably shift before we get downstairs, though, for both our sakes."

"Hmm? Oh." He grimaced. "You are certainly right about that. A soldier letting a Syldrari get away with wearing his true form in public…yes, I do get the impression that could be even worse for you than it would be for me. Will you be staying for lunch?"

"Mhm. My patrols were canceled in favor of sending me to show you *that*. They gave me leave to have lunch before coming back, though I was warned not to dawdle."

He nodded understandingly. "I'll make your lunch to go, then. Mind if I surprise you this time?"

"Sure?" I asked, and he grinned.

"Excellent. I think you will enjoy this immensely." He cracked his knuckles as he headed behind the counter.

It wasn't too long of a wait before I had my lunch in hand, so I said my goodbyes and before I knew it I was on my way out of the Syldrari sector. It wasn't until I was sitting in the craft speeding back to headquarters that it finally hit me.

…Shit. Syldrari eyesight let him see something about 'Lethe' that links her to me, didn't it? I gnawed nervously on my lower lip. I wasn't sure how to pursue that line of thought, especially when I didn't even know all the spectrums Syldrari could see. There were only so many ways I could believably blow off similarities as a coincidence. Fuck.

Or…was he bluffing to try to get an answer out of me? After all, he didn't say or ask much of anything aside from telling me to relay his appreciation…

"Ma'am, we've arrived." Someone coughed, startling me out of my reverie. How long had we been sitting at HQ? "Better get that food in you fast if you're spacin' out like that. Er…that *is* food, right?"

"Sorry about that—and thanks for the lift. And yes, it's food. It's surprisingly good." I hurried off the craft and into HQ, making my way straight to the elevator and down to the basement levels where we all lived. I needed to figure out how much to filter out of my report to Zafir—and quickly.

CHAPTER FIVE

"What's going on?" I inquired as I walked into the lounge. Zafir, Sarah, Diana, Amara, Calder, Nikolai, and Maelor were all crowded around the television.

"Some reporters are going around the Syldrari sector and interviewing people live," Sarah answered, glancing back at me with a worried expression. "We don't know how, but they got permission to let the Syldrari drop their disguises, too!"

"Is it true there's an Imperial soldier who has been coming to this sector lately?" A female reporter's voice drifted to me as I drew closer. *"Don't you find that strange?"*

"Strange? It's not that unusual. There are humans coming and going all the time, like yourselves," a familiar voice answered.

My suspicions were confirmed when I walked around Sarah and got a good look at the screen.

Oh man...those pants are doing things to me. I crossed my arms over my stomach. Rel was wearing tight black leather pants and a loose white tank top. Simple, but effective enough. His blue-grey skin glimmered faintly under the camera lights, though the crew's lighting couldn't compete with the luminous sections in his blue-black hair. "They're interviewing *Rel*? Do we think someone's been following me?"

"And is it true this soldier has been dining at your establishment?" the reporter prompted. *"I thought humans couldn't eat Syldrari fare?"*

"It is rare, yes, but not unheard of." Rel answered the question with such a charming smile that the reporter *and* my fellow viewers seemed a little taken aback. *"Our differing palates are an evolutionary nuance, certainly, but it isn't unusual for those who have lived by the sea to have similar tastes to Syldrari."*

"Syldrari are so odd," Diana murmured softly. "They almost sound like they're singing when they talk. Then there's how he looks…"

I glanced over at her. "Hmm? What's wrong with how he looks?"

Diana shook her head quickly. "Nothing is wrong, it's just so…*strange*. I don't understand why they look so different from us."

"Odd? I dunno, I think he's pretty— You know what? Never mind." I decided to stop that train of thought there. They didn't need to know that I found Rel attractive, or the kinds of places my brain was going with him in those pants.

"Pretty?" Zafir asked dubiously.

I sighed and pressed my fingers to my temples. "That wasn't the end of the sentence. I was going to say he's pretty handsome, though I guess 'pretty' works, too. Especially if you consider the other alien species we have wandering around in the city. Syldrari may actually come the closest to looking like us—and even a lot of humans don't really look human anymore."

"It may be the similarities that put people on edge," Zafir offered, rubbing his chin. "Some humans experience the feeling of 'Uncanny Valley' when they meet other species who look similar to us but *aren't* us. With some, the more you look, the more they look like us. It is the opposite with Syldrari. Their more aquatic evolutionary path and likely different origins have made them *more* unlike us."

"You think he's *pretty?*" Sarah peered at me doubtfully.

I tilted my head slightly. "You don't think all the glowy shiny stuff is pretty?"

She quickly held up her hands. "I mean, it is, and it's a really pretty shade of cyan, but—"

"Ahhh, I see," Zafir remarked, glancing my way. "Due to your loss of memory, you haven't been trained to see inhuman species as grotesque. Our colleagues here are likely too well-trained to admit that they find a Syldrari, for example, attractive."

…Yeah, let's go with that. I smirked. "If being untrained means I

have a more open mind and can enjoy more things, I don't mind."

"*—think Lethe and this soldier girl may be the same person?*" The reporter's question made our collective attention snap back to the television.

"*Why would I think that? Friendly humans are not particularly rare.*" Rel rubbed his chin. If he was faking being unaware, he was doing a damned good job of it. "*Besides, the government is hunting Lethe, is it not?*"

"*The government rarely finds the time to protect its Syldrari citizens—perhaps this soldier was fed up and hatched a plan to take matters into her own hands?*" the reporter suggested excitedly. "*It can't be a coincidence—*"

"*Their friendliness and speech rhythms may be similar, but that is where the resemblances end, I'm afraid.*" Rel fastened his gaze on the reporter. "*Rhythms are determined by where one lives the longest. It is likely they grew up in the same city, and nothing more.*"

"*Oh? Well, last question—if you had to choose between the two of them, who would you pick?*" the woman asked, an oddly sadistic grin spreading across her face.

"*…Pardon?*" Rel asked slowly.

"*You know, if you got the chance to stick that—*"

Thankfully, Zafir promptly switched the television off. Within moments, he was on his phone with someone, giving them a rather impressive tongue lashing for allowing the reporter to conduct herself in such a manner.

"Wooow…" Sarah inched away from Zafir and toward me. "That was really weird. What the heck were those reporters after?"

"Mmm… Hey, Amara. Amara, what did he answer?" Diana tugged on the woman's sleeve as she tapped away on her data pad.

"Looks like he acted appropriately offended and a producer dragged the reporter offscreen," Amara answered, turning the pad first to Diana and then to me and Sarah. Sure enough, a now-dark blue Rel was fuming, his arms crossed and his glow a pretty shade of red, while the producer repeatedly apologized.

"That was suspicious as fuck," Maelor stated flatly. "That woman had some other motive."

"Yes, sir… I'll send her right away." Zafir hung up his phone and sighed heavily, looking over to me. "The higher-ups want you to go patrol the Syldrari sector as Lethe. They're concerned that the reporters were sent to distract us from some other issue. You have full permission to intervene in any conflicts you encounter, with however much force you deem necessary."

"Guess I won't be stuffing my face with candy all night after all," I remarked dryly. "Alright. To the garage I go."

A short while later, I found myself perched atop a roof and gazing down at the busy streets of the Syldrari Sector. It was much busier in the evening than it was during the day, and most of the people were still Syldrari. There were a few, however, who clearly belonged to a much more…*amorphous* species, though I got the impression they weren't exactly welcome.

Look for signs of conflict, huh… I stood up and quietly paced along the roofline, looking for potential fights.

After a few blocks, I came across the reporter and her camera crew arguing with one another. Rel was still there, though two more Syldrari men had joined him. They were hanging back, as if waiting for trouble to break loose—and a producer was still attempting to rein in the reporter. *That's odd, why are they still…?*

I narrowed my eyes at the group and my visor zoomed in. Sure enough, the strange shape I'd spotted on one of the camera men turned out to be the barrel of a gun. A quick survey revealed that all the humans except the producer were armed.

Capture targets if you can. Otherwise, eliminate. Zafir held up a sign with the written instructions before disappearing from the in-visor feed. I was just glad he'd remembered my suggestion—no talking, since the Syldrari might be able to hear what was said over comms.

I crept closer toward the human group, doing my best to keep out of sight. Once I was close enough, I channeled electricity around my gauntlets and dropped into their midst, landing on and disorienting a few, and swiftly striking out to punch the closer others.

"Stay back!" Rel barked to the terrified producer, moving the human behind him. "Lethe, what—"

"Guns." I leapt at the 'reporter' and punched her hard enough in the gut to make her keel over. After tossing her toward Rel, I turned to face the remaining humans. "Keep an eye on *that* while I take care of these bastards."

I strengthened the charge around my gauntlets and dashed toward my opponents. Soon, with just a few well-aimed strikes, every member of the crew was laid out on the ground, unconscious. For a moment, I considered fully overloading their neurochips, but then I stopped myself. They might have useful information.

"Now then." I shook out my hands, letting the gauntlets retract up my forearms, then turned to face Rel and the producer. "I'll… Really? A human holding a Syldrari at knifepoint?"

I crossed my arms over my chest and stared at the 'producer.' The Syldrari looked similarly unimpressed, though they appeared to be playing along for the moment. Zafir flickered into my feed again, holding a sign that read, ***They will get into trouble if they attack a human, even in self-defense. Kill or capture the producer. Be advised, the camera feed is still projecting to live television.***

Wonderful. Just what I needed. I considered my various abilities for a moment, unsure whether I wanted to reveal any more than my lightning and water abilities.

"I-If you want him t-to live, show your face! To the world!" the producer stammered, seemingly unaware that his blade was doing literally nothing against Rel's neck. Even though he was pushing hard, there wasn't so much as an indent in the Syldrari's skin.

I rolled my eyes behind my mask and started walking toward the group. The producer spluttered in terror and pulled his arm back as if he'd decided to stab Rel in the neck after all – but that gave me all the space I needed. I dashed in, squeezing past Rel, and grabbed the human's arm. With a savage yank, I dislocated his shoulder and used my momentum to spin him around, sending him toppling face-first to the ground. A nice jolt of electricity knocked him out cold and I dragged the bastard over to the pile of other humans.

"Good thing I brought zip ties, I guess…" I muttered, glancing over at the fallen cameras. Only one was still running, so I promptly strode over and stomped its lens out, then looked for the controls to turn off the broadcast entirely.

Military is waiting until you zip tie them to move in. Suggest you hurry. Zafir's sign popped up again. As if on cue, I heard sirens approaching in the distance.

"Found their behavior that offensive?" Rel inquired, amused. I glanced to the side, finding a long pair of leather-clad legs filling my view. Hooboy.

"I was checking around to see if anyone was causing trouble. Saw you seemed to be having an altercation over here and noticed their guns." I withheld a grimace upon hearing myself. Changing my speech patterns was difficult, and I got the impression from his smirk that it wasn't actually helping any.

"Rel—" One of the other Syldrari spoke up in a chastising tone, spewing out a long series of sounds I had no hope of replicating. "—thank the woman!"

If *that* was his full name, I understood why he'd said a human couldn't pronounce it. Even thinking of trying made my jaw hurt, and half of it had sounded more like music than actual words.

"Ah yes, my manners. Thank you, Lethe." Rel chuckled and crouched down beside me, his long tail swishing behind him. He held up his hand, from which dangled several zip ties. "I believe you dropped these."

"…Thanks." I snatched them from him and returned to securing the idiots. "I need to get out of here before the military shows up."

"You're looking a little flushed. Is using magic really so difficult for *interesting* humans such as yourself?" He tilted his head faintly as he examined me, looking more like a lurking predator than a concerned acquaintance.

"No." I returned my full attention to securing the humans. For some reason I had an incredibly strong urge to jump Rel's bones on the spot, and looking at him just made it so much worse.

I never feel like this around him in the café. Is this the suit's fault, or is he pulling some kind of Syldrari mind control bullshit to try to get info?

"You said you were looking for conflicts?" he probed as I stood up, rising to his feet alongside me. "For what reason?"

"This city is a cesspool. I'm doing whatever I can to stop criminals in the act, whenever I can find them." The sound of soldiers marching down the next street over caught my attention. I scowled, then turned and scaled a nearby pipe up to an overhanging balcony. "That's my cue to leave!"

"Be safe." He shot me a mischievous, borderline *evil* smile before turning his attention to his comrades. "This is going to be a long night. Answer the humans' questions honestly, and we might just get some sleep before morning."

What the hell were those reporters up to? I ground my teeth as I sped over the rooftops in the direction I'd left my bike. However, after just a few blocks an unfamiliar cloaked Syldrari dropped from somewhere *above* me to block my path. A quick glance upward showed nothing but open sky. *A cloaked shuttle…?*

"You're this 'Lethe' we've been hearing so much about?" The distorted, digitized voice somehow managed to sound condescending. "I suggest you stay out of Syldrari affairs."

"…You want me to just *let* idiots pull guns on innocent Syldrari?" I growled, feeling anger—and my feral—rising within my chest.

The Syldrari turned his head, as if listening to something, or as if he'd sensed something near us. After a moment, he returned his full attention to me. "The Syldrari do not need your protection. Humans who interfere in our matters will only die in the crossfire—or get more Syldrari killed. Stick to your own sectors."

"I'm not going to turn a blind eye to absolute *imbeciles* doing stupid shit like… Ugh!" I winced, bringing a hand up to the side of my head as a piercing whine drilled through my skull. When I recovered, the cloaked Syldrari was no longer in front of me.

I whirled, summoning my gauntlets, and caught a *sword,* of all things, against them. This close, I could see the lower portion of the man's face, along with the infuriatingly amused smirk resting there. I couldn't, however, ascertain the color of his skin in the low light, not with the color tint my visor gave to everything.

"Interesting…" He pressed down against my gauntlets, holding his sword one-handed. "Alas, your strength is still no match for a Syldrari's. What do you think you can offer that we do not already have?"

"*I* don't give a shit if the military dislikes my interference. Someone has to do their job for them, and I know damn well the Syldrari aren't allowed to protect themselves." I twisted out of the deadlock, whiffed a kick to the man's ribs, then punched his sword out of my way.

"And if a Syldrari dies trying to protect you from other Syldrari?" His tone shifted from amused to cold and deadly, his voice reverberating through the air as though coming from multiple angles.

"I'm not worth dying for, but sitting on my thumbs doing jack shit is criminal." I growled in frustration. "You seriously want me to just *ignore*—"

The man's hand flashed out, grabbing me by the face and lifting me off the ground. Though his hands weren't much larger than a human's, he seemed to have no issue with my weight. I had a feeling the energy I could feel bouncing between his fingertips was the reason. Letting out a low growl, I grabbed his wrist and attempted to dislodge his grip.

"The R'selkti will protect the Syldrari sector. Keep your nose out of it." His fingers twitched against my face. "I could kill you right now without even needing to squeeze. Each and every Syldrari is capable of such force. We are only permitting you to continue living because you genuinely wish to help."

"R…selkti…" Intense, nearly blinding rage clawed at my chest as my feral attempted to take over. The Syldrari's lips parted briefly before he dropped me and leapt back. "You're the ones who *turned an entire city into human jelly* and I'm supposed to trust *you* to do *anything* protective?"

I winced, my head spinning as my anger threatened to spiral out of control.

"We—" His tone turned placating, his hands raising in an attempt to calm me.

"Get out of my way." My voice was deadly calm, and I watched him stiffen and freeze like stone. A second later, he nodded as if responding to someone else and moved aside.

"A…human with…" he whispered, but the rest shifted to Syldran. I gritted my teeth and stalked back to my skybike. *Fucking hell.*

<—ethe? Lethe? Do you cop— There you are!> Zafir exclaimed, leaning forward on his desk and looking worried. <We lost all contact! What happened?>

"I'll brief you once I'm back and I've cooled off," I stated in a tone that I hoped left no room for further discussion.

The next day, I found myself in the training room at HQ. As I gnawed irritably on one of my Syldrari candies, I watched Calder, Nikolai, and Maelor go through the drills I'd assigned them. Off to my left, Zafir was watching as a data pad streamed the three men's vitals.

"Want one?" I offered the jar to Zafir, who answered with a dubious stare. "What? Not going to expand your horizons by only ever eating human stuff. You never know, you might like it."

"…A small piece, then," he relented. He hesitated before putting it in his mouth, and a few seconds later he was scrambling for a glass of water. "I thought that was *candy*, why is it spicy?!"

"Huh. It tastes sour-tart-sweet to me. Like how lemon or lime candy does, except it doesn't taste like citrus." I glanced down at the stuff, then back over at Zafir. He'd taken the candy out of his mouth, but looked like he was contemplating putting it back in. "Well?"

"Have you ever tried candied ginger?" He glanced at me.

"Yeah?"

"It tastes like that, but with much more heat. It's… good, but painful." He placed the candy in a napkin, then an idea seemed to strike him. "Ah, but like candied ginger, I bet I could put this in tea or coffee. I will report back on that later."

"See? Expanding horizons," I remarked dryly, turning my gaze back to the training boys. "So, any verdict from the bosses yet about last night's disturbance?"

"The humans you caught are still being questioned." Zafir shook his head. "Another city was destroyed by Resonance yesterday, so their focus has been on that. They're currently transporting the survivors to a facility for recovery and stabilization."

"They're not coming here?" I asked. *Another? Really? Was it the R'selkti, or…?*

"No, the attack was on the other side of the planet. The survivors were seriously injured, so the response teams deemed it necessary to stop at a base closer to the strike zone first. Once the survivors are stable, they'll be transferred here." He sighed. "We haven't the faintest idea why they chose to attack that particular city…"

"*Tch*, damn R'selkti!" Maelor snapped, a particular brand of rage gleaming in his eyes. I knew that look, and I tensed in my seat as he continued his tirade. "They aren't gonna stop until they've destroyed every city on this planet! Those bastards—"

Before he could finish his sentence, Maelor's rage engulfed him and the feral took over. I leapt to my feet, summoning my battle suit. "Zafir, get out of here."

Darting forward, I kicked Maelor across the chest and spun into an uppercut, sending him sliding across the floor on his back. When I heard the doors to the training room close, I summoned a lightning strike to see if I could startle him out of his feral haze. Nope.

Hard way it is, then.

He conjured a boulder and hurled it at me, forcing me to dodge around it. As I came back into view, I visualized a pit of dark sludge behind Maelor and ran at him, kicking him hard in the chest. He fell back into the sludge and began to panic as tendrils of the dark goo latched around his limbs and sucked him into the floor, covering his face and probing at his body.

It wasn't until his panic had him screaming and begging for me to spare him that I let the illusion disappear. Maelor cowered on the floor, shaking, and dry heaved a few times. My head spun and I staggered backward, landing on my butt. Wincing, I shook my head, trying to clear it.

"You okay, Elara?" Calder knelt next to me while Nikolai tried to calm Maelor down.

"Yeah, I'll be fine. Go check on your buddy." I shook my head again, trying to dislodge the odd feeling that had come over me. It had made me feel…like a god. Like I could crush them in an instant if I wished. *That's new…maybe I'm still a little shaken from last night? And why am I so dizzy…*

I dragged myself to my feet and fetched my candy, then exited into the hallway where Zafir was waiting. He looked much less worried than I'd expected. Instead, he looked mystified.

"Was that real, or an illusion?" he inquired with a frown as I leaned back against the wall.

"Illusion."

"I feel there must be more to it. I've never seen a feral submit, let alone behavior like that. *Begging* before fully leaving the feral state? That's unheard of. The other two should have gone feral as well—a chain reaction—yet…" He looked and sounded baffled. It was kinda cute. "You look tired. Should we call it for today? There are less tiring subjects we can attend to if you aren't feeling up to it."

"Just dizzy, but something less active would probably be a good idea," I suggested.

"Indeed… And you don't intend to visit the Syldrari sector today?"

"Either I, or Lethe, needs to chill on visiting there." I made a quoting gesture with my fingers. "I'm still waiting for you to pick."

"Ah… I believe we should have Lethe work elsewhere for now in order to prove this isn't specifically about the Syldrari." Zafir adjusted his glasses before swiping through his data pad. "You as Elara are more likely to pick up useful information during your visits. However, I would ask you to wait a bit. The higher-ups are debating one of my proposals. If it goes through, I want you to deliver it."

CHAPTER SIX

Later that week, I wandered through the Syldrari sector, feeling oddly disoriented. One of my ears was even ringing, and trying to shake it off only made me feel worse. If any of the Syldrari noticed my behavior – or anything odd going on at all – they didn't show it. Something just wasn't right.

I nudged the door of Rel's café open and came face-to-chest with a surprised Syldrari. Though he was in human disguise, his hair was striped with sections of white and black, his sclerae were black, and his irises were a pearlescent white.

I bowed slightly. "Sorry, sir. I wasn't paying attention to where I was going."

The man glanced behind him when several others burst out laughing. "Did a *human soldier* just apologize to me?"

Rel smirked from his spot by the counter. "Elara, isn't it a little late for lunch?"

"You're the Elara I've heard about?" The white-eyed Syldrari's attention turned to me, though he continued to block my entrance into the café. "What's in the bag?"

I shrugged one shoulder. "The idiots higher up are too scared to send someone official—read: important—so they have me playing delivery girl. I mean, it's good news, I think, but..."

"Hmph." The tall Syldrari crossed his arms and gave me a challenging look, one that made my inner feral want to drag him out into the street for a brawl. I narrowed my eyes and he did the same, his glow shifting closer to red. "You're human. Back down."

"I don't *care*. *You* back down," I growled back. *That* garnered an outright laugh and his glow returned to cyan, which seemed to shock the people in the café.

"Fine. Show us this so-called important delivery of yours." He gave me a smug look before placing a hand on my back and nudging me toward the counter. It probably looked rough to the others because he didn't tone down his strength much, but I still got the feeling he was holding back. He moved to block the doorway again, his arms crossed.

"Don't mind him." Rel shook his head slightly before placing a *bright* purple drink on the counter and nudging it my way.

"Oooh, what's this one?" I came over, watching as he finished it off with a skewer of what looked like blue cherries.

The tall man behind me scoffed. "You're giving the human

traditional fare now?"

"She's *been* eating and drinking our food each time she comes here. I don't serve anything else." Rel shot the man a foul look. "If you're going to play spectator in my establishment, then behave."

I ignored their exchange, mostly, and picked up the drink, giving it a tentative sip before downing half the glass and picking up the skewer of berry-things. After popping one in my mouth, I chewed, swallowed, then smiled. "You know, you're making it difficult for me to pick a favorite."

"What…" The tall man stalked over, snatching my glass and drinking the rest himself as if he didn't believe it was what he'd initially thought. He gave me an incredulous stare. "You're not vomiting."

"Really? Is that seriously the usual human response to that one?" I glanced over at the sheepish Rel.

"I'll give you another jar of candy as recompense…and a new drink." He shot the tall man a dark look at that last part.

"Ohhh, you mean the candy that one of my colleagues described as 'tasty but painfully spicy'?" I remarked dryly. "I get the impression you're having fun trying to see just how similar my palate is to yours."

"Well, yes. It isn't every day we get to serve a human Syldran fare." Rel laughed. "Now, what's this about a delivery?"

"Right." I hauled my bag up and pulled a folder from it, placing it on the counter. "After the broadcasts from last night, civilians started pressuring and threatening the government, so a bunch of departments got together to review the complaints and figure out what to do.

"Even though the citizens are still…" I reread the line a few times and rolled my eyes. "'Cautious and nervous of all alien visitors,' they're displeased with the unfair treatment of the Syldrari, and that this treatment has spawned a vigilante."

The tall man snorted at me. "I didn't think delivery girls were supposed to roll their eyes when delivering messages."

"You want to take this outside?" I growled at him. He just shot me a small smile, patted my head, and sat down at the bar. I reined myself in with a twitch. "…*Anyway*. Starting roughly ten minutes ago, Syldrari are no longer forced to remain in human disguise, and—"

"Thank the fuckin' ancestors!"

Several similar declarations rose from other customers, and I remained silent as everyone in the café *immediately* dropped their disguises.

Rel's skin was back to its normal dark blue-grey, while the tall man's was a variegated grey that reminded me of a shark. I certainly wasn't going to admit that the tall, irritating man was also pretty. Nope. Nuh uh.

"*And* on top of that, self-defense restrictions are being lifted. Most of the human viewers were distressed that Rel couldn't do anything even when a knife was pressed to his throat." I scoffed.

Sure, I was ignorant, but what did that make the human civilians? "They don't seem to realize it doesn't actually *do* anything, but hey. They freaked out so bad that they bullied the government into letting the Syldrari defend themselves. 'For the people' and all that bullshit. If it works, I guess…"

"Staying for dinner?" Rel gave me an amused look when I started fanning myself with the folder.

"Let me see that." The tall one snatched the folder away from me, leaving me hot and without a fan. Great.

"Yeah, well, now that's done, so I'm technically off duty." I began the arduous process of unfastening and pulling off my damned uniform jacket. Once it was finally off, I tied the arms around my waist and perched on a barstool.

"You feeling alright? It's freezing in here." Rel swiveled a circular thing on the counter toward me, revealing that the room's temperature was indeed quite low.

"I get hot when people *aggravate me*." I glanced pointedly in the tall Syldrari's direction, then back to the amused-looking Rel. "You look like you're up to mischief. Planning to surprise me again?"

He chuckled. "Indeed. Any requests?"

"Mmm… Something sweet and fruity for dessert?" I stretched my arms over my head.

"By human or Syldran standards?" Rel teased.

"Syldran, of course. I think I'm just as curious as you are at this point to see if the Resonance altered my palate entirely." I shrugged.

Seriously, though, how much did the Resonance change me, and why? Is this just a weird side effect, or is there more to it?

"The… I see, you are a survivor?" The tall Syldrari's tone suddenly shifted into something a hair gentler. I glanced over at him, but he was now looking at Rel. "You didn't tell me she was involved."

"It doesn't define her, though it has certainly made her a bit…quirky," he answered.

"Hey!" I pouted.

"Resonance survivors… How odd," the tall Syldrari murmured. "A supposedly flawless weapon of destruction leaving survivors…?"

"I'm not permitted to go too much into it, but the reigning theory within the military is that destruction isn't the weapon's only purpose." I swiveled on my stool to face the now-pensive Syldrari. "In scientific terms, the weapon quite literally 'resonated' with something in our genetic makeup, altering our cellular structure. Now, some people only survived because they were on the fringes of the blast and were merely hit by flying debris, but others were at the epicenter.

"Due to the rather pronounced cellular changes, the military believes that the R'selkti are intentionally changing people at the price of murdering all the others in the area of the blast. They're still working on the 'to what end?' part of their theories."

"And you're allowed to share this information?" The tall

Syldrari gave me a suspicious look.

"From what I understand, a lot of this information is available to the public—it's just that most people either don't want to read research papers or else just don't care." I raised my hands in a shrug. "From what I'm told, there are multiple papers publicly available at universities both online and off, if you want to verify what I said."

The man immediately pulled out a data pad and began flipping through it. Since our conversation seemed to be over, I turned my attention back to Rel.

"Any new theories about this Lethe woman?" he inquired, a mischievous sparkle in his eyes.

"Not really, they're all too busy scrambling to track her down." I leaned back in my chair with a sigh. "Which kind of brings me to my less favorable news. I've been tasked with attempting to find amiable soldiers to patrol the Syldrari sector with me. It seems to me they're more worried about finding this 'Lethe,' and think she may live in this sector, than they're concerned about troublemakers."

"What, exactly, is a fragile creature like you meant to do on a patrol?" the tall man asked disbelievingly, unaffected by the sharp glare I shot him. "You are *human*. Your kind break far too easily to be entertaining, but that doesn't mean there aren't those who won't fight back if you attempt to butt into Syldrari business."

"Hey, I'm just an Imperial soldier. You realize what that makes my options, right?" I narrowed my eyes. To my surprise, he looked to Rel questioningly.

"It means she can obey, or…" Rel hesitated, then continued in Syldran.

The tall Syldrari bristled, his grip cracking the casing of his data pad. Based on that reaction, I figured I could trust well enough that Rel had made the consequences of disobedience quite clear.

"And you would have to obey despite the physical danger?" the tall man asked dangerously.

"I'd rather die in battle—no matter how little I could do against a Syldrari opponent. The other option is…undeath, in a manner of speaking? Losing everything that makes me *me*, and being tossed into one of those places… I'll pass on that." I crossed my legs at the ankles and leaned forward to grab my drink. "I don't really consider it an option, given how clear the choice is."

"Die in battle…heh." The tall man shook his head and grabbed his own mug. "I can drink to that."

"Rel! Keep the human there!" A panicked-looking woman dashed into the café, drenched in what appeared to be luminescent nervous sweat. "We think we found the queen!"

"Take me to her." The tall man was out of his seat and heading out the door in what looked like the same movement, such was his speed.

"Elara," Rel began.

I shrugged. "I know. I'm planting my ass here until it's safe to do otherwise. Besides, I haven't had my dinner yet."

"*Do you think it's Lethe?*" I heard whispers start up in the café, though Rel released a low laugh.

"They think that, due to her use of Syldrari technology and the hiding of her eyes, that Lethe is actually a Syldrari pretending to be a human vigilante." Rel placed a bowl containing some sort of vibrantly colored soup in front of me, then returned to the stove. "With the eyes being something we cannot hide…"

"Even with lenses?" I inquired.

"No. To my knowledge, no such lenses have been created. There were some groups who were seeking ways to hide our eyes without obscuring our vision, but their research hasn't borne fruit. Or if it has, they haven't made it public.

"Given our…edge over other species, *hiding* in such a manner is not something we tend to do. Our shapeshifting originally emerged as a chameleon-like mechanism to trick natural predators on Syldra. Our ancestors later guided that ability into what it is today, but only because other species tend to find us incredibly startling upon first meeting us. As such, we often observe a planet's species first in order to approach them in a form they are familiar with."

"Huh. Guiding evolution?" I murmured, intrigued. "That's something human researchers have been theorizing about but haven't been able to realize yet."

"Thus, their interest in resonance?" Rel nodded in understanding. "As interesting as the concept is, I'm inclined to say the cellular changes are an unintended side effect. Otherwise, why wouldn't the R'selkti have used such knowledge to enhance their own people?"

"Maybe they have, and we just don't know it yet," I countered, shrugging. "After all, it could be another way of 'guiding evolution,' right?"

"I see your point, but I don't like it," he muttered, his tail flicking briefly in agitation.

"You seem rather informed on and interested in the topic for someone who is, to quote, 'just a café owner,'" I remarked dryly.

"And the same applies to you, Miss 'Just a Creshe Imperial Soldier,'" he countered, shooting me a small smile. "Speaking of, are you certain you shouldn't be rushing to see what this 'queen' commotion is about?"

"I may prefer to die in battle, but I'm not suicidal," I answered flatly. "Besides, as a survivor of the Resonance, I'm ordered to put self-preservation over solving conflicts or continuing missions. They don't want to lose any of their precious research samples, abilities or no."

Rel stroked his chin thoughtfully as I finally dived into my soup. "Let us hope that the queen truly has been found. If she has, she will be returned to our home planet for her own safety and tensions here will fade. I'd had my suspicions that a queen was the cause of the increasing disagreements, but now that we have confirmation, all should be well."

A Syldrari woman with neon green skin stepped over and asked Rel something in what sounded like a concerned tone. He nodded, and she trotted out the door at once.

"Let me guess—she's going to go check?" I asked when Rel opened his mouth. He shot me a surprised look. "I heard something along the lines of '*fis*.' That means 'go,' if I'm not mistaken?"

"You're picking up on words you *hear*?" he asked, clearly astounded.

"Well, they're shouting it in the streets a lot, along with making motions like the ones humans make. Put those together with other context cues, and we arrive at my conclusion." I motioned vaguely, miming the arm and hand movement people made when telling someone to go first.

"You pay much more attention than most people, human or otherwise." He raised an eyebrow when he caught me tilting my bowl around with a frown. "What's wrong? Finally find something you dislike?"

"All gone." I pursed my lips and angled the bowl toward him. "For the record, the only things I don't like so far are those things that taste like some kinda medicinal root vegetable. They're *seriously* bitter."

"Medicinal is precisely what they are," he agreed, taking my bowl and filling it partway with more of the tasty soup. "We utilize a great deal of beneficial ingredients in our fare. Some, admittedly, more pleasant than others."

"Where do you source your ingredients, anyway? It's not like any of this grows wild here." I happily picked up my fork and spoon to tackle the noodles and other bits in the soup.

"Ah, at the center of the sector, that big building you can see from the more open spaces? It has floors for…well, essentially, land and sea." He picked up a spherical vegetable that looked like it was covered in scales. With a flourish, he sliced it in half to reveal a glowing orange interior. "This, for example, is a vegetable found deep within the ocean caverns of our planet—with great difficulty, mind you. The difficulty and danger of sourcing ingredients led us to develop ways to farm them at the very early stages, and now our technology permits us to grow crops at any depth or altitude we wish."

"Oooh, that's really cool." I caught the half of the vegetable he tossed to me. "What about meat, then? Most of what *we* eat is cloned or lab grown."

"Bah, we are capable of doing such if we like, but we prefer to raise food creatures when we can." He paused, contemplating something. "Though we are thankful for our technological advancements, we also appreciate the natural order. Gathering, hunting, fishing, making things by hand—these are all things we appreciate and don't wish to lose."

"Huh, I guess that's in line with all the art and graffiti I see all over the district…" I eyed the interior of the veggie, prodding it a little—I was mildly alarmed when I realized it *felt* like pudding, and yet didn't drip out of the shell when tipped. Rel reached out a hand, waiting for me to give it back. I decided to ask another question.

"Okay, I have a question I've been meaning to ask. Given how advanced the Syldrari are, and how much more powerful than humans you are, why haven't you just...conquered us?"

"That is a *very* human question." Rel laughed, returning to the stove yet again. "I hope you take no offense to this, but quite simply, humans enjoy murder. War. Subjugation. My people do not enjoy those things. We enjoy the arts in all forms, exploration, hunting, gathering, and expanding our knowledge.

"Our conflicts are few and far between. Personal conflicts are settled by debate or duel, depending on the individuals involved and how serious their quarrel. Clan or species-encompassing conflicts usually only arise when a queen has appeared but gone undiscovered for a long period of time."

So, humans have a murder boner and Syldrari don't. Makes sense. I watched as he brought a large plate over to me, complete with some sort of medium-rare blue steak thing and multiple sides. "I get the feeling this is more than one serving."

"Indeed, though I'm sure you'll find time to eat the rest." He smiled, then glanced over my head when the door opened again. "Well, what is the verdict?"

"Child queen. She and her family are being returned home immediately," the bright green woman reported with a faint nod.

"She didn't destroy much; repairs should be done by morning." She paused to look at me, then noticed my empty bowl and the rest of what I was eating. "...Elara, right? You mentioned something about candy earlier?"

"I gave her a jar of the ludrán you make," Rel answered for me as I nodded around the fork in my mouth.

She frowned in thought. "You...liked it? And your human friend said, 'spicy but tasty'?"

"Yeah, he compared it to candied ginger, just a lot spicier. I think if whatever is spicy to humans was toned down, it'd probably work. For me, though, it's great as-is." I glanced over at Rel when I heard him sigh. "What?"

"You finished it all already, didn't you?" He crossed his arms.

"Uh...*nooo*? Maybe? ...Yes?" I grumbled, stabbing at a black veggie with my fork.

"I can go get some more?" the woman offered, and I glanced back at her. "They're nine hundred credits each, and I've got other flavors. How many do you want?"

"Oooh, how many flavors?"

"Fifty?"

"One of each, please!" I grinned.

"One of... Are you serious? That's..." She blinked, and I nodded. "I, uh, alright then! I'll be back shortly with your box!"

"Well, I'd wager you made her night," Rel remarked dryly. "She's been trying to bridge human and Syldrari tastes with sweets. After all, sugar is sugar. You probably gave her ideas for tweaks."

"I'll make sure to report back to her, then." I grinned. "So, things should calm down now?"

"Indeed they should. With the queen relocating, there's nothing to spur us into competition."

I let out a relieved sigh. "Well, I sure hope so. There are other problems I'd like answers to, and I doubt they'd get addressed if you're all trying to prove yourselves to a queen."

"Says the woman who was prepared to brawl with a Syldrari soldier earlier," he remarked dryly.

"Bleh. Sometimes I meet people and their behavior makes me want to beat them until either their manners improve, or they prove their superiority complex isn't just a complex." I munched on a bit more of my dinner, watching as Rel placed a to-go box to my left. "You're really good at telling when I'm almost done."

"You get this look like you want to keep stuffing your face, but also want more for later." He placed a large glass filled with layers of *stuff* in front of me. "And you *did* request dessert."

CHAPTER SEVEN

"The queen was found?" Zafir muttered for the umpteenth time since the previous day's events. He paced his office while I lounged in a chair. "It's all well and good that she's been relocated, but if the conflicts don't die down then we have another problem."

"I think we already have enough on our plates," I remarked. "There's way more crime in the other sectors, at least according to the reports you showed me. I can't stop all of it myself, not while also patrolling the Syldrari sector and training the others. Something has to give."

"Training can wait. I have plenty of study material I can give them." He pivoted to look at me. "I've decided. You will make nighttime activity a pattern for Lethe. People will be less likely to suspect 'Elara' due to your day and afternoon patrol schedule."

"Okay. And if people still press that angle?" I frowned.

"We can fake footage of you elsewhere at the same time as

Lethe's activity. To be safe, said footage will show you in headquarters and not out in other sectors, which could be easily disproved."

I nodded faintly. "Okay. We'll see. So, off to do Lethe things?"

"Indeed. And be cautious. There are already plenty of humans who want to capture you," he warned. "If they try, you have permission to kill them."

"Right. Will do." I stood and made my way to the garage, summoning my suit as I went. Despite being human—or however human I actually *was* after the Incident—I hadn't had much interaction with the human sectors.

My hopes weren't very high.

I was almost all the way to the garage before I heard rapid footsteps closing in behind me.

"Lethe, wait!" Sarah called. "Are you sure about this? Once you kill people—"

"I've killed people before. This time at least I'll have control over who I attack." I mounted my skybike. *Guess Sarah didn't go feral after the weapon was fired?*

I sped off without giving her time to respond. People needed to stop questioning my choice, as if there'd been another option. The best I could do was try to keep my morals straight. Kill criminals and monsters, try to manipulate the government into treating non-humans like people... *Fuck. I'm not sure which one's harder.*

My skybike took a sudden turn toward a section of the city where no lights seemed to be on. I frowned as Zafir popped into view in my peripheral.

<Sorry, change of plans.> He nudged at his glasses, his expression concerned. <Our bosses want us to look into rumors of a rogue faction taking up residence in the dead sector. We aren't detecting any humanoid life signs, but if there are people using it as a base you should be able to find evidence.>

"Dead sector? What is it, a cemetery?" I glanced around, noting that both lights and other vehicles were becoming sparser by the second.

<Nothing quite so pleasant. There was an accident there decades ago, rendering everything in the blast radius aetherically inert.> Zafir skimmed something before continuing. <The details are above my clearance level. My impression is that something went awry with a prototype magitech weapons platform, but that's merely a guess based on the extent of the damage.>

"Well, guess I'm taking a look regardless…"

The skybike slowed to a stop beside an imposing gate. A lone pair of soldiers hastily opened a side door, permitting me to walk through. *Idiots. Do they want my connection to the military to be discovered?*

Once inside, it took my eyes a moment to fully adjust to the darkness. As far as I could see there was just…wreckage. There were a few buildings that had kept their first and sometimes second stories, but most of the sector had been completely obliterated. Despite the sheer amount of warped and broken concrete, steel, piping, and other building materials, the place felt oddly empty. Silent. So silent, in fact, that I realized I couldn't even hear the bustling city behind me through the massive walls hemming in the ruined sector.

…They really think a rogue group is out here? I carefully started picking my way down segments of a broken street that looked as if it had fallen from somewhere above. *Or are they perhaps putting me out to pasture?*

<Anything?> Zafir prompted.

Well, maybe not yet. I released a small sigh. "I'm barely fifty feet in, and you're making it hard to see."

<That place is dangerous, it's important that I—> Zafir's voice and image glitched out, then disappeared entirely. All that remained on the inside of my visor was the faint trace of alien language and icons I didn't know the meanings of.

Great. I quietly adjusted my stance, letting my gauntlets slide into place. Even if a rebel group *wasn't* out here, that didn't mean there weren't beasts, monsters, or some other problem.

The ruins of the sector struck me as more and more bizarre as I made my way further in. Dozens of war-torn machines littered the ground, giving it the feeling of a graveyard. The hollow, rusted vestiges ranged from the size of cats to taller than some of the smaller buildings in the area. Their damaged shells had long since been stripped of usable parts, leaving only their frames to loom in the dim light.

Despite all the devastation, there were no traces of decay. No organic remnants whatsoever. There weren't even weeds growing out of the cracks or in the dirt.

My curiosity growing, I decided to make my way up to what looked like a newer, less damaged construction. *A dam…?*

I made my way along the top of the dam, my gaze scouring the ruins below. There were no signs of activity in the sector aside from me. It was a wild goose chase…but an interesting one.

Rumors of renegades, my ass. Something else was going on. I placed my hands against the rail and looked out over the sector, then further to the bustling city beyond.

Such devastation… Such fun. I gripped the rail more tightly and pulled myself back. *No, not fun. Tragic. The people here would have been helpless, like—*

The faint sound of movement behind me, of boots landing quietly against the concrete, was followed by a deep, melodic voice colder than any I'd ever heard. "It was probably like shooting fish in a barrel for your government. Or perhaps even easier. Your kind do so adore giving up their lives for fleeting, half-understood ideals."

I slowly turned to find a cloaked man standing a few feet away from me. He pulled down his hood, revealing a smirking *human* face. *Right. The guy bashing humans is human. I highly doubt that.*

"What do you—" I cut myself off when I realized my voice modulator wasn't active. *What? Just how much else is nonfunctional? The fuck is going on?*

"What do I want? Many things." He smiled, beginning to walk toward me. "Right now, I want an interesting fight—and since you need to be dealt with…" He flourished a hand, summoning a vaguely familiar longsword. At the same time, his human pupil elongated into a slit and several smaller pupils opened around it, each a different size until suddenly they stabilized. "Entertain me."

Fuck, Syldrari! I darted to my right to evade a swing of his sword, then pivoted into a defensive stance. His blade hadn't touched anything, yet several inches of concrete hurtled through the air away from us. *What…how am I supposed to fight that? Fuck it!*

Focusing, I launched into a punch aimed for his head. I couldn't afford to be distracted or curious. Not if he could turn concrete into shrapnel without physically touching it.

"That was a quick turnaround," he remarked idly, catching my fist in one hand. "You made a mistake involving yourself in Syldrari affairs. It's past time I fix that mistake for you."

"I just want to *help*!" I snapped, twisting out of his grip and aiming a kick at his solar plexus—assuming he even had one. "If surviving a Resonance Incident means I get stuck with a weird suit and inhuman abilities, then I—"

My head swam briefly, disorienting me long enough for the Syldrari man to grab me by the wrist and fling me into the nearest wall. I managed to catch myself and spring back at him, punching his sword out of my way in the process.

"So entitled." He slashed at my shoulder with his sword, narrowing his eyes when no cut appeared. "So it's true. The suit you survivors manifest is Syldrari technology. I wonder…are you mere thieves, or…?"

Fuck. What is wrong with my head? I shifted into a defensive stance. It was almost like his presence alone was disorienting and disarming, and every word out of his mouth only made it worse. At the same time, I could feel my consciousness attempting to slip into its feral state.

"I believe I told you to entertain me." The man took a few steps toward me, then stopped for some reason. "That aura—"

"Shut up!" I snarled, launching at him with more speed than I'd known I had. My fist slammed into his shoulder and I followed through, using momentum to forcibly turn him from me. He recovered quickly, swiping lazily at me with his weapon. The lack of effort made my blood boil.

He easily blocked, parried, and sidestepped my barrage of strikes, and the more smug he looked, the angrier I got. Finally, something in me snapped, and with my next punch, a cacophony of elements exploded down my arm and into the Syldrari's chest.

"Hmph." He smiled, not at all the desired effect, and took a deep breath. When he refocused, there was a look in his eyes that made my feral recoil in fear. Without any other warning, he moved fluidly into a series of strikes so smooth and precise it was like he was dancing.

I instinctively blocked with my gauntlets, doing my best to guard and deflect against the rapid onslaught of attacks. He didn't stop until my feet were close to the far northern end of the dam and I'd caught the sword between my palms. Where we'd fought, pieces of the structure were cracking and falling apart.

"Why did you sto—" A sudden urge to cough interrupted me, and I hacked with so much force I nearly keeled over. When the fit subsided, I saw splatters of red and blue all over both the concrete and my gauntlets. *What...*

"Hmph, so concussive force still penetrates your armor." The Syldrari stepped forward, his boot landing in one of the stains. He gripped me by the neck, lifting me up to his eye level. I dug my fingers into his forearm, the urge to fight nearly overwhelming all thought.

"Ah, so you adore fighting, do you? How endearing. So weak, yet you don't let that impede your feistiness." He paused, glancing at my gauntlets and down my body, then finally to the blood on the ground. His lips parted in surprise before a serious, dangerous expression overtook his face and he slammed me back-first into a wall. "What are you?"

"Resonance…survivor…" I barely managed to get the words out.

"That isn't an answer. Do you *have* another answer?"

"…No…" I choked.

"The government doesn't know, the military doesn't, *you* don't…*tch*." His gaze filled with ice again. "We'll meet again, when you're more entertaining… I'll do you a favor this time and get rid of these hints that you may be more than human. After all, breaking you out of a test tube would be far more effort than I care to exert."

"I'll—" I started with a snarl.

"—Kill me? How quaint." He dropped me to the ground. "Stay put."

I, apparently, had no say in the matter. A high-pitched sound pierced what felt like my very being, and my brain just…shut off.

CHAPTER EIGHT

"*...Internal damage...negligible...*" A distant voice reported. "*Conscious...soon. Aftereffects shouldn't last more than...*"

I drifted in and out of consciousness for what felt like an eon. At several points, I could have sworn there was a Syldrari in my room, but that seemed highly unlikely. It had to have been my groggy mind messing with me.

"Elara?" The question, though quiet, made me wince, and I covered my eyes with my forearm when the lights flickered on. My left arm felt like it was asleep and didn't respond when I attempted to shift it. "Sorry, I'll dim the lights."

Zafir quickly tapped at his data pad, then set it aside. As the lights dimmed, he carried a bottle of water, complete with straw, over to me. He helped me sit up, offering me the bottle.

After consuming nearly half the water, I grumbled, "Thanks. How long have I been out?"

He set the bottle aside, then took a seat in a chair next to my bed and adjusted his glasses. "A few days, though not due to whatever conflict you found yourself in. The doctors sedated you so you'd remain still long enough for your internal injuries to mend."

"I feel like I got hit by a cargo liner," I whined.

"The doctors said your injuries weren't caused by *human* weaponry, Elara." He gave me a pointed look. "Did the renegades—"

"It was a Syldrari who was pissed about me interfering in Syldrari business," I interjected flatly, causing Zafir to go silent. "He was able to hide his eyes, somehow, but for some reason he revealed them to me before attacking. I didn't get enough information on his true appearance to identify him, but I know damned well I haven't encountered someone like that in the Syldrari sector before."

"You're certain?" Zafir murmured.

"Yeah. He has a presence to him unlike any of the rest of them. He nearly subdued my feral with a *look*." I frowned, attempting to analyze the man's behavior. "He was trying to 'deal with me,' as he put it, but was also looking for entertainment."

"Then... Why didn't he kill..." Zafir paused, a look of recognition dawning. "He didn't think you were entertaining enough...*yet?*"

"Mhm. I think he'll continue to be a problem." I rubbed my aching temples, debating how much else to say. "Whoever he is, that sort of power is more what I was expecting when everyone kept telling me Syldrari are infinitely stronger than humans. He was clearly toying with and testing me… And I think venting some frustration, too."

"Frustration?" Zafir gave me an odd look, as if I shouldn't have been able to understand my opponent's state of mind.

"He was pissed off that me, the military, and the government didn't have answers to any of his questions." I shrugged and leaned forward, noticing that Zafir had gone slightly pale. "Care to explain what's up with my left arm?"

"What—Ah." He composed himself before answering. "The doctors injected the sedatives and treatments into your left shoulder. It will probably take a few days to fully work itself out of the muscles and return to normal. I've been debating what tasks to have you handle in the interim. The bosses want you to go to the Syldrari sector—"

"That would be fucking stupid. I'm pretty sure going there like this would fully out me as Lethe," I stated irritably. "Absolutely not, even though I could seriously go for some lunch right now."

He gave me a lopsided smile. "*Fully* out you, you say?"

Well, shit. Guess I may as well get into that… I sighed heavily before explaining to Zafir how my battle suit had basically stopped functioning when the mysterious Syldrari appeared.

"I see…" he murmured, running a finger down his chin. After a moment, a sly smile spread across his lips. "I think we can keep that our little secret. Perhaps, while you remain on the mend and under house arrest, we can see about furthering our study of your suit. If it's truly Syldrari tech, and they have a way to control the suits of others, then it's imperative we discover a way to modify yours and those of your potential team members."

"Our secret? Really?" I stared at Zafir in disbelief.

"Indeed. It wouldn't do for the other survivors, or our bosses, to begin questioning the validity of your battle suits—or worse, scrap them and this project altogether," he answered innocently. He crossed one leg over the other and leaned back in his seat, his hands folded in his lap. "*My* priority is keeping you and the others safe—mentally and physically—to the best of my ability. That I get to research fascinating subjects at the same time is merely a bonus. Or, perhaps more accurately, if researching interesting things wasn't my role in life, I wouldn't *be* here to keep you all safe."

I rubbed my temples. "Please just don't start doing the whole 'you're all like sons and daughters to me' bullshit Abel pulled."

"You don't need to worry there." He made a sour face. "Now then, we should discuss how we're going to keep you occupied while you heal."

"Fine," I grumbled, giving him the side eye. "Can you get me more water first, please?"

Zafir did as I asked, then got comfortable in his seat once again. "Since you will be remaining at headquarters while you recover, I think it's time we started working with some of the more troublesome survivors we have isolated here. The ones you've met so far are on the cusp of mastering their ferals, but there are many more in isolation who are still stuck in that state."

"*Stuck?*" I echoed. "I can't say I'm familiar with that, as I never was."

"Yes… Abel's reports said you merely had a hair trigger." Zafir frowned. "The ones who are stuck were victims of the more recent incidents, and the damage to their cities was different. The varied strength of the weapon leads me to believe they're still in the testing phases."

"So you think I can do something about it? On an empty stomach?" I shot him a pointed look.

He laughed, then tapped a few buttons on his communicator. "Sarah, come to Elara's room, please."

A few minutes later, Sarah peeked in, a questioning look on her face.

"*Her Highness* is hungry and demands Syldrari food." Zafir's eyes twinkled with amusement, even as his voice dripped with sarcasm. "You expressed interest in the Syldrari sector, did you not? Take Nikolai and see if you can grab her something to eat from Rel's place for breakfast."

"Wait? Really?" Her eyes brightened and she turned to me.

"What should I ask him for?"

"Tell him I said to surprise me, and that I feel like I could eat a…" I paused, struggling to find the word. It was on the tip of my tongue, but…nothing. I couldn't even picture the creature I'd been going to reference. "Uh, just say that I'm really hungry. He'll probably make multiple dishes or something."

"Okay! I'll go grab Nikolai!" She promptly darted off.

Zafir watched the door slide closed, then returned his attention to me. "Are you feeling up to walking around while waiting for your food?"

"Yeah, sure." I nodded, wincing when my shoulder pulled. "Think you're gonna have to help me up."

"A change of clothes?" he suggested as he helped me to my feet. He seemed to be doing his best to not look too closely at either my cropped shirt or my undergarments, to his credit.

I gave him a sour look. "I'm not getting dressed, and I'm not letting you dress me. You may help me put on a robe, but I'm only putting one arm through it."

"Fair enough." He assisted without complaint, then fetched me a pair of slippers without prompting. "You're confident you can help them without putting on more daunting attire?"

I considered it for a moment, visualizing the myriad ways such encounters could go wrong. If they were stuck in feral mindsets, wearing intimidating or professional clothing wouldn't mean jack shit. "I don't need to wear costumes in order to put them in their places."

Zafir shook his head in disbelief. "Losing didn't damage your confidence at all, did it?"

"Of course not. I had no reason to think I could defeat a Syldrari in a proper fight. Whatever I did after the Resonance Incident was an extreme circumstance, and not something I can replicate at will. My physical ability may be far above the average human's, but it is still in the same range, as far as I've been told." I shifted my gaze sideways, giving the clearly uncomfortable Zafir a pointed smile. "I would have to lose to one of those 'average humans' for my confidence to be shaken."

"…Point taken." He waited a moment, then cleared his throat. "Anyway—"

"One more thing." I held up my good hand to stop him. "Since when are Sarah and Nikolai allowed to go to the Syldrari sector? I thought Nikolai was too unstable to go *anywhere*?"

"They're allowed ever since I impressed the importance of maintaining an image upon our bosses," Zafir answered innocently, a very *not* innocent smile on his face. He brushed his pewter hair out of his eyes with a flourish. "As of a few days ago, I may permit people under my care to travel to various sectors—at my discretion. More importantly, our bosses believe it will help encourage the Syldrari to think of you and Lethe as separate people."

"And how did you manage *that*?" I asked, flabbergasted. "Or are you telling me that the government and its military branches are both run by utterly incompetent fools?"

"I can be *very* persuasive." He waved his hand in a dismissive motion. "Now then. The subject I need you to help stabilize is being held two floors down. She is close to you in danger levels—perhaps worse since the feral has taken over completely. She's destroyed her bedding and clothing in favor of a…nest, if you will. We're struggling to keep her fed, as we have to tranquilize her in order to access her room."

"Huh. Alright then." I raised an eyebrow. "Nesting?"

"Indeed, her behavior is the strangest we've observed thus far." He nodded as the elevator headed down. "She is highly aggressive and attacks on sight. Are you sure you're up to this without protection?"

"Trust me." I glanced at him long enough to see his skeptical expression before the doors opened and I stepped into a sterile white hallway. "*Tch*, would it kill the military to make things look a little nicer?"

"They *are* quite obsessed with making any medical or research facilities depressingly *white*." Zafir sighed, running a hand through his hair. "I've asked for permission to make changes, but I've been denied every time. They do not care if the blandness makes our subjects depressed or agitated, so long as they get the results they want."

"By that same logic, shouldn't they not care if we make changes?" I rubbed my temples.

"No one has ever accused the military of being sensible." Zafir scoffed as he led me down the hall and around a left turn before we finally came to a door at the very end of the hallway. Each door in this section was guarded by a pair of soldiers holding tranquilizer rifles. Shock batons rested on their hips, and real weapons hung at their backs. "Here we are. Ready?"

"Straight to it, then? Sure." I turned to face the door, listening for movement.

The guards hesitated, then moved further to the side of the door to access a pair of hidden panels. Several readings were taken before I heard the hiss of hydraulics disengaging, followed by a series of dull *thunks*. They had this woman under a much more secure lockdown than I'd ever needed.

When the door opened, it revealed a mostly empty room, save for the large nest Zafir had mentioned tucked into a corner. So, she was hiding in a blind spot. I listened carefully as I stepped through over the threshold, considering saying something aloud to potentially startle the woman.

I heard the rushing of air first, then my gaze found what I could only describe as a rippling in front of me. A rippling in the shape of a woman. Either her control was lacking or she sensed that I was aware of her, because she unstealthed as she rushed me.

Now then, what was that feeling again…? Ah, yes. I locked eyes with the woman as I grasped for the same sort of sensation I'd felt from the Syldrari who'd scared my feral. "*Sit down and behave.*"

The woman flinched and skidded to a stop, her eyes going wide with terror. Urine soaked her pants and pooled on the floor as her gaze flickered and the proverbial lights came on.

She fled to a back corner of the room and huddled into it, mumbling to herself. I caught a few curses directed at me as Zafir cleared his throat and took a few tentative steps into the room. "Sydney? My name is Zafir, and I am in charge of this facility—and seeing to it that you and those like you don't hurt yourselves or others. This here is Elara. She will be helping you all learn to control your abilities."

Sydney shivered with fear. "Control? It can't be controlled. It's a demon, inside me, I—"

Oh, please. It's the things outside yourself you should be afraid of. I held myself back despite the strong urge to simply walk up and slap her. I wasn't sure what it was, but I instantly disliked the woman. "It isn't a demon. It's *us,* but with a primitive, feral mindset. We're reduced to our most basic instincts, with a hair-trigger desire to fight. Fight for territory, to protect ourselves, and so on. We're little better than animals, mentally, in that state. If you learn to control it, you can make use of its powers without the negative impact to your mental functions."

When I finished talking, I noticed Zafir watching me with an intense expression on his face. His arms were crossed as he stroked his chin with one hand. It struck me as strange that he was watching *me* instead of the woman he'd wanted me to subdue.

"Control it?" Sydney snorted. "Why not kill it? A thing—"

"Then I suggest you acquire a jug of bleach from the cleaning staff and drink it." I gave her a cold look, feeling *my* feral stir in agitation. "You are your feral and your feral is you. If you want to kill off your last remaining brain cells—"

Zafir cleared his throat. "That's enough. Sydney, someone will be along to show you to the shower and give you a change of clothes. Once you've learned to control yourself and aren't a danger to the others in this facility, you will have a proper room and free run of the residential floor—well, aside from rooms that don't belong to you, of course."

"Can I go see about breakfast now?" I asked, crossing my arms over my stomach.

"Indeed. I will join you." He nodded.

"W-wait! Food?" Sydney protested.

"You will be well taken care of, worry not." He glanced back at her. "If you are still in control after you bathe and change, you may even have pleasant company for your meal."

I followed Zafir out of the room and down the hall, feeling more agitated than before. If I never had to interact with that woman again, it would be a blessing.

"Where did you learn that?" Zafir asked quietly.

"Hmm? What?" I looked over at him—that serious expression was back.

"The way you subdued her."

"Oh. It's similar to how that Syldrari I met earlier scared my feral. I figured I'd see if I could reverse engineer and replicate the effect." I paused for a moment, considering an explanation, then motioned with one hand, palm-up. "The feral may seem fearless, but that just means that when it *does* get scared, it gets very scared. A non-violent solution seemed ideal given the small space."

When no reply came, I looked over to see that Zafir had crossed his arms again, his brow furrowed. I had a feeling he would have walked smack dab into the elevator door if I hadn't opened it before he reached it. Once we were on the ascent, he heaved a sigh.

"You are full of surprises. Next time, do try to have a more solid plan. That should not have worked." He gave me an unusually fiery look.

"I did have another plan—I just changed my mind when I saw what I was working with," I answered sweetly. That, at least, got a short laugh out of him, though he still looked concerned. "You said you're joining me for breakfast? I thought normal humans dislike the smell of Syldrari food?"

"It isn't an offensive smell, it's just strong," he replied, as if I needed placating. "And yes, we will eat in the mess hall. I should have the reports from your medical treatment, plus the analysis of your suit, so we can discuss things over breakfast. We'll figure out what you're doing next after I've gone through the reports."

CHAPTER NINE

"How are you feeling?" Zafir asked as we got comfortable in a plush corner of the mess hall, him taking up a seat on the sofa and me in a recliner. When I gave him a questioning look, he smiled and clarified, "Your arm and shoulder."

I glanced at the sling on my arm, then nudged off my slippers and pulled my legs onto the chair. "Oh. Still no feeling from the shoulder down. It's really strange."

Zafir sighed and scribbled something on his data pad. "I wish they would listen to my warnings. Such strong doses are liable to do more harm than good. You have interesting abilities, yes, but that doesn't mean you need a deadly-to-humans dosage."

"I don't blame them, considering how much tranquilizer they had to use to subdue me after the Resonance Incident." Zafir frowned slightly as he swiped through the records.

"That should have killed you," he murmured after a moment. "I see here that abnormally large doses are their norm with you. They've never even tried smaller ones. Honestly. I must wonder if your persistent amnesia is due to the stress these dosages have been putting you under..."

I raised my hands in a loose shrug. "Who knows. I'm not exactly worried about recovering my memories. Anyone I knew is dead."

"You don't wish to remember the dead?" He frowned.

"I don't particularly see a point in remembering or mourning people who have already moved on to their reincarnation," I countered.

"Reincarnation? Have you been hanging around other alien races too?" He gave me a lopsided smile.

"Huh?"

"Elara, humans don't really believe in reincarnation or life after death. If the— If we did, then we never would have pursued ways in which we could upload our consciousness to virtual reality and later to new bodies." He stroked his chin thoughtfully. "Re-uploading to a *body* may only be available to those who can afford it, but it is still common practice. On the other hand, there are still species who live out their lives mostly naturally.

"Then there are the Syldrari. To our knowledge, they live forever—or at least until they die in battle or grow too bored. I can't say I know anything about their beliefs on the afterlife."

"Uh huh… But reincarnation makes *sense*. Our energy has to go somewhere when we die—and re-uploading a consciousness is essentially synthetic reincarnation." I leaned forward in my seat. "Besides, if—"

"Our bosses would be very upset with you for calling it that," he remarked with a lopsided smile, glancing somewhere behind me. He lowered his voice immediately. "The others are back, and it appears Calder, Maelor, and Amara are with them. Further discussions will have to wait. They're not privy to most of what we need to talk about."

"Fine." I sat back and crossed my arms.

"The Syldrari sector is so cool!" Sarah called from somewhere behind me, followed by the sound of several large boxes being placed on a table—and Zafir's dubious expression. "Mr. Rel is so nice! We have food for everyone here. He said Elara's is more 'challenging,' but the rest is entry level. Come on, you two! Sit at the table with the rest of us!"

I bit back a groan and let Zafir help me to my feet.

"Here you go, Professor. The reports you asked for." Amara plopped a stack of folders down in front of Zafir's seat. "I didn't peek, promise."

"They threatened you, I take it?" He walked over to his own chair once I was situated, grimacing when she nodded. "I am sorry for that, Amara."

"So, you gonna explain what Elara did to subdue that chick

downstairs?" Maelor crossed his arms.

"You saw that?" I frowned.

"We saw it on Amara's monitors, but we also *felt it*." Calder turned his attention to Zafir. "You said she's got more control of her feral, but whatever that was didn't feel like a feral. It felt like some other kind of power."

"It will require more study," Zafir answered dryly. "She stated that it is the same manner in which her attacker subdued her—she merely mimicked it."

Amara rolled her eyes. "'Merely,' he says."

"Well, whatever. We brought the food, Sarah and I got to see the Syldrari sector for the first time, and it sounds like you guys weren't bored either. Win-win?" Nikolai shrugged, his hands in his pockets, and dropped heavily into a seat. "Those Syldrari are way nicer than any I ever heard of. Why is the Empire so scared of them? On the list of scary-looking aliens they're at the bottom for me."

"Well…" Zafir sighed. "Simply put, Syldrari are so much more advanced that the Empire is automatically inclined to see them as a threat."

"But they're so artsy. What are they gonna do, murder us with a paintbrush?" Sarah asked sarcastically.

"Their planet sounds pretty dangerous. I'm sure those hunting and self-preservation skills are what translate into their ability to destroy a human if they need to," I pointed out. "But enough of that. I'm *hungry* and all this smells *good*. Which one is mine?"

"Oh, these." Sarah pulled a good twelve of the boxes along the table to me. She nudged me with her knee, drawing my attention to an envelope in her hand. Unfamiliar handwriting scrawled the word 'Elara.'

"So, when I told Rel that you were super hungry, he kinda smirked and said he had an idea. We ended up with all this for you, and all the other ones to cover the rest of us. Let me know if you need help with anything? You can't cut up your food while your arm's in a sling."

While she was speaking, I took the envelope and sneaked it into my robe, then reached out and pulled the lid off one of the boxes, revealing another cut of the blue meat Syldrari seemed so fond of.

"Whoa, that color!" Maelor balked.

"It's basically steak." I glanced at him. "I've noticed most of the meat they utilize bleeds blue."

"Copper instead of iron," Zafir murmured absentmindedly while he skimmed his reports, though he must have sensed us all turning to look at him. "Ah… There are a few creatures native to our own planet that bleed blue too. It is usually due to the blood's copper content being higher than its iron. That could explain the Syldrari and their fare."

"The Syldrari too?" Sarah asked.

"Yes. You may recall that the university I studied at predated the

Empire's current levels of paranoia. One of my Syldrari classmates broke a beaker and cut his hand on the glass—blue *everywhere*." Zafir stroked his chin in thought. "The Empire has tried to replicate the diet and atmosphere of the Syldrari home planet in an attempt to create super soldiers. They're quite desperate to surpass the species. There are rumors they've even attempted to replace someone's blood with that of a Syldrari."

"Not at the table!" Sarah whacked Zafir with a stack of napkins. "Time for relaxation, not work and nauseating theories."

"Ah, fine…" he sighed.

"So, uh…" Maelor stared blankly at the many boxes of food still left to open. "Help?"

"Um, let's see…" Sarah pulled a crumpled paper out of her pocket and skimmed it a few times. After she was done, she stacked five boxes in front of each remaining person. "There. He even wrote on the boxes which one is for which part of the meal. Rel is seriously nice!"

"Syldran hospitality—" Zafir started.

"Come on, man, it's too early for lectures!" Maelor whined.

"…*I* wanted to hear about it." I pouted and rummaged through more of my boxes. "You know, I'm starting to think the only thing challenging about *my* food is the quantity."

"Mmm?" Sarah glanced over, mid-bite on a piece of bread. "Maybe he wanted you to have enough for later?"

"It *is* an odd amount of hospitality…" Zafir murmured, walking over to get a better look at my boxes. "It's more a meal fit for a… Hmmm." He fell silent and nudged his glasses absentmindedly, though I noticed his attention drifting to my dumpling-looking things.

"You want one?" I pointed to the dumplings. "I can't eat fifteen by myself."

"Ah…" He looked surprisingly conflicted for a moment, then gave me a sheepish smile. "Please."

I handed him a dumpling and watched him return to his seat. He didn't so much as hesitate before biting into it, and I shot him an amused look. "I take it you also grew used to their food while you were attending this odd university of yours?"

"Ah, yes." He shot me a wary look. "Part of our activities was cooking and sharing traditional foods among the student body, to promote cultural understanding and friendship."

"So, this must be what, your fourth or fifth body?" Calder asked bluntly. "I can't imagine the Empire supporting that any time recently."

"Something like that," Zafir answered with a mysterious smile. I wasn't buying it, but I wasn't ready to pry yet, either—at least, not into that part.

"Fourth or fifth body? What?" I stared at the two.

"Yes, as I mentioned earlier, re-uploading to new bodies is common practice." He glanced at me again. "Some people refer to it as re-sleeving, others call it ascending, and I've heard some of the more rural systems in the Empire call it rebirth. It is a process that allows the transfer of your neurochip and a digital backup of your mind to be transferred to a new body. Of which there are many kinds, though the Creshe Empire favors clones, as our other technologies aren't yet consistent enough for the more designer options some species offer."

"Okay..." I tried to process *that* onslaught of information. The idea of essentially body hopping infinitely upon death wasn't appealing to me. At least, not in my current state. If I were free to explore the universe, then it'd be a different story. Maybe.

"Alright, this isn't half bad..." Nikolai muttered from nearby—*that* surprised me. "It's kinda spicy, though. He said they usually put *how* much seasoning on this, Sarah?"

Sarah counted on her fingers as she talked. "Uhm, like five cups for the whole cut of meat, I think? Granted, what we have here is like a quarter of the thing he showed us. I'm glad he was willing to chop off part to make a milder version for us."

"Syldrari like their food strong," Zafir remarked. "I'm uncertain if it's a similar phenomenon to fluid shift in early space travelers, or if perhaps it's something more permanent in their physiology, but most humans can't handle the strong flavors— let alone taste them correctly."

Sarah was silent for a moment, then she looked at me and

pointed to the potato-things on her plate. "These taste kinda like potatoes with butter, lemon, salt, and pepper. Right?"

"Mmm…" I snatched one with my fork. "Wow, when you said mild…"

"Huh?" She promptly stole one of *my* potatoes. "Holy flavor overload! How can you eat that so casually?!"

"How indeed…" Zafir murmured, rubbing his chin.

"So, how was the Syldrari sector?" I asked, picking up a slice of pale pink bread.

"Oh! Once we told them we're friends with you, they were all really nice to us. They were super wary at first, though." Sarah smiled. "A few helped us carry all the food back to our vehicle, and this really nice lady gave us free candy to try."

So, every single Resonance Incident survivor here is fine with Syldrari food… I peered around the table, noting that everyone was happily chowing down. "Prof… Doc… Fuck it. **Zafir**. We should see what that captive thinks of this food."

Zafir shot me a smile. "I have several doctorates and I have taught in universities. Call me whatever you like. Zafir is fine as well.

"You want to determine if this oddity is due to the Resonance? I am in agreement. Usually it takes months for humans to grow accustomed to even the mildest Syldrari food. Something must be different about you all."

"I'll make a plate for her. I definitely can't eat all this," Sarah volunteered, and that was that.

I fell back into silence to enjoy my mountain of food, eating around half of everything before finally going for dessert. Once finished, I went to excuse myself so I could read Rel's letter, but Zafir stopped me.

"I want you to spend the day teaching Calder, Nikolai, and Maelor methods for controlling the feral," he informed me. "Our bosses are growing more inclined to send them out on missions before they're ready."

"Alright…" I turned to look at the three men. "Are you done eating? Good. Let's go, then."

CHAPTER TEN

Zafir watched in silence as Elara taught breathing methods to the men struggling to control their ferals. With each breath, they calmed further, despite the agitating noise from the speakers that was meant to trigger the change. After a moment's hesitation, he turned and began walking away from the viewing area.

"Professor? Where are you going?" Sarah called in surprise.

"Elara has their training well in hand. I'm going to go rest in my quarters." He paused to glance back with a smile. "See to it everyone knows not disturb me, please, Sarah."

Sarah nodded her affirmation and he took his leave, though there was no one to see his expression change to one of determination. He set off to his suite, locked the door behind him, and carried a stack of folders with him to a room barely larger than a closet. The doors slid shut behind him, and he sat on a low stool, placing the folders on a dark blue device to his left.

The odd machine whirred, engulfing the documents in cyan light. When the light abated, the folders and their contents were gone, leaving Zafir to place both his hands against an ornate console in front of him.

Within moments of touching the device, his consciousness swirled out of his body and into a virtual meeting space. The room was dark, its walls appearing to be made of a dark blue-green alloy etched with intricate, purposeful markings. It was void of any furniture or decoration, giving him the impression that his superior was too impatient with him to give a damn about hospitality.

"I told you not to contact me until you made progress," the Syldrari man on the other side of the room stated tiredly.

"I *have* made progress." Zafir stepped forward, calling the folders he'd transferred to hand. "You just won't *like* the progress, or my hypothesis."

The Syldrari sighed and made a motion with one hand, placing a table and two chairs between himself and Zafir. "Fine. Show me your progress."

"I believe Abel faked Elara's original diagnostics." Zafir placed a single sheet of paper in front of his superior, followed by a second. "I took the liberty of taking my own readings while she was unconscious. Not only did Abel lie about her neurochip being without detonation properties, he also lied about her human origins. This physiology is *not* human. It's…"

"She's experiencing cellular dissonance?" the Syldrari interjected, tracing his fingers over the chart. "Would this be due to the Resonance weapon? Or…no. *This* is destabilization here."

"She's been forced to appear human for long enough that her body is starting to grow…confused, at a cellular level." Zafir grimaced. "They're starting to 'learn' to be human. The humans are giving her a medication that perpetuates whatever *originally* gave her this form—though I'm not convinced they're aware they're doing this.

"My current hypothesis is that she and her family were in hiding, pretending to be humans. The Resonance Incident may have caused the beginning stages of cellular confusion and some of the other problems she's experienced."

"What species was she, and why would she be— You think she's *Syldrari*?" the man demanded.

"I believe this is why she was in hiding." Zafir placed a sheet of black paper in front of his boss. His tone shifted to one of immense annoyance and he gave the other man a sour glare. "This was taken while she was unconscious after her little spat with you. Her signature—"

"You truly believe she might be a queen? With a signature like this, she could overthrow—" The Syldrari cut himself off with an agitated twitch, quickly regaining his composure. "We must both be careful. No one can learn of this. If she is a queen, and has this much potential, my entertainment and your research will be the least of our concerns—to say nothing of my ongoing investigations."

"Then I am to continue as I have been?"

"Yes. And do something about her neurochip, would you? Such a distasteful, inelegant invention." The Syldrari eyed the information on the Creshe chip. If something like that were to malfunction, the resulting detonation could kill more than just the person it was attached to.

A mischievous smile spread across Zafir's face. "Not to worry. I've already taken the liberty of changing it out for one of Syldrari design—all with my superior's approval, of course."

"*Tch*. Anything else?"

"If you could refrain from thrashing Elara and giving her ideas, that would be fantastic." Zafir's expression changed to one of bemusement as he went on to explain how Elara had managed to reverse engineer the Syldrari's ability to terrify ferals.

"I see nothing wrong with giving her interesting ideas or suggestions, but I will keep your counsel in mind. Some caution would probably be prudent."

CHAPTER ELEVEN

"Sarah said you wanted to speak with me?" I strode into Zafir's office and closed the door behind me. He looked mildly surprised to see me at first, but a welcoming smile soon took over. Considering *he'd* called *me*, I had to wonder what that expression was for, but he looked ready to talk and I didn't want to interrupt.

"Yes... We have much to discuss." He watched me carefully as I sat down across from him. "First and foremost, I should inform you of Abel's lie and the steps I've taken to fix what he'd done."

"Oh lovely. I can't wait." I leaned against the armrest. "*Do* tell me of your noble deeds, O great hero."

A short laugh escaped him before he settled back in his seat with his hands steepled in his lap, his voice all business. "To the point it is. Abel, contrary to both his reports to me and what he told you, had you fitted with a manner of brain chip that can be detonated remotely. The military recently began investigating Abel's activities due to his sudden—*classified*—disappearance. As much of his misconduct was in relation to the other survivors, I took the liberty of ordering additional scans while you were unconscious."

I gave him an impatient look when he paused for a swig of water. "Which showed the chip. And?"

"I took the liberty of replacing it. After some discussions with our bosses, I educated them on the nuances of survivors such as yourself and acquired permission to use a Syldrari-made chip." He gave me that mysterious 'I know you're overthinking every word I say' smile of his. "The survivors, and especially you, require more processing power than the Empire's chips provide. Luckily for us, the Empire has no qualms about stealing technology from others and refitting it to suit their own purposes."

"Why Syldrari, specifically?" I inquired curiously. "There's plenty of races more advanced than us."

"Because the Syldrari are the *most* advanced species we've encountered, and because the Syldrari chip was the only one you showed compatibility with. I imagine it must have something to do with the Resonance Incident and your Syldrari suit." Zafir shrugged, seemingly unbothered by my suspicions. "With that explained, we come to the primary reason I sent for you: I want your permission to run further tests. I'm not confident that Abel didn't fake more information. Specifically, I would like to run blood tests."

"I mean…fine?" I glanced around, then back at Zafir. "Here, or one of the labs?"

"Here will suffice." He motioned for me to roll up my sleeves before standing and beginning to rummage in the nearby cabinets. "How is the training progressing?"

I shook my head. "It's going. There's not really much to say on that front until they can start actually going out to do…whatever it is we do."

"I'm still waiting to hear back from our bosses, but I *did* send in my request that Calder, Nikolai, and Maelor begin working." Zafir pulled a chair up next to me and rolled a tray over, motioning for me to give him my arm. I eyed the tray, taking stock of what he'd laid out. There were several black vials, plus an odd black band embellished with a darker black pattern in a slightly different material. After a moment, I relented and let Zafir take my arm in his hands. He smiled and continued on. "Speaking of which, they want you to resume patrolling the Syldrari sector during the day. They believe we've given it enough time—"

"I'm not so sure about that," I interjected, thinking back to the letter Sarah had brought from Rel. "From what I understand, the Syldrari are already convinced that I'm Lethe, and it may be dangerous for me there as a result."

"And you have this on good authority?" he inquired as he gently prodded at my arm, sanitizing it before strapping a thin black band around the crook of my elbow.

I grimaced. It was too late *not* to elaborate. "Rel sent a letter along with our meal the other week. He warned me that I should stay away because multiple clans, including the R'selkti, are looking for me due to these rumors."

"Of course…" Zafir sighed, his expression falling. "I'm afraid there's nothing I can say at this point to make them reconsider… at least, not without putting you at greater risk. Tomorrow you will begin your patrols again, though I will see if I can convince our superiors to permit one of your colleagues to join you. Either way, I am planning to have one of them act as our 'vigilante' in the sector for a time, while you focus elsewhere. Who would you say is the most stable?"

"Nikolai, for sure. He's naturally more level-headed than the others, and he's shown far fewer signs of feral thoughts." I gave Zafir a questioning look as he took the band off. "Done already?"

"Indeed. It's much more efficient than a needle." He tilted one of the black glass vials, peering into it briefly before capping it off. The other three were quickly sealed as well, and if there was anything off about my blood, he didn't comment or show it. A pity, that. I was curious to know if there were still traces of blue in it, like I'd seen while fighting the mysterious Syldrari man.

"Now then, I recommend you rest for the remainder of the day. I want you at your best when dealing with the Syldrari. Perhaps you can do some reading up on their culture while you relax?"

I arrived in the Syldrari sector early the next morning just as the shops were opening and people were beginning to drift into the streets. Though it was still early, there seemed to be an unusual number of people out and about. They were all so distracted that I managed to make it all the way to Rel's café without anyone acknowledging my presence.

"Elara? You shouldn't..." Rel released an aggravated sigh. "You don't have a choice and that's why you're here. Of course. What can I do for you, then? Are you feeling better?"

"Better...ish?" I shrugged, giving him a small smile. "What can I say? It's one thing after another. I'm just trying to roll with the punches at this point."

"Understandable." He nodded, smiling tiredly. "Will I be surprising you again today?"

"Can you stop spoiling the *graekstidat* fodder for *one second*?" a grumpy voice demanded. I glanced over to see a Syldrari man with pale grey skin approaching. His black hair obscured one eye, its cyan underside glowing gently against his cheek. His eyes were among the oddest I'd seen, right up there with Rel's—minus the glow. While his pupils were consistent with Syldrari patterning, their deep mauve, yellow, and jade green colors blended together similarly to human hazel.

"A what fodder?" I looked over at the aggravated-looking Rel. "And since when do you have an edgy teenager working for you?"

"Ah, think of it as an amphibious, furry shark hybrid the length of, oh, several train cars," he answered, pressing his fingers to his temples. "Furthermore, Aldiner is old enough to be your great-great-great—"

"I'm working here to pay up for pissing off the *Elder* here," Aldiner interjected with a snort as he pushed his hands into his apron pockets. He leaned over me, examining me from a few angles. "You don't have that military air to you. Are you sure you're a—"

I gave Aldiner my best cold, intimidating glare as he reached out and poked my cheek. When he went for a second poke, I knocked his arm aside, spun behind him and elbowed him – *hard* – where I hoped his kidneys were. He grunted, and I moved to take him down. Alas, an arm wrapped around my waist and lifted me clean off the floor—and didn't stop until my butt was planted on a broad shoulder. I looked down, startled enough to forget about beating the crap out of Aldiner.

"Ignore Aldiner. He likes to annoy everyone he sees and hates being ignored." The much-larger Syldrari glanced up at me. I certainly hadn't expected it to be the grumpy soldier from earlier, seeing as he'd appeared to rather dislike me. "You're fast, for a *strigaella*."

"A human woman." Rel answered my inevitable next question with a sigh. "Aldiner, *behave*. Humans are much less...ah..." He motioned with his hands and wiggled his fingers as he searched for the word.

"You don't touch humans unless invited to," the Syldrari soldier grunted.

"She invited ya?" Aldiner leaned forward, peering first at the soldier and then at where I was currently perched on his shoulder.

"I didn't, but I can appreciate that he was stopping me from starting a brawl with you right here and—" I cut myself off with an aggravated sigh when I felt the feral attempting to push forward. All three Syldrari went still, watching me warily. What exactly they sensed, or how much, I wasn't sure I wanted to know. "Set me down, please...uh..."

The large Syldrari helped me down off his shoulder and carefully set me down, looking a tad bashful. Considering our initial brusque interactions, I found his sudden gentleness both strange and amusing.

"Heh, always bitching about manners and you never introduced yourself, did ya?" Aldiner gave the soldier a cocky grin.

"...Call me Casair." The soldier glanced away. He seemed a little disgruntled, but the patterns of light on his arms didn't so much as flicker.

...Aldiner, on the other hand... I glanced at the self-contained

rave fish and the way his glow was strobing numerous colors, then back to Casair. "And you can call me Elara, though I suppose you knew that already."

"Awww, Casair is shy!" Aldiner teased. "Suppressing—"

"Quiet, *vlerst* bait." Casair crossed his arms at the strobing Syldrari, then glanced over to me. "Back to patrolling needlessly?"

"Something like that. I was sitting around recovering for so long that my boss's bosses started thinking up other uses for me." I grimaced before walking over to the counter and hopping up onto my usual seat. "As for surprising me, Rel, yes. Though I'd like a glass of…" I paused to reference the menu. "*Jiirst~nil?*"

Either I said it very right or terribly wrong, because all three men stopped what they were doing to stare at me in shock. Well, Aldiner had already been staring, but he didn't count.

"Ah, there you are, Rel my dear!" A woman's voice rang through the room as the doors banged open. "I've been looking everywhere for you!"

"Mother, please…" a familiar voice groaned, and I glanced back to see the bright green candy girl, who perked up and waved when she spotted me.

"Careful you don't become the queen's snack," Casair muttered into my ear. He moved away to a booth in the corner, settling into it in a way that allowed him to keep an eye on everyone.

Queen? I eyed the flamboyant woman and the three people with her. If one was her daughter, I had to assume the other two were guards—they had weapons holstered at their hips, at least.

"I'm honored by your visit, but please refrain—" Rel began.

"So, when will you become one of my consorts?" the… queen? demanded with a bright smile—one that faltered when Rel placed the drink he was making in front of *me* instead of her. I half-expected her to be angry, but instead she studied me for a moment, her head tilting as she examined me from head to toe. She pressed a finger against her full, black-painted lips.

"A visitor in the Syldrari sector… Are you an *iri, sen'iri, sol'iri, anad'iri, sora'iri,* or *lun'iri*? I can never tell with you humans…"

"Elara is an *iri*, honestly…" Rel rubbed his temples. "How many times must we explain to you that the humans are binary in their biological—"

"And that is just the problem! *Biological!* If they didn't hop around between bodies and swap out prosthetics constantly—no offense—perhaps I could more easily identify who they are!" The queen *hmph*ed, crossed her arms, then finally seemed to spot my uniform. "Ah, a military girl—my *favorite*. If Rel still refuses to become my consort… How would you like off this planet, sweetie?"

"Mother, please!" The candy girl moved between her mother and me. "Elara is the nice human I told you about! She likes the candy I make, and her friends are going to help give me ideas for ones more humans will like! Plus, you haven't even introduced yourself! Humans can't sense a queen's identity!"

"Speaking of my colleagues." I pulled out a stack of folded papers. "They may not be able to come to the sector for a while, so they asked me to deliver their notes to you."

She took them and skimmed the first page, the glowing sections of her skin pulsing faster the further she read. "This is… This is great! I'm going to go work on the next batch!"

And with that, the excitable candy girl darted out of the café, practically skipping as she went.

"I'm Xilen, I run the mercantile Dvarl Clan." Xilen offered me her hand. When I shook it, she paused to study my face and search my eyes. "If you ever want off this planet, Rel knows how to contact me. It wouldn't do for a pretty little thing like you to be wasted on the humans."

"…I'll keep that in mind." I gently reclaimed my hand while Aldiner snickered from somewhere behind me.

"Do you find women…?" Rel raised an eyebrow when I shook my head. "Then you are merely being polite."

"I'm keeping my options open," I countered. "If the military can't recreate the Resonance phenomena—and maybe even if they can—their next step is going to be breeding our mutations down to offspring. I want no part of that, so having options is good."

"Ahhh, she's so smart!" Xilen leaned over to squeeze me, rubbing her cheek against mine. To my surprise, the Syldrari in the café all looked ready to start a fight over it—with *her*. I got the distinct feeling it *wasn't* jealousy, though, which made it all the more confusing.

"You just say the word and I'll have you off this planet and into my arms! Why, we could take the nearest intergalactic gate straight back to Syldra and go shopping! I'd love to see how such a cute human would look in Syldrari clothes—you don't mind translucency, do you? I'd imagine not—"

"Elara needs to have her meal before she returns to her duties." Rel suddenly appeared behind us, his hand on the queen's shoulder and his voice cold as ice. "If you're here to discuss trade, you can wait for me in the usual room."

"How dare—" One of the men I assumed to be the queen's guards started to raise his weapon. I figured this was as good a time as any to make my point.

I was out of my chair and twisting the weapon out of the man's hand before he could finish his sentence. Using his body weight against him, I took him to the floor and twisted his arm behind his back, placing my booted foot against the back of his shoulders.

"You— Ugh!" The other guard grunted as Casair's fist met his stomach.

"Please keep in mind that my *job* is to keep conflicts in the Syldrari sector to a minimum, and I am authorized to use lethal force if you pull a weapon on anyone, regardless of their species." I spoke calmly, grinding my heel into the Syldrari's back for emphasis. "You may keep your weapons and use them for defense if necessary. If you pull them again for any other reason..."

"Cuuute!" Xilen squeezed me in another hug. It took most of my willpower to beat down the feral, especially since I happened to agree with the idea of fucking ripping her arms off if she hugged me one more damn time. She leaned down to speak quietly into my ear. "Be careful, dear. If you ever suspect you're in trouble or in over your head, I'm sure you know how we can get them to come running to save you. And stay far, far away from the R'selkti and their queen."

"Uh—?" I didn't get to ask her what the hell she was on about before she'd fetched her guards and led them into a back room, leaving me confused and a little unnerved.

"I apologize for Xilen's...eccentricities," Rel offered when I finally turned around to return to my seat.

"Are all queens so goddamn pushy?" I snorted irritably, trying to shove her insinuations out of my mind.

"Ah...with *iri* being the rarest of the six, they tend to act however they please..." he murmured awkwardly. "It is not uncommon for Syldrari women to turn their rarity into a form of power over others. Most *iri*, even if they are not queens, have many... I believe the human word is 'spouses'?"

"Long story short: Most recent queens have been groomed to see the other sexes as playthings to collect. Some of them even collect other *iri*, but it's generally frowned upon," Casair piped up. "Xilen is of a different type. She's lasted so long because she can pretend. Whatever she told you, I'd wager she was bein' honest."

"Blah blah blah." Aldiner rolled his eyes and leaned toward me. "You know, being a queen's pet has its perks."

"Aldiner!" Rel barked, his markings flaring brightly. "*Go wash the dishes!*"

"Fiiine." Aldiner sauntered off toward the back, though just before he disappeared through the door he turned and stuck his fingers up in a V, flicking his surprisingly long forked tongue between them.

…I have a feeling it's a good thing Rel didn't catch that… I eyed the door for a moment, then turned my attention back to Rel. "So, are there any other developments I should know about before I start my patrols again?"

"Just…be cautious. Someone has convinced the people here that you are Lethe – and that she may be either a queen or related to one." Rel sighed heavily and pushed his hair back. "Aside from that, things have been calming down since the little queen was found, though with Xilen here… who knows. Her unannounced visits always cause trouble."

CHAPTER TWELVE

"Can you wait a damned minute?!" Casair demanded as he followed me through the streets of the Syldrari sector. What I guessed to be curses streamed from his mouth when he finally caught up to me, giving me an agitated glare.

"I'm on duty, so if you want to talk, keep up," I countered, not giving him a second glance. "You're a soldier yourself, right?"

"Patrols are a thing of the ancient past—or only used in interspecies cities," he snapped, shaking his head. "We have better things to spend our time on. Walking in circles gets nothing of value done…" He trailed off into a disgruntled growl and rubbed the back of his neck. "…But I understand that orders are orders. Humans closely monitor performance?"

"Especially the performance of *oddities*," I answered pointedly. "I think we came to an understanding that I was going to patrol even if it isn't necessary, due to my other non-options. Since you're going to follow me, can you answer a few questions?"

He shrugged. "Depends what they are."

"Xilen rattled off a bunch of things she thought I might be before Rel told her I'm an *iri*," I started, frowning. "I know '*iri*' translates to 'woman,' but she listed off, what, five other things?"

"Ah…that." Casair raised an eyebrow. "Those are the biological sexes that Syldrari mature into when they reach adulthood. Our young folk are usually sexless, though queens who come into power early also become *iri* early.

"To humans, *iri*, *sen'iri*, and *sora'iri* look like women. *Sol'iri*, *anad'iri*, and *lun'iri* look like men. *Lun'iri* are the closest thing to a human's understanding of 'male,' and they're the most common sex in our species."

"Uh…" I stared at him in disbelief for a moment. "How the hell do you tell who is who? Or does that not matter in your culture outside of identifying queens?"

"Goes back to the whole bit where our senses are better than yours," he answered with a grin. "We can see their aura and hear certain layers in their voice that explain who they are. When dealing with other races, we just tell 'em to base it off…uh…" He flushed a little and patted his chest.

"Right. If it has boobs, call it she or her?" I asked dryly, and he nodded in response. "I think I follow, and I'm glad going with something so simple is acceptable."

"We learned a damned long time ago that we can't expect

other species to see or hear the universe the way we do," he remarked, nodding. "Now, if you don't mind, uh…"

"Let me guess—you wanted to discuss something, and that was your main reason for joining me?" I asked dryly, watching as he gave me a sheepish smile. "I thought as much. Figured it was only fair I have you answer something for me first. So, what is it?"

"Right…" he grumbled. "Can you find out if Xilen told any of the humans that she's coming? It's considered common courtesy to inform a planet's officials ahead of time, due to the effect a queen can have on any Syldrari there."

Doubtful, I pulled my communicator out of my pocket. "She didn't seem to have much of an effect on you all, aside from annoyance."

"That's…" Casair trailed off into thought, frowning, as I dialed Zafir's number.

<Elara? Did something come up? Do you need an extraction team?> he inquired the moment he answered. <You—>

"Do I need to start calling you Mother Zafir?" I asked dryly, shaking my head. "Nothing is wrong, I just need some information. Were we aware a queen was coming to visit?"

<A…> He paused, and I heard him tapping away at his data pad. When he spoke again, his tone had grown more serious. <Are you alone right now?>

"No."

<Do you need an extraction—>

"For fuck's sake, Zafir. I just need you to answer the damn question!"

"Allow me." Casair took my phone and raised it to his ear. "'Zafir,' right. My name is Casair. *I* asked Elara about the queen's visitational status. You see…"

Over next few minutes, Casair explained the encounter in the diner and his concern that the queen's visit was unannounced. After he was done, he handed my phone back to me.

"Uh, you get all that?" I questioned when I heard nothing but tapping.

<Yes…ah. Here it is. Marked as *unimportant*?! Those fools! Are they trying to undermine—> Zafir reined himself in with a sigh. I could practically *hear* him rubbing his temples. <Continue your patrol for the day; I'll arrange for a relocation for the duration of the queen's visit if I can. You're lucky they aren't already ornery. Hmmm…>

"What is it?" I found his shift in tone a little strange.

<Just a theory. One I can explore later.> He chuckled. <Be careful, and don't hesitate to call back if you need to get out quickly.>

"Your boss seems…eccentric." Casair snorted, the luminous patterns on his skin glowing a brief pale purple before returning to a calmer light blue. "I'll accompany you for the remainder of your patrol."

"Weren't you *just* saying that patrols are a waste of time?" I shot him an amused look.

Both his cheeks and the tips of his ears flushed blue as he looked away with a quiet grunt, his glow shifting rapidly between cyan, pink, purple, white and…off? before finally phasing back to cyan. He let out a slow, measured breath.

"Making sure the nice-but-overly-confident human stays alive isn't a waste of time. And if the rumors about that vigilante are true…"

He gave me a pointed look, but I appreciated that he didn't push the matter.

"Well, I can understand that. Plus, it's a nice change of pace. After all, I don't want to drag you out for a stupid brawl now," I remarked thoughtfully, shooting him a mischievous smile. "Though I *am* curious what sparring with you would be like."

"Heh. Don't get ahead of yourself, *yir~stryta*." He patted my head. "If you don't want people thinking you're Lethe, going a round or two with a career soldier like me isn't a good idea."

I sighed in disappointment and linked my hands behind my back. "You have a point there, I guess. Still, I can't help but be curious. We're told Syldrari are *so* much stronger than humans, that we don't stand a chance even with augmentations. Yet we're not shown why."

"Ahhh, so the lack of information makes the curiosity of a hunter come out in you. Dangerous, unknown prey for you to challenge yourself against." He nodded faintly and rubbed his chin. "I thought such instincts were dead in humans. Well, I can tell you we *are* dangerous, when we must be. You would be too if your home planet was akin to ours."

"Yeah...I've gotten the impression that your planet is something of a death trap." I shook my head. "Well, I won't press you for a match, but I am disappointed that it's ill-advised."

"Heh. Maybe one day you'll get a chance. I don't mind giving curious humans a taste of our differences." Casair smirked. Noticing my expression, he added, "Don't be so eager to prove your ability. If you hold your own–or *win*–against a Syldrari, *you aren't human*. Given which government's leash you're on, I don't think those are implications you want to explore."

"Why do you have to be so damned...*reasonable*?" I let out an agitated sigh. "Fine, *fine*, I get it. What's a girl gotta do to have an interesting, *friendly* fight for once..."

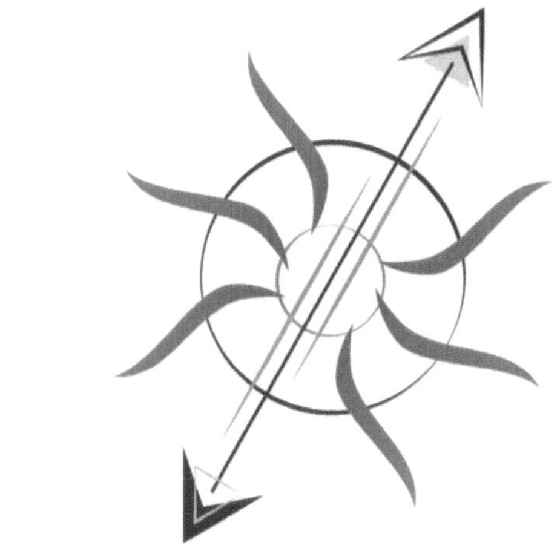

CHAPTER THIRTEEN

"Okay, Nikolai, how does the Syldrari sector seem to you?" I asked, watching the feed from his visor on the screen before me. He whipped his head around a little too much for my taste, but at least he was trying to stay alert. "The area you're above now is where they've been having issues with other aliens coming into their territory."

<It seems kinda dead? Shouldn't a visiting queen make it livelier?> Nikolai peered over the edge of the building he'd perched on. Sure enough, there was no one on the street below him. <Orders?>

I glanced back at Zafir, who just smiled and made a flourishing motion with one hand. Great. He'd meant it when he said I'd be in charge of this one.

"Keep patrolling. Just because nothing has gone wrong yet doesn't mean it won't." I tapped a button on the console to remove my image from the inside of his visor and crossed my arms. "If you notice any part of your suit malfunctioning or glitching, come straight back to HQ. We think some of the Syldrari have the ability to disable the suits—or at least some of their functions."

<Right. Which is why I need to find non-Syldrari troublemakers, give them a reason to like me…> Nikolai sighed, then nodded. <Understood. Continuing to patrol.>

I muted my mic before glancing at Zafir again. "Is this really necessary? I have studying to do."

Zafir adjusted his glasses and came to join me at the monitors. "Absolutely. You should be prepared to oversee your teammates or the other teams. I can't direct them all at once."

"Right." I stuffed my hands into my pockets. "Nikolai is right, though. The sector should be livelier. It was buzzing with activity before the queen even showed up at Rel's joint."

"It does seem a bit too— One moment. I'm getting a call." He turned away, likely pulling up his AR interface. "Sir? Yes. Mhm. But she's oversee— …I understand."

"You sure backed down quick," I observed, stepping around the obviously disgruntled man to peer at his face. The expression I saw there was, in a word, *dangerous*. "Work for me?"

He took a steadying breath before turning to look at me. "You are to break into an underground fighting ring near the slums and free the alien slaves there. A politician who is…no longer needed runs the ring. Our superiors intend to use you busting the ring as a way to remove him from his position."

"Making themselves look better at the same time." I pulled a sour face as Zafir nodded. "When?"

"Now."

"Seriously? *Now*? Without preparation or any intelligence to—"

"I will send the maps to your suit. Contact me if you need me— I'll be remaining voice-only this time." He shooed me toward the door.

"Good, it's a little hard to focus with holo-you waving your hands around in my retinas." I gestured briefly at my eyes and stuck my tongue out at him. "Make sure Nikolai doesn't get into too much trouble."

"Elara, you're dealing with—" He cut himself off, his tone one of exasperation.

Slaves. You said it already. I get it. I clenched my hand into a fist, feeling my blood boiling. *Sometimes joking around is the best way to cope with a dark situation, you know? There's no telling what kind of slaves they have there. I doubt it's just the fighters.*

Once I was suited up, on my bike, and headed for the slum border, I connected to Zafir's communication line. "What species are being held captive, and how am I meant to subdue them all on my own?"

<Let's see...> He paused, tapping away. <...They look to be primarily Syldrari and humans. There are a few others as well, but

the Syldrari will be the most dangerous. Ah… Unless the humans are drugged, perhaps. That could be unpredictable.

<As for keeping them in line, it says here that an informant has been leaking tales of Lethe's justice endeavors to the slaves, along with pictures from the media. Your identity will hopefully make them less agitated.>

"And I'm escorting them where?"

More tapping, then an answer. <The Syldran Embassy. I'll send you the coordinates now in case Nikolai's little problem isn't over by then. Now, if you'll excuse me…>

I grimaced. It was nowhere near as much information as I wanted, though it sounded like he was in the same predicament.

Shortly thereafter, I parked my bike on a rooftop, eyeing the streets below before turning toward the horizon. The slums in the distance had buildings, at least, but it looked like they hadn't received any maintenance in decades—or longer. It looked more like the ruins of an old city center.

A few buildings over from me, according to the overlay in my visor, was the main entrance to the fighting ring. No other entryways were marked. I rubbed my temples and sighed, debating looking for possible other entrances. Or maybe I should just barge in through the front door.

…*Or can I bluff?* I scanned the entrance again, along with the two human bouncers standing at the front. They were average in size, without the sort of bulk I'd come to expect from guards. They did, however, have various cybernetic implants, according to my visor. One had a mechanical arm, and the other had had both his legs replaced from the hips down.

"Uh…" One of the men hesitated as I strolled casually toward them. "You got an invitation… Lethe, was it?"

"The vigilante? Great…" The other one groaned. "Look, if you're going to beat us up, at least leave me fun bits alone, alright? The missus—"

"Maybe I just want to see if I can find myself an interesting opponent?" I suggested with the sweetest smile I could muster.

"You're…not gonna hurt us?" They exchanged glances.

"You're military, aren't you? Working an extra job to pay the bills, I understand. Perhaps even being coerced by a corrupt politician…" I let my words hang in the air, then took another step forward. "You can let me in and go home, or you can test the lightning resistance of your cybernetics. Which will it be?"

The one with the bionic legs slumped. "If we just let you go…"

"A light singeing it is, then." I snapped my fingers, sending electricity arcing over their skin—and only their skin—until their clothes were torn and scorched and they each had a few minor burns.

They, understandably, freaked out and flailed back, making everything more dramatic than it really needed to be. I was already in the building before they finally seemed to realize I wasn't going to kill them.

I sighed. *Any guards inside, though… This is going to be a mess.*

Loud music and the voice of an announcer competed in the dim establishment, while white neon lights and signs strobed everywhere, indicating the direction to the gambling tables and other…services. A large variety of different species surrounded a massive arena, which was set into the floor and sealed off with a thick, clear substance.

Hanging from the ceiling were females of various species in little-to-no clothing, whose job was apparently to dance. Most numerous among them were Syldrari with vacant expressions in their eyes, the glowing parts of their bodies strobing more drastically than any of the lights in the room.

Of the Syldrari…women? I noticed no small few of them had penises, and some had both male and female genitalia. Only three appeared to be women as I currently understood women to be. Upon even further inspection, I realized some of the caged Syldrari were entirely masculine except for those bits.

I think I'm starting to grasp why Xilen listed so many sexes… I shoved the confusion and curiosity from my mind and refocused my attention on the scene closer to ground level. The guards hadn't noticed me slipping through the crowd, but I wasn't entirely sure what to do. *If I'm supposed to rescue the slaves, do I just kill everyone else?*

I slipped closer and peered down at the arena, eyeing the fight below. Utter brutality. The human fighting a red-skinned, four-armed giant of a man was about to be quartered—and the audience was *screaming* for it to happen. A flicker of regret, then acceptance, crossed the giant's face as he started to pull.

No. Stop them. Something not wholly unlike the feral burst forth from within me. I had to stop the murderous humans, without causing harm to the slaves.

A foreign feeling overcame me, like a cold, dead calm, and my visual and auditory senses dulled for a few seconds. Arcs of lightning and whips of starry darkness tore through the crowd around me, arcing through every non-slave in the room. I heard platters drop and glasses break, and my pulse raced as blood pooled around me.

As the last of the humans crumpled to the floor, my senses returned and went into overdrive. I looked around my immediate field of vision, double-checking that it was only humans who'd fallen. I'd just…reacted. It almost felt as if I'd fallen unconscious for a moment, despite seeing my abilities still writhing in the air around me.

Thank goodness… Just the humans. I need to be more careful. I clenched my eyes shut, forcing myself to focus. My work here wasn't done.

I heard footsteps splashing through the blood, and the music stopped. Sensing someone carefully inching toward me from my left, I turned to spot a Syldrari girl glowing grey.

"U-um…" she stuttered.

"Can they hear us?" I pointed at the clear barrier of the ring below.

"Y-yes, but don't break it. The security…" She gulped. "Y-you're… That vigilante human, right? Are you… You're here to…"

I took a deep breath and reabsorbed the energy still hovering around me. Someone had to stay calm for these people. My frustrations could be vented later.

"I'm here to take you all to the Syldran Embassy. Finding where you all belong is a touch beyond my expertise, so they will be taking care of you all once I've freed you."

The girl said nothing, just started shaking, so I turned back to the barrier and gave it a few good knocks before yelling down at the hesitating giant, "I'm here to get you all out of here, so don't kill the poor bastard yet! I have questions for him!"

With that, I turned and went to frisk the bodies of the guards in the room, collecting the devices off them that I figured I might need to bypass the inevitable security measures. One of the guys had been on the phone at the time and dropped it, so I gave it a quick search for any functionality that might allow me to disable the security systems within the building.

"They…um…" The girl pointed up at the cages.

"They will need medical assistance and detox, I assume?" I pressed a button at my wrist to make certain that line made it to Zafir, then released it to send. "Is anyone else drugged that you know of?"

"Humans." She nodded. "But sedatives, until made to fight.

They try to hurt themselves otherwise. Rest of us knew it waiting game."

"Waiting and humans don't mix. They don't live as long naturally." I shook my head faintly and made my way toward a locked door. "What other security—?"

"Here." The girl offered me a red keycard, her eyes shining with determination. "I stole it from one of the guards when…um. Red cards can go anywhere! The security room is downstairs near all the cells."

Do I trust her? I studied the girl for a moment, then nodded. "What's your name?"

"Qiis! Call me Qiis!" She perked up a little. "The fighting slaves are scary. Can I…can I wait until you help the…not fighters? Sorry, human sex-gender concepts confuse me… Um…"

I glanced up at the caged people, then back to her. "I think it's safe to say the Syldrari sexes confuse me just as much as the human concepts confuse you, if not more. I'm just going to guess that all the fighters have neither breasts nor, uh…"

Not sure of a polite way to say it, I motioned up at one of the people above us who had a vagina and no other equipment. Qiis' cheeks turned blue and her glow changed to a deep yellow.

"Yes… Uh… Customers don't like to play with…" She pointed down at the fighters. "Woman?"

"Man," I corrected. "Are you sure they can wait?"

Qiis nodded. "Yes, keep fighters from fighting, please. Guards below, too…"

The more stressed she became, the more her grasp of the human language seemed to slip. I nodded to her and set off down to the prison below. Now that I had blood on me, I doubted I'd have any issues figuring out who was an enemy. I'd be shot at before I could even open my mouth.

While the club above appeared relatively welcoming, for its guests at least, the underbelly was little better than a cage. The black metal walls had large spots of rust peeling off them, old bloodstains marked nearly every surface, and in many places electrical wiring and panels remained exposed to the elements. It looked more like an old, decrepit maintenance tunnel than a place to keep people.

Why are they all so easy? I smashed a man's head against a wall, letting him drop limply to the ground. Despite the commotion, most of the men were still sitting in their cells, doing nothing but staring at the ground.

I decided to head to the arena first. The large, circular arena was walled in with seamless clear material, giving spectators a clear sightline to the violence. Inside, the flat floor was covered in sand. There was a section with nasty-looking water off to the side, lined with fake trees and a few boulders. Bloodstains on the objects made their purpose all too clear.

The red giant of a man was still holding the human at arm's length, but given the crazed look on the man's face, I could see why.

"I'm Lethe. I'll be taking everyone here to the Syldran Embassy once I've gotten those restraints off you all. You should be able to contact your own embassy from there." I adopted a matter-of-fact tone as I approached the giant and the human.

"Lethe…?" the giant asked suspiciously, slowly examining me. Finally, his eyes went wide. "You're here to free us? Truly? Marvelous!"

"I'm going to need help, though. I need to know everything you can tell me about your restraints and how I might get them off you without causing damage." I nodded to the oddly dapper-sounding giant. "And I suppose I'll have to knock out the drugged captives."

"Certainly! I will tell you all you wish to know!" He stepped over to me, kneeling so he was closer to my level – though it didn't help much. "Please, permit me to show you to the security room. I believe that is where their equipment is stored—or the access to it, at least."

Without further prompting, the giant began to tell me everything he knew about the restraints as he escorted me through the building—the deadly shocks, their ability to inject drugs of various kinds, and the difficult-to-damage metal alloy. The adjustable shock was such a high voltage that it posed a threat to even the Syldrari—though personally I wanted to know how they'd been captured in the first place if they were so superior to humans.

It took me a good half an hour to find the tools used for placing and removing the restraints. By then, Zafir had sent a brief message to my visor to let me know he'd returned to observing my work, but was remaining silent due to the captives' hearing abilities.

"Where to start..." I sighed, looking at the intersection of hallways. The bastards had sorted the slaves by species.

"Syldrari would be my suggestion, Lady Lethe." The giant bowed, flourishing two of his hands. "They will be able to assist in freeing more of the captives, and their harmonic abilities will allow them to soothe those who might otherwise lash out."

"Good point." I nodded, looking up at the giant with a smile. "Your name...?"

"Ah! Forgive my poor manners, Lady Lethe!" He bowed again. "I am Gixorbilav."

"Nice to meet you. Could I bother you to guard the stairs for me, Gixorbilav?" I gave him an exceedingly polite smile, seeing as he'd been almost overly polite thus far.

"It would be my honor, but will you be alright alone... Ah." Gixorbilav looked down the hallways and nodded his understanding. "Of course—I will not fit down most. Should you need my assistance with the others of my kind, you know where to find me."

We parted ways, and I steeled myself as best I could before heading into the Syldrari cellblock. Most of the prisoners stirred at my presence, a few even creeping closer to the bars. Bars I knew damn well they could break if they wanted. Why hadn't they?

"My name is Lethe and I'm here to return you to the Syldran Embassy," I announced in my best commanding tone. It seemed to have some effect, at least, since many of them straightened and appeared more alert. "The device I'm holding allows me to remove your restraints. If any of you are willing, I'd be grateful for assistance in freeing the other captives."

"Huh...cute," a Syldrari with pale purple skin murmured as he examined me. His tail swished back and forth, his glow shifting between various shades of purple. "A debt should be repaid and all that. I'll help. Whatever powers you have, there's some people down here they just won't work on."

A few other men voiced their agreement, and once I'd released all of them from their cells, I set to work removing their restraints. They all seemed more...relaxed, or perhaps acclimated, than the other captives did.

"So, have you been down here too long, or are you new?" I inquired, not quite sure what to think of their collective demeanor.

"Long enough to know how to avoid problems," the purple one answered with a sly grin, revealing shark-like teeth—very different from any Syldrari I'd met thus far. "You're human, huh? I'm not buying that. Humans don't smell or look like snacks."

"You sure you're not just hungry, Yeriphe?" a Syldrari the color of slate asked sarcastically.

"There you go. All done." I removed the last set of restraints from my volunteers. "Are there any less well-adjusted Syldrari I should be careful with?"

"There's a new *sol'iri* in the back," one of them offered, glancing down the hall. "They've been trying to break him in, and he's been in a few fights. Got upset and went…what do you humans call it? Feral? They've been keeping him locked up between fights since they can't deal with him but they still want to keep him. If they don't get him fighting again soon, they're probably going to make him one of the dancers upstairs."

…*Feral?* I wondered uneasily. "Okay. I'll see what I can do and will call for help if I need it. Now, here's how these devices work…"

An hour, maybe more, had passed before I'd worked through all the restrained Syldrari and found myself at the final door in their cellblock. Constant vibrations rattled the metal, a melodic humming coming from inside the room itself. I opened my mouth to call out, then paused. Perhaps speaking in my own language first would make things worse.

"*Vilam n~t bukairda?*" I did my best to hum the appropriate syllables, then listened for a response from inside, or any change at all. "I'm here to free you, and I'm opening the door."

I sensed the presence of the Syldrari in the room shift, darting somewhere above the door as the sound and vibrations abruptly stopped. However, his presence, rather than calming, became murderous. It most definitely reminded me of the so-called 'feral phenomenon.'

When I opened the door, I was prepared for the Syldrari to mindlessly rush me, which he did—but much faster than I'd anticipated. He collided with me and I felt his teeth sink into my shoulder as I was bowled over—something my own feral didn't appreciate at all.

I connected my foot with his gut, forcing him to continue over until he was on his back. My shoulder, unfortunately, was still in his mouth. I placed a hand on his chest and let electricity tingle beneath my hand. "*Let go.*"

His jaw tensed, and I felt blood trickle down my skin...then suddenly, he froze. The color of his skin abruptly changed from deep red to white, then to a very light blue-grey. Stuttering something in his own language, he daintily released my shoulder. He looked up at me with wide, vibrant blue-green eyes, all his pupils dilating further than normal.

He said something again, then seemed to realize I couldn't understand him. "I-I'm sorry, I wasn't in—"

"Are you confident I can let you up?" I asked, less bothered by his attack and more bothered by the fact that I could *feel* my shoulder and suit repairing themselves. He nodded meekly. "Like I said, I'm here to free you. Stay still so I can take your restraints off."

"Um..." He struggled to find words, his white skin turning progressively bluer. He seemed embarrassed, much like the girl upstairs, but instead of glowing yellow, he went a sort of pinky-purple color. "I didn't think anyone was really going to come for us. That guy who was always talking about Lethe, I thought he was just spreading false hope. But you're...you're really..."

He turned a darker blue, and any part of him that had been white before definitely was not now. Poor thing seemed oblivious to the fact that my bicolored blood was still painting his mouth. Or that the underside of his pastel pink and blue hair had started strobing.

"Hmmm, you should probably wash the blood off so the others don't get angry," I suggested, though it was more a foolish hope that Zafir hadn't yet noticed what was going on.

The foolishness was almost instantly confirmed by the brief **Another 'our little secret'** scrolling across the corner of my visor. Cheeky bastard. He was lucky he was smart *and* good-looking enough for me to let him get away with it. For the moment, anyway.

He promptly flicked his long, bright blue-to-black tongue out and licked the blood off his mouth and chin, leaving a faintly luminescent layer of fuchsia saliva in its place. He caught my incredulous stare and wiped his mouth on his sleeve, giving me a sheepish grin.

"That works. Let's join the others, then." I stood, and he followed. Despite being taller than me, he trotted after me like a loyal, happy puppy the whole way.

After meeting up with the rest of the Syldrari, we freed the remaining few fighters and made our way upstairs, with the Syldrari assisting with the more damaged captives. Their harmonic abilities allowed them to quell the fear, anxiety, and hatred whirling around in the other captives' minds; an aural tranquilizer, in a way. It allowed us to clear the cells of the other species with minimal issues.

Another message from Zafir guided us to a ship waiting on the roof. A ship piloted by someone I was apparently meant to threaten.

"Take us to the Syldran Embassy, or I'll kill you." I briefly encircled the pilot, who was waiting outside his ship, with lightning and gave him a frigid smile. Even though Zafir had supposedly told him I would threaten him in order to be convincing, he still turned deathly pale.

Eventually I climbed into the ship with the last of the freed prisoners, finding a spot in a corner near where the Syldrari had grouped together...but it wasn't peaceful for long. A pair of hands gripped my thighs and I felt a long tongue slide up my inner thigh, bringing my attention immediately downward. The white Syldrari was there on his knees, looking fully prepared to put his long nubbed tongue to use.

Startled, and with no idea of what to do in such a situation, I grabbed him by the hair on top of his head and yanked him away from my groin. "What do you think you're doing?"

"Isn't...this how we're supposed to thank a queen?" He blinked up at me, his expression oddly innocent.

He seriously believes what he's saying? I stared at him, flabbergasted. "I'm not a queen. I'm human. You don't do these things to a human unless you're asked and you both want to."

"Am I not satisfactory?" he murmured in confusion, his expression falling. "Human? You're... Humans can have queens?"

"Uh... You're very handsome, but in my culture you don't just..." I struggled to find the words to explain just how inappropriate his attempt had been.

"Ahem." Yeriphe, the purple Syldrari from before, carefully pulled the white one away and said something to him in their native tongue. Whatever it was seemed to get the point across, so Yeriphe addressed me next. "I think we'd all appreciate it if you could forget what he said about repaying queens..."

"I can overlook it." I shot the disappointed white Syldrari a concerned look. He was clearly sulking, as he'd taken to drawing patterns on the floor with one finger. "Foreign cultures are difficult to understand, and I can tell he meant no harm."

"He apologizes for startling you," Yeriphe offered, then leaned forward, his expression inquisitive. "You didn't say 'alien culture.'"

"Eh, people are people." I shrugged, relaxing back against the wall again. "Humans would be the aliens on your planet, right? And I can't imagine *they* would like being referred to as such all the time. You have an identity, and that is Syldrari. Not 'alien.'"

"M-Miss Lethe, we'll be arriving at the Syldran Embassy in five minutes," the pilot stuttered over the intercom.

"Lethe." Yeriphe took on a serious, hushed tone and moved closer. "There's another prison you need to know about."

CHAPTER FOURTEEN

"Elara, wait!" Zafir exclaimed, attempting to block my way to the door. "You can't handle such an enormous prison by yourself, nor are you in the right frame of mind to try! You've been awake all night!"

"I'm going." I pushed Zafir out of my way and yanked the door open. "I may not be able to do anything about it personally, but that doesn't mean there's nothing I can do."

He attempted to follow after me, but I fused the door to its frame as I left. Sure, I'd been at the fighting arena for a good five hours and it was now well into the wee hours of the morning, but I wouldn't let *that* of all things stop me. Especially not when I had a good idea who to turn to.

I parked a few buildings down from Rel's café and walked the rest of the way. The main floor was closed, but the lights upstairs were definitely on, so I ascended the stairs to the outer door of his apartment, knocked twice, and waited.

A moment later, the door swung open to reveal a mostly unclothed Rel. Underwear and an unfastened robe counted as clothes, right? He was much more sculpted than I'd realized, and his skin had a faint iridescent sheen depending on how it caught the light. Instead of the bulky musculature humans typically had, his build was closer to that of a swimmer. Balanced, defined… I found myself following his torso down to the V-lines that disappeared into his boxers. *Oh no, he's hot…*

"E—*Lethe*?" he questioned, bringing my attention back to his face. "What… Come inside."

He stepped aside and I silently accepted the invitation. When he opened his mouth to speak again, I motioned subtly to my visor, hoping he'd get the idea that our conversation wasn't exactly private—and to do something about it if he could.

"I've already taken care of that." He waved a hand dismissively. "My question is why you're here. I thought you'd be at the embassy still, taking care of matters."

He motioned, and I glanced in that direction to see a screen with the news playing on it—news that showed the rescued slaves being delivered to the embassy in question.

"You've been stubborn about maintaining your disguise and separating 'Elara' from 'Lethe,' so what changed?" He took a step closer and leaned down to peer at me, his glow turning a dark, almost black, blue-grey.

"I… You have many contacts among the different clans, right?" I asked quietly.

Something about my tone must have caught his attention, because he straightened, his expression becoming more serious. He considered something for a moment before answering, "That I do. Are you thinking about taking that invitation off-planet already?"

"I have intel that I'm not allowed to—and can't realistically—act upon." I sighed and crossed my arms. With or without voice modulation he clearly fucking knew who I was, so I figured I should just speak as myself. "I need you to deliver a message to someone who has the manpower and *can* act."

"How much manpower?" He frowned, seeming to contemplate something.

"Uhm…" I thought for a moment. "With Syldrari strength, I'm not sure, but with humans, it would take a military offensive."

"…One moment." He walked over to a bookcase and pulled out what I initially thought was just a decoration, until it expanded into a blue-green communication device. After he was done conversing with whoever was on the other end, he glanced at me apologetically.

"You won't like this, but I'll see to it that he behaves himself."

"Who—" I sensed movement behind me and promptly turned, bringing my hands up instinctively to catch the blade of a sword. At first, it appeared to be merely a sword with no one wielding it—until the air rippled and the owner of the blade appeared. It took most of my self-control to keep lightning from arcing down the blade when

I saw who was at the other end.

He, however, wasn't having it. The Syldrari, disguised as a human *again*, twisted his sword out of my grip and launched himself at me, the blade slicing past my head. I spun into a kick, which he caught easily, his single hand encompassing my entire ankle. He discarded his sword, shifting instead to punch me in the gut. I knocked his hand away and carried through with my momentum, spinning behind him and dropping into a leg sweep. He managed to bring me down with him, but I landed on top with my hand poised at his throat, electricity crackling around my fingers.

I sensed power welling up within the Syldrari as he snarled, but it was *Rel* of all people who spoke.

"**Enough**. Kindly refrain from destroying my apartment."

"*Hmph*. Is that all the strength you have?" the Syldrari under me sneered.

"You were holding back, so I did as well." My response earned me a deadly glare. "Why would I waste my strength on someone who doesn't take me seriously?"

"*Lethe*." Rel bent down beside me and offered me a hand. "Let him up."

I hesitated before dismissing the electricity and letting Rel pull me to my feet. The other Syldrari climbed to his feet with ease and adjusted his long coat, then turned to glower in my direction.

"She's bringing us information. Settle down." Rel stepped past me and toward the annoying Syldrari.

"You believe her?" the man asked, looking to Rel in disbelief.

"She's telling the truth. Hear her out." He pointed to a nearby seating area. "Sit. Both of you."

"Fine, but if she lies, I will kill her."

"Oh yes, I'm sure you'd find it so thrilling to kill the dainty human you find so uninteresting," I snapped, rolling my eyes as I plunked down into a seat. "I'll cut to the chase. One of the Syldrari I rescued earlier tonight informed me that there is another, much larger prison in one of the territories north of here, and this one contains *only* Syldrari. Some appear to be simply prisoners, and others are being experimented on. According to rumors he heard, there is at least one queen imprisoned there – but some of the others claim there could be as many as five.

"From what he told me, the complex sounds just as large as some of the government's smaller military installations. There could be a few hundred to a few thousand prisoners, and an unknown number of human guards and employees. There are also robotic defense systems patrolling the prison and its grounds. I've been ordered to stay far away because I can't possibly deal with the issue on my own."

"Yet you wanted to do something." Rel nodded faintly, then looked at the other Syldrari. "You know as well as I do she isn't lying."

"Her source could have been." The man shook his head. "I refuse to send my people charging in without—"

"Do I look or *sound* like I'm asking you to go rushing in like an idiot?" I demanded hotly. "What I *want* is for someone to be able to determine on their goddamn own if it's true—and act on it if it is. Considering you say you want me to keep my nose out of Syldrari business—"

"Is that what you call your antics earlier? Keeping your nose out of our business?"

"Would you prefer I'd left the Syldrari and rescued everyone else?" I snapped.

"…No. But your masters must have had an ulterior motive in—"

That was the last straw. "Listen, you paranoid, xenophobic prick," I snarled, "I have a fucking job to do, if I don't want 'fuck puppet' to become my new one."

"Being able to perform her job while upholding her personal morals is integral to her survival," Rel added, turning to look at the annoying one. "She could be a great ally—"

"Why should I make concessions for one person who, in the grand scheme of things, doesn't matter?" The man eyed Rel, then looked over at me. "Those who separate from the pack are the first to get picked off. That is the way of nature."

"She isn't asking for concessions and neither am I," Rel answered before I could snap back. "You are needlessly antagonizing someone who could be a valuable ally to the

Syldrari. She has been kind to us and given us information that others wouldn't risk delivering. Only criminals need to fear crossing her path…and even then, a Syldrari could easily overpower her." Rel glanced at me and added, "No offense."

"None taken. I'm aware Syldrari are superior to humans in every way—and that's why tonight's events and this tale of another prison worry me so much." I took a deep breath, forcing myself to calm down. "I don't like the idea that they've found a way to capture and subdue Syldrari. Experiments are even worse. I know our government is trying to unlock the ways of targeted evolution, and I wouldn't be surprised if they think you physically hold that key— and that they can take it."

"See? She even accepts our superiority. And you wonder why she said *you're* the xenophobic one…" Rel rubbed his temples. "Lethe has had a long night. Are you or aren't you going to investigate? I'll contact another clan if—"

"Fine. I'll look into it," he snapped. "Anyone else is prone to politicize it, which is why you called me first. Right?"

"Ah so the lights *are* still on when Lethe is involved." Rel tapped his own temple, smirking at the other Syldrari. "You're correct. With a queen recently removed from the planet, another visiting, and rumors that there are more in hiding, the other clans are scrambling for leverage."

"Why *this* planet, though?" I muttered, garnering an odd look from the sour Syldrari. "What? Females are rare in your species, right? And I'm under the impression that queens can *only* be female. If that's the case, isn't it statistically improbable that there would be so many queens on this planet? After all, I would think being closer to the Empire is dangerous for them."

"'I'm just a soldier,' she says…" Rel shook his head, shooting me an amused smile. "If we're talking statistics, yes. It *is* strange for there to be more than one queen here. All queens who have visited this planet in the past are accounted for, which means any *captive* queens were undiscovered. That the Syldrari population hasn't reacted to their presence, however…"

"The humans must have found a way to dampen their abilities or camouflage the presence they radiate." The other man sighed heavily. "Or it's a trap. Still, no Syldrari in their right mind would leave a queen in the humans' possession. Trap or not, it should be dealt with before someone younger and dumber tries."

"Good. We agree, then." Rel put a hand on his hip. "Now, what are you planning to do about the slaves at the embassy?"

"They aren't being sent back to Syldra?" The bitchy one frowned and shot me an accusatory glare.

"Hey, I just dropped them off. The suits there were muttering something about there being no trips to Syldra until one of the gates is repaired, though. They stopped talking when they spotted me, so it seems as though they're trying to keep something quiet."

"I'll look into it." Rel glanced at the other Syldrari. "Go make your preparations. Lethe should be going home for rest."

"Hmph." The bitchy one hesitated, giving me an odd look. Then he stood, fetched his sword, and disappeared from sight.

"You need an escort back." Rel turned to head into an adjacent room.

"I'm fine, I've got my bike, and HQ's location is supposed to be a secret," I protested, rising to my feet.

"You're sure?" He paused, turning to look at me. "Many people will be looking for you now."

I sighed and crossed my arms. He was right about that. I considered for a moment. "You can escort me to my bike if it makes you feel better; it's just a few blocks from here. Figured I shouldn't park on your roof or outside your door."

"An acceptable compromise. One moment." He disappeared into the other room and came back a few minutes later dressed for work. "I have to get the café ready for business soon anyway. Don't worry about it—I've already slept."

"Early riser, huh?" I gave him a half-smile.

Rel laughed, glowing yellow-green like summer grass. "A hazard of the trade, I'm afraid." He rummaged around in one of his pockets, then pulled out a medallion with a round blue-green crystal set in the center. A faint glimmer of electricity flickered within it. "Here. Use this for practice. It will help you get that lightning of yours under control."

"Uh…thanks?" Mildly confused, I took the medallion and turned it over in my hands, looking back up at the amused Syldrari. "How?"

"Think of it as a battery." He gestured loosely, motioning for me to follow him outside. "You can charge it with as much energy as you want and teach yourself how to control the amount and intensity of your power. You're lucky you haven't fried yourself yet."

I nodded and slipped the medallion into a pocket. "Yeah… I guess it isn't exactly normal for humans to have magical powers."

Rel remained silent, looking lost in thought as we made our way to my bike. Once we got there, I hopped onto the bike and he finally spoke. "Lethe. I know Casair told you not to question anything, for your own sake, but I'm going to give you different advice.

"Question. Everything. Skepticism is healthy. It's how you react to the truth and what you do with that knowledge that is important. You aren't a normal human—that much is clear."

"I'll keep that in mind." I nodded and he gave me a small smile before stepping away from the bike. I pointed at my visor. "Mind undoing the…whatever it is you did?"

He chuckled and stuck his hands in his pockets. "Of course. And I'll leave you with an answer. Your suit, much like your neurochip, is of Syldrari design—and your bosses appear incapable of truly tinkering with it. Disrupting the communications and modulator they added is a simple matter of conflicting frequencies—ones too high for human ears to hear.

"Any Syldrari can hear through the modulator. Disabling the rest requires a more experienced touch."

"So, I need to be more careful. I'll keep that in mind." I nodded, and he moved away to let me leave. As the bike rocketed away, my earpiece crackled.

<There you are!> Zafir exclaimed. <Where are you? I swear, if you're on your way to—>

"Cool off. I'm on my way back. Someone with the knowhow and manpower will be looking into it," I interrupted. "Do me a favor and have a hot meal waiting for me when I get back, alright? I'm fucking hungry."

CHAPTER FIFTEEN

"Elara?" Zafir knocked on her door with his free hand, his data pad gripped in the other. He waited a moment, but there was no response. The room was dead silent. *Something isn't right...*

Closing his eyes, he concentrated briefly, catching the sound of oddly slow breathing. Suddenly, the scent of blood filled his nose. Decidedly inhuman blood.

Damn it! He swiftly disabled the security for the room with his data pad, sending a harmonic pulse through the immediate area to fry anything that might be lurking. "Elara, I'm coming in."

He braced himself for the worst, concerned that perhaps this new life and the confrontation with the slaves had been too much for her to handle. He closed and locked the door behind him, set the data pad aside, then carefully searched the room—finding Elara on the opposite side of her bed. She was sprawled facedown on the floor, blue blood splattering the floor, her hands, and her mouth.

Did she push herself too far? He frowned and carefully pulled her from the floor, setting her upright against the side of the bed. There were no obvious injuries, so she hadn't attempted to harm herself, as he'd initially feared. Nor had she seemed anything other than tired during her meal. He swiftly pulled a set of linked rings over the fingers of one hand and faced the sensors in Elara's direction. As he scanned, he paused by her right hand. Her veins had become much more pronounced, and were a darker blue than they should have been.

[*High levels of toxins detected,*] a synthetic voice reported from his Syldrari neurochip. [*Noting twelve different varieties. Analysis: Sloppy attempt at murder. Subject's system is slowing down. Rate of cellular dissonance increasing. Recommendation: Dy'zglit and tyhtor to counteract the active toxins. Cellular dissonance has progressed too far to be halted. Suggestion: Subject should learn better control.*]

"Easier said than done…" He let out a soft sigh, then turned his communicator on. "Amara, I need you to acquire a few things for me and bring them to Elara's room—and keep quiet about it."

<Yes, sir!> Amara answered, followed by the sound of her chair swiveling. <What do you need?>

Once he'd listed his requirements, he set to work cleaning first Elara's face and then the floor of her room, removing every trace of blood. He sighed, hands on his hips, as he looked down at the bottle of cleaner. *Good thing I hid these around the place. I never would've gotten the blue out in time…*

There was a knock at the door, and he crossed the room to allow Amara in.

"Here you go! Two vials of nigh-unpronounceable whateverthefuck!" Amara handed off her cargo, then looked over at the collapsed Elara. Zafir gave the woman a sympathetic look. He'd known her long enough to understand her seemingly cheerful behavior was how she coped with stressful situations. "Someone tried to poison her? Who do you think did it? Do you need me to look into it? I checked her room on the cameras on my way here, there weren't any obvious intruders. When I get back I can do a more thorough analysis."

Rel and the others wouldn't have done it, not after she brought them such important information, so… Zafir's chest clenched and his blood boiled. "We're looking at an inside job. Someone who can get their hands on alien substances. The cocktail they used includes toxins from five different planets—all ones we are at odds with, but none ruled by any of the Syldrari clans.

"Go take everything out of her bathroom and analyze it for contamination."

Amara narrowed her eyes. "An inside… I'll investigate the kitchen, too. She might not be the only target."

Are they trying to kill her, or reveal the subjects for what they are? He sat back down on the edge of Elara's bed and prepared the dose of antitoxin. *They're sloppy. Half of these toxins cancel each other out. Should I report this…?*

He finished administering the antitoxin, then picked up his data pad, sending a message to his Syldrari contacts to inform them that someone had tried to assassinate Elara. He hadn't expected any response, let alone so soon, but the reply was almost instant.

<Find this would-be assassin and bring them to me. I won't suffer anyone hunting *my* prey.>

Zafir sighed and rubbed his temples. *Prey? By the ancestors… She is an* ally *and not* prey, *you dolt. It doesn't matter if she intrigues you or not.*

CHAPTER SIXTEEN

There was a knock at my door, followed by Zafir's muffled call of, "I'm coming in!" right before it swung open. I lowered my book with a sigh. He could've at least given me a chance to grab something other than a tank top and panties. My mild irritation shifted to curiosity when I caught a rather pleasant scent from him.

"Are you wearing cologne? Got a date tonight or something?" I watched him close the door, seemingly steeling himself before he turned to face me—but my question made him falter.

"I'm not wearing anything…? Never mind that." He shook his head and placed a hand on his hip. "We have much to discuss. One moment."

A small smile pulled at his lips right before I felt a sensation akin to a mild static shock sweep through the room. Though I couldn't hear it, I certainly *felt* it.

I watched as Zafir shut his eyes briefly and concentrated, the air around him appearing to swirl, glitch, and fade. When it had settled, I found myself staring at… Well, a *Syldrari*. But he still looked like Zafir. A few years older than me in appearance, though his hair was still pewter. His skin, however, was greyish lavender and his eyes a piercing topaz blue. A long tail uncoiled from his waist and he stretched his arms above his head, as if working out the kinks.

Finally, he focused his eyes on me and I saw his pupils dilate slightly—but he said nothing.

I set my book in my lap, unsure of what to say. While I'd begun to suspect that he was more than he appeared, I hadn't expected him to reveal himself outright. "You're trusting me?"

"Yes. I need to." He took a step closer. "For your safety and for mine. I've observed enough to believe I can trust your interactions with other Syldrari aren't merely an act."

"*Need* to trust me?" I frowned. "Not sure I like the sound of that."

"Yes…well…" He hesitated as if searching for the right words. "We need to discuss the results of your blood tests, this offer I hear Xilen gave you, and…"

I raised an eyebrow, watching his glowing bits swirl through too many colors and shades to track. "You wanna sit down first?"

"…Thank you," he answered with a small sigh.

However, he staggered first, dropping to a knee on his way to the chair. Taken aback, I hopped off the bed and moved to help him, crouching down to see what was wrong. "Zafir? You feeling alright?"

"It's been a while since I've been able to drop the illusion," he answered, a bitter edge to his tone. "It's more of a relief than I expected, and a drain."

I went to help him stand, but he finally seemed to notice that I wasn't exactly dressed. "Oh…ah… I suppose I should have asked if you were presentab—"

"I'm presentable enough. Up you go." I pulled him to his feet and deposited him in a chair, then grabbed a robe from the end of my bed. Admittedly, it didn't cover much more than my underwear. "How much time do you have before you have to leave? I'm assuming you knocked out the cameras, so—"

"Amara has a replacement loop running. We can take our time." He shook his head to clear it and leaned forward. "You, Sarah, and Amara are the only ones here who know I'm Syldrari—and I would appreciate it if we could keep it that way.

"We need to discuss your options, Elara. Your blood tests have come back with an alarming detail, and our superiors are now discussing the method of your…retirement."

"Retirement? Really? I figured they'd wanna keep me around for murdering purposes a while longer." I narrowed my eyes at the clearly uncomfortable Syldrari, watching as he shifted under my gaze. He was a lot more fidgety and…colorful than I was used to. "You know, I'm going to need a guide to Syldrari mood colors at the rate you're going."

He flushed blue, his glow rapidly shifting to deep yellow. "I-I'm afraid it's been quite some time since I had to consider controlling my displays of color. Hopefully I haven't offended—" He paused and adjusted the glasses he was still, for some reason, wearing. "I suppose even if I have displayed an offensive color, you wouldn't be aware of it. This is more troublesome than I anticipated…"

"*Zafir*," I sighed. "Can you please elaborate on this retirement thing before giving me a lecture about Syldrari colors and anatomy?"

"Anato—? Ahem." He cleared his throat, his glow shifting from yellow, to bright pink, to a more neutral sage green. "According to the tests, the brain chip isn't the only human tech you're incompatible with. You are incompatible with all their life-prolonging technologies.

"They want to test you for compatibility with Syldrari equivalents—which they can't acquire. Since they can't guarantee they'll be able to make you live for centuries or longer, they've returned to discussing the idea of a breeding program.

"I'm doing what I can to convince them that they need you alive, happy, and healthy, but there are many who believe you could bridge the gap between human and Syldrari strengths. Several have posited that you may be biologically compatible with both species.

"I'm pushing for them to keep you on this project to train other fighters, but we need to have options if they don't—"

"Hold on, hold on, hold on. Slow down." I raised my hands to stop him. Not only had he just dropped my incompatibility with life extension tech on me, there had been all the other stuff, too. I felt like if I didn't stop him, he was going to unload a college course's worth of material on me. "They want to turn me into breeding stock to produce powerful, potentially hybrid soldiers? Seriously? Hey, don't give me that look. You think I don't already know my blood is more than red? Huh?"

He gave me a half-smile. "Sorry to dump so much on you."

"So, what, you're concerned about how to keep their distasteful plans from happening?" I murmured mostly to myself, tapping my fingers against one arm. "No. There's more to it, isn't there? Otherwise you wouldn't have revealed yourself."

Zafir let out a slow, shaky sigh. "I've taken it upon myself to make certain you and the other Resonance victims remain safe. That said, in a worst-case scenario, I've thus far only been able to secure passage off this planet for you. Xilen has taken quite a liking to you but is uninterested in the others.

"I am negotiating with other sources, but taking my roles into account, I will need to leave with you if you evacuate."

"You will?" I asked, but he glanced away. "What exactly is it you want me to do, then? Be a good girl and keep quiet while you negotiate, to avoid pissing off our superiors?"

"I'm less worried about our human superiors and more concerned about the attention you've been drawing among the Syldrari…" He sighed, rubbing his temples. "With any luck, I can direct your missions to sectors where certain individuals will know better than to test you. However, with someone having made an attempt on your life…"

"Any progress on that front?" I prompted. "Being under house arrest sucks. I'm more bored than I was back in my cell at Abel's facility, for fuck's sake."

"Ah, if your accommodations and entertainment are unsuitable…" His eyes glazed over as he reached up to toy with the buttons of his shirt. "Perhaps I…can…be…"

His gaze flickered, clarity returning. In an instant, he turned away and his glow swirled once more with chaotic colors. I narrowed my eyes at his sudden embarrassment. *That* was nothing like the Zafir I was getting to know. "Forgive me. As a Syldrari, dealing with women is…a struggle."

I tilted my head briefly before walking over to get a better look at him—though he promptly shifted to continue hiding his face. Given that that tips of his ears had turned a solid navy blue, I had a good guess as to why.

"Is that so?" I inquired with an amused smile. "And somehow this has only become an issue in the past…however long since you dropped your human disguise?"

"The device that disguises me also dampens Syldrari

instincts, so we don't…" He hesitated when he glanced at me, his pupils dilating even further. "Syldrari *lun'iri*, what you would call men… Women and queens hold a certain power over us. Those I serve are attempting to break free of the cycle of oppression we've found ourselves in, but…"

"Uh huh. Is that why you're so chatty with me?" I leaned over to meet him at eye level, but his eyes snapped to my cleavage instead and he flushed. This time, I could see his visible struggle to return his gaze to mine. Sighing, I grabbed him by the chin and lifted it up. "Hey. Snap out of it. I'm sure I look nice, but let's discuss the issue at hand—keeping the humans from turning me into a human cow."

In an instant, full clarity returned to his gaze, as if my order had actually worked. He stared at me in silence, mouth agape, for a moment, then reached up and gently removed my hand from his chin.

"…Elara, we may also need to discuss how you phrase things when speaking to Syldrari. If you were to command someone like that publicly—"

"I'm not really the commanding sort, but I'll do it when I have to." I gave him a pointed look. Though I kind of wanted to tease him, my curiosity was winning out. "This…innate subservience, if I can call it that, would that be why one of the rescued prisoners thought he needed to go down on me to show his gratitude properly? Ah, although, he did mention it was how he was expected to repay queens…"

"Someone… Did you let him?" Zafir asked, aghast.

"Hell no! I had no idea what was going on, and it would've been in front of all the others. Plus, damaged person and all that." I crossed my arms. Just what kind of woman did he take me for?

"Ah… Queens generally get whatever they want, from whomever they desire." He shook his head slowly. "He likely mistook you for a queen because you were able to save them singlehandedly. As *lun'iri*, we are expected to give a queen her every desire—regardless of whether she's saved us or not. We're meant to be grateful that she'd pick us out of the millions of others she could choose—especially when competition is so fierce.

"Of course, intimacy, pleasure and adoration are all valuable currencies. If I must offer any of them for you to keep my identity a secret, or to earn your cooperation—" He cut himself off and raised a hand to the side of his head, wincing.

"Uh huh…" I frowned at the struggling Syldrari, not exactly sure how to console him. "Well, fun as I'm sure it would be, I'm not exactly in the market to be breeding with *anyone*. I'd rather remain fit to kick ass, if it's all the same to you."

"I apologize. This is more of a struggle than I'd anticipated." His shoulders slumped. "To be more precise—we need to prove to our superiors that they *need* you as a soldier or a trainer. To that end, you will be taking on more responsibilities as Lethe. Calder, Nikolai, and Maelor should be cleared for service by next week."

I nodded. "And the training angle?"

"Pending the release of more victims, I'm afraid. I've put in several requests, but none have been approved yet." He paused, frowning slightly. "Wait a moment. You have qualms about breeding. If I recall…" He conjured a data pad out of nowhere and pulled up a document. "Hmmm…they tested human contraceptives on you but not Syldrari ones… Ah. Of course. It was during Abel's era."

"Do you want to fuck me that badly?" I asked bluntly. *That* he seemed to take offense to.

"That isn't what prompted this search!" he snapped back. "If Syldrari prevention methods work, then we can guarantee interference with any meddling or…"

He faltered, clearly uncomfortable with voicing the numerous things the humans might try to do to me.

"Right. I get it." I tapped my foot against the floor, thinking. "Well, what's involved with Syldrari prevention measures? I'm down to ruin the government's plans—and those of anyone else who wants to get out of line."

"I will make the arrangements." Zafir stood abruptly, adjusted his glasses, and re-summoned his human disguise. "I should be returning to work. You're remaining under house arrest for the time being—Amara is trying to pinpoint who may be attempting to kill you."

I moved to block his way out of my room, giving him a playful smile. "If I'm stuck in here, maybe there's something you can do for me after all."

"Elara, I—" Zafir stuttered.

"If I'm going to be stuck here… Then you can send someone to get me food from the Syldrari sector!" I informed him cheerfully. As I moved past him, I smirked. "What, did you think I was going to say something else?"

A long stream of agitated Syldran spilled from his mouth before he adjusted his glasses roughly and took his leave. I laughed to myself, bringing a finger to my lips. *Oh, this could be so much fun…*

CHAPTER SEVENTEEN

I walked into Rel's café with a very, very agitated Zafir behind me. Rel and Aldiner both looked up eagerly when we came in. At first, Rel looked happy to see me—until he noticed Zafir. I had to assume he could see through Zafir's disguise, or at least sense it.

"This is my boss, Zafir," I offered when Rel shifted his questioning look to me. "Given recent events, I'm not allowed out without an escort...and *his* bosses want to confirm something."

"Is that so?" he inquired dangerously. "Your boss, is he? An ally, or one of the ones..."

"An ally." Zafir stepped past me and toward Rel, but not far enough to keep me from noticing that he briefly revealed his eyes. "I'll be blunt, as Elara assures me unfiltered honesty works best here.

"Someone attempted to murder Elara. They used a cocktail of hazardous toxins—in an admittedly sloppy manner—and our mutual bosses want me to inspect the places she frequents to rule out the possibility of outside tampering."

"You're accusing us—" Aldiner started to snap, but Rel grabbed him by the scruff of the neck and kept him in place. The ruckus, however, caused a familiar face to poke out of the back room.

"What's all the…" The pale white Syldrari trailed off when he spotted me, his jaw going slack. Then, suddenly, his glow swirled between pink and yellow and he fled back to where he'd come from.

"What…" Zafir stared after the shy Syldrari and I let out a low chuckle, glancing over at Rel.

"Taking in some interesting rescues, are you?"

He sighed and gave me an amused look. "Yes, well…with the gate broken, the embassy can't ship them back home. A few of us have offered to take on the rescues as employees while they find their current again."

"Was that the one…" Zafir trailed off when I shot him a smug look.

"Wouldn't you like to know?" I laughed and moved to perch at the counter, then rested an elbow on the surface. Cupping my face in one hand, I gave Rel an amused smile. "We'll have whatever the chef suggests."

"I *suggest* you tell me what's going on." He planted his hands on the counter and leaned down. "Someone attempted to poison you? How bad—"

"I walked in to find her unconscious on the floor, covered in blood. It appears she passed out when she started coughing it up." Zafir finally made his way over to the counter. "The issue is that our labs stopped studying those toxins ages ago and the samples were destroyed. Since our bosses can't determine how someone on the inside could have—"

"She looks fine to me." Casair's voice came out of nowhere moments before he lifted me out of my seat and onto his shoulder. When I looked at him, I couldn't read the expression he was giving Zafir.

"A feat of Syldrari technology," Zafir answered pointedly. "If my neurochip hadn't been able to identify—"

"Hmph. I'll have to report this to the boss." Casair grunted, though he made no move to put me down.

"Are you well enough to be wandering around?" Rel frowned at me.

"She may be demanding, but I wouldn't have let her out if she wasn't recovered." Zafir sighed and massaged his temples. "Since she demanded Syldrari food and everyone else is busy, the options were to either let her go alone or escort her myself."

"Or keep her under house arrest," Casair pointed out dryly, and Zafir stiffened. I had to wonder what color he'd turned under his disguise, seeing as several of the Syldrari were smirking at him.

"Casair, set her down." Rel gave him an agitated look before turning his attention back to Zafir. "I'm sure she's a handful. I can give you instructions for handling her type if you need it."

"Absolutely not!" Zafir fidgeted with his glasses. "She may have caught me off guard, but I won't let—"

"Hey, Rel, I've been meaning to ask about the different colors Syldrari glow." I interrupted Zafir's babbling with a smile. "It's gotta be linked to something, right?"

"Moods and emotions." Rel smiled and spread his arms out to his sides, palms up. "What do you want to know?"

"Is there some kind of guide to Syldrari colors, then?" I asked. He shook his head. "Okay… Zafir, hand me your data pad."

Zafir let out a heavy sigh, but did as I asked. I promptly pulled up a program that allowed me to select colors.

"Okay, what about a grey like this?" I turned the screen so Rel could see it.

"Someone would be trying to go undetected if they turned that color. In water, it best simulates and reflects the surrounding ocean." He tilted his head faintly, watching as I moved on to a particular shade of yellow—for a second, he looked concerned. "Ah, a yellow like that shows embarrassment."

"Hmmm, okay…" I moved on to purples next, several of which were suspicion or confusion-related emotions. Then I pulled up pink and he started to look *very* concerned. "How about this?"

"Oooh, are we playing Teach the Human again?" Aldiner rested a forearm on Rel's shoulder, while both Zafir and Casair remained quiet.

"This?" I held up a soft, pale pink and Rel let out a relieved sigh.

"Adoration. Were it closer to red it would be mixed with some degree of lust or sexual aggression." He pointed to several sections of the hue bar. "Closer to certain shades of pink, purple, or orange would be concerning. The former because it would indicate someone trying to get something out of you, such as information. Were there a mix of blue and orange… I believe you humans call them love-hate relationships?"

"Okay, and this?" I moved over to a bright, pure neon pink that almost hurt to look at.

That got quite the reaction. The wooden spoon Rel had reached for snapped the moment he grasped it, and Aldiner's face lost all traces of amusement. Hell, the eavesdropping customers even walked over, looking like they were ready to beat the snot out of something.

"Who has been showing you that color?" Rel demanded, discarding the broken spoon and leaning forward on the counter. "Don't try to say it was just a random choice, either."

"Uh…" I stared at him in confusion, though he quickly caught on that both Casair and Zafir were being too quiet.

"Was it you two?" Rel straightened to his full height. The corner of his eye twitched and his mouth pulled into a smile somewhere between sadistic and angry.

Aldiner called for the translucent white Syldrari, and together with the angry customers they dragged Zafir and Casair off into a back room.

"Uh, what was that all abou—" I started, turning to follow.

"Sit down and have a drink." Rel ordered sharply, slamming a drink down on the counter. When I hesitated, he narrowed his eyes at me. "*Sit* and *don't ask*."

"Um? Okay?" I inched over to my seat and sat down again.

"Some colors are…offensive," Rel stated flatly when I opened my mouth to ask again. He leaned over the counter and gave me quite the intimidating-but-hot look. "There's a few in particular that look bright pink to the human eye."

"Offensive colors? I hadn't considered there might be—" I fell silent as Rel held a finger to my lips.

"Which is why we learn to *control* which colors we show. Now, enough questions." He took a step back and pointed down at my glass. "*Drink.* If there are any remaining toxins in your bloodstream, that will take care of it."

"Uh…right." I picked up the glass and peered over the rim at the agitated Syldrari. "Sooo—"

He gave me a firm side eye. "No."

"I was going to ask why those two specifically," I continued anyway, watching as he pinched the bridge of his nose.

"Of the people you've been with, unsupervised, the two of

them— What?" He stared at me when a giggle escaped me.

"You're my supervisor now?" I teased. "If we're going off people I've been alone with, you'd fall into that category too. And then there's…"

"Ah…" He took a moment, then called something in Syldran into the back room. A moment later, the white Syldrari came out and gave Rel a curious look—though his face promptly turned blue when he spotted me. Rel cleared his throat pointedly and said something curt to the shorter Syldrari.

"There's my two favorite people!" a female voice exclaimed from somewhere behind me. I grimaced and glanced over my shoulder to find Xilen prancing over with her entourage of questionably-clad…guards? "I came running the *moment* I heard you were here with some strange man no one had ever seen before, darling!"

"He's my *boss*," I informed her flatly, as the man in question staggered out of the back room, along with Casair. Both of them looked like they'd been chastised thoroughly. "Zafir, you gonna have anything to eat, or am I hogging all the food?"

"I'll have—" Zafir fell silent and tensed when he spotted Xilen. She gave him an amused smirk and crossed her arms.

"Ahhh, he's your boss, is he? Not your plaything?" Xilen asked me innocently. "I'm sure he'd be a *fantastic* stress reliever, dear. You really should consider acquiring his services."

"*Xilen*, please. Humans—" Rel started, but Xilen waved a hand to shush him.

"Please. Human or not, Elara should have all the relief she desires! Being a soldier is such strenuous work, after all." Xilen put her hands on my shoulders as if she were planning to give me a massage, her bust pressing against both sides of my neck. She laughed when most of the men present tensed. "Ohhh, so *that's* why you deny me! Well, I can't blame you. She's just so damn cute."

"Uh…" I attempted to escape the woman's cleavage. "Maybe, *just maybe*, they deny you because you're so pushy? I mean, they're people. Not objects. You don't just 'acquire' them."

"If only that were true, dear." Xilen let go of me and patted my shoulder with a smile. "The other queens take whomever they want and control their lives completely. I try to spare mine that fate, but…" She glanced between Rel and Casair. "Some desire a degree of freedom that the R'selkti matron simply won't allow anyone to have."

"So, she's a tyrant?" A collective flinch passed through the men and Xilen's mischievous smile broadened.

"You could say, in her greed, she tips the natural order toward the unnatural. She wants to make certain her offspring have their choice of the best males. She believes the power of a queen is hereditary." Xilen perched on a seat beside me and propped her cheek against her fist, examining me. "When her spies realize that so many unclaimed males are hiding on this planet…"

"Enough." Rel spoke quietly, placing a drink in front of Xilen. "We don't need—"

"Please. Whether you ask for it or not, you have my support." Xilen gave him an 'I'm done with everyone's shit' look. "*I* hear that even the R'selkti here have split off and severed their ties to her. Do you think that will go unnoticed?"

Casair gritted his teeth and crossed his arms, but Rel shot him a glance and the man remained silent. I glanced between them all, debating whether I could diffuse the situation, before I realized Aldiner was missing.

Well, missing until he suddenly appeared next to me with his arm around my shoulders, that is. He released an exaggerated sigh before speaking. "Come *on*. You flip-flop between doting on her and ignoring her—what's it gonna be, huh? You gonna get her some food, or should I take her upstairs and entertain her until you're ready to do your jobs?"

"What—" Rel cut himself off into an uncharacteristic snarl, his eyes narrowing. I had an inkling this time just what sort of gesture Aldiner had made.

"Don't be greedy!" the white one exclaimed, latching onto my other arm. "Together, we can—"

"Get back to work. Both of you." Rel's unnaturally calm voice sent a chill down my spine, as did the outright murderous look he gave the other two Syldrari. Both of them immediately fled for another room, though Aldiner was laughing.

"Aw, I'm sure they could have used the practice!" Xilen teased, giggling.

"Honestly…" Zafir collapsed into a seat to my right.

"Regardless of what they could use, I won't permit my employees to use Elara for such purposes, especially when they don't seem to realize that she has a say in the matter!" Rel snapped, turning toward Xilen. He placed his hands on the counter and actually growled, though Xilen just gave him a dreamy smirk that said, 'yes, show me more.'

"Yes, they do seem intent on treating her as though she's a *queen*, don't they? Poor things have been indoctrinated already…" She shook her head and gave Rel a sly smile. "I'm sure you're doing your best to reeducate them."

"Like a…" Rel promptly shut his mouth, spun around, and went back to cooking.

With her previous target now occupied, Xilen turned to me and Zafir. "Now then. Zafir, was it? Might you know how I could contact *Lethe,* or at least a branch of the government who can provide me an escort? I've been invited to a party, you see. They require that I have a 'proper' guard…whatever *that* means."

"It means they don't recognize your men as guards because they aren't armed and wearing uniforms." Zafir pressed his thumb and forefinger to his temples. "I'm not sure a military escort is a good idea, and we don't know how to contact—"

"Of *course* you don't." Xilen rested a forearm on my shoulder. "Not. At. All."

"Ah…" He hesitated.

"Is she coming to play guard to the queen? Yes or no?" Xilen asked sweetly.

He sighed and slumped back in his chair. "I'll see what I can arrange."

CHAPTER EIGHTEEN

"So, what's the target?" I tugged at my gauntlets as I walked into the garage. Zafir turned to look at me, though Calder, Nikolai, and Maelor kept seeing to their own preparations. Nearby, a woman I didn't recognize lurked beside a bike, crouching down to examine it.

He gave me a tired smile. "We received reports of R'selkti deserters harassing people in several districts. There have been several reported rapes, but..."

"But?" I prompted. He didn't strike me as the sort of filth who would invalidate someone's claims.

"While the victims were most certainly attacked, none of the evidence points toward Syldrari attackers." Zafir, thankfully, voiced his disagreement with the reports. "You see, Syldrari...secretions? Are bioluminescent, and—"

"If you were tryin' to find a polite word for jizz—try again." The woman by the bike strode over, hands on her hips. When she reached us, she held out a hand to me. "Name's Aisu. I'm guessing you're Elara?"

"Aisu is another survivor. She was being studied at another facility until recently." Zafir nudged his glasses further up his nose, apparently eager to leave behind the subject of Syldrari jizz. "As she showed promise, our bosses decided to see if she could learn to rein in her feral herself."

"My town was a few over from yours—we got pulverized too." Aisu shrugged, grimacing. "Not that I remember a damn thing about it, mind you. I've been patrolling some of the other sectors the last few weeks—mainly the Brihl areas. Girls there are real nice, and the guys ain't half bad, either. Real dapper, the lot of 'em. Great at givin' hugs."

Zafir chuckled when I shot him a questioning look. "I believe you met one of their kind—tall, four arms, incredibly polite despite looking like they could wrestle any monster in this half of the galaxy…"

"Ah, right. Them." I nodded.

"You wanna feel appreciated? Just go in there as a girl in uniform!" Aisu laughed. "Real ladylike, their women. 'Cept they have a real thing for strong women from other species. Had a gaggle of them after me the first time I went! Something about strong women really gets them goin'."

"…Anyway," Zafir began, clearing his throat. "Your next

few missions will be conducted as a group. I was hoping a few more women would stabilize before we reached this stage, so we could even out your numbers, but this will have to do. If you work well together, your team will become permanent. Newly stabilized individuals will be assigned to a Team B, if you will."

"Yeah, yeah, yeah. We both know our bosses just want to retire us and shove us into the breeding pit sooner rather than later." Aisu snorted and flapped her hand. "Get to the point, will ya? What do the bastards want us to do this time?"

I grinned crookedly. "I think Aisu and I are going to get along just fine."

"*They* want you to kill the R'selkti deserters. *I* want you to work smarter, not harder." Zafir crossed his arms and went silent for a moment. "As I said, all Syldrari bodily fluids, aside from blood, glow. Blood is only an exception due to bioengineering, as luminescent blood apparently made Syldrari easier targets on their home planet.

"The victims were covered in decidedly human fluids, and they aren't showing the usual signs of trauma. They did, however, all have an unknown chemical compound in their bloodstream."

"You think they were drugged into submission and assaulted by humans, but somehow got around to blaming Syldrari?" Nikolai joined us, looking disgusted.

Aisu shrugged. "Sounds like the government, alright. Framing 'aliens' at any cost."

"A sedative that makes them susceptible to suggestion, maybe? Under the right conditions, that would've allowed them to hallucinate that their attackers weren't human." I crossed my arms, contemplating the idea. Pharmaceuticals weren't exactly my forte, but it sounded possible enough.

Zafir grimaced. "The point is, we need to confront the R'selkti deserters in a way that satisfies the military *and* chases the deserters out of our jurisdiction. Since we don't know if their loyalty has been pledged to anyone new, we can't take a more political approach via Elara's contacts."

"Let's get to it then." I started heading in the direction of my bike. "I swear, this damn thing gets more action than I do."

Aisu laughed. "You too, huh? See, that's what's great about the Brihl girls. Our bosses don't care if I get it on with girls. No 'breeding risk,' and all that. I can introduce you to a few, if you like?"

"No thanks, Syldrari are really more my thing." I hopped onto my bike, shooting Zafir a sly look. "You know, *boss*, if we're not allowed to get laid—the least you could do is order me something fun to play with."

Zafir faltered. "U-uh…that's against regulations. I can't—"

"Is it now? Or are you just worried about what you'll overhear since your room is down the hall from mine?" I asked sweetly, earning a snort of laughter from Aisu. "Tell you what. I'll let you think about it and decide for yourself what you think is worse."

"Can we focus on the mission, please?" Maelor glanced between me and Zafir, looking totally lost. Then he perked up. "Though if Elara is getting toys, I want some too!"

"For the love of…" Zafir brought his hand up over his face. "Did acquiring a feral side throw you all back into the ages of breeding seasons?"

"Waaait! I'm coming too!" A soft voice, accompanied by quick footsteps, reached our ears. A petite woman, clad similarly to the rest of us, skidded into view and paused to catch her breath.

"Uh…" I wracked my brain for a moment, trying to identify her. Finally, it clicked. "Diana, right? Where've you been? I haven't seen you at train—"

Zafir stepped closer to Diana and sighed, crossing his arms. "Diana has been under medical observation. She can control her feral well enough, but her health is—"

"I won't fight if I don't have to, I promise! But they can use my abilities!" Diana clenched her fists and glared up at Zafir. "If anyone tries to ambush or sneak up on us, I'll know it. Who else can do that the way I can?!"

"…*No fighting.*" He glared back at her, then glanced my way. "If you have to engage the R'selkti deserters, all of you will be *silent* and let Elara do the talking. Her identity may already be compromised. If it is, then the Syldrari have some reason for tolerating her. That said, there's no reason for you to give yourselves away."

"Can we get going yet?" Maelor growled in irritation. "The more time we waste here, the more likely we're too late to save tonight's victims. Right?"

"I'll be careful, and make sure we all come back safe," Diana reassured Zafir, then darted over to me. She gave me a sheepish smile. "Can I get a ride?"

"Sure." I nodded, shooting Zafir one last look. "Try not to hog too much of our visual and auditory senses. It seems like we're going to need both for this mission."

He shrugged and slid his hands into his pockets. "I'm hands-off with this one; the higher-ups want you to run it. I'll be monitoring everyone's vitals and communicating with our military allies in the event you need to be extracted, but that's it. This is all you."

"Right." I revved the engine. "We're off, then." As we sped off into the night, an important question came to mind. "What are everyone's code names? Mine is Lethe."

"Cocytus," Calder answered.

"Erebos, whatever the hell that means," Nikolai offered.

"Styx." Maelor grunted. "Why I gotta be named after a damn stick—"

Nikolai sighed irritably. "It's S-T-Y-X. From some old dead planet's ancient mythology. Not 'sticks.'"

Diana giggled from behind me, clearly just as amused as I was by their exchange. "Mine is Hypnos. Zafir suggested we should all choose code names related to yours, Lethe. Team cohesiveness. *Styx* couldn't pick, so Zafir chose for him."

"Damn, wish I'd been in on that conversation," I snickered.

Aisu spoke up next, her tone making it clear she was grinning like a wild woman. "Mine's Acheron. Figured it sounded badass enough."

I nodded to myself. "Okay. Stick to code names until we're back. The Syldrari may be able to hear through the voice modulators or hear the feed from our comms. We need to do what we can to preserve the secrecy of everyone's identities, especially since we're not supposed to reveal our military ties. Everyone remember our cover story?"

"We saw each other's good deeds on the news, arranged a meeting, and decided to team up for bigger projects," Diana answered in what sounded vaguely like an attempt at a Zafir impression. Vaguely.

"Right. And if we find our targets…in the act?" I grimaced at the thought.

"We bash their skulls in and drag 'em back to HQ for study, while you guard the victims until help arrives." Aisu sounded a little too excited about the bashing heads bit.

Calder sighed irritably. "We should cut the chatter to a minimum considering Lethe's info. Until we can confirm there's no Syldrari around, keep quiet and stick to hand signals."

"Well, Lethe can talk considering her cover's already blown.

May even speed up the process," Maelor pointed out. "I dunno about you, but I could really go for a brawl right about now."

When we reached our destination, I let Diana hop off my bike before climbing off myself. The first thing I noticed was that the sector smelled oddly perfumed. Frowning, I reached up and nudged a button on the side of my visor. "Analyze air samples."

A few moments later, I heard a faint beep and the analysis streamed across the corner of my visor. There was nothing out of the ordinary.

Is it me? I sniffed at myself, then shook my head faintly. It wasn't. "Stay on alert. It may smell nice, but it doesn't smell *right*."

We made our way methodically through the streets, clearing each area before moving on to the next. The deeper we went, the stronger the scent became. Then, what I could only describe as a melodic chiming sound came to accompany the scent. However, unlike a typical chime, the notes were constant and didn't sound as if they were produced by hitting something.

My teammates didn't seem able to detect the smell, but they could certainly hear the sound. I hushed them and crept toward the next corner—this one leading to a plaza that should have been empty so late at night.

Should have been, but most certainly wasn't. Across from me, three barely conscious women were propped up against a retaining wall, their clothes dirty but still intact. They were being guarded by two seemingly unarmed Syldrari in unfamiliar uniforms.

A little way off from them, I spotted more Syldrari soldiers, plus the cloaked man who'd pissed me off so much. His head turned just enough for me to catch the smirk on his lips, then his attention returned forward to a group of beaten-looking human men.

We walked right into his web. I let out a soft sigh and motioned for my comrades to follow—*quietly*. There was no point in hiding now.

"I see you beat me to the hunt."

"I do believe I told you to stay out of Syldrari business." The annoying bastard linked his hands behind his back, not even bothering to turn and face me. "Though you are smarter than I gave you credit for. You recognized that we already knew you were here."

"Yes, well, the sector doesn't smell right. Then there's that sound…" I trailed off and motioned with one hand. "Syldrari business, though? Those victims aren't Syldrari."

"Perhaps…but the attempt to frame us *is* our business." Suddenly, the cloaked man disappeared, but not completely, and when his sword came down I batted it aside with my armored forearm. "Mmm? Are you so eager to make yourself interesting to me?"

The corner of my eye twitched. "What, you think I'm going to just stand here and let you cut me down?"

He leaned down a little with an amused smirk. "Most *humans* would. Now that you have my attention, why don't you tell me why you're here, and why I shouldn't paint this sector with the blood of you and your companions?"

"We're here to stop the attacks that have been happening in this sector—*regardless* of the species of the attackers." I prodded him in the chest and held back a growl. "Human or Syldrari, the kind of filth that would—"

"Oh? You claim you have the stomach to give them their comeuppance?" He shoved me in the direction of his soldiers and their captives. "Then show me what this punishment of yours looks like. If it is enough, or at least entertains me, I'll forget you and yours attempted to interfere in our business tonight."

"Interfere? Hardly." I snorted, crossing my arms. "And which one are you so *graciously* giving to me?"

"Lethe, you don't have to—" Calder raised his hands and backed away when one of the Syldrari moved toward him.

"Which one? Why, I'll let you have your pick, of course. Which one do you sense may be the most vile?" The cloaked man made a sweeping motion with one arm.

I sighed and examined the beaten human men. Several immediately began shouting loud, raunchy things about what they wanted to do to me...but no. The vilest of them all would be silent. Aware enough of his own twisted mind and its abnormalities to know he'd survive longer by hiding his nature.

Finally, I shifted toward the second-most quiet and reserved of the bunch. He looked to be in his forties, likely unable to afford transference into a new body.

"Not the loudest or the quietest?" the cloaked man murmured.

"The loud ones are just socially inept weaklings who were manipulated by the right people during the right circumstances. The quietest one is clearly in a state of shock, likely traumatized by the events he's found himself participating in despite his guilt." I shook my head, then looked at the one I'd chosen. "Then there's the ones capable of hiding or masking their nature."

The cloaked man chuckled and came to stand beside me, towering over me and the cowering humans alike. "And what do you think is an appropriate punishment for their crimes?"

I considered for a moment, before a fitting option finally came to me. I gave the Syldrari a mischievous smile. "We'll put their corpses on display in the plaza…after removing their most treasured parts, of course. Though I'm not certain what to do with said parts. Clearly no one wants them."

"You bitch—" One of the men lunged against his restraints but fell flat on his face.

I promptly placed my foot on his skull, keeping his face smashed against the ground. Then I looked to the smirking Syldrari. "Did you get the information you needed, or do I have to wait?"

"Oh, I got *plenty* out of them," he mused.

"Did they get to do anything to those women?"

The smirk dropped off his face and he shook his head. "Beyond frightening them half to death, no. One of my men is analyzing the drugs they were given so he can set them right. It may be a while."

So he's serious about more than just the Syldrari. I sighed in relief and turned my attention back to the humans. I wanted to know if the irritating bastard had followed up on the intel I'd given him, but before I could ask he suddenly stepped forward and plunged his sword through the torso of the man I had my foot on.

"Not that I'm complaining, but why—"

"Don't. Ask." He turned away sharply, his glow turning a deep red. "We're sending a message with this filth," he called to one of his men. "Fetch something we can pin them to."

I took my foot off the human and peered down at him, trying to figure out what could have prompted the Syldrari's response. Suddenly, I realized that one of the man's hands was suspiciously obscured. "Gross."

"I did say not to ask."

"You did. But you didn't say 'don't think,' and even if you had, I would have told you to fuck off."

"You are making me question my decision to be lenient." He raised his fingers to somewhere inside his hood.

"Do you really think we would have interfered if you tried to punish these assholes?" I rounded on him with a growl. "First off, we aren't idiots. We know we couldn't take down one of you, let alone all of you. Despite how much fun it might be to try. Second, I'm not going to complain if you execute trash like them. Third, we're here to put a stop to these attacks and the bullshit framing of the Syldrari. So—"

"Yes, yes, mouthy as ever." He made a dismissive motion. "You said something about scents and sounds being off in this sector. Explain."

I shoved down the urge to slug him. "Ever since we arrived, I've noticed that the air in this sector smells heavily perfumed. However, the analysis came back with nothing. As for the sound…"

After I fumbled through explaining what I'd heard, the cloaked Syldrari remained silent, smirking and rubbing his chin. Finally, he spoke again. "And these enhanced senses are supposedly the cause of the Resonance Incident? No, I doubt that. *Human* tissue—even most human augmentations and structures—can't withstand that accursed weapon."

"Uh…" I wasn't quite sure what to say to that. My shoulders slumped and I sighed. "Hey, I only know what I've been told about the Incident, okay? The last thing I remember is my consciousness slipping and my fingers tearing into…someone."

"It may be for the best that you don't. It is a gruesome weapon. One that should never have been deployed on this planet." The cloaked man briefly placed a hand on top of my head, as though trying to comfort me, then moved off somewhere out of view. "You lot—Lethe's companions. Make yourselves useful while we wait and guard the entrances to the plaza."

I half-turned to nod at them. "Do as he said."

"Six 'humans' wearing Syldrari under-armor… How very strange." His mutterings caused me to whirl in his direction.

"*Under*-armor? Seriously?" I asked, aghast. "I mean, I guess a body suit doesn't make much sense for actual armor, but—"

Some manner of viney, biological-looking material erupted around the cloaked man and engulfed him, obscuring him from view. When the vines retracted somewhere into his back, I was faced with a man clad in what I could only describe as biological light armor. Every nook and cranny emitted a glow, while the tendrils shone a glossy black. The top part of the armor formed a trench coat-like piece of attire, with a split in the back to make room for his armored tail.

The glow shifted from a rich violet to spring green as he stepped toward me, sword balanced on his shoulder. "Well, well, the *sviirti* has nothing to say? Your masters haven't unlocked the secrets of your stolen armor yet?"

"It isn't stolen." I bared my teeth at him. "Must you always be so damn smug?"

"I have to find some manner of entertainment while we wait." His armor appeared to retract and disappear as he turned to look at the humans, then he smiled icily and glanced my way. "Or, perhaps you can get started on earning my forgiveness. Will you be needing to borrow a knife?"

"No. I'll use mine." I turned to face the cowering humans.

I'm going to savor this.

CHAPTER NINETEEN

The horizon was starting to glow with morning light, yet my team and I were still stuck with the bastard Syldrari and his men. He stood a few feet from me, rubbing his chin as he looked over my work. Once I'd gotten started with the dead human, I'd…I'd gotten a little carried away.

"Did you *have* to make a *garland* out of their testicles?!" Maelor groaned, clutching his own groin and cringing. "T-that's…"

"Aren't you supposed to be keeping your mouth shut?" I flapped a hand at him and turned to grimace at the display of dead humans. Most of my teammates looked nauseated, but I…

"You're relieved, aren't you?" The cloaked Syldrari shifted his head slightly to smirk at me.

For how poorly we get along, he sure does seem to know what I'm thinking a lot of the time. Maybe that's the problem?

I sighed in exasperation. "Why wouldn't I be relieved? I'm sure there's a boss who was pulling their strings, and he'll need to be taken down, but for now this should bring some stability back to this sector."

"And *you* will stay *out of it*." He turned and walked toward me, stopping a little too close for comfort. "I won't interfere if you need to take out more scum like them…but leave their masters to us. Their attempting to frame Syldrari, no matter which clan, is none of your business."

"Lethe!" Aisu rushed over, clearly panicked. "I need to get to the Brihl sector!" She glanced at the Syldrari beside me. "Now! Please!"

"Calm down. Deep breath. What's wrong?" I raised a hand. Something about my tone seemed to make the Syldrari swallow whatever quip he'd been about to make.

"There's been an explosion. Someone attacked them— maybe a xenophobic group?" She clenched her fists. "I need to go—"

"Her friends are there." I shifted toward the cloaked Syldrari.

He let out a small sigh and glanced over at one of his men. "Go with her. Determine whether this attack has anything to do with the Brihl's relationship with the Syldrari and see what aid they need."

I watched Aisu and the assigned soldier run off, then listened as the cloaked Syldrari ordered his men—and my team members—to go back to their sentry positions.

"Given the circumstances, I won't be letting you and your team go just yet." He turned to look at the maimed human corpses again, his expression a mixture of disgust and confusion. "The anatomy of human males is so… fragile."

"Uh…?" *That* comment caught me off-guard.

"What? Did you think Syldrari would be made like humans?" He chuckled. "Humans were made in *our* image. Not the other way around. We have been traveling through space since before your ancestors left their caves."

"Made in your image? Why do I get the sense that you mean that literally?" I frowned at him, though he seemed surprised by the question. "Humans are clearly inferior to Syldrari in most, if not all, ways. I can't say I'd be surprised if you're being literal."

"…You are inquisitive. About the right things, for once. That is good, I suppose…and it explains *much*." He pressed his fingers to his temples. "Humans may multiply quickly, but yours is a rare species. On most planets, humankind self-destructed before they were capable of even the most primitive kinds of machinery. In the cases where they didn't destroy themselves, the superior species on the planet did—whether it was another intelligent species, dangerous wildlife, or…concepts I will not spend the next four days explaining.

"One of the ancient Syldrari found humans interesting. As a scientist, he was curious to see how human evolution would differ from ours, as the planet he'd found had much more land than ours ever did. Carefully, he and his team planted the knowledge and tools the humans would require for survival. There were some genetic modifications as well.

"What you would call 'humanoid'… Bah, I hate the human languages. They are so lacking."

"Syldroid?" I offered with a smile and a half-shrug. Again, he looked surprised. "I follow you so far. Essentially, humans on most planets were too weak to survive and evolve without outside assistance. A curious researcher decided to render that assistance…and I'm assuming took a hands-off approach with everything else?"

"Yes. Once it was clear the humans had a chance to survive, his team merely observed." The cloaked man let out a heavy sigh and placed a hand on his hip. "That planet has long since been given back to nature, though such research continued elsewhere."

"Hmm…" I considered the information for a moment, thinking back to a question I'd asked Rel and never gotten a good answer to. "Can I ask you a question? Perhaps an odd one, but the last answer I got was pretty dissatisfying."

"You're asking for permission now?" He scoffed. "You have at least some capacity to think critically. I'll humor you."

"Why is it that the Syldrari don't simply conquer the Empire?" I held up a hand when he immediately opened his mouth to answer. "Last time, the answer was left mostly as 'that is a very human question.' But I'm quite serious. Wouldn't that be less, well, tedious, and come with a lower cost of life?"

He laughed outright at that. "You must have asked Rel. Sounds just like the sort of answer he'd give."

"I figure not everyone shares the same opinion. My experience with the clans may be lacking, but it's clear they're all very different." I shrugged.

"To put it simply, the cost will be much less if we simply wait for the Empire to self-destruct." His lips pulled into a chilling smile. "Haven't you ever wondered why all the off-worlders you hear about aren't human? It's because the only humans capable of flight—let alone space travel—are already part of the Empire.

"Most of the others glassed themselves when they discovered nuclear capabilities—some by accident, others due to war."

I rolled my eyes. "Let me guess, even the ones who didn't die to nuclear crises, died from more, uh...*traditional* or primitive warfare."

"Well, a good many wiped themselves out with biological weaponry or warfare, too. A few managed to create deadly plagues in the process of trying to cure disease... Humans are sloppy creatures. They tinker and interfere before they know anything about what's going on."

"So, what, instead of ending the Empire and taking back however many queens—" I went silent when the cloaked man leaned down and put a finger over my lips.

"Don't give me ideas. Letting the humans do as they please is…trying. Alas, for now, it is much saner and smarter to play from the shadows." He straightened again. "We have a saying on Syldra, though I'll spare you from attempting the pronunciation yourself. The translation is essentially, 'Remain in the shadow of the beast in order that you may strike its soft underbelly. When the beast is gone, its tyranny will collapse and the trenches will be free.'"

"Hmmm… A hunting-related saying that turned out to have practical applications in other settings, I take it?" I murmured, mentally repeating the translation.

"Indeed. Some opponents are best dealt with using strategic precision." He gave me an amused smile, possibly the least-smug version I'd seen yet. "You and yours are free to go. Do *try* to keep your nose out of our business."

"Yes, well, I'm not the boss. So, no promises there." I sighed heavily and crossed my arms, then glanced back at the display of dead humans. "With any luck, neither of us will do something that results in us getting in each other's way."

"Ahhh, yes…your life is owned by the Creshe Imperial Military," he mused. "In which case, I'm sure we'll get to play again soon. Perhaps you should train while you can."

I bit back a snippy remark and watched as all the Syldrari disappeared in an upward burst of blue-green particles.

"We should get out of here. People are going to start waking up soon." Nikolai hurried over to me. "Zafir wants us to come back *now*. Acheron can handle things in her sector."

"Right. Let's go."

I watched Zafir pace irritably around his office. As he did, I leaned back in my seat with a sizeable mug of Syldran tea. I'd made some for Zafir too, but clearly he was too preoccupied to sit down and drink.

"Honestly, Elara! Putting the humans on display like that…" he muttered, shaking his head. "No, no. You did the right thing, of course. If you'd refused, your team would likely have had to fight *him* and his men. Even so…didn't you take it a bit far?"

"Oh, that reminds me," I swirled my tea in its mug. "He made an odd comment about male anatomy. Something about human males being particularly fragile?"

"Yes…humans are quite strange to have evolved in such a way that their innards became outards," he murmured, bringing a hand up to rub his chin. "A rather odd evolutionary trait, really. Much different from many other alien species. Most evolved so that their reproductive organs are protected rather than shown."

Aw, he's not easy to fluster anymore? Or is he just that *preoccupied?* I shifted in my chair and propped my cheek against my fist. "Well, from what I've read, ancient humans ran around naked and were rather animalistic. Perhaps in lieu of more complicated methods to attract a mate, they evolved to…shall we say, put themselves on display? After all, it isn't like they have colorful feathers to display."

Zafir paused and glanced over at me. "That is an interesting theory. Yes, perhaps you are right. It would certainly explain why human males have been so prone to photographing and sharing their genitalia since the inception of early cameras. Even now, from what I understand, it is quite common for them to send photos to women they fancy. Is this a valid tactic, I wonder? Or…"

"Not particularly, I'd imagine," I stated dryly. "I'm sure you could ask some of the female staff how they feel about that. Anyway, what I'm gleaning from your musings is that Syldrari anatomy is fully internal?"

"Ah. No." He walked over to a shelf and pulled down three books. "Since you have practically become our liaison to the Syldrari, I suppose it's past time you studied the anatomy of the six sexes. Should you ever find yourself needing to offer assistance—or fight one in earnest—this knowledge should help you."

"Sounds like something you should've given me weeks ago."

He gave me a sheepish smile. "Perhaps, but I was still gauging your ability and intentions. Now then, I will do what I can to calm our superiors. The media has already jumped all over your little display. I'm not sure if making it appear to be solely your team's doing was a good idea, but it is too late now."

"It'll catapult us into the fray in one way or another, yeah." I shrugged and gave him a small smile. "If that's everything, I would like to get *some* sleep."

"You aren't concerned?" He frowned.

I shook my head. "I don't see much point in worrying about what's already done. It seems more logical to get some rest. If things do go over poorly, I'd like to have my strength and wits about me."

"Perhaps, but…" His lips parted, an inquisitive, concerned look on his face as I stood, walked over, and patted his shoulder. "Elara?"

"Drink your tea, and get some rest, too. You've been awake even longer than I have." With that, I left his office and made my way to my room to get ready for bed. Sure, the sun had already been up for a few hours, but I was mentally and physically exhausted.

CHAPTER TWENTY

Several weeks had passed since my team and I had encountered the cloaked Syldrari. I'd seen the guys intermittently for training, but Aisu and Diana were nowhere to be found—though Sarah and Zafir had both assured me they were fine. Just busy with their assigned sectors.

"Elara, open up." Zafir knocked on my door. Thankfully, he had apparently learned not to just barge in.

"Hold on. Not dressed." I grabbed my pajamas and pulled them on, then opened the door, squinting into the light at Zafir. "Ow, bright…"

"I brought you some things for your headache. Hope they kick in before you need to go to work." He stepped into my room and placed a glass of bright pink liquid on my nightstand. Next to that, he set what looked like a jar of hard candy. "Take *one*, and finish the drink."

"You said something about work?" I grumbled as Zafir made himself comfortable in a chair.

"More like a personal request."

"Huh?"

He pulled out his data pad and continued, "I need you to deliver a message for me, and I don't think you are going to like who to."

"What now?" I sighed heavily, popping a candy into my mouth. Immediately, my entire body tensed. "Oh my fucking… That is *sour!*"

"Contend with it." He waved a hand. "Nothing better than that to mend your headache. The drink is to get rid of the taste.

"Anyway, as I was saying. I've received concerning information, and I can't get ahold of any of my contacts. I'm hoping that Rel will have better luck—but he is *your* contact, not mine."

"And this message is going to…?"

"…The R'selkti." He raised a hand, clearly expecting me to fly off the handle. "Our bosses finished a prototype resonance weapon and intend to test it on the orbiting R'selkti city-ship. I finished my calculations a few hours ago. We can't let them fire that weapon."

"Show me." I extended a hand and wiggled my fingers. He hesitated, then handed me his data pad. I skimmed his notes, my stomach sinking. "The millions on the city-ship is bad enough, but take into account the aftermath and chaining events…"

Zafir nodded. "There is also an approximately eighty-two percent chance that the weapon will not survive after the first shot. If it explodes, we will be looking at a catastrophic loss of life on the surface as well."

I frowned at him. "But they're still going to fire it?"

"Ah, their calculations are flawed due to missing information." Zafir's shoulders slumped and he shook his head. "They believe their success rate to be ninety-eight percent—rounded down. However, that is due to their lack of knowledge regarding the Syldrari components used in their version of the weapon. Components they shouldn't have been able to acquire unless someone on the inside has betrayed the R'selkti."

"And you think *I* can deliver this info to them?" I gave him a dubious look.

"The rumors about them may be foul, but their motivations always come back to their desire for honorable and interesting battles. While yes, that means bloodshed is ingrained in their history, it also means they feel intense guilt over the first Resonance Incident. Thus the lengths their young master went to in order to right the wrongs of his father."

"No promises, none of the people in the Syldrari sector seem too fond of the R'selkti." I rubbed my temples and the back of my neck, then glanced over at Zafir. "I'll take payment in the form of a neck rub. I swear my muscles have turned into stone overnight."

He hesitated, but finally he sighed and moved over to do as I asked. After a moment, he spoke, his tone concerned. "Have you not been taking proper care in your training? You should not be this tense."

"I'm careful." I arched my neck. "Right there's good…"

"It's no wonder you have a headache." He gave the back of my neck one last squeeze, then stepped away, adjusting his glasses. "If this problem persists, we will need to take a look and see whether something is wrong, or if you simply need better physical therapy care."

Who said you could stop? I whined internally, choosing to keep the thought to myself. In the absence of my teasing and deliberate phrasing, Zafir's professional air had returned and the flustered Syldrari persona had vanished. I felt the latter was probably closer to his actual personality, but I didn't want his reactions to raise suspicion with anyone.

"What is it?" He nudged his glasses up his nose, looking at me with a concerned expression.

"Maybe I need a different pillow?" I shrugged. "When do you want me to leave? I should get dressed—and am I going as Lethe?"

"Go as Elara to Rel's café, and to the R'selkti as Lethe…but you may have to reveal your face to make an impression." He lifted his tablet out of my hands and rapidly typed something, then ejected a tiny disc of some material I didn't recognize. He placed it in a case and handed the case to me. "Everything they need to know is there—including the consequences for betraying your identity."

"Okay. I'll behave." I nodded to Zafir.

Not quite how I thought I'd be meeting the R'selkti...

The moment I walked into Rel's café, I made eye contact with him and spoke in the most commanding tone I could muster. "Rel, we need to talk and it's going to take a while. You should close for the day."

"Hey! What about my lunch?!" one of the customers protested when Rel promptly pulled off his apron.

"Aldiner, Ciheri—take over while I'm gone." He looked to the rave fish and the ghostly one. "Close up at the usual time if I'm not back by then."

He led me upstairs to his apartment but backed me into the door after it shut, resting his forearm above my head. "You have my attention. Now, I suggest you think carefully about what you are going to do with it before you take that tone with me again."

"I need you to get me an audience with the R'selkti," I stated, meeting his gaze unflinchingly. "And before you ask, no, it isn't for some half-baked idea of revenge."

"...When?" Rel frowned, though he didn't move away. "I would rather not expose you to each other any further."

"Now." I narrowed my eyes, summoning my battle suit just in case he decided to comply without warning. "We may not have long to prevent a cataclysmic event. If you know where they're hiding—"

He sighed heavily and leaned a little closer. "What kind of cataclysm, Elara? You will have to be more specific if you want my cooperation."

"The humans are going to fire a resonance cannon at the R'selkti city-ship."

In an instant, Rel's demeanor shifted completely. His expression turned fierce, all his pupils shrank, and his glow became what I could only describe as storm-colored. I'd never seen anything like it.

"Where did you get this information?" he inquired in a quiet, dangerous tone. Lifting his hand, he removed my visor.

"My boss is an informant working for the Syldrari. He's lost communication with all his contacts, and hoped you would be able to help," I answered plainly, watching as he studied me a little too intently. "What?"

"…Keep this on." He set the visor back in place. "And don't take it off until we've returned here and you can dismiss your suit. I will handle the R'selkti if they protest your appearance as Lethe."

"Um, okay?" I asked, puzzled. "Can you at least tell me

why?"

"No." Rel finally moved away from me and walked over to the nearby closet, pulling out a harness with some kind of gun and a short sword strapped onto it. He offered me a hand. "I'll transport us to their base. If you must be sick after, try to aim *away* from me, please."

The moment I took his hand, my vision exploded into a burst of colors and chaotic shapes. I clenched my eyes shut against the vibrant barrage, stumbling when I felt my feet hit the ground again. Thankfully, Rel had a good grip on me. My stomach lurched as I opened my eyes, but I managed to keep what little was in my stomach from ending up on the ground.

"Oooh…dizzy…" I crouched in place, holding my hands to my head.

"What in the…" a familiar voice exclaimed, and I peeked around my forearm to see Casair standing next to a man with a rather familiar sword—and face. "Rel, what is the meaning of this? She shouldn't be here. At the very least, you should have warned—"

"Related? That explains a lot…" I muttered, glancing between Rel and the now-*un*cloaked bastard. They had the same slate blue skin, the same blue-black hair, and the same beautifully eerie hazel-patterned eyes of variegated blue and burgundy. Hell, even most of their facial features were similar. And hearing him speak again, I realized that the uncloaked Syldrari must have been using a voice modulator before. He sounded *so much* like Rel.

"Related?" Rel raised an eyebrow, then offered me a hand. "Can you stand?"

"...Maybe." I let him pull me to my feet. "Are you saying you're *not* related?"

"The usual guess is twin," he answered dryly, looking past me to his apparent brother. "Which we are. Most humans can't tell the difference between us."

"Most *anything* can't tell the difference between these two," one of the soldiers muttered.

"And...you're R'selkti?" I asked pointedly.

"Rel saw our father's insanity sooner than I did. He left and formed the V'shir...centuries ago, now." The uncloaked one made a dismissive motion before stepping around the table he was standing behind and approaching us. "Give me one good reason I shouldn't kill you where you stand."

"Zafir sent me because he can't contact you." I crossed my arms as his pace slowed.

"This human could still be lying, sir!" one of his men exclaimed. "If Zafir was compromised—"

"I can assure you I'm not here to exact revenge for turning me into what I am," I stated flatly. "I may be pissed off about the Resonance Incident, but that doesn't mean I want to see millions die, either. So. Are we going to talk or not?"

"Please. We were only responsible for the first time, and—" The soldier fell silent when he received a sharp look from both

Rel *and* his twin.

"Which one did you think I survived, dumbass?" I raised my hands into the air, sighing dramatically. "My hands are stained with both Syldrari and human blood thanks to that. Let's not add any more just because you're an even bigger stubborn pain in the ass than your boss is."

Rel let out a short laugh, while the stubborn pain in the ass in question shot me a foul look.

"*Fine.* Speak."

"We're going to need something that can read this." I held up the tiny disc, and he sighed.

"Casair, halt ongoing procedures until I've dealt with the human. Keep the men busy, but let them know they aren't to attack her...*yet*." He turned to look at me and motioned down a long corridor. "This way, then. It's a long walk, so start talking."

"Jysel." Rel gave his brother a reprimanding look. "I can vouch for the importance of her information."

Jysel sighed irritably. "Yes. Otherwise you wouldn't have brought her here."

I shrugged and began talking. "The military has been working on their own version of your father's resonance weapon for several years now. Unfortunately, it has reached its completion."

Jysel snorted. "You don't make it sound complete."

"Remember our conversation about how humans tinker with things without any grasp of how something works or what they're doing?" I asked dryly. The twitch of his tail was answer enough. "There's several issues. Do you want the bad, the idiotic, or the worst first?"

"I want whatever prompted this visit."

"Okay. Worst it is. The military plans to test the weapon by firing it at your city-ship. Their projections suggest a slim margin for error. However, Zafir's more informed calculations guarantee that the weapon will not only destroy your city-ship, but the debris will take out many of the other ships in orbit, as well as pelt the surface of the planet. Furthermore, there is a high probability that the weapon will overload and explode after firing. He estimates a severe loss of life on the surface from the explosion alone."

Jysel slowed to a stop but didn't turn to look at me or Rel. "And why are his projections so…severe?"

"The cannon is a mixture of human and Syldrari technology, all spliced together. As far as he can tell, the majority of the Syldrari tech is pieces that were salvaged from the original R'selkti weapon." I crossed my arms, my stomach turning. "Due to the particular human tech it's been paired with, he believes the initial explosion will destroy the parts that give the weapon its directional aim. It will likely get several seconds of resonance off in every direction before the vibrations obliterate the weapon entirely. The final explosion itself will also release a massive amount of toxins into the atmosphere, but there won't be many people left after the resonance to begin with."

"Why haven't they fired it already?" Rel frowned, stroking his chin. "It's unlike them to wait."

"They're waiting for signs that all the R'selkti have returned to the city-ship." I scowled. "They're planning to put out a broadcast banning certain clans from visiting the surface. Their intent is actually to make certain they destroy most of the clan in one strike."

"That should be easy enough to get around." Rel tilted his head thoughtfully, then shifted his gaze to Jysel's back when he didn't make a move to start walking again. "I told you she's a valuable asset, as did Zafir."

"She is *troublesome*." Jysel raised his fingers to his temples and slowly rubbed them. "But not as troublesome as the Resonance Project. A minor mercy. This way now, there's a secure computer back here. What is on the disc?"

"Zafir's full report and his calculations, along with the weapon's details. As interesting as I find…well, most things, if I'm being honest, I don't have quite the grasp necessary to explain these things fully." I followed Rel and Jysel into the room and handed the disc to the latter. A low whine had me glancing off to my left.

A massive furry…*thing* that looked vaguely canine padded over and stuck its nose against my torso with enough force that I would've toppled over if Rel hadn't caught me. The creature took a few sniffs, then sat back on its haunches, looking a tad confused.

"Not going to go running in fear?" Jysel remarked, glancing at me before patting the creature's shoulder—which rested roughly at his eyelevel.

"So *cute!*" I balled my hands into fists to keep myself from darting over and burying myself in the thing's fur. "What is it? What's its name? Can I pet it? Are they from Syldra? What—"

"Uh…" Jysel looked taken aback by my sudden excitement.

Rel, on the other hand, laughed and placed a hand on my shoulder. "Sal'aphel is a *nyndsh~r*. Whether you may pet it is up to Jysel. Yes, they are from Syldra—the colder reaches, to be more precise. Their thick fur helps to regulate their temperature in the frigid waters, though they can function just fine on land, too."

"If it will keep her occupied…" Jysel shrugged and looked up at Sal'aphel. "Be nice to the human. For now."

Another whine, and Sal'aphel laid down on the floor, four of its six legs tucked up underneath it. I scooted over as it watched me, its head laying on the floor. Reaching out to scritch its head, I found its fur was so long it went up almost to my elbow.

"How is Zafir?" Jysel asked after a moment.

"Tired and distressed, though he remains focused and professional," I answered, then tilted my head and frowned. "Although he's been on edge the past week or two. The moment anything is even slightly wrong with us, he wants to run a full docket of tests to make sure we're okay. The only reason *I'm* not back at base and in bed just for having a headache this morning is because delivering this information was clearly more important."

"Ah. He must still be concerned about the attempted murder," Jysel muttered, causing me to glance toward him. "Someone among your superiors seems to quite dislike all aspects of the Resonance Project..." He trailed off and reread a portion of the report several times. "Rel."

Frowning, Rel joined his brother, leaving me to lavish the fluffy thing with attention. A moment later, I heard Rel say, "They're going to fire from there...? The entire city will get caught in the explosion! What little of the Empire is left would be thrown into war with each of the different species—"

"Avoiding a test of the weapon won't be enough. We're going to have to infiltrate the weapons platform and disable it." Jysel flipped through a few schematics, glancing back at me. "You won't be able to create a distraction large enough to get in...ah. I know what we can do."

"Hmm?" I gave the smirking Syldrari an inquisitive look, but he just turned back to his screen. Sal'aphel butted me with its snout, demanding more attention.

"Are you just going to keep pretending you don't see that Sal'aphel likes her?" Rel asked dryly, making his twin twitch.

"I'm *working*."

Rel laughed. "That's a yes, then."

He walked over and crouched next to me and Sal'aphel, reaching out to give the creature several pats. However, when there was a noise at the door, Sal'aphel abruptly leapt to its feet and put itself between us and the door, snarling.

"And that is why he isn't the best guard—everyone but me and Jysel are his enemies." Rel chuckled and shot me an amused smile. "Well, until now, I suppose. Perhaps you have certain *traits* he likes."

"Sal'aphel, settle down. Let them report," Jysel murmured distractedly. "Come in."

Casair inched the door open and peeked around it, then paused when he saw that Sal'aphel had padded back over to me and put his massive head in my lap. "What in the name of the…"

"What is it, Casair?" Jysel prompted. "We're very busy—"

"Sir. Our scouts have confirmed the number of queens the military has captured, experimented on, and hidden from us." Casair hesitated, then glanced toward me. "Am I to report here, or…"

"Considering the huma—*Elara* is trying to prevent the humans from wiping out our city-ship, not to mention she is the one who delivered the information about the queens, I will let it slide. This time." Jysel rested his head against his fist and swiveled his chair to gaze at Casair. "Continue."

"Sir. I'll be blunt. The humans have fifty-three queens spread out across Creshe in various facilities," Casair spat venomously. "Most of them aren't in our databases *or* Xilen's.

The humans, or perhaps one of their allies, may have found a way to discover queens faster than we do."

"All the more reason to stop this attack…losing fifty-three queens would be… Ah." Jysel glanced back at the screen, then brought up a second document. "That would be perfect. Casair. Begin drafting plans for an invasion of the facilities—and Elara, keep your mouth shut about this. Don't tell Zafir."

"Um, alright?" I gave him a puzzled look as he stood up and strode over.

Jysel made a face when he saw Sal'aphel snuggling into my lap. "Another reason he can't guard—"

"Hey! Sal'aphel is a good boy!" I protested, smooshing the creature's cheeks and massaging its jaw muscles. "Or girl. Or, uh…do the various creatures on Syldra have as many sexes as Syldrari do? Whatever Sal'aphel is, they're a good that!"

"Of *course* he's good. He's been trained well. He just isn't—" Jysel started, but Rel stopped him, murmuring something in their own language. Jysel stiffened and looked away before finally answering. Whatever he said, Rel didn't look happy.

"It's time you go back to your headquarters." Jysel gave me a pointed look. "If you utter a word of any of this—"

"I won't." I nodded and stood up. "They're liable to act early if they suspect anything, and I'm not keen on helping them to begin with." I paused and glanced toward Rel. "I have to wonder. Are you regretting advising me to take their deal yet?"

"Not at all." Rel smiled. "You've proven yourself to be a great ally. Even this dolt recognizes it."

"I do not—" Jysel started to protest, and Rel promptly put an arm around his twin's neck, forcing him to practically bow. "Be *nice* to the nice human lady who gave us vital information."

"Are they always like this?" I asked, looking over at Casair.

"You could say that..." He shrugged slightly. "Elara, I should have told you I'm—"

"Please. And go against your orders?" I flicked his arm. "I think not."

"Sal'aphel, stay. Elara has to—" Jysel started, but a moment later I was lifted into the air and dropped onto a sea of fur. "For the love of..."

"Aw, are you going to miss me?" I cooed, scratching the back of Sal'aphel's neck. He made a sound somewhere halfway between a dog and a bird as he trotted in the direction of the main cavern I'd entered from.

Jysel took on a commanding tone as he addressed his soldiers. "There's been a change of plans. Call back a portion of our forces from our ships."

"Let's go." Rel nudged my leg, then looked at Sal'aphel. "Come now, Sal'aphel, set her down."

In response, Sal'aphel showed his teeth and growled—a response that caused everyone in the cavern to freeze and turn to look at us. Sighing, Rel placed a hand on Sal'aphel's leg and said something in his own language, using soft, soothing tones. Sal'aphel hesitated, but finally crouched down. Pale purple energy coiled around me and lifted me off his back, setting me carefully on the ground.

"Mmm? Was that...psychokinesis?" I peered at Sal'aphel curiously, then at Rel when he nudged me again.

"Come along." He reiterated quietly, taking me by the wrist and transporting us without warning. "Yes, *nyndsh~r* are psychokinetic. That, I suppose, is a decent glimpse into the many ways Syldra is dangerous. It isn't simply tooth and claw we must be wary of."

"So, what now?" I murmured, watching as Rel put away his harness and weapons.

"Dinner, on the house, if you like." He motioned toward the door, then paused. "Once you dismiss your suit, that is… And I feel as though I should apologize for my brother's behavior. He—"

"He's a pain in the ass, and not your responsibility," I interjected dryly. "He said you left the clan to form the V'shir?"

"Yes. Our father was… Well, I suppose the best translation for it would be 'queen drunk.' He would do anything to please the R'selkti queen." He grimaced and crossed his arms loosely over his stomach. "Admittedly, that was not actually her fault. He was unstable long before he met her, from what we understand. Exposure to the queen's power simply twisted him further. He became obsessed."

"And I take it stopping him wasn't exactly a simple matter." I leaned a little closer, curious. "You also said that humans have a hard time telling you and Jysel apart? Why?"

"Yes, stopping him back then would have been— What do you mean *why?*" He stared at me in disbelief. "As the soldiers were muttering, *most* people can't tell the difference between us. The Syldrari only manage to do so because of our ability to see other spectrums. You shouldn't be able to—"

"Your voice is a little deeper than his, your face is narrower, his eyes are set a little further apart. You wear your hair completely differently. He carries himself with arrogance, you carry yourself with confidence. You smell different. Your presences feel different. You..." I trailed off and gave him a questioning look when he placed a hand on my head.

"And those sorts of detailed observations, my dear, you need to keep private. They are not the sort of things *humans* notice so easily." He patted my head and moved past me to the door. "You need to take more care protecting yourself, and that begins with pretending to be more human than we both know you really are."

CHAPTER TWENTY-ONE

I walked into the lounge section of the mess hall with a cup of coffee in hand and sank into a chair with a small sigh. It was pretty early, but Zafir was already there, mulling over his data pad. Sarah and Maelor were there as well, busily stuffing their faces with breakfast as they watched TV.

"What are you working on, Zafir?" I inquired after a few moments.

"Ah, Elara. Good morning." He glanced at me briefly before returning to his work. "I am reading reports regarding the most recent Resonance Incident. I believe I mentioned it to you...?"

"Happened a bit over a month ago, right?" I nodded and leaned over my armrest to get a peek at his screen. "Do they usually take so long to report?"

"No, but I can understand their hesitation. The effects of this weapon are vastly different from the previous attacks. The victims were torn into large chunks—not reduced to goo. Parts of some buildings are still standing, while others went completely unscathed. There are more survivors, most of whom show no signs of change…" He trailed off into a tired sigh, his voice dropping to a barely audible whisper. "Something isn't right. This isn't Syldrari work."

"Eep! What the—!" Sarah let out a sudden yelp when an obnoxious screeching sound, accompanied by brief static, came from the TV, interrupting the morning news.

My heart stopped for a moment when the screen filled with an intricate spiraling gold-on-black logo, which promptly slid out of frame to reveal a very familiar face.

Jysel's piercing eyes were focused straight at the camera, showing every detail of their variegated pupils. His blue-grey skin shimmered faintly under the lights, making it clear the texture was not human. His hair was parted off-center and swept into a somewhat formal style, the underside glowing with what I'd come to know as their 'passive' cyan.

The look on his face told me that passivity was the last thing on his mind.

"I am Jysel, formerly of Clan R'selkti. It has come to my attention that this planet's government has been terribly naughty…" He shifted slightly, giving the world an alluring, dangerous glare as his lips pulled into a smile. *"You have taken many of our queens*

and their guardians captive for experimentation. We will not stand for this insult. You have a week of this planet's time to return them all to us—or we will not hesitate to use force to reclaim all the poor souls you have stolen from us.

"I recommend you comply before more clans begin to intervene."

With that, the feed cut off—but the previous show didn't come back on. Instead, it was merely static. As if on cue, Zafir's communicator began ringing and Amara came trotting into the room, still wearing her pajamas. Noting that our boss was busy, she motioned me over instead.

"That was a prerecorded address. I just picked up hits at several facilities—they're already on the move." She showed me her screen, which was playing a video feed of Syldrari infiltrators. "Rather, that's what I'd say if I hadn't zoomed in. I'm pretty sure they're from some other clan, and they're acting weird. They seem to be looking for chemical compounds, not weapons or queens. Think you can get this verified for me?"

"I'll arrange for Xilen to meet Elara at Rel's café," Zafir interjected, walking over to us. He gave me a stern look. "Or rather, she will be meeting *us* there. The party is still on for this afternoon. The only change is that the higher-ups want me to act as your handler, just in case."

"Going to handle me, are you?" I gave him a pointed look. "Then you'd better change into something more suitable. Off you go."

He frowned down at his lab coat. "This isn't...?"

"Zafir, please. It's a party featuring government officials from multiple species—including a Syldrari queen. *Of course* that isn't suitable." I placed my hands on his shoulders and guided him in the direction of his room. "Now, go find something formal. Don't make me dress you myself."

Once he was in his room, I turned and leaned back against the wall by the door. *I* would be going in military dress. There had been some discussion about the possibility of bringing me as Lethe, but Zafir wanted to try to keep Xilen from realizing who I was. While we both agreed she probably already knew, *he* claimed there was a chance she didn't.

A tenth of a percent of a chance is still a chance, I guess… I shifted to glare at Zafir's door in irritation. "Come on. You have to have some sort of business suit or otherwise-snazzy attire, right?"

"I hate human clothes." He opened the door sulkily, apparently entirely unaware of me checking him out from top to bottom. "So infernally *itchy* and *tight* in all the wrong places…"

"You could get a tailor to fix that last problem." I nudged him with my elbow, earning a disgruntled pout. "Your glasses are crooked."

He sighed and adjusted them before straightening to his full height. Or, well, what his human disguise made his full height appear to be. He'd seemed much taller the one time I'd seen him in his true form.

"We will need to discuss this morning's news, but later, of

course, after we've attended to formal business." Zafir crossed his arms and narrowed his eyes at me. "What are you staring at?"

I gave him a light smack on the ass, then began to head in the direction of the lobby. "Good choice of pants. We should probably get you some more options, though, if you get dragged to formal events often."

"*Elara*," he reprimanded. "Such behavior toward your *boss* is incredibly inappropriate. You should refrain from—"

"Oh, I'm sure it is." I made a dismissive motion as I listened to him hurrying to catch up to me. "Consider it part of my payment."

He sighed in aggravation. "Payment for *what*?"

"For dragging me to this bullshit formal party nonsense!" I held up a finger and gave him a bright smile, waiting for my very deliberate phrasing to register in his brain.

We'd gone up four floors in the elevator before he finally asked, "What did you mean by *part of* your payment?"

"That depends on how much this affair bores and/or offends me!" I gave him an innocent smile before stepping out of the elevator and into the main lobby.

He slumped, putting a hand over his face. "I'm cursed..."

"Or maybe you're blessed?" I winked at him. "We'll just have to see."

He let out a distressed groan and followed me out of the building, where we caught a hovercar that would take us to the Syldrari sector. I figured I'd see how long it'd take to make Zafir realize that my uncomfortable uniform was the reason I'd decided to torture him.

Uniform, my ass. Should be called 'that thing you put an escort in to make her look military-but-hot because she's just a cheap side piece.' I glanced down at my thigh-high boots. *Or, well,* expensive *side piece, in my case.*

Zafir got out first, offering me a hand up despite my teasing. I accepted the help and led him through the Syldrari sector to Rel's café. To my surprise, no one whistled at me, though I got plenty of strange looks. Strangely, that was about where it ended. From what I'd read, I'd expected a much more pronounced reaction.

"Ah there you two…" Rel's glow turned brilliant scarlet tinged with traces of pink, and the glass in his hand shattered. "Elara, by the Abyss Father! *What are you wearing?!* Zafir! *You allowed this?"*

"What… Ah, are you referring to her uniform?" Zafir glanced at me, then back at Rel. "This is standard issue for—"

"Elara, dear, let's go get you changed." Xilen walked over and pulled my arm into her cleavage. "Rel, perhaps you can *educate* Zafir while I take care of this little problem, hmm?"

"Hold on. There's stuff we need you to look over first!" I protested, attempting to reach for the footage Amara had given me.

Xilen shook her head at me and loosened her grip to move

my hand away from my pocket. "Absolutely not. It can wait until after you've changed, and after we've been to the party. We are cutting it close as it is."

"If she wears something else—" Zafir started to protest. This time, the flames of the grill leapt into the air. "E-Elder, please calm down. This—"

Aldiner and Ciheri poked out to see what was going on, spotted me, seemed to think twice about saying anything, and immediately retreated.

"Come along, dear." Xilen guided me to a private room where several outfits were already laid out. "I had a feeling this would happen—I've seen this 'standard issue' before. Luckily for you, I have just the right contacts. You won't get into trouble for wearing something *I* personally requested."

"Xilen, that footage—" I tried to change the subject, but she shushed me. "It's *important!*"

"I'm sure it is, dear, but the consequences for being late to or missing a party like this are not good for your health, mine, Rel's, or Zafir's." Xilen crossed her arms and blocked the door. "We can look it over after, I promise."

Sighing, I turned to look at the multiple outfits laid out in the room. I knew better than to ask just *how* it would make things worse for us with the Imperials.

Finally, I forced myself to focus on selecting one of the outfits she'd apparently acquired for me.

"Still a little on the sexy side…but at least they've got pants."
I immediately gravitated toward an outfit with a pair of shiny
black leggings. Then I felt the material and sighed. "Or not. I
wouldn't be able to fight in this."

"Come now, darling! It's a party!" She dragged me over to a
black and gold ensemble, a playful smile tugging at her lips.
"What about this? They're less shiny, but will these leggings
suffice? Ah, and don't you worry. They're made of the *finest*
materials on Syldra. I'd wager they'll protect you more than
human armor would!"

Doubt that, but… I glanced around, noting that the other
options were all dresses. The black and gold ensemble seemingly
had cutout panels, but after a few prods I realized they were in
fact made of a clear material that I simply couldn't see. "What
about this part?"

"The same material as our under-armor," she answered
sweetly. "We understand the tastes of humans and other lesser
species, dear. They love to show off certain parts of the body.
With *my* designs, you can flaunt yourself in such fun ways…"

"Alright, this set it is. Though, with a revealed back and
cleavage…" I shrugged to myself and then started stripping. It
wasn't my problem if Rel decided to rage at her too.

"Goodness! Those bruises!" She traced her fingertips down
the left side of my back. "You're turning *blue*, dear. Get into a
nasty fight?"

Bruises? From what? I thought for a moment, my stomach tightening. "I sparred with the guys yesterday for a few hours to work on their training. Probably from the grappling."

"Oh? Is that all?" Xilen murmured slyly.

Here we go again… I pulled the leggings on, eyeing the transparent panels running from ankle to waist. I definitely felt some kind of material there, even if I couldn't see it. The tight top required Xilen's assistance to get into place, and once it was, the hem appeared to *fuse* with the pants. "Uh…"

"And now you're suited up." She winked, then nudged a pair of shoes with manageable heels at me. "These will do the same. I figure these should allow you to look 'correct' to the humans while still letting you do your thing if you have to."

"And you said this material is strong like Syldrari under-armor?" I questioned, backing away when Xilen pulled a knife out of seemingly nowhere and sliced it across my arm. "Hey!"

"See? So strong!" She tossed the knife aside. It stuck tip-first into the wall, and she clasped her hands together. "Now then! The party awaits! Let's go show them our beauty can be just as deadly as our…well, everything else, I suppose."

She dragged me back into the café. Zafir promptly buried his head in his arms when he spotted me, as if he could hide in the bar. Rel covered his eyes with one hand and massaged his temples, his tail swishing back and forth.

"Why did I trust *you* of all people with this matter…" He

groaned as several shades of pink, fuchsia, and yellow fought for dominance.

"Careful there, you're turning awfully pink," I teased, crossing my arms under my bust in a way I knew would lift it up a bit more.

"Oh my, I'm going to have to let you go shopping through my ship's wares at some point!" Xilen giggled, circling me once before turning to look at the poor flustered men. "Come now, centuries old and an Elder? The only thing that should be able to fluster you at *this* point is a quee—"

"Whoa! From monster bait to seductress, huh? That sure is an upgrade!" Aldiner declared a little more loudly than necessary as he came strolling out of the back room, hands in the pockets of his apron. He grinned at me, looking me up and down as his colors sparked all over the damn place. "Heh. Maybe I should come along to this party too. Xilen's usual guards might not be enough—"

"I'll be joining them," Zafir and Rel said in unison.

Of the pair, though, I looked over at Rel and raised an eyebrow. "Are you, now? Won't that be problematic due to the whole…"

"My ID clearly differentiates us, and I was already invited," he stated flatly. He stepped around the counter, his clothing shifting into a looser garment that I had no name for. It revealed part of his muscular chest and abs, and the sleeves stopped around his elbows, yet somehow the ensemble still came across as formal.

"Aw, and here I was hoping you'd try to impress us!" Xilen whined with mock disappointment.

Rel, however, gave her a serious look. "Were there only one of you, yes, though I believe you're already well aware it wouldn't be you."

"Yes, yes, we're better as friends and business acquaintances, I know." She motioned to her to guards, glancing back at Zafir. "Aren't you coming as Elara's handler, dear?"

"Abyss Father lend me strength…" Zafir slumped briefly in his seat before reluctantly leaving it to join us. "Not a word, Elara. Not a word."

Once we were all seated in the shuttle that would take us up to the party, I crossed one leg over the other and looked between Rel and Zafir a few times. Both were doing their damnedest to look anywhere that wasn't at me.

"Sooo, about this party… What am I doing, exactly?"

"Ah! Well, you see," Xilen began cheerfully, "you will be acting as my Imperial escort and guest. You have full authority to drop anyone who tries to attack me or treat me like meat! The Imperials are *so* keen on making it appear like they're cracking down on xenophobic and xenophilic assholes, you know."

"So, what? Zafir is here to keep a leash on me so I don't kill anyone important or go feral? What about Rel?"

"A reluctant, but official, guest," Rel answered with a grimace. "None of the other V'shir Elders wanted to go."

I'm never going to get used to him being called an 'Elder.' I eyed Rel up and down, then studied his face for a moment. Sure, all the Syldrari I'd seen looked to be the human equivalent of in their twenties and thirties, but I knew that sure as hell wasn't the case.

On second glance, that outfit isn't half bad. I do miss the leather pants and tank top, though… Hmmm.

"The poor dear could use some pleasant company to cheer him up!" Xilen gave Rel a mischievous smile. "If he didn't shrug off anyone who might have power over him, anyway."

"I mean, I can kinda understand that, though. Isn't it better to know you're attracted to someone—physically or otherwise—because they're your own feelings, and not whatever it is Syldrari…" I fell silent when Xilen pressed a finger over my lips.

She smiled cheerfully and shook her head. "Syldrari… men? Ah, no, but them too… Ah, I know!

"Any Syldrari who has a *dick* and nothing else are on the lowest rungs of our society. Compared to human societies, of course, Syldra is still a utopia of freedom. Alas, *iri* are just so rare… If you were to visit Syldra, you would meet people who had never met an *iri* before—you would be their first!

"It isn't merely a queen's draw that flusters them so badly, you see. Many simply don't know how to react to an *iri* beyond reverence and desire. Even if you took a queen's power out of the equation, there would still be many…problems, if you will."

One of Xilen's guards spoke next, nodding at me. "It's why so many of 'em end up tricked into serving ladies of the court or working in brothels on other planets—like this one. It's an issue, for sure. But that's why Xilen is out here buying up anyone she can rescue—and trying to keep all her friends safe. Don't let the sultry persona fool you."

"Oh, ruin my fun, why don't you." Xilen pouted.

Even so, I don't think any of those issues quite explain Rel and Zafir… I glanced at the two men. Rel had stopped pouting and seemed to have sunk into intense thought, his glow swirling lazily between shades of blue and green in a way that reminded me of someone tossing a ball back and forth between their hands. The pattern compelled me to ask, "Rel? Are you *playing* with your glow?"

A jolt went through him and his color abruptly stopped at sage green. He looked up in surprise, the lower portion of his tail smacking into the base of his seat. "Ah…yes. It helps me stay focused when I think. More importantly, how did you…?"

"I have a far-fetched idea." I leaned forward in my seat, watching as his pupils briefly fluctuated in size and his demeanor shifted back to the one I was more used to. "Humans are stupid, right? If you can control your glow, why not pick a color other than the color your brother showed on TV? If the color's different, that may be enough to make the humans understand you're totally different people."

"I don't know if they're *that*…" He sighed and gave me a sheepish smile. "I don't think I can convince any of you even if I *do* finish that sentence. Well then, what color do you suggest, seeing as this is *your* idea?"

"Well, you don't have to convince us of *that*, at least." I gave him a sweet smile when he bristled. "Let's see… What emotions can result in deep purples?"

"Various forms of arrogance, confidence, suspicion, god-like delusions…" Zafir muttered, finally returning to the conversation. He looked over at Rel. "She's right. The color would likely be enough. Most humans I've met assume the color is dependent on the individual or the clan—and nothing has ever been done to reeducate them. We just need to find something you can sustain."

"I have just the thought for that!" Xilen exclaimed, leaning over to put an arm around me. "Just think of how much discipline this cutie pie needs for all the trouble she's put you two through!"

"Or how much *you've* put them through," I growled back. In an instant, Rel's glow turned a vibrant royal purple. *Huh. So, I'm more well behaved than Xilen. Good to know.*

Xilen pouted, though the corners of her mouth still curled up, giving away her amusement. "Aw, I guess I haven't rubbed off on you enough yet. Don't worry, we can fix that and have them *begging* to—"

"Thanks, but I don't like my men to beg." I'd dismissed the notion before I fully realized the words were coming out of my mouth. ... *Too late to take that back now, I guess.*

"Ahhh, I see, I see. Yes, giving them power from time to time can be fun, too." She leaned in a little closer, apparently crossing some distance threshold that earned her glares from both Rel and Zafir. "Now, now, weren't you boys trying to be discreet?"

She says, as if I wasn't already suspicious of multiple things before ever meeting her. I kept the thought to myself and instead glanced out the nearby window. "Let's keep it professional, shall we? We're there."

"Oh, boo. Professional? And here I was hoping someone would start a brawl for the right to dance with one of us!" Xilen sulked briefly before grasping my arm. "Oh! Or you and I can dance!"

"I don't dance." I brushed her off easily and rose to my feet. Xilen's guards *and* both Rel and Zafir promptly blocked my way.

The quieter guard bowed slightly. "We will make certain it is safe. Please wait here until we've finished."

Xilen pulled me back down onto the seat with a smile. "Now, now. You're with a queen today. You must be patient."

"...Fine." I crossed my arms.

"They're not just driven by the fact that they're male and you're female, you know." Her voice took on an oddly serious tone.

"Does it have anything to do with all these queen insinuations?" I shot her a foul look.

"They are both more than capable of protecting themselves from most queens if they need to. You have a certain…presence to you. One I have no doubt the R'selkti queen would notice were you to have the unfortunate pleasure of making her acquaintance…" She studied me, her pupils flaring slightly. "You don't approve of the power imbalance among Syldrari. That will attract certain types of men to you more strongly than queenship would. You should be careful how freely you speak about your beliefs. There are rogue Syldrari, and they could be just as dangerous to you as the R'selkti queen would be."

"And why is she so dangerous?" I frowned at Xilen, who hesitated.

"She…would be considered an extremist, perhaps, had she not gained full control of our government," she replied carefully. "I get away with what I do because I'm *buying* the poor souls. It is a troubling situation, but not one for you to concern yourself with. Keep the people you like close and stay as far from that woman as you can."

I wanted to ask her more, but a soft knock on the shuttle door made it clear our time was up. Xilen went first, escorted by her guards. Zafir and Rel both seemed to consider offering me assistance, but stopped themselves. While I might have enjoyed the attention under other circumstances, it struck a bit of a sour note after my exchange with Xilen—plus, I was supposed to be playing guard dog.

"I hate to say this, but our bosses want you to play the silent type…" Zafir murmured to me, earning a sharp look from Rel. "They're terrified about letting a Resonance survivor roam free for an event like this. They've given strict orders for Elara to remain silent unless it's imperative that she talk. I'm meant to speak for her."

Rel glanced away, his jaw tensing.

I shrugged and followed the group through the drab ship and into the main room. Dozens of humans were present, but only two to five members of any other species. There were quite a few humanoid species present aside from Syldrari, including the Brihl. Then there were other things, more *unique* species, who either carried portable tanks or rolled around inside clear, gas-filled orbs.

Noting me glancing around, Zafir leaned down to murmur into my ear.

"Many species do not contend well with the type of atmosphere humans require, nor with that of their neighbors. Thus, they designed ways to bring it with them, much like humans will bring oxygen down into the depths…as if it can help them there."

I glanced to the side at him as his voice took on a darker tone. He smiled slightly, looking more sinister than anything else, and straightened.

"My! Zafir, dear, you should do that again. Those pants pull in all the right ways," Xilen teased as she fell into step with us. I did my best to maintain my role as a stoic, silent soldier as she continued, "Rel, you should have— Ah, where did he slink off to now?"

Damn, he ran off somewhere? I crossed my arms and propped my cheek against my fist. *Ugh…and why is it so hot in here?*

I followed Xilen and Zafir to their table, which they shared with several Syldrari I didn't know—plus an empty seat for Rel. Looking around, it became quickly apparent that the tables were assigned by species. Some part of me wondered if it was for security purposes, or perhaps to allow them to quell any problems more efficiently by annihilating a single table.

The conversations were oddly quiet. Multiple representatives came over to speak with Xilen, but their voices were always so hushed I couldn't determine what was being said. Meanwhile, I was feeling hotter by the moment. But my outfit breathed well enough and no one else appeared to be overheated, so I did my best to suck it up.

"Here," Rel murmured by my ear, surprising me into turning toward him. He smiled in amusement and grabbed one of my hands, placing a bottle of water into it with a knowing smile. He left it at that and wandered back to his seat at a leisurely pace.

"This should be over soon." One of Xilen's guards gave me a small smile. "These dinners are always just that…dinners."

Sure enough, about half an hour later people began leaving to return to the surface. Xilen pranced over and put an arm around my waist. "Aw, were you lonely over here without me?"

"No," I stated simply, eliciting a giggle out of her.

"Let's head back." Rel gave Xilen an unamused look. "You can tell as well as I that her issue isn't loneliness."

An older male voice rang out over the comms system. <Honored guests, I regret to inform you that the shuttles are experiencing delays… Thankfully, we have plenty of food, drink, and entertainment on board for you to enjoy while you wait for this hiccup to be dealt with.

<Please return to the main hall and your tables and enjoy the rest of the party.>

"Zafir?" I glanced at him as he whipped out his data pad to scroll through his messages.

"A system malfunction in the shuttles. No one's been injured," he answered after a moment, lowering the data pad. "They're working on repairing the affected shuttles and bringing others in from other parts of the city. *After* checking that their systems are in working order, of course."

Xilen hung onto my arm and pulled me back in the direction of her table. "Well then! We'll just have to make the most of our time together, won't we, dear?"

"I'm on duty, ma'am," I answered flatly when I noticed several of the military brass eyeing us.

"Come *on*," she purred, squeezing my arm into her chest.

Zafir followed my glance and promptly took the hint. "I'm afraid that is against regulations, ma'am. Elara must be allowed to do her duty—which is to protect your party, should you require it."

Xilen let go of me with a bratty sigh and plopped into her chair with another huff, shooting me an amused smile. However, she thankfully said nothing, and I returned to my post.

"Here—Ah..." Rel was about to offer me a new bottle of water, but a grinning human man stepped between us.

"The girl is on duty. She can wait until she's off the clock."

"Sir..." Zafir let out a soft sigh and bowed slightly. "Is everything alright? Should you need assistance, I can have Elara oversee me as I work on a solution."

"Bah, it's nothing to worry about. Enjoy your wine and company, lad." The man's grin broadened as he glanced at me. "So, this is the Resonance survivor I've heard so much about? She certainly seems well-behaved enough."

Zafir nodded slightly and pushed his glasses up his nose. "Indeed, sir, and as I've attempted to explain to the brass, she's plenty capable...so long as regulations are followed."

"Ahhh, I see, I see. Then we have filth wanting to *break* regulations, do we?" The man rubbed his chin, scowling. "I will look into it. Castrating the project just because they want to go a few rounds... That won't do..."

Without another word, he wandered off. I kept my expression passive, as the other humans present were still keeping an eye on me – a little fact I was disliking more and more by the moment.

"I suppose this means our dance will have to wait," Rel remarked, bringing his forefinger and thumb to his chin and resting the elbow of that arm in the hand of his other. He examined me, his lips pulling into a mischievous smile. "I know, I know. You don't dance. That merely means you need a good teacher…and I can teach you *many* things."

With that, he pivoted with a flourish of his tail and returned to his seat. I did my best to shake off the deep, soothing tone he'd shifted to.

Ugh… If he's trying to get payback, I think it's working.

CHAPTER TWENTY-TWO

An hour passed before there were any further updates regarding the malfunctioning shuttles, and even then, it was a 'please wait a little longer' sort of answer. I'd begun to wonder if the humans were just stalling, trying to see if they could catch me going feral in public, because now and then someone would come by and make infuriating remarks about me, Zafir, or our Syldrari guests.

I fidgeted occasionally to keep my limbs from falling asleep, and because I was so infernally hot. In the hour I'd been wallowing silently in my own misery, I'd narrowed the cause down to either Rel or Zafir. If I paid any attention to either of them, my temperature seemed to skyrocket and my mind wandered. If I ignored their existence, I mostly returned to normal...until Rel's voice hit certain low pitches, anyway.

After careful observation, I realized that one of the two—if not both—appeared to be having the same effect on Xilen, her guards, the other Syldrari representatives, and even some of the other guests. If either Rel or Zafir were aware of the issue, however, they didn't show it.

Okay, this almost never happens. What else could be causing this? I wiggled my toes inside my shoes to keep myself from squirming too visibly. Thinking back on the rare instances I'd felt overheated, I couldn't think of any consistent factors other than Rel's presence—though he'd only ever shown concern over the matter. He was good at bluffing, though, so I had to keep him as a possible instigator.

"Elder Rel, please," one of the other Syldrari implored. "I know you're young and wish to wet your fin with whatever strikes your fancy, but you should return to Syldra. Your mother *needs* her elder sons—"

"She needs to give us away as political currency to other queens, you mean?" Rel shifted in his chair in an impressively dismissive fashion. "I have my own ambitions and desires—ones she clearly approves of, seeing as the V'shir haven't been declared rogue."

"Speaking in front of a queen with such neglect!" An annoying woman I didn't know leaned toward Rel as if chastising a child. "You should be grateful that—"

"I agree with Rel—Clan V'shir is a valuable asset to Syldra. Without them, we wouldn't have any trade agreements with the

Empire, nor a foothold here." Xilen crossed one leg over the other, a dangerous smile coming to her lips. Rel looked away, clearly disgruntled, but wise enough to know when to shut up. "And you are forgetting an important fact. If his mother decides to…*arrange* for him to serve a queen, Clan V'shir would be part of the agreement. It gives her great political leverage. As such, Rel is unfortunately quite correct that he is political currency. After all, how many of her children *weren't* given to other queens?"

"E-even so…" The other woman wilted.

"You should be applauding his intelligence and thorough grasp of his situation," Xilen continued, her smile becoming slightly sadistic. "It is rare for a *lun'iri* to understand and accept their situation with such grace."

Zafir abruptly rose to his feet without a word and strode straight past me, heading for the buffet. I glanced after him briefly, then back to the troublesome queen I was supposed to be escorting. *I really hope they fix those shuttles soon…*

After several minutes of awkward silence, Rel pulled out a communicator and scanned something on the screen, then stood and approached another guard—who promptly escorted him over to our rather standoffish hosts.

Zafir returned first, toting a questionably large slice of chocolate cake and a glass of red wine. Xilen giggled at the sight, then shifted her attention to me.

"So, Elara dear, what do *you* think we should do to pass the time?" she asked sweetly.

Considering I didn't want to be here at all, and the brass were pissing me off just by existing, images of the room littered with human body parts briefly filled my mind's eye. I shook my head slightly to clear it. Remaining silent, I simply shrugged. After all, I wasn't supposed to talk, and by now my throat was so dry I didn't even want to try.

"I have a matter I must attend to on the surface." Rel spoke formally when he returned, two human guards accompanying him. "Queen Xilen, if you and your party would like a ride down…"

"Certainly!" Xilen smiled cheerfully, pulling herself to her feet. She *thwack*ed Zafir on the back. "Bring your cake. I'm sure they have boxes."

Everyone stayed mostly silent on the way to whatever shuttle Rel had managed to acquire. The moment I sat down inside, he tossed me two bottles of water—both of which I quickly drained.

"It's as if they were *trying* to make you ill." Rel's face twisted with disgust. "Damned creatures…"

"They wanted her to break role," Zafir spat, clearly just as agitated. "Someone amongst the brass doesn't like the project, I'd wager."

"I just want to know who to kill for making it so damn *hot* in there," I grumbled, crossing my arms and turning to look out the window as we descended toward the surface. It might have been beautiful if the city below and the surrounding industry hadn't marred the surface so vastly.

"It wasn't," Rel stated flatly. "Quite frankly, you should have been shivering, not melting."

Xilen smirked and looked like she was going to make a sly comment, then appeared to change her mind. Instead, she leaned toward me with a small frown. "More importantly, your clothes are self-regulating and don't appear to be malfunctioning. So—"

"I'll be fine. Let's just get somewhere we can talk in private about the footage we need to have Rel look at." I crossed my arms and gave them a mildly frustrated look. "Maybe we can find something a bit looser and lighter for me to change into."

Rel and Zafir both studied me, odd expressions on their faces. When they realized I had noticed them staring, however, they both abruptly looked away.

Xilen leaned up against my left side and giggled. "Now, now, boys. You'll get to see her unclothed soon enough. There's something you need to see."

"You said yourself it's a bruise. I'm sure it'll be *fine*." I shifted to give Xilen a challenging look, which just made her smile.

"What do you mean, a bruise?" Zafir was suddenly all business. "There haven't been any activities in the past two weeks that should have resulted in bruising. Where is it? Does it hurt? How—"

"It's on her back," Xilen offered with an amused smile.

"On her back…?" Zafir frowned at me. "Elara, I don't recall you getting thrown or grappled in a way that would cause such a bruise."

"Bruises are *normal*. I'm sure it's nothing to worry about." I flapped my hand dismissively, though even I didn't believe the words coming out of my mouth.

"Are you sure it isn't just…" Rel paused as he seemed to search for a word. "I believe humans call them 'love marks'?"

Zafir twitched. "What *you're* implying is against regulations. None of the survivors are permitted to have relationships—romantic or physical—with each other, the staff, or their bosses. There's surveillance everywhere to ensure they don't."

"Is that so?" Rel scoffed at Zafir, his expression one of disdain. "Then you just naturally behave like a *taruc*?"

"I. Do. *Not*," Zafir growled. "The well-being of the survivors is my responsibility. If Elara has been hurt in some way—"

"Ah, so you meant yes." Rel nodded sagely and patted Zafir's head, giving him a dangerous smile. "How about you fill Xilen and I in on what has you so concerned."

"Ah… That's…" Zafir struggled with himself for a moment. "Ask your brother."

"I'm asking *you*." Rel turned in his seat and gripped the nervous Zafir by the chin. "Start talking."

Zafir appeared to comply…but in *their* language, leaving me utterly in the dark. For *that*, I snatched Zafir's box of cake and helped myself to the contents, earning an amused glance from Rel and an agitated sigh from Zafir. Unfortunately, they didn't finish their conversation until we'd reached the surface.

"Did you leave any… *Elara.*" Zafir groaned when I tossed the box into a trash can. "I wanted to finish that."

"It was awful. Have Rel make you something instead." I made a dismissive motion. "His cooking is much better, and it won't be *stale.* Now then, you said you need to attend to something on the surface, Rel? Should we wait—"

"Your business is what I needed to attend to." He gave me an amused look. "We can talk after you've changed into something more comfortable."

"That *is* comfortable," Xilen pointed out.

"Yet she is overheating again. Find her something else," Rel shot back.

"Wow, I bet he only gets away with talking to a queen like that because he's one of Jalan-ki Citomy's sons…" I heard someone murmuring. I glanced over to see a group of younger, purely androgynous Syldrari.

"He gets away with it because we're old friends and he's right." Xilen rounded on the gossiping group. "If your friends won't tell you off or call you out, they're not your real friends. Now. Shouldn't you *vir'ildrod* be in school?"

"It was canceled today… 'cuz of…" The kid trailed off when Xilen crossed her arms.

"Then go study at home!" she ordered. "You have so many resources at your fingertips! Use them!"

The kids fled, and the fuming Xilen returned to us. We made it back to the café without further incident, and Rel promptly locked the doors and shut the curtains. Xilen's guards, for whatever reason, took up positions outside.

Next, Rel turned to me and narrowed his eyes. "Strip."

I glanced over at Xilen when a giggle-snort escaped her. "How do I do that, exactly?"

"Ah, of course. Here, dear." Xilen tugged the fabric at my waist and twisted, which seemingly told the fibers to let go of each other. I promptly pulled my top off, then turned so my back was to the trio.

"*Xilen*, you know damn well that isn't a bruise," Zafir hissed. "*Tch*, how are we going to hide this from our bosses?"

"Clothes that cover?" Xilen offered.

"That won't help when it comes to her monthly physical examinations." Zafir let out a frustrated sigh. "I need a drink."

"And we could also use some real food," Rel added. "Elara, why don't you go with Xilen and get changed. We can review the footage while we eat."

"Sure…" I glanced over my shoulder at him, only to realize he and Zafir were making their way toward the bar. As they walked, Rel's outfit morphed back to his customary leather pants and long-sleeved shirt. *Goddamn. That ass.*

"Off we go." Xilen promptly dragged me into another room to change. "Let's try…hmmm. See about peeling the rest of that off while I look for a replacement, dear. There's no way we're letting you saunter around in your 'standard issue.'"

Sighing, but with no reason to argue, I proceeded to pull off the black and gold ensemble. I laid the pieces out over the back of a piece of furniture, then turned slightly when I heard the door to what I thought was a closet rattling. Before either of us had time to react, the door swung open and a furious-looking Jysel stepped out of the space. I noticed some manner of glowing rune on the floor behind him before the door shut.

"Rel, we need—" Jysel raised his voice to call to his brother…then stopped abruptly when he spotted Xilen. He started to scowl at her before noticing me—and the fact that I wasn't wearing anything other than my panties. His glow shifted from scarlet to a more fuchsia color as he slowly realized just what he was looking at. "What exactly is going on here?"

"Jysel, what have I said about dropping in unannounced?" Rel demanded, storming through the opposite door. He, however, was much quicker to realize the situation—and the color his twin had turned. His glow flared a dark garnet red and he stepped aside, pointing to the door he'd just entered from. He narrowed his eyes at Jysel and spoke in an utterly murderous tone. "*Out.*"

The annoying twin hesitated for less than a second before stalking past me, his slate blue face flushed slightly darker than usual. Rel didn't even say anything before following his brother out and slamming the door shut. I stared after them, then glanced at Xilen when an unfamiliar laugh escaped her. A laugh that told me I was in trouble, Rel was in trouble, we were *all* in trouble.

"Well, well," she remarked playfully, eyeing me up and down as though seeing me for the first time. "I think that gives me the perfect idea for what you should wear. Be a good girl and play along."

"I can already tell you're not planning to give me much choice in the matter." I crossed my arms and gave her a lopsided smile. "You should know that Jysel and I don't get along well. It would probably be best if Zafir and I concluded our business here quickly."

Xilen smirked. "Oh, is that so? Perhaps you should rethink his reaction. What he doesn't like are women who wish to mindlessly exert power over him—like his *mother*. You see, queens have this terrible habit of using their power to get everything and everyone they want…"

"And you don't?" I challenged her.

"I do my best not to." Xilen chuckled as she turned to rummage around in a bag. "Of course, it would be for the best if you kept your distance from Jysel, but he's taken an interest in you. I can tell. You won't be getting rid of him for quite some time, so do your best not to anger him."

"Oh yeah? And how do I do that?" I sighed heavily. "All he ever goes on about is keeping my nose out of Syldrari business."

Xilen shook her head. "Hah! Just be you without trying to sway him in any particular way, and don't try to get something out of him. He'll come around eventually. The both of them are usually quite standoffish, and Rel is generally the more difficult of the two. Considering you've already won him over… Ah! There it is! Here, you'll wear this."

"Uh…that looks really see-through. I'm not so sure—" I held up my hands and leaned back when she rounded on me, moving a little too close for comfort.

"You're wearing this and that's final! Don't worry about showing too much. There are pieces that go over the top. Get this on while I fetch the rest." Xilen shoved what, to me, was essentially a full body stocking into my hands.

I swallowed an agitated sigh and did as she asked. The material was a little thicker than a pair of tights, and more opaque, showing just the barest hint of skin even when stretched over my hips and chest. Next, she helped me into a little leather one piece with short sleeves, a plunging neckline, and very short shorts. Over that, attaching to the shoulders, she draped an asymmetrical cape thing with curving patterns reminiscent of a sliced open seashell.

For the finishing touches, she fastened a belt around my waist, then pulled out a pair of ankle boots with metal high heels. They were taller than my last pair, but still manageable, thankfully.

"There you are—one of my favorite pieces of hybridized fashion!" Xilen clapped her hands together excitedly. "On Syldra, we have widely varied fashions—it depends on more than simply region and season. We also have to take ocean depth, function, ranking, and work into account in our personal designs. In regions where swimming from place to place is still common, you'll find that all our clothes are formfitting to reduce drag.

"On land, however, we express our artistic freedom. We've been experimenting with incorporating fashion elements of other species—granted, those pieces are more popular with my alien clients and not the Syldrari, but…"

I arched an eyebrow at her. "So what was that thing Rel was wearing before, then? Not exactly conducive to sea life."

"Bah. He chooses the most *unsightly* things for formal events. Whatever he can do to make himself less desirable to power-hungry queens, the better." Xilen threw her hands into the air in exasperation. "With just you and I there, he should have embraced his *daring* side. Leather isn't the only thing he looks good in."

She winked and shot me a knowing smile before walking over to the door and motioning for me to follow. "Oh! And you can keep both the outfits, dear."

"Oh, thanks." I moved to follow her, not entirely surprised by the offer.

"Well now!" Xilen declared as she looked from Rel, to Jysel, and finally to Zafir. "Why do you all look so glum? And where are those cute boys you've got working here now, Rel? Don't they live with you?"

"They're…" Rel trailed off, glancing past Xilen and straight to me. After a moment, he tore his eyes away and gave Xilen a suspicious look. "Just what are you up to?"

"Darling, when am I *ever* up to something?" Xilen smiled sweetly.

"I think the better question at this point is, 'What *aren't* you up to?'" I shot her a sidelong look as I walked past her and over to the bar, then shifted my attention to Rel. "Should we attend to business before or after you've seen to whatever Jysel needs you for?"

"He decided we should wait for you to finish." Jysel swiveled his chair to look at me and rested his chin against his fist. He slowly looked me up and down, though this time his glow remained a passive bright cyan. "According to these two, it is related to my reason for being here."

"How is Sal'aphel?" I put a hand on my hip and leaned forward slightly.

"What—"

"You'd better be giving him plenty of attention." I prodded Jysel's shoulder. "In fact, you should give him a juicy treat on my behalf, since he's such a good boy. What's his favorite?"

"He's *not* a 'good boy,' he wants to eat half my comrad—"

I crossed my arms and gave him an impatient look. "Yes, yes, like master like cute-fuzzy-murder-thing. That doesn't answer my question."

Jysel slumped back in his seat and sighed irritably. "*Jihgsar.* He likes *jihgsar.*"

"That would be the blue meat you yourself are so fond of." Rel's tone was dry as he slid from his seat, offering it to me before moving behind the bar. "I'm sure you're still parched after what the humans put you through. I'll make you a drink."

"Thanks." I shot him a smile, then took the empty seat *next* to his instead. "Though, should we really conduct our business here? I don't exactly see any secure computers or monitors."

"I need a drink," Zafir whined after staring at me for a moment. He collapsed on the bar counter with his head in his arms.

"Not a chance. You're still on duty." Rel smirked at the miserable man, then shot me an even more amused look. "Besides, if you keep that up, Elara here may get the wrong impression from us all."

"Did someone say Elara?" Aldiner crept around a corner, Ciheri right behind him. "Oooh, you're all back! Now then—"

"Back to your room." Rel shot the pair a sharp look.

"B-but…" Ciheri started to inch toward me, but when he finally spotted Xilen, he *hid* behind me instead. Almost too quietly to hear, he murmured, "E-Elara, I apologize for the other day. I was inappropriate. Um… I wanted to talk more, but…"

He peeked around me at Xilen again, glowed grey, and fled back to wherever he and Aldiner had come from.

Aldiner sighed and shrugged, stuffing his hands in his pockets. "Well, *that* was what we'd come back down for. I guess it'll suffice. *I'll* just be getting out of the way now before certain people kill me with a look. Yup. Later."

"What was *that* about?" Xilen remarked, sounding mildly concerned.

"From what I understand, Ciheri was sold by his clan's queen to the fighting arena Elara saved him from," Rel answered after a moment, then looked to me. "Though I'm not exactly sure what he's apologizing for."

"How about we don't go into that? Seems he's learned his lesson. That's not the first time he's apologized." I leaned forward a bit. "Enough distractions. Zafir and I have been waiting all day to show you this footage. We recorded it around the same time as Jysel's address was happening."

"I don't recall giving you permission to call me by name," Jysel remarked.

I gave him a sour look. "I recommend you don't bitch about it. You won't like any of the other things I'd consider calling you, and with *that* attitude, I'm pretty sure I'd stab you with every pointy object in this sector over any of your recommendations."

"Hmph." He glanced away from me.

"Here you are." Rel chuckled as he placed a large neon blue drink in front of me. "As for your original concern about screens—here. This will suffice. You have the disc, I assume?"

I pulled it out of a pocket and handed it to him, then turned my attention to my drink. After Rel had finished setting everything up, a large screen slid down from the ceiling. He walked back around the bar with two large platters in hand, both filled with what I had to assume were some sort of cookies. One of the platters, he placed on my half of the bar; the other, by Zafir and Jysel. Xilen hesitated for a moment before coming over and sitting on Jysel's right, leaving the three men sandwiched between us.

When I was confident that Jysel was done with his comments for the moment, I started talking. "This footage was captured at one of the Imperial facilities outside the city. Initially, our colleague thought Jysel's faction was getting to work early despite the content of his address. On closer inspection, though, she recognized that their behavior was strange—and the test subjects weren't the focus of their hunt."

They all remained silent for the first two plays of the footage. When someone finally spoke, it was Rel. "All former R'selkti, certainly, but no one I recognize...and I don't recognize this bond they now have."

"Agreed," Jysel murmured, his eyes narrowing at the footage. He glanced down the bar at me, seeming to consider his phrasing before stating, "I would like to see the controller."

He may have left out 'please,' but it was still an improvement. I slid out of my seat and walked over, offering the controller to him. Jysel hesitated to take it directly from me, seeming to take extra care to make certain he didn't come into contact with my skin at all. When I turned around, I noticed Rel scribbling something on a napkin—which he slid in front of my seat when he was finished.

I returned to my stool and perched on it, then read what Rel had written on the napkin. *'Some women exert more power through touch. He's being cautious out of fear.'*

Huh. Really? Some women…or some queens, *I wonder? Have they not realized that they just keep making me more and more suspicious?*

"Elara, about your 'bruise,'" Zafir began slowly, finally looking toward me. "We still need to discuss a way to hide it. However, it will likely spread. Especially as you spend more time—"

I shook my head, and he fell silent. Turning slightly in my seat, I decided to give him a partial answer. "I'm confident in your ability to falsify whatever records you have to send in for the higher-ups. Keeping it secret from the other survivors and others is going to be difficult if it really does spread. However, given your skittishness, I have to assume you knew this was going to happen."

"Of course he did. A *human* doesn't simply cough up blue blood," Jysel muttered absentmindedly as he re-watched the footage in slow motion. He was so focused that he didn't catch the others all turning to give him sharp looks. "Are they searching for some manner of military pharmaceuticals, perhaps? If they're a new group and wish to acquire funding…"

"Blue blood?" Rel demanded. "What else are you not telling me?"

Zafir coughed into his hand, drawing Rel's attention to him, as Jysel clearly wasn't paying attention. To my surprise, Zafir slid his data pad over to Rel. The agitated Syldrari skimmed what I assumed was my medical record—though I couldn't read a damn thing on the page.

I felt pressure against my arm and discovered that Xilen had gotten out of her seat and circled over to my left at some point so she could lean against me and peek at the data pad. Something caused a look of surprise to cross her face, her lips parting.

"I see—hiding it should be the least of your worries, dear." She patted my arm before sliding the platter of cookies over to me, as if hoping it would distract me from the issue.

"Care to explain?" I asked, the corner of my eye twitching.

"There is no point in worrying you with it right now." Rel gave me a dangerous look. "Allow us to look for a solution. *You* should focus on doing your job and making certain the Imperials don't retire you early. Until a solution is found, refrain from showing your colleagues more of your body than necessary. You can trust Zafir to inform you of any spread. In fact, Zafir, I would recommend you begin regular checks. Perhaps once per week?"

"I might be able to swing something, if I suggest *all* the survivors undergo more thorough checks…" Zafir pressed his fingers to his temples and sighed heavily. "Elara, Rel is right. Let us worry about this matter—*you* should worry about keeping up appearances and training the others. If they don't fully tame their ferals—"

"*Must* you keep calling them that?" Jysel turned sharply and glowered at Zafir. "You and I both know the correct term is *kuhir-dal*. This 'feral' nonsense…"

"Yes, yes, *kuhir-dal*. And how, exactly, am I meant to propose to the Imperials that they use a *Syldrari* word for *anything*?" Zafir slammed his hand against the bar and turned to glare at Jysel. "I am supposed to be *undercover*. If I begin tossing Syldrari terminology everywhere, especially for such a prominent hurdle of the Resonance Project, the brass will begin to suspect me, and all the survivors— *especially Elara*—will be in greater danger. That is an unacceptable risk. You can spout off about *kuhir-dal* all you like, but I have habits that I *must* maintain."

"Sooo." I leaned forward on the counter and peered down at them. "*Kuhir-dal*, you say? And this is more accurate than 'feral,' because…?"

Zafir groaned. "Elara, please. Do not get him started—"

"*Kuhir-dal* doesn't translate into other languages. *Kuhir-dal* is *kuhir-dal*," Jysel stated flatly. When he turned to me and saw my expression, though, he became slightly less defensive. Perhaps he realized my question was genuine. Or perhaps he just wanted to talk about it that much. I wasn't sure.

"It is the word we use to describe the phenomenon where a specific section of the mind has separated itself from the whole. *Kuhir-dal* encompasses all primal instincts—such as fight-or-flight and the need to gain, protect, and fight for territory—as well as more complex feelings and instincts that humans simply do not share with Syldrari.

"Various forms of accidents can result in the separation of the *kuhir-dal*. Most commonly, those who are exposed to certain types of resonance and harmonic weapons. The phenomenon was first encountered when our engineers were developing a harmonic art illustration for the capitol building—during testing, they misaligned several key components, and the frequency caused the *kuhir-dal* to separate in those exposed to it."

Rel sighed heavily and rested his head in his hand, his eyes focusing on me. "And you've witnessed firsthand what that same frequency does to humans and their cities. However, the *kuhir-dal* is a distinctly Syldrari trait. Or, at least, we thought it was. Zafir?"

"Evidence suggests that not all the survivors share Elara's…unique traits," Zafir answered after a moment, his delicate tone making me want to punch him. But he was way over there, and I didn't want to get up quite yet. "Most of the ones I suspect of being human are still in isolation because they have yet to stabilize. However, given Elara's strong negative reaction to one of them… I am working under the assumption that anyone she reacts to in such a way is likely truly human."

"I wasn't that bad," I scoffed.

Zafir shot me an unamused look. "You wanted to kill her, decided she wasn't worth the effort, and told her to *drink bleach.* Care to claim that again?"

"Like I said! I wasn't that bad." I shot him a small smile and watched him grow pale. "That was me being *nice.*"

Rel let out a long sigh and put a hand on top of my head, giving me a reprimanding look. "You should try to behave in a manner that is *actually* nice, if you're going to maintain your cover *and* Zafir's. Shall I use positive reinforcement with you, or do you require a…*different* method?"

I pouted slightly, then motioned at the screen in front of us. "Weren't we supposed to be discussing that?"

"Don't change the subject." Rel leaned a little closer and narrowed his eyes at me. "*Behave.* For all our sakes, but especially yours."

"I will *try*," I grumbled, relenting, before reaching for a cookie and focusing my attention on that.

"I'll have my men look into this supposed new clan, but it is likely a new group of outcasts instead." Jysel motioned loosely at the screen. "Either way, it is distinctly business for Elara to *keep her nose out of.* If the Imperials *must* send her to interfere, I would appreciate a warning first. It's so very hard to tell when she's been sent versus when she's simply being a pain in the—"

"Trust me. You'll know when she's being a pain in your *anything,* dear." Xilen spoke slyly, leaning around me with a smile. "From what I hear, none of your encounters with her have been the result of her meddling. Each and every one has been while she was attempting to work. *In fact*, it sounds to me more like *you* are always getting in *her* way. Ah! Don't tell me—you have a crush? Is getting in the way of her work your way of—"

And just like that, Jysel got up and stalked out of the room. A moment later, I heard a faint sound that I could only assume was the transporter he'd used to get to Rel's café in the first place. Xilen burst into delighted, malevolent laughter. Rel and Zafir, on the other hand, both looked thoroughly *done* with playing host to the troublemaking queen.

"Well. That wasn't exactly as productive as I'd hoped it would be." I crossed my arms and let out a soft sigh. Sure, I'd learned a lot—too much, even. Too much to process all at once. Yet what I'd wanted to talk about the whole damned day? Barely touched on. I doubted it was even enough for Amara's needs.

"I'm afraid it's difficult to give you more, when we ourselves don't know who these Syldrari are," Rel offered in a mildly apologetic tone. I glanced at him and he gave me a faint smile. "I can only speak for myself, but I will assure you that, once it is safe to do so, I will answer whatever questions you have. You've proven that you are a true ally to the Syldrari, and though you may be playful, you don't have ill intentions.

"For now, however, it is getting late. You and Zafir should return to headquarters before your superiors grow suspicious about your extended absence."

"Ah! I'll go put your things in a bag for you, dear," Xilen exclaimed, tapping me briefly on the shoulder before hurrying off into the other room.

"Elara." Rel spoke quietly as he stood up, and I gave him a questioning look. "I meant it. Be careful. You need to pretend, as best you can, that you're merely a human who's acquired more power. It doesn't take much for the wrong people to begin asking questions, and rescuing you is nowhere near as easy as Xilen likes to make it sound. Promise me."

I stared at him for a moment, a little taken aback by his seriousness, but even more so by him asking me to promise. Finally, I gave him a lopsided smile. "Alright, I promise I'll be more careful."

"I half-expected her to say *no*," Zafir muttered bitterly.

He's just asking for me to torture him more, isn't he? I eyed Zafir for a moment, though my attention turned to Rel when he cleared his throat. Perhaps he knew what I was thinking, seeing as he was giving me a rather stern look. But he left it at that and returned to fetching the disc for us. Unfortunately, we all agreed that taking dinner home would be too suspicious, for multiple reasons.

"We can pick up some *human* fare for you on the way," Zafir informed me as we walked through the Syldrari district to where a craft would be picking us up. "It would do the others well to see you eat something other than Rel's cooking for once."

"It's not my fault he's so damn good at what he does," I pointed out.

"Yes, yes, I'm aware. However, there are plenty of others who excel at the culinary arts. Perhaps it's time I introduced you to them."

CHAPTER TWENTY-THREE

"Sit. We're going to go over the remainder of your test results." Zafir pointed at a chair the moment I entered his office. I closed the door behind me as he continued, "You are experiencing what I will call 'cellular dissonance.' Upon further investigation, I've found that your genetic makeup was introduced to foreign cells—in this case, Syldrari cells.

"The human and Syldrari genetic data are vibrating at separate, varying frequencies as they vie for dominance. This is likely the cause of the blue patch of skin on your back. Several other survivors are showing this same dissonance phenomenon, but not to the same extent. It's possible that exposure to Syldrari and their food hastened its progress. Furthermore—"

"Zafir," I interrupted, placing my hands on his desk and leaning over it. He glanced up from his papers, his eyes widening slightly.

"Let me guess. You're telling me a believable half-truth because telling me *the* truth is more likely to cause problems with your bosses. The *actual*—"

"Sit. Down," he reiterated, the corner of his eye twitching. When I didn't budge, he made a subtle motion and I felt as if a set of weights *made* me sit. "As I was saying. The dissonance doesn't appear to be harmful—yet—but I will be closely monitoring it among all subjects.

"We currently believe that the resonance weapon somehow…how should I put it…? It has created a 'wall' between the human and Syldrari data. It will require further study, but we believe that the weapon's purpose may be to turn humans into Syldrari hybrids."

I massaged my forehead with one hand as Zafir shifted through his papers to a new page. *Okay. So, by the sound of it, our Imperial bosses are now in on the 'mutation' that's happening. In which case, Zafir is giving me information that is consistent with what the Imperials think and therefore what I 'need' to know. It's probably all a half or reversed lie to circumvent the risk of my skin turning blue. Okay, I can sort of get behind that…but how much is a lie? Should I operate under the assumption that the human genetic material is the actual foreign body? In which case…*

"Elara, pay attention." Zafir whacked the top of my head lightly with his stack of papers. I glared at him, strongly debating whether I should try to give him the spanking of a lifetime for that. "We need to determine how the foreign cells were introduced. I'll be needing to draw a few new samples of blood and take some other samples.

"I'm not convinced that the weapon itself is what introduced them. Likely, it was some time beforehand. Which only raises more questions, admittedly. It means someone would have had to know about the resonance weapon and that it was going to be fired."

Well, that part seems truthful, at least. I let out a small sigh as Zafir stood and began rummaging around for his kit. "Am I still required to hide it?"

"Yes. They're concerned that it could destabilize the others if they were to see, and recognize, the change." He nodded without turning around. "Given its rather striking color, I'd say it can't be passed off as a bruise. You would sooner be able to pass it off as a bad tattoo, were removing such things not such a simple matter."

"Great," I muttered, watching out of the corner of my eye as Zafir came over, rolling a tiered tray behind him. He sat next to me and began pulling a pair gloves on as I watched. "You know, I didn't agree to this."

He hesitated briefly, then sighed and continued preparing. "And we both know that you don't have much choice in this matter, and neither do I. All I can do is promise you that I will seek out a solution. I would prefer to solve the problem instead of discovering whether it is fatal the difficult way, and the patch's proximity to important organs is making me anxious. Please, cooperate."

With that, he held out a hand and gave me a gentle look. I reluctantly complied, choosing to stare at a wall while he collected what he needed: blood, skin, nail clippings, even a bit of hair. I was a little surprised he left it at that, honestly.

"Now then, about your patrols for the week," he began, offering me a sheet of paper. "I want you to continue overseeing the Syldrari sector, especially where it borders the other sectors. We've seen a spike in crime since Jysel's address, so it's a good opportunity for you to make more appearances as Lethe. The others will be on standby in case you need backup."

"You owe me a massage after all that," I complained, slumping back in my chair.

"I will *consider* it if you continue to both behave and perform well," he remarked in a tone that made me suspect he thought I was joking. "Now then. We should review your schedule. Morning through afternoon, you will be patrolling the Syldrari sector as yourself. You will return here afterward, have dinner and a nap should you need it, then you will deploy as Lethe.

"Aisu and Maelor will also both be awake and prepared to come to your aid if you need it. You will do the same for them if something goes amiss in their districts.

"I've decided to, ah, *scramble* your schedules. Our bosses have delayed my plan for the military to publicly accept your team's actions. As such, you need to appear disorganized."

"Now you also owe me a strong drink." I propped my elbow

on the armrest and gave him an unamused look. "If you keep up these overly long explanations—"

"Behave." Zafir bristled, shutting his eyes briefly and taking a calming breath, then continued like nothing had happened. "You will be on duty tonight, tomorrow night, and Eoriad night. Your weekday schedule remains unchanged, for now. If tensions rise, you may have to patrol the rest of the weekend as well, but for now, you have the daytime on weekends off. I'm hoping you can focus on training the others on those days, since our bosses aren't giving you time during the week."

Which one was Eoriad, again? I mulled it over irritably. Whoever was in charge of naming the days of the week needed to be hauled outside the city and shot. I snuck a peek at the nearby calendar, confirming that was the first day of the weekend. So, I would be working from then until Aeriad morning, then have the last day and night of the weekend off.

I gave my annoyance a mental shrug and leaned forward. There were other questions I wanted answers to before he started rambling at me again.

"*Zafir.*"

"*What?*" He gave me an exasperated look.

"I have a question I've been wanting to ask since the party," I informed him. He looked oddly relieved, motioning for me to continue. "This overheating thing. Are any of the others experiencing it, and do we know what causes it, or how to stop it?"

"Ah. I'm afraid that depends," he murmured, rubbing his chin. His eyes seemed to lose focus. "One possibility is that it's caused by the cellular dissonance. Were the vibrations between cells to increase to higher levels, you could experience that as a form of overheating. The issue is that there's no real way to predict what could trigger your cells to do that. Especially not in such a setting.

"The other options come from the Syldrari side of your current genetic pool. However, most are merely unconfirmed theories. The only confirmed source of rising body temperature would be arousal, but it's safe to say that the overheating you experienced was too extreme to be that—and I find it hard to imagine you were aroused in such a place to begin with.

"I'm afraid the rumor-related options aren't something either of us could easily ascertain. I am disinclined to inform our mutual acquaintances either, due to the nature of those rumors. They are...somewhat taboo."

I sighed in disappointment. "Well, thanks for answering, even if it boils down to 'I don't know, and even if I did, I couldn't say.'"

"Elara, I—"

"Yes, yes, I know you're playing mama...bear." I frowned slightly. I'd wanted to go for another type of animal, but it refused to come to me. "Is that all? I should get ready for my patrols."

"There's one more thing we should address," he murmured, hesitating slightly before placing a sheet of paper in front of me. At a glance, I could tell by the icon in the corner that it had something to do with neurology, but none of the imagery on the rest of the sheet made any sense to me. "I finished analyzing the various scans I took of your brain and compared them to those of the other Resonance Incident survivors.

"Those of you who are showing signs of cellular dissonance also have no memories from before the Incident, but your case is the most severe. That is to say, the sections of your mind that should exist with that information just…don't. There are only so many governments with the technology to actually remove sections of the mind, and fewer still who are willing to use it."

"Which, given various other implications…" I motioned loosely and he nodded, his jaw clenched and his gaze fiery. "We're keeping this bit quiet, I take it?"

"Yes."

I sighed and slid my chair back, rising to my feet. "Alright. Need anything before I get to work?"

"I would appreciate it if you would ask Sarah to bring me my lunch in a few hours; I have too much work to do…" He sighed, then murmured some unrecognizable sound. A moment later, he pulled out his wallet and offered me some of the money in it. "If you could pick up a few things for me from the Syldrari sector while you're there, I'd be quite grateful. I'll jot them down for you."

I nodded to him. "Sure. Anything I need to be worried about?"

"No. They're teas and medicinal herbs that I learned about during university. Syldra is home to flora with some incredible properties."

"Uh huh." I raised an eyebrow as he scribbled a list of things and handed it to me. "Try not to go too crazy all holed up in here working. Take a walk later if you need a mental break."

He gave me a lopsided smile. "I will try to remember that."

"I'll have Sarah remember it for you," I informed him as I left his office and made my way straight to the lobby. Sarah was behind the counter as usual, though her attention appeared to be focused on a book instead of potential visitors. I couldn't blame her. "Yoo-hoo."

"Oh, hi, Elara." She glanced up, smiling sheepishly. "What's up?"

"Zafir asked me to ask you to bring him his lunch in a few hours. He's gonna forget otherwise," I answered dryly. She rolled her eyes, and I got the feeling this was a fairly common occurrence. "He's swamped with work. Think you can force him to go take a walk sometime this afternoon?"

"I can try." She nodded. "I swear he's gotten more stubborn this past week."

"If he bitches, remind him he can't take care of us if he doesn't take care of himself." I grinned, placing a hand on my hip. "He's given us plenty of ammo to use against him, but we can start there. Now! I'm gonna go get ready for work. If you need me to pick up anything on the way back, make me a list. I'll check in with you before I leave."

Even at such an atrociously early hour, the Syldrari sector was abuzz with activity. The main topic of the day appeared to be Jysel's address...which the locals were *not* happy about. From what I gathered, they felt that the 'foolish boy's' demands were only going to make their lives harder. They didn't believe his claims regarding captured queens in the slightest. Too improbable, they claimed.

And I can't exactly go around telling them it's all true. I sighed faintly before returning to the stoic expression I was expected to maintain during patrols. Granted, the Syldrari were in such an uproar I was starting to think I'd complete my first lap without a single greeting.

"Ah! Elara! Over here!" A neon green Syldrari waved to me, raising up on her tiptoes. It took me a moment to realize it was Xilen's daughter, to whom I hadn't yet been properly introduced.

"Hey. On patrol, so I can't linger long," I informed her as I strode over.

She smiled brightly anyway. "I realized that I didn't introduce myself! My name is Ceyoh, I'm Xilen's...uh, let's keep it simple.

Daughter. I wanted to ask how you and the others are enjoying the ludrán."

"Oh, that's a little complicated, actually. Let's see here…" I pulled out my communicator and swiped through a few menus, finally finding my notepad and glancing up at her. "I can send you the notes, though I'd appreciate it if you kept certain details quiet."

"Hmm?" Ceyoh peeked over my shoulder, so I showed her the two columns—one for Incident survivors, the other for the numerous guards at the facility I'd been foisting pieces of candy on. "Oooh, I see. Understandable. Mother's first rule of business—if your client wants you to keep quiet, keep quiet!"

With that settled, I sent her the file, then checked the time. "I should get back to my rounds, I'm afraid. You still going to be open in a few hours?"

"Sure will!" she answered with a smile. "Well, unless mother calls me for something. You want more ludrán?"

"Yeah, uh…" I pointed out six different flavors. "Can you save me a jar or two of each of those?"

"Of course! I'll set them aside so you can swing by later." Giving me a brief wave, she disappeared behind her stall to tuck things away.

With that done, I moved deeper into the district, feeling a twinge of concern when I came across Rel's place. The café was closed and all the curtains upstairs were drawn shut, with no hint of light peeking through. But I couldn't afford to linger. I needed to keep chugging forward.

On my third lap through the main section of the sector, I was stopped by a familiar, rifle-toting figure. At least, I was pretty sure it was a rifle.

Casair was in full uniform, the tip of his weapon aimed toward the ground. He looked to be on patrol himself—yet he seemed surprised to see me. A second later, though, he looked relieved, then all emotion left his face.

"Elara. Thank goodness—come with me, we need to speak privately." He motioned for me to follow him, and I did so—despite how nervous it made the onlookers.

I couldn't exactly blame them. The giant Syldrari leading an apparently human soldier into a back alley had to look a little odd.

"What's wrong?" I asked when he stopped and conjured a couple of floating energy-seat things, one of which he sank into with a sigh. I sat across from him and crossed one leg over the other.

He gave me a serious look and leaned forward. "We're running into issues due to the rogue clan that's been going around looting military installations. Moreover, we think they may be targeting yours next. We can't spare anyone to try to disrupt them yet, so you're going to be on your own. I'm concerned. I think Jysel is, too...not that he'd show it, and he'd just say it's because Sal'aphel likes you, anyway."

"Any idea when?" I murmured.

"Not a damn clue. But here." He offered me a small disc. "One of our scouts recorded that. Given how you helped us… I thought we'd return the favor."

"Mhm. No loose ends, right?" I asked dryly.

He grimaced. "There's such a thing as understanding him too well."

<Elara? You've stopped moving. Is everything alright?> Zafir asked over my earpiece. I rolled my eyes and put my head in my hand, while Casair snorted.

"Yes, *mother*, I'm quite fine. I'll resume patrolling shortly."

He hesitated. <You don't need extraction?>

"I don't. I followed a cute little birdy. I'll get back to work soon." I grinned when Casair turned blue and huffed. Zafir sighed in my ear, and there was a *click* as he hung up. "Okay. If there's nothing else, I should—"

"Keep an eye on him, will ya?" Casair shook his head and stood up, offering me a hand up. He looked me up and down, giving me a mildly concerned look. "You been eating alright? There's a hunger in your eyes I haven't seen before."

"Yeah, I've been eating fine…it's just my lunch plan is currently closed." I half-shrugged, though he didn't look convinced. "See you around, maybe, and thanks for the heads up."

I made my way out of the alley without waiting for a response and promptly resumed tracing my steps around the sector. All in all, it was uneventful as ever. The Syldrari appeared to be some of the politest, most well-behaved people in the city.

On my last loop, I lingered by Rel's place for a moment, then started walking away. Still closed. As I turned away, however, I spotted Rel strolling toward me with a veritable mountain of boxes and bags in his arms.

One of these days, I'm gonna find out what's under those leather pants. I eyed his legs and crotch, then the off-the-shoulder sweater he was wearing. For a moment I considered slapping some sense into myself but opted for shaking my head clear instead. I needed to stop letting my mind wander so much when he was involved. Finally, I started walking toward him. "Afternoon, Rel. Need some help?"

"If you would..." He paused long enough for me to snatch the top four boxes, which I tucked under each arm. His vision no longer obscured, he sighed and gave me a small smile. "Thank you, Elara. How goes your patrol?"

"Uneventful," I answered, following him into the café once he'd unlocked it. "You should've had Aldiner and Ciheri help you carry stuff."

"Ah, but then you wouldn't have been able to swoop in and save the day," he remarked dryly. "In all seriousness, they're out tending to other errands for me. It's stock-up day, as it were. These are the ingredients I use that need to be imported from off-world. A few planets in this system are capable of supporting some of the more unique flora and fauna we like, so we have farms and facilities there."

"Oh? What are the boys out getting, then?" I inquired.

"I have them scouring the markets in the other sectors for some spices I would like to try from non-Syldrari cultures. I want to see if I can come up with some interesting fusion dishes… Ah, but I'm probably boring you, aren't I?" He hesitated, glancing back at me.

"Not at all. Though I imagine *I* am in *your* way. Where would you like these?" I awkwardly indicated the boxes I was still holding.

"Here." He started toward me, clearly wanting to take them. After a little work, he had all four boxes stored in the freezer under the bar. "Hmm? Where are you going, Elara?"

"Well, you're closed, and I helped, so I figured I should—"

"Close the door and come sit down. I can hear your stomach growling from here," he stated. "You should have time to join me for dinner, right?"

"If it's not too much trouble," I answered, linking my fingers behind my back as I walked over to the counter.

"It's no trouble at all. Trust me—if I didn't want you to join me, you would know already." He placed two glasses on the counter, then hesitated, giving me an inquisitive look. "Are you fully off-duty after this, or…"

"I'm afraid not," I replied as I perched on a stool.

"Very well, then. Alcohol for me, and for you…let's see…" He opened a cabinet full of colorful bottles and scanned them, his expression surprisingly intense. After a moment, he glanced back at me. "Any aches or pains lately? Or anything else feeling off?"

Right. Medicinal ingredients and whatnot. I eyed the cabinet—more than half its contents glowed damn near brighter than my battle suit did. "Intermittent headaches. Have had some general all-over aches too, though I think that's just the standard-issue bed being standard-issue awful."

"Of course," Rel muttered. He pulled down several jars and set about dosing them out. Finally, he began to brew what I had to assume was tea from the custom blend. To my surprise, he then walked around the counter and over to me, motioning to my shoulders. "If I may? I'd like to double-check that general aches are truly all it is."

"You can do that?" I tracked him curiously, though I had to stop watching when he disappeared behind me and placed his hands on my shoulders.

"Quite easily…if you do not mind touch. I can see where some of the aches are, but I can better identify them if I use touch and sound to see how the muscles respond." His voice had taken on an ethereal, calming tone. "There are some illnesses that occur in those capable of wielding elements. I simply wish to make certain it isn't one of those."

"Sure." I nodded once.

"Good. Now, stay quiet…if you can," he murmured, the sudden shift to a suggestive tone throwing me off guard. He had a voice *made* for that kind of tone. Smooth, deep, commanding… Goddamn.

Alright, quiet time. You too, brain. I listened for whatever Rel meant by 'using sound,' but whatever it was, it was beyond my range of hearing.

His fingers worked fluidly over my shoulders, then down my back and sides at a slow, careful pace. He paused in the few places I was feeling most tense, and I heard a faint sigh of relief each time before he moved on to the next spot. Finally, he stopped at my lower back, then stepped away and back into view, looking contemplative.

"Well, my concerns were for nothing, at least, but thank you for letting me make certain. You should feel a little better now…though I'm afraid, short of getting a real bed, the problem will persist."

I couldn't help but laugh. "A real bed, huh?"

I managed, just barely, to keep myself from reacting to my own tone. I sounded *horny*. I crossed my toes in my boots, hoping Rel hadn't caught it—or, if he had, which I had to assume, I hoped he wouldn't comment. *His hands are really nice, though…*

"Yes, a *real* bed. Though I can't imagine your superiors would be happy if you suddenly brought in Syldrari furniture."

He shook his head faintly as he resumed searching through the cabinets. "That said, I think I have the perfect dish in mind for dinner. I was wanting something hearty anyway, and you could use the energy."

Thankfully, I was able to shrug off any awkwardness I felt and instead focus on conversing with Rel while he cooked.

"So, what's troubling you?" he inquired as he waited for a cut of meat to sear. "You're not quite yourself today."

"Oh, you know, a heavy amount of information from my boss, then *receiving* information I need to show him..." I smiled and shrugged. "There's just a lot going on that I'm aware of but not actively involved in. It's a lot to track."

"Care to share?" he offered, leaning over the bar slightly. "Freely, of course."

"Without any prying ears?" I mused, earning a mischievous smile and a faint nod in response. "Sure. You seemed displeased with the amount of info you got from Jysel and Zafir. I can regale you with what Zafir dumped on me this morning."

I explained my extended exchange with Zafir from earlier, and my suspicions that the information wasn't quite as truthful as I might have wanted. Rel listened attentively, even when his back was turned and he was making our food.

By the time I was done, he'd plated our meals and taken a seat next to me at the bar.

"I see. That *is* concerning." He poured me a fresh drink, then topped off his glass of...beer? Wine? Booze of some sort. Glowing red booze. "If he is twisting the truth for your safety, I can't fault him, and it would be best if you didn't openly question it. That said, I'm more concerned about this neurology report. Few species are capable of something like that. Of course, the technology could have been stolen, but..."

"But it's also a very deliberate thing to have done. Yeah." I grimaced and picked up my fork and knife. "It doesn't sit well with me. I've never been too bothered by my memory loss—I don't see much point in worrying about memories of a place that was so thoroughly obliterated."

"But any family you had—" He cut himself off, clenching his fist. "Though perhaps I am the last person who should speak on the matter. Even if I left long ago, I'm still from—"

"I'm told the only biological data there that matched mine *is* mine, and none of the people who knew people there recognized me in the slightest." I gave him a firm look. "And hey, I'm not going to blame you for any part of that shit. So don't start blaming yourself, either."

"You're right." He sighed and gave me a small smile. "You need to come back on a night you don't have work so we can share a proper drink."

"I'll consider it—but let's *not* test if my alcohol resistance is human or Syldrari, alright?" I laughed, shaking my head. "That sounds like it'd be a recipe for alcohol poisoning—maybe for both of us."

"Elara." Rel spoke quietly.

"Hm?" I glanced to my left, finding him leaning a little too close.

"There's still something we really should discuss—"

"We're back!" Aldiner called cheerfully as he threw open the front doors and breezed in, Ciheri in tow.

Rel must've realized it looked like he was trying to kiss me, because he moved back into place so quickly that all I saw was a blur. His glow wavered briefly before settling into its usual lazy coils of cyan. I held back a laugh and turned further in my seat to look at Aldiner and Ciheri.

"Sheesh, you two have a lot of boxes," I remarked, raising an eyebrow. They, at least, had something to roll the boxes with, rather than trying to carry them. Raising an eyebrow, I looked over at Rel. "Maybe you should get a second dolly."

"Perhaps." He shrugged, though he flushed slightly. "Or you could just help me again."

"Elara!" Ciheri called, looking surprised to see me. "Were you patrolling today?"

"Aww, how did we miss her?" Aldiner paused and eyed me, his lip curling with distaste. "Okay. Might have something to do with the atrocity you humans call a uniform."

"Yes…quite the contrast to your 'standard issue' dress uniform," Rel remarked, eyeing me. "Come to think of it, I don't believe I've seen you wear much other than uniforms and training clothes."

"Shopping is a little…overwhelming." I let out a reluctant sigh. "It also gets old really fast when people ask what styles you like, and you quite literally don't know."

"Xilen could—" Rel started to suggest, though he rethought it before I could even start to protest. "Actually, we've already seen how she would dress you, and I don't think that would go over well with your superiors. Never mind."

"I'll get around to shopping for myself eventually. I just need a day where I actually have enough time to sit down and browse online." I stretched my legs out briefly and sighed. "For now, though, I should go make my report before I see to my other work. I'll have to pass on dessert this time."

Rel caught me around the waist with one arm after I stood up, stopping me. He leaned a little closer, a tempting smile on his lips, as his glow shifted to a rich fuchsia that radiated a blue halo of light. "You could always come back for dessert later tonight."

CHAPTER TWENTY-FOUR

Don't think about the hot alien guy, don't think about the hot alien guy, I repeated to myself as I walked away from Rel's café. Aldiner and Ciheri had done a pretty decent job of distracting Rel from whatever thoughts had been going through his tipsy head, but that hadn't stopped him from giving me incredibly intense, inviting, hot...mildly enthralling...glances as we finished dinner. Then there was the whole glowing various shades of reddish-pink thing. I had a pretty decent idea what that meant now, though I wasn't sure about the blue halo. Or how pink could even *cast* a blue aura to begin with.

I paused briefly as I stepped into the main market street. *Right...need to pick up some things and grab my ludrán.*

After double-checking how much time I had, I spent a while getting everything Zafir wanted, then made my way to Ceyoh to pick up my candy. *Hmm, Rel had candy on hand before. If he likes it, I wonder if…*

I hurriedly squashed that train of thought. There were places my brain wanted to go with it, and it involved a lot of tongue.

"Hey there, you look rough. Feeling okay?" Ceyoh leaned forward worriedly. "Need to eat or drink?"

"I'm good, just had dinner. Uh…why? That's the second time today I've been asked if I need to eat." I placed a hand on my hip as I watched her start boxing jars of candy.

"Hmm? Do humans care so little about each other, that they don't ask each other if they're alright or check in on more detailed things?" She frowned at me. "Oh! Is that why humans are always so grumpy?"

"I…don't think so?" I hesitated, realizing I couldn't say for sure. Sighing, I gave her a small smile. "Well, it's not that way in the military, at least in my experience. Maybe it's different for civilians. I wouldn't know."

"Ah, did you grow up in the military?" She shot me an inquisitive look.

Really? I thought half the sector would know by now. I shook my head. "No. I just don't remember anything from before the Incident. That's all."

"'That's all,' she says!" she exclaimed in disbelief, crossing her arms. "Doesn't it bother you sometimes?"

"Well, yeah, but it's pointless to worry about something I

can't change—and before you say my memories could come back, no, they can't." I gave her a firm look when she opened her mouth to protest. "Anyway, self-rediscovery and all that. Figuring out what food I like, clothes, music, even smells… It's interesting and overwhelming, sure, but I can't *not* do it. And I don't think I'd want to go back now."

Ceyoh blinked at me, before slumping slightly and uncrossing her arms. "Well, if you ever need to hear more about the Syldrari sector or have other questions—I'm your *sora'iri*! I'll happily help you get your bearings any time you need."

"Thanks, I'll keep that in mind," I murmured, handing her the cash for the candy.

"Come on, say it you like you mean it!" she demanded, leaning forward. "I'm being serious. There are things people like my mother and Rel wouldn't dream of telling you! They're too old and stuck in their ways—"

"Too old?" I raised an eyebrow. "Never mind that for now, actually. I have to get back to HQ. I can have you explain some other time."

"Right." Ceyoh smiled, then offered me a small slip of paper. "Here, my number. Shoot me a message when you're free."

"Sure, thanks." I collected the box with my ludrán in it, then wandered off with that and Zafir's goodies.

I hesitated as I walked down the main thoroughfare and toward the sector's border. An alluring scent filled my nose, making my thoughts hazy for a brief moment. The next thing I knew, a cloaked Jysel was beside me, hand on my shoulder.

He gave me a brief sideways glance. "Keep walking. This doesn't concern you."

"I wouldn't have stopped in the first place if you hadn't—" I started, but Jysel took another step closer and leaned down close enough that I could see his eyes within his hood.

"And later tonight?" he asked pointedly. I broke his gaze with a small sigh.

People were starting to notice our presence, and given how empty the street had become I couldn't just answer him outright. After a moment, I had an idea. Taking a step toward him, I leaned in suggestively. "Yes, I'm afraid I have plans tonight. Maybe some other time?"

He looked briefly taken aback, but then recovered, his gaze flicking from side to side as he registered how exposed he was. His jaw clenched and unclenched a few times before he spoke quietly. "Then be prepared for a fight. I can't realistically let you walk away if our paths cross again tonight."

"Oh, I'm always prepared for a fight," I answered, giving him a sweet smile and stepping a little closer. "I'd have started one with you already for stopping me on my way back to base, but I need to get these medicines to my boss."

Jysel didn't take kindly to my reaction. Or at least, that was the impression I got as he reached out and gripped me tightly by the jaw. He narrowed his eyes as he studied me, and I glared back my challenge.

"I could kill you right now," he snarled, his tone shifting to something oddly accepting, cold and inhuman. Almost as if he'd rationalized that doing so would be best for us both.

"Yet you're not going to." I reached up with my free hand and wrapped my fingers around his wrist. His eyes, now dead, met mine again.

"Don't touch me." He spoke very quietly.

I exerted pressure on his wrist and narrowed my eyes at him. "Maybe you should consider that sentence again before putting your hands on someone else."

The feral stirred within my chest as we glared at each other, but I stuffed it down. The last thing anyone needed was for me to start a brawl with this bastard in the middle of the Syldrari sector.

"How charming," he scoffed, exuding a brief wave of what I could only describe as pressure. His lips shifted into a faint frown. "You felt that."

"Of course I—" I started to snap back, then sighed irritably. "You're saying I shouldn't have been able to, blah, blah, blah, reasons you won't explain because you're a secretive bitch like everyone else. Can I go now, *Your Majesty*?"

"*Sir*," I heard Casair call from the mouth of an adjacent alleyway. "Can you please refrain from antagonizing Elara for one damned day?"

I glanced over to see Casair and several more of Jysel's men tucked into the alley, weapons in hand.

One of the men beside Casair laughed. "Can't decide if the boss wants to kill her or fuck her."

Jysel twitched, his glow turning a deep red-pink for a split second before returning to its usual cyan—though his face stayed slightly flushed.

"Maybe both?" I shot Casair a sidelong glance. "Even the people who like me aren't nearly as forward."

"Did you just compare me to Xil—"

"Hardly. She deserves her own bracket," I stated flatly. When he still didn't let go, I sighed and took a step closer, a little surprised he didn't simply stop me with his continued grip on my jaw. "Listen. Can you hurry up and decide if you're going to kill me, capture me, fuck me, use me for leverage, tie me up and drop me off somewhere, or let me go? I have work to do and I'm expected to be places soon. The longer you delay me, the more suspicious my superiors will get—and they're already problematic.

"I really don't give a shit why you're in the sector right now, so long as you don't intend to hurt any of the Syldrari here. So make up your damn mind before—"

"Can you not embellish my thoughts?" Jysel twitched.

"Real convincing there." Casair walked over and nudged Jysel. "Sir, *you* keep challenging *her*. What do you expect? For her to just cower or 'offer services' like a human would? She's a soldier. One who wants to test herself. Stop making yourself a target, and she'll ignore your presence like you want."

Jysel hesitated, his gaze flickering with uncertainty, before he carefully let go of my jaw and returned his hand to his side. "I don't..."

"We have a schedule to keep to. Sorry about this one, Elara," Casair offered, turning to me and nudging Jysel out of the way as if it'd distract me from his murmuring. "Where are you gonna have to work?"

"Around," I remarked, glancing toward a nearby sign that indicated the nearest border. "All around."

"Hmm. You may cross paths, then..." He glanced over at the now mildly distressed-looking Jysel. I raised an eyebrow and looked between the two a few times when I saw Casair frown at him. After a moment, Casair led me a little way down the street, to what I assumed was out of earshot due to the quiet tone he continued in. "Can you pretend that exchange never happened? Women, Jysel... It's complicated, especially with parents like his."

"I can, but can *you* get him to stop attacking me as his first response?" I countered dryly.

"I can try, it's just..." He glanced back to make sure his boss was still distracted. "His biggest fears are being ignored, forgotten, or abandoned. You have a certain...*draw* because you're unusually similar to a Syldrari, but your behavior isn't colored by our social culture—or by the interference of queens. I don't know if he can come to terms with his attraction to that, or if he realizes it doesn't have to mean…"

He trailed off and glanced to the side as Jysel shambled dejectedly into the alley to wait with the others, seeming a little lost.

"I think I get it, in theory." I tapped Casair's shoulder. "Don't worry. I won't be around forever; I'm sure he'll be back to normal soon enough. Now, I need to go before my boss calls in an extraction team due to the *delays*."

"Elara, what—" He seemed taken aback as I turned away and started walking.

I ignored his protest and kept going. A short walk later, I was perched in my waiting transport and my communicator began to ring. Raising an eyebrow, I turned it on and brought it to my ear. "Yes?"

<…I'm afraid there's going to be a little detour,> Zafir told me hesitantly. <Are you…never mind. Something happened. I need you to pick up our dinner on your way home.>

Something about the way he said 'never mind' made me feel guilty, and my heart clenched. If Ceyoh was right about what she'd told me…

"Yes, Zafir, I'm fine. Just a small hiccup we can discuss later," I answered after a moment. I hesitated before adding, "What about you? Did you remember to take a break?"

<There wasn't a chance to. I'll brief you when you arrive.> His flustered tone had me raising an eyebrow at the empty wall across from me. <I-I'll wait for you at the front desk. You should be arriving at the restaurant now—I already paid. See you when you get home.>

There was some hurried fumbling, then a *click* and the connection ended. I lowered my phone, giving it an incredulous look. *Are all men so weird? Is it just a Syldrari thing? Furthermore, why can't I just have a normal conversation with someone?!*

Sighing heavily, I disembarked to fetch our food. *'Just because I'm a woman,' my ass. Syldrari society couldn't function if everyone with a dick acted like that. Do they really think they can hide that there's clearly more to it than this?*

CHAPTER TWENTY-FIVE

I flipped through a few apps on my communicator as I reclined back against the side of my transport. When I finally found the one I was looking for, I pressed the call button and waited a moment.

"Hey, Zafir? It's going to be a bit. This place is swamped," I said the moment I heard him pick up. "You going to be alright if I have to wait ten to twenty minutes?"

<Will I be…?> He hesitated, and I bristled with faint suspicion. What the hell had made him so nervous? <Yes, that will be fine. The situation here has stabilized for the moment…the concern is you. Are you feeling alright? Any symptoms, or anything strange at all?>

The hell? I frowned slightly. "I take it this is an in-person only conversation?"

<Yes.>

I sighed reluctantly. "I'm fine, Zafir. My delays were due to a stop at Rel's, picking up your medicines, buying some ludrán, and getting annoyed by the usual source of my irritation."

<That's...odd.> Zafir hesitated before continuing in an unusual tone, giving me the impression that he had company. <Have you checked the news?>

Considering I was one of the few people at HQ who avoided the news like the plague, I had to assume this was important, rather than just small talk. "No, I haven't had a chance."

<Well, it will certainly explain a few things if you found that people were agitated,> he suggested. There was a muffled sound in the background, and he sighed softly. <I have to go, Elara. If I don't greet you at the door, wait for me in the mess hall. Furthermore, you're off duty for the night. I'll see you soon.>

The fuck? I looked at my communicator, then over at my driver. He was standing just a few feet away, his rifle aimed at the ground and his eyes sharp. "Hey, Erik, right? You have a TV or radio in this rig?"

"Yes, ma'am— Uh..." Erik narrowed his eyes and glanced past me.

I turned, finding a group of very drunk humans making their way toward us.

"Heeey, military girl! That's cute!" One of them laughed. "Man, why'd they decide to waste good pussy on—"

"Turn around. Now." Erik stepped past me. His gun was still

aimed at the ground, but his shift in demeanor made him seem ten feet tall. The drunkards hesitated, then suddenly went running. I had to wonder just what sort of face he had made at them. "TV is in the back. The boss suggest you take a look?"

"Yeah. He's not in a position to tell me what's going on… I assume it's the same for you?" It didn't seem likely that the base was under attack. Was it simply a high-ranking visitor? I doubted it.

"Yes, ma'am." He watched me hop into the vehicle, then turned to keep watch. "The situation has been diffused, but the boss is still shaken. All I can say is that it's unrelated to the matter that's showing on the news, ma'am."

I grumbled complaints under my breath as I turned the TV on and navigated to a news channel.

"*—due to his abandonment of his clan and these outrageous demands, I am forced to disown my son. Jysel is no longer of Clan R'selkti, and I have canceled his pending sale to the F'rsze Queen. He and those who support him have been cast out and will now be treated as rogues.*"

The interviewer leaned forward excitedly, seemingly enraptured by the veiled Syldrari woman she was interviewing. "*Are you saying that your government doesn't believe in or condone these threats, Jalanki?*"

"*I didn't say that.*" The R'selkti queen shook her head slowly. "*Any Syldrari queens—and their servants—should be returned to* me. I *dislike thieves. Keeping Syldrari prisoners will be treated as a declaration of war.*

"However, my idiot son's threats were unnecessary and unrealistic. You will find me to be much more reasonable and cooperative…"

The show cut for a break, and I scowled. I instantly disliked the woman much more than the more annoying of her two sons. Even on the TV, there was just something about her that didn't feel right. Plus…*his pending sale?*

"Order for Elara?" a slightly mechanized voice questioned from outside. I shifted and walked past Erik, finding a person in the restaurant's black and orange uniform waiting.

"That's me." I flashed my ID, and the person nodded—though I could have sworn I heard motors whirring.

"Excellent. I have your order here. Would you like me to load it for you?" They stepped aside to reveal a dolly with several bags of takeout boxes.

"Military craft—sorry. I'll handle it." Erik stepped forward, and there was another nod.

I took a better look at the person, noting that they had faint seams running down their neck and forearms. Their eyes, upon closer inspection, seemed to be mechanical as well—the components just *looked* like a human eye at first glance.

Is this one of the non-biological vessels I've heard about? Are they a cyborg or an android? Human, or some other species of origin?

"Thanks," Erik said, offering the person a tip once he was done loading. I nodded, echoing his sentiments. Finally, we hopped in the vehicle and Erik started driving toward headquarters. "Haven't seen one of them before, I take it?"

"No."

"Androids—real common to see them working in the minor roles humans used to," he offered. "The government halted its android research in favor of researching the Syldrari, so the androids aren't complex or sturdy enough to serve military purposes. My guess is they want to create human-Syldrari hybrids and then design a new line of androids with their capabilities. The old android systems aren't compatible with any aetheric tech."

"Huh. Is this common knowledge, or…?" I tilted my head as I studied his muscular build and his uniform. "Or are you more than just a mere soldier?"

"The android department was repurposed into the Resonance Project HQ," he answered with a short laugh. "Been working at the same location for a little over a century now. Working at these kinds of installations is the goal of just about any of us. Guarding researchers is a damn cushy deal."

"Huh, I could see that." I considered for a moment as he slowed the vehicle and navigated us into the underground parking garage.

"I'll go get something to carry the food," he offered after hopping out. "It'll give you a minute to prep for dealing with the boss man."

Hmm, and Zafir isn't upset because of the R'selkti queen? I leaned back in confusion. Honestly, the interview snippet had bothered me. *What was it Casair said…right. Abandonment. …Oh. Jysel's seen her broadcast already, hasn't he…oh boy.*

I poked through my communicator in search of an interview transcript and quickly found one. I skimmed it, my unease growing. She'd talked about Rel, too—how his 'endearing game of playing clan leader' was beneficial, but she hoped to find a buyer for him too. Apparently, leading the V'shir and being the queen's eldest son made him expensive. She was eager for him to continue building the clan so that she could command a higher price.

From there, I attempted to find what the fuck she was talking about. The closest explanation I could find online was a comparison to ancient human practices where a groom—often betrothed—would pay the bride's parents to be able to marry her. The article's writer theorized that it was a similar practice, but with reversed genders due to the Syldrari's more matriarchal society.

However, commentators on the article claimed that the R'selkti queen spoke similarly of her non-male children. It was just that the males were harder to get rid of.

"Here, this should do the trick." Erik returned with a large empty cargo box. "You can stack the food in here and carry it, that sound like something you can do? I've got orders to go fetch more stuff."

"Yeah, I'll unload real quick." I hopped to it, said a quick goodbye to Erik, then hurried off to the mess hall. To my surprise, Zafir and a man I didn't recognize were waiting in the lobby.

"Elara, this is my boss—and yours—General Crowe." Zafir motioned to the unfamiliar man.

I glanced down at my box, then back to Crowe. "I hope you'll forgive me for not saluting, sir."

"Of course! Let's walk and talk. Zafir here could stand to get some food in him." Crowe clapped Zafir on the back. "Surveillance is currently disabled throughout the facility, so I'll get straight to the point. All the members of your team and the ones displaying cellular dissonance were poisoned while you were on patrol.

"They'll all be fine, but we have them in isolation and under guard. We believe this was an inside job, and I'm bringing in an external team to investigate the staff. You two are off the hook, but everyone else can't be accounted for."

"We jointly proposed new uniform protocols for the guards and research staff so that it's more difficult to hide facial features," Zafir muttered, plopping down at a table. "Amara is going over a copy of the security footage in search of suspicious behavior."

"We should really turn surveillance systems back on." I paused in placing the food on the table and gave them a stern look. "I have it on good authority that we're the next target of the rogue Syldrari attacking the different research installations. Poisoning most of our strongest fighters sure seems like a good distraction to me."

"What…" Zafir's eyes widened momentarily before he seemed

to switch into 'on' mode. He turned and narrowed his eyes at Crowe. "Sir, Elara has made reliable connections in the Syldrari sector. I don't believe they'd tell her this lightly. We should prepare."

"You trust this info-giver?" Crowe looked to me thoughtfully.

I shook my head before giving a proper reply. "I don't trust anyone, sir, but my gut says he was telling the truth. Furthermore, I don't think a Syldrari would say to be careful when trying to set someone up."

"And this contact has *connections* you'd rather not talk about?" Crowe laughed when I grimaced. "I know the type, girl. Got plenty of contacts like that of my own. Keep 'em close, they're invaluable.

"Zafir, eat. Elara, keep an eye on him and make sure he doesn't let his dreamy skull detach from his shoulders." Crowe paused, then motioned loosely as he addressed Zafir. "We're going to go ahead with relocation plans early. Enough is finished to house your current staff and survivors, so we should have everyone out by the morning. After you eat, go with Elara and pack everyone's effects."

"Sir—" Zafir started to stand and protest, but Crowe put a hand on his shoulder and gently pressed him back down.

"We don't know how long it will take for them to recover. You and I can't afford to have the Syldrari attack and destroy all our work here with this installation." He glanced pointedly at me, then back to Zafir. "Keep her alive. Bail early if you have to."

"...Yes, sir." Zafir slumped back in his chair, and silence fell as the general took his leave. He waited a little longer before muttering, "Damned bastard, leaving *me* to be the bearer of bad news..."

"Zafir. Zafir? *Hey*, enough with the pouting. I'm not gonna shoot the messenger." I sat down across from him and started making him a plate of food, since he still hadn't moved to do so. "What? Okay—I won't punch you, kiss you, kick you, or stab you either."

"Even so, it still isn't—" He paused, shifting in his seat. "...One of those was not like the rest."

"I have no idea what you mean." I shrugged, lifting the plate of food and placing it in front of him. "Talk or eat—pick one."

"I don't know if I have the stomach to..." he started, before a loud gurgle from said stomach interrupted him. "Of all the times for my body to betray me..."

"Oh yes, how terrible that your body is trying to keep you fed," I commented, rolling my eyes as I propped my elbow on the table and rested my chin in my palm.

"Before this chaos, I received orders from the brass—they had me cancel all patrols for your team, day and night, because they want you to work on team building exercises and training together while things are still calm." He grimaced and paused, as if expecting me to immediately start bitching. When I said nothing, he hesitated, then continued, "You were all to be on emergency standby, of course, but now the situation has changed. Brass has ordered you to remain in and keep an eye on the poisoned ones. They're concerned a more direct attack may be in order now that your team members are incapacitated and easier to deal with—and of course, the information you brought will only make them more confident an attack is coming. I doubt they will change their minds."

"Okay."

He blinked at me. "That's it?"

"Well, it makes sense. If you can give me a rational explanation as to the *why* of something, I'm significantly less likely to get pissed," I pointed out, watching as he glanced away in discomfort. "You just need to get more creative in telling me the reasons for *other* things. Clearly you have it in you—which is why it's infuriating when you don't do it.

"Plus, how would you feel if you came to the realization that everyone you talk to is keeping things from you *all the time*?"

Zafir's gaze drifted down to the floor as he sighed, continuing to look away from me. "Yes… I'm sure your patience is quite short by now."

"*Eat,* before I feed you myself." I kicked his foot lightly under the table. "How about I ask you questions I think you *can* answer?"

He made a sour face. "You can try."

"Okay, how can some Syldrari colors glow pink, but still have a blue sort of halo?" I asked, and Zafir's hands twitched so hard he dropped his silverware. In an instant, he was on his feet, grabbing my wrist and dragging me to the residential quarters. *Uh...oops?*

He pulled me into his office and then to the room in the back, which looked like a small lab. Pointing at an examination machine, he spoke flatly. "Let me see your eyes. Sit."

I decided to cooperate, since this time he appeared unnerved instead of grumpy. There'd already been a faint trembling to his hands since I'd come back, but now it was worse.

Seemingly not finding what he was looking for, he crossed his arms and ordered, "Suit up and take your visor off."

I did as he asked, and his lips immediately parted slightly, his eyes widening. He inhaled shakily and carefully reached his hands up to my face to cup my cheeks. I watched as his gaze became hazy for a brief moment, then he regained control.

"Oh...that...is not good," he murmured in a breathy, half-excited, half-distressed tone. "Your eyes, they— Don't look!"

He pressed me back into my seat, hands on my shoulders and one knee up on the seat cushion beside my thigh. He sounded genuinely panicked, though now that he was closer he appeared to be struggling more to stay out of his hazy state.

"But you're clearly distressed, so something must be wrong," I protested. Still, he easily kept me in place.

"Elara, please, don't look," he pleaded in almost a whisper, his forehead resting against mine. His eyes clenched shut as though he were in pain. "I'm afraid that seeing your real eyes may trigger an acceleration in your condition, and there is no way to predict how dangerous that might be. Not to mention the potential psychological ramifications, there's just too much…"

He moved back abruptly and shook his head hard to clear it. I hadn't seen a Syldrari react to anyone like *that* before, and that was having met a queen. *The hell is going on? I'm not exactly surprised that I might be Syldrari. Not by any stretch. But why am I having such a strong effect when Xilen doesn't?*

"Here." He handed me back my visor and sighed quietly. "Put it back on and de-suit. I should find Crowe and—"

Since he still seemed a little out of it, I thought my choice of words over carefully before speaking. "What about your food? It's going to get cold at this rate."

"Hmm?" He shot me a questioning look. "That much thought for such a short question?"

"Uh, well, you said I need to be careful about wording in certain situations, so…" I grumbled awkwardly, crossing my arms and glancing away. "Is all the food yours?"

"No, no, you're welcome to join me," he answered quickly as he fetched a small device by one of the machines. "To check the food, just in case."

"Good idea." I nodded, following him. The praise appeared to put some spring in his step, though after we'd gone a few feet, he raised a hand to his face and rubbed his temples. After that, he slowed and became less bouncy. I opened my mouth to ask a question, but then stopped myself.

No, no, hold it back. You know he'll be compelled to answer. Don't do that to him. You know his intentions are good even if he makes you want to throw him out of a window sometimes...

"Hmmm..." he murmured, scanning each dish quickly. "All clear. Shall I grab you a drink?"

"I don't know how to answer that." I sat down with a sigh, considering it. *Will a yes compel him and a no upset him when he's been exposed to...whatever it is I do?*

"Ah..." Zafir rubbed his chin, sinking into thought. "Thank you for being considerate, but I don't believe we can afford to be awkward when more people show up. Much like I can't yet explain what it is I was looking for, I hope you can be patient with me so we can discuss it later."

"Then I'll grab the drinks, *boss*," I stressed, hoping to remind his silly Syldrari brain that he was supposed to be the one in charge. "What would you like?"

"What I would *like* is—" He cut himself off abruptly and placed a hand over his eyes, both hiding his face and rubbing his temples again. "Just...fill a kettle and bring it here. The herbs I requested are in one of these bags, right? I'm going to make some tea. You are welcome to try some."

I fetched the kettle and grabbed the little basket of strainers and fillable bags we kept handy. After placing both next to Zafir, I pulled over the bag he needed since he was too distracted to find it, then sat down across from him again.

"Thank you," he murmured as he set about making the tea.

I wonder, is this how they all react, or are there a variety of potential responses? I considered what little I knew of the other Syldrari, especially the most frustrating one. *Huh. Could Jysel be worse? That might explain his seeming fear of abandonment and how it's contrasted by the anger he has toward so many things. Just what has that woman put them through? Jysel is always cranky, but I don't think I've ever actually seen Rel drink before.*

Moving forward, I should probably assume they've both seen the interview with their mother. That may be why Jysel was so...odd today. Same for Rel. I bet Jysel was looking for a fight to blow off some steam. Rel, though...maybe I should get his number next time I talk to him.

Hmmm, is Rel more amiable because he's been away from R'selkti control for longer? If I have my series of events straight, it was only within the last five years that Jysel killed their father and ordered their resonance weapon destroyed. Is he struggling to find his place away from his parents' control? Then again, didn't someone say Rel is usually the hard one to win over? Hmmm...

"Elara," Zafir asked in a manner that suggested he had called my name multiple times. When my gaze flicked to him, he frowned. "What's on your mind?"

"I was contemplating some of the personal quirks I learned about a few of the Syldrari today during my patrols," I answered vaguely, having caught the sound of footsteps approaching the mess hall. "Many of them seem like they've been treated poorly by any and every queen they've encountered. I was wondering if that's why the V'shir are a queenless clan, but I was also thinking that it's odd that others would be so strongly driven to rescue the queens they claim are missing."

"Sharp one. I see why Zafir speaks highly of you," Crowe remarked as he approached. "There's only rumors and theories, but some believe the Syldrari programmed their men to be mindlessly subservient to their queens. I find it believable—imagine the wars they would wage among themselves if they had to compete for such a small number of women. Human history has seen how few people have to be involved for something to escalate into war."

Zafir doesn't seem to agree with that... I nudged his foot under the table so he could correct his expression before Crowe fully reached us. "That's difficult to believe, sir, but I suppose if it was well done it could be undetectable."

"Not done yet?" Crowe nodded his sympathies to Zafir. "I know you're worried. The best thing you can do for them right now is to keep yourself well-fed and healthy."

"Which is why Elara escorted me to fetch a tool I could use to scan the food before we ate it." Zafir brandished the small device briefly before pocketing it. "One of the Syldrari inventions I managed to recalibrate. They use it when exploring undiscovered planets, as a quick way to determine what is and isn't edible."

"Why haven't we reverse-engineered this yet for ourselves?" Crowe asked irritably as he sat beside Zafir.

"Ah… I have proposed as much many times, but…" Zafir made a show of sulking. "Eddard, well, you know how he is. Not to speak ill of one of my superiors, of course, but I have to wonder about his intentions sometimes, sir."

"Bah, that old fool is a purist through and through. Believes in making our own way through the universe—without any alien tech." Crowe grimaced in disgust, though something appeared to dawn on him. "I wonder… Zafir, Elara, finish up and get packing. The transports will be here soon. I'll tell my men to look to you for instruction."

He stood abruptly and exited the room again. I glanced over at Zafir just in time to see a rather villainous smile on his face—which he quickly hid when he realized I was looking. I made a dismissive motion.

"I can guess. There's some things you just can't research in your position." I gave him an amused look. "Maybe save the triumphant 'ha, fool, you are my pawn!' looks for when you're in private? It's usually right after that sort of behavior that villains either fall or become the pawns themselves, you know."

"Ah yes, but that is fiction, and I have quite the charming sidekick." He laughed, shooting me a wicked smile. "I appreciate your concern, Elara. But for now, perhaps we should hurry, as he suggested."

CHAPTER TWENTY-SIX

"Zafir? Where's Elara?" Casair stood abruptly and left his desk when Zafir emerged from a portal.

Zafir glanced around the cavern-turned-staging point, frowning as he took stock of those present—Casair and one other guard. "Where—"

"Where is Elara?" Casair repeated dangerously, taking several steps toward the smaller Syldrari. "She never showed up for her patrol last week, and we haven't seen her since. Rel said he hasn't seen her either. Rel and Jysel are both ready to dissect the whole damn city!"

"Oh…" Zafir adjusted his glasses. "When you last saw her, she wasn't yet aware that the brass had canceled *all* my plans…and then the situation escalated. It would be best if Jysel were here for this."

"Not going to happen. He won't be back 'til tomorrow or the

day after." Casair grabbed a data pad. "Report. I'll see to it those two don't do anything else stupid."

Zafir frowned, concern gripping his chest. "What do you mean by that?"

"Elara told Jysel off pretty damned good when we last ran into her. The problem was the timing. He's been acting like a shell-less *glusyx* since. Doesn't know *what* to do other than throw himself into every damn mission on the list.

"Rel caught the stupid a few days later, and now he's convinced himself that Elara is avoiding him due to either his tipsy behavior and/or his suggestion that she should have a drink with him when she's off duty sometime."

"Please…" Zafir groaned. "I thought they were better than this."

"They are, but we haven't been able to contact any of our agents within the Resonance Project—*including you.*" Casair's tail whipped back and forth, nearly tossing a chair halfway across the cavern. "So, like I said: **Report.**"

Zafir hesitated momentarily before filling Casair on the events that had transpired, leading to the project's relocation and the ongoing medical treatment of the subjects. By the time he'd finished relaying all the information, the sun was setting.

"Do you think we're going to have to perform an early extraction?" Casair inquired, skimming his notes. "If they're all showing signs of more dissonance, it's only a matter of time before it's no longer hideable—or worse, they cause each other to spiral into full reversion. Curious as I'm sure we all are about Elara at this point…"

"I think we're quite some time from needing extraction; my primary concern right now is her team." Zafir leaned back against a table. "It's possible, of course, that Elara was an undiscovered queen. The events of the past few years could be what have made her allure so strong.

"…Or she was an established queen, and something happened. Her current team might get along so well with her because they were originally her guards or servants. I took some extra scans—her team hasn't been nearly as tampered with. I believe they may be able to recover some of their memories of the past."

"But she can't? *Tch*. Just what is going on in that damn—" He stopped as a melodic sound rang through the area, his eyes snapping past Zafir. "Sir? What are you doing back already?"

Casair hurried past Zafir and over to the portal, Zafir following behind him. Jysel looked between the two in silence as he removed his equipment and took off his sword belt. Finally, he looked to Zafir. "Why haven't we been able to contact you or the others?"

"We haven't been able to reinstall our equipment at the new headquarters yet. Everyone involved with the Resonance Project is currently under investigation aside from Elara, her hospitalized team, and myself." Zafir hesitated, expecting some manner of reaction from his boss, but there was nothing. Though Jysel was attempting to keep his expression blank, he couldn't hide his downtrodden demeanor or the dark yellow, almost black, color of his glow. Zafir glanced over at Casair, who half-shrugged and shook his head. "If you would like my report—"

"Is Elara alright?" Jysel interrupted. His expression stayed the same, but his glow began to shift between various forms of dark purple and grey.

Zafir stared at his boss for a moment, taken aback by the hints of concern. How rattled *was* he by his mother's dismissal, and just what had Elara said to him? "Sir, she's fine aside from being, in her words, 'unbearably bored.' Because her shift started in the early morning that day, she wasn't poisoned at lunch like her team was. We're currently waiting for them to recover so they can begin—"

"I see, another poisoning?" Jysel frowned slightly. "Then I assume this relocation is due to the warning Casair gave her of the impending attack."

"That was you?" Zafir glanced at Casair, then back to Jysel, narrowing his eyes. "Given your demeanor toward her, *sir*, I thought the warning more likely to have come from Rel."

"Hmph. She may...*frustrate* me, but I am invested in your infiltration of the Resonance Project. I can't deny the evidence you've given that indicates she might be Syldrari— What?" Jysel narrowed his eyes when Zafir shifted in discomfort. "Yes, yes, you told me about the cellular dissonance and her skin changing color. That alone doesn't mean anything other than that her cells are vying for dominance."

"She *is* undoubtedly Syldrari, Jysel," Zafir informed him with a sigh. He rubbed his temples before continuing. "And a queen. Undeniably a queen. She asked me how pink could glow blue."

"And?" Jysel crossed his arms.

"I took her to my lab to check her eyes. They're indistinguishable from a human's…until she suits up." He sighed heavily. "Her eyes are Syldrari when suited but they're not functioning fully yet. However, the effect she has on—"

"What did she do to you?" Jysel demanded, stepping forward.

"*Nothing*. She has no control over her allure, but she was cautious—perhaps overly so—about her phrasing of both questions and answers." Zafir offered a half-smile. "She's unsettled by the way I react to her power, and perhaps she should be. She doesn't want it. Alas, I can't arrange for her to learn from Xilen given the current circumstances."

"…Just how powerful is she?" Jysel asked quietly.

Zafir considered for a moment before offering, "I haven't met a queen like her—in power or personality. She's had me under her sway several times, though she immediately becomes distressed when she realizes it. She wants to be able to joke, tease, and banter with people like anyone else, but she's realized that's dangerous in her position."

"A queen who cares? Hmph." Jysel paused, processing the

information. "You've met the R'selkti queen. Are you implying—"

"I believe that is part of Xilen's interest in Elara, yes." Zafir nodded.

"I have to agree. Xilen warned Elara to stay far away from that woman during their first encounter," Casair offered with a grimace. "At first I thought it was just the usual, but we'd have to be imbeciles to not recognize there's more to it."

"Another queen to rescue, then…" Jysel sighed irritably.

"You and I know it's not that simple. We need her if we want to continue investigating the Resonance Project." Zafir frowned deeply. "Without her and her team—"

"You want me to rescue the other queens, yet leave her behind?" Jysel asked, a dangerous rumble tingeing his voice.

"I've done some looking around. She isn't one of the queens on their list—even they didn't know about her." Zafir narrowed his eyes. "*None* of the Resonance survivors are catalogued queens. There's something else going on, and I would like to find out what it is. Preferably before there's a *successful* murder attempt."

Jysel sighed heavily. "When will we be seeing her again?"

"Not any time soon if the brass has anything to say about it. They have every survivor under house arrest now, under the pretense of team building exercises," Zafir answered venomously. "Why you *want* to see her is another question. Do you *enjoy* antagonizing her?"

"No, I just…" Jysel sighed, his shoulders slumping and his glow turning a rich yellow. "She's…refreshing. Even if her acceptance of Syldrari culture may not be as unusual as we first thought, she's still different from both humans and from us. According to you, she is atypical as a queen as well. *That* would be quite welcome after the week we've had."

"You've begun finding queens?" Zafir frowned.

"Yes, though tonight's excursion was a miss. They appear to be relocating their captives." Jysel winced and rubbed the back of his neck with one hand. "*Tch*, the queens we've been finding… I was of half a mind to leave them in their cells once they started talking."

Zafir grimaced. "I understand your frustration, truly I do."

"But we can't leave them to the humans or my mother. I'm aware." Jysel's voice was dry. "Most of those we've found thus far, however, will be returning to her. They're already loyal to her without even meeting her. It's infuriating. We hope to find more reasonable queens as we continue to work, but—"

"We already know a reasonable queen—Elara." Casair crossed his arms over his chest and looked between the clearly uncomfortable Zafir and Jysel. "How long until her cellular dissonance progresses too far, and she becomes the next queen we need to save? I don't trust what the humans may do if she becomes more clearly Syldrari. They could choose to kill her. Get rid of the danger."

"And we know someone is already trying," Zafir murmured, his brow knitting with worry. "If General Crowe's suspicions are correct…"

"…What is it?" Jysel prompted. "Do we or do we not need to get her out?"

"You can't keep her…" Casair paused and shot Jysel a grin, then added, laughing, "Sal'aphel might, though."

"I'll let you know as matters progress." Zafir rubbed his chin, a smirk spreading across his face. "We may be able to lure the bastard out. I'll keep you informed, but for now, I'm late to return. Casair has my full report."

Jysel reached out to stop Zafir, then pulled his arm back. "Tell Elara I— Never mind. You're free to go."

Casair smirked and half-shrugged at Zafir before leading his boss deeper into the cavern. Shaking his head, Zafir returned through the portal to the new Resonance Project HQ.

CHAPTER TWENTY-SEVEN

I rummaged around in my new room in search of my snack stash, groaning when all I pulled out was an empty box. Gone. All gone. I didn't *want* to leave my room in the middle of reading, but I was *hungry*. Frustrated, I tossed off my pajamas and got dressed. Pulling my hair into a messy bun, I stalked out of my room and down the hall.

Our new HQ was a high-rise apartment building, with all living quarters above ground. The main floor lobby was connected to a mall that formed part of our building, providing us with access to whatever shopping we might want to do. My target, though, was the food court.

Our labs and training areas were still underground, but the rest of it was meant to simulate real living conditions. Plus, the mall was popular and gave us some interaction with civilians. For those of us who wanted that, anyway. Personally, I'd been keeping to myself...and, admittedly, that was likely one of the reasons for my increasing boredom.

After getting off the elevator, I started to wander toward the food court when a familiar voice caught my attention. "What... *Elara*? What are you doing here?"

"Hmm?" I glanced over my shoulder to find Rel, Aldiner, and Ciheri. They were dressed casually, and Rel had a few shopping bags on one arm. "Oh, hey! You guys here shopping?"

To my surprise, Rel stalked straight toward me and abruptly leaned down to hug me. "Elara, we were so worried... Where have you *been*?"

Considering where we were, I was thankful he kept his voice to a whisper...even if it sent tingles down my spine.

"I'm under *house arrest*," I answered quietly, hoping that my tone would convey the gravity of the situation. "I was just about to get breakfast. Want to join me?"

"Breakfast? It's five in the afternoon." Rel straightened to his full height and gave me a concerned frown. "Just what—"

"I've been in my apartment reading all day." I made a show of stretching my arms over my head. "If you wanna talk, join me. Of course, you don't have to eat anything if you don't like human food."

I started walking and the three of them promptly followed. They seemed much more concerned than I'd expected. Ciheri's expression put me in mind of a worried puppy, and even Aldiner had a look of concern on him. Hell, he wasn't even flashing a bazillion lights everywhere, for once. *Does Zafir only report to Jysel?*

"House arrest?" Rel murmured. "Why? Did you get into an altercation after leaving?"

"Nope." I glanced at him, raising an eyebrow. "I think we both know who you can ask."

"I see. Then by house arrest…this is all…" His voice went quiet. "You are alright? When you stopped coming by, I thought perhaps I might have offended you."

"I'm quite fine and you didn't offend me. At the rate things are going, it's going to be a while before I can take you up on the offer of a drink, though." I watched as he released a sigh of relief, the tension leaving his body. I gave him a pointed look. "How are *you* holding up?"

He grimaced. "Ah, yes. I'm sure you saw *her* address."

"Not until after I was off duty, but yes, I eventually saw it." I nodded, but he shot me a puzzled look. "What?"

"Then…you stopping by and offering me assistance…" He paused, a hopeful smile coming to his face. "Ah. That was not out of pity? You were simply…being nice?"

"Welcome to what we've been dealing with for weeks." Aldiner threw his hands into the air, rolling his eyes. "You know, he can be really dumb for an Elder. I guess some people just—"

Ciheri glared up at Aldiner. "Stop it! You were just as worried!"

"…Right." I raised an eyebrow at the pair, then looked back at Rel. "I wouldn't say I was just being nice. I do enjoy your company, plus it would've been pretty asshole-ish of me to *not* offer to help."

"Hmmm…how strange," he murmured, hurrying to follow me around a corner. "To answer your question, I am doing fine. I've known since the founding of the V'shir how she views my endeavors."

"I can't claim to understand how any of what she said is acceptable." I shot him a sidelong glance. "If you're not busy, how about you regale me with the details while we eat. While I eat? You didn't say if you'll be joining me, come to think of it."

"We'd be happy to." He glanced back at Aldiner and Ciheri, who appeared to be arguing in Syldran, then looked back to me. "What did you have in mind?"

"There's this restaurant on the other side of the food court that serves human food from different planets. They've got private rooms and automated table delivery. That should work. We've got an arrangement where they turn off the in-room surveillance when military members request a private room." I motioned for him to follow me, and a few minutes later the four of us were settled in a dim lounge room. Rel gave me a faint nod after I'd sat down, indicating he'd disabled anything that might be listening in.

"I can catch you up on my problems quickly enough. My

teammates were poisoned at lunch while I was on patrol, and they've been in medical isolation undergoing treatment ever since. Since they're down to one combatant—aside from the human guards— and combined with the warning I received from Casair regarding an impending attack, our bosses decided to move HQ. That said, I had already been put under house arrest because they want me on hand to deal with my teammates—if they get attacked again, or if they lose control of their ferals while weakened. Zafir doesn't want them tranquilized, so I'm the only reliable way to subdue them."

"Someone wants to kill the Resonance survivors?" Rel murmured.

I nodded. "Inside job—and currently under investigation. Zafir and I are the only ones in the clear and allowed to leave our rooms right now. Amara is confined to her rooms, but she's otherwise fine. The guards you see everywhere are from the investigation team, not the Resonance Project."

Rel sighed and walked over, taking a seat beside me—so close his hip was pressed up against mine. He leaned back, resting his head against the top of the upholstered backrest. "And this has all been reported?"

"Mhm." I eyed him as his glow swirled to an orangey red. "I take it you weren't informed."

"That *utter imbecile* excludes me from a great deal," he answered flatly. "He thinks he can avoid taking me down with him if things go poorly. As we're twins, we've always been held accountable for each other's actions. Originally, *she* was trying her damnedest to treat Jysel and I as a package deal. However, after he killed our father several years ago, she decided it would be easier to sell us separately. Of course, the price she's set is much too high for any of the queens or their clans to pay. She doesn't understand any form of trade—that is what one of her other *lun'ithero* is for."

"Her…what?" I asked blankly.

"I sometimes forget you aren't acquainted with our language." Rel gave me an apologetic look. "I believe the closest human word is 'husband,' but it is a poor translation. A *lun'ithero* is essentially, ah…"

"A breeding male. It's what she's trying to sell Rel and Jysel as," Aldiner interjected flatly. "More specifically, it refers to a breeding male who is descended from a queen. It's theorized that the necessary genes to become a queen are hereditary."

"But that was debunked…" Ciheri added quietly, earning an odd look from Rel. "Um…the clan I belonged to was heavily focused on research. Our queen wanted to discover what makes queens the way they are, why there aren't queens of other sexes, and why we haven't been able to artificially create queens.

"They determined that the genetics aren't hereditary, but were ordered to keep that knowledge to themselves because it hurts business and contradicts millennia of beliefs."

Rel released a soft sigh. "Yes…many of the queens can become testy when their beliefs are challenged. It's a shame they let such things get in the way of progress. Though perhaps I can't say much, since my mother is the cause for much of the current state of stagnation."

"Even the Syldrari don't quite understand what makes a queen a queen?" I murmured, stirring my straw in my drink.

"You could say that. There are some theories that queens were created, and other documents imply that we once had full control over the phenomenon. If either is true, that knowledge was lost." Rel shook his head slightly before shifting his gaze to me curiously. "You asked me to regale you. What exactly is it you want to know?"

"I want to know why it's an acceptable practice in your culture to sell off one's children," I answered flatly, giving him an unamused look. "Listening to her talk about you and Jysel made me want to torture and kill her as slowly as possible, and in the most humiliating way I could think of. Granted, my fuse may be a little too short to keep from just chopping her head off and mounting it on—"

"Keep that up and all three of us are going to want to kiss you," Aldiner interrupted slyly. "Seriously, if you can get away with doing that—*please do?*"

"Uh...oh." I flushed, realizing I'd gone off on a bit of a tangent—and that all three of them were glowing some variety of pink to reddish-pink.

Rel cleared his throat. "Anyway, to answer your question, the practice is only common among queens. Traditionally, clans are led by queens, and they believe that keeping their bloodlines pure is the best way to produce more queens. They avoid inbreeding by marrying their offspring off to other queens and descendants of queens.

"Jysel and I have the highest worth of her male children, as we are the eldest and I have my own queenless clan—a rarity among Syldrari. Were I to be married off, the queen would pay my mother a price that reflects both my status *and* the size of Clan V'shir. The clan would then become hers to do with as she wished, and I would only remain in charge if she permitted me to.

"Mother has yet to have any *iri* children. Thus far, her *lun'itheroi*—that is the plural term—have only given her *lun'iri* such as myself, and *sol'iri*. *Sol'iri* are more valuable than the males, but…"

Aldiner shrugged and spoke up when Rel went silent. "Those of us who aren't queen-spawn live more or less like humans do—except we're culturally driven to try to make ourselves appealing to queens. 'Marry up,' and all that—humans marry up for money and status, Syldrari marry up for status and the hope of *more* status. Second to queens are whoever can 'bless' their partner with a queen."

"Not quite right, but accurate enough," Rel remarked dryly, earning a questioning glance from me. "I believe I've mentioned before that our culture is heavily focused on the arts and sciences. If we take queens and those uncontrollably obsessed with them out of the equation, the highest-status members of our society are those with beautiful and complex minds."

"Who usually catch the eye of a queen or dozen, and get put in a cage to try to breed a queen with that kind of mind," Aldiner countered flatly.

"You know he's right." Ciheri peered over his crossed arms at Rel, who sighed heavily. Next, the shy Syldrari turned his attention to the menu, glancing at me. "Um... I've never had human food. We order from this? What should I get?"

"Elara's clearly been eating here—let's make her order." Aldiner linked his hands behind his head and leaned back in his seat, shooting me a grin.

"Yes, let's," Rel agreed, much to my surprise. He gave me a mischievous look and leaned a little closer. "Can Ms. House Arrest have a drink, or..."

"Sadly no, but I can think of something you might like." I picked up the data pad that acted as my menu and swiftly scrolled down the list. Clam chowder for our appetizer, grilled steak and lobster for the entree, and molten chocolate lava cakes for dessert. I paused over the drink menu, then glanced up at Rel—he was still a little close, but I decided to ignore that. "Are those two old enough to drink?"

"Yes. They're actually not much younger than me...not that anyone would be able to tell from their behavior," he answered, shooting Aldiner and Ciheri an amused look.

"Okay, that will go well with the entree... Oh, and this with dessert." I finished placing our order and swiped my card to pay before he could see the total. "I'm guessing Syldrari hold their alcohol better than humans do, but these will taste good, at least."

"How's your stock of ludrán holding up?" Rel teased, a knowing smile spreading across his face when I shot him a disgruntled look. "Ceyoh told me she'd sold more to you, and given the rate you've been demolishing her stores thus far, she's concerned by your absence as well."

"All gone, but I can't exactly get more—and I'm not permitted to give anyone my room number. So deliveries are out."

"And with you and Zafir the only ones allowed out of your rooms... I take it you can't send Sarah to play fetch?" He shot me a frown when I sighed and slumped back in my seat. "What is it?"

"Sarah's one of the ones who were poisoned. Though she's not on a team, she *is* a survivor of the Incident. It just didn't give her powers like it did us," I muttered irritably.

"Interesting... So, she too may be..." he murmured curiously.

I nodded. "Yeah, that's my theory. Everyone who was poisoned was confirmed to have been experiencing cellular dissonance prior to it happening. Zafir didn't say outright that Sarah was in the same boat, but his choice of words implies it."

"Cellular whatsit?" Aldiner narrowed his eyes.

"I will explain when we're back home." Rel shook his head at Aldiner, then glanced to me. "We've been making weekly trips to this mall for a while. I'll see if I can bring you some ludrán when next we visit."

"Oh, I'd appreciate it." I smiled at him. "Don't feel the need to go out of your way, though; I'm not sure if I'd be able to get it past security right now. They've got Zafir scanning anything that comes into or goes out of the building right now—consumable or not. They've even got him scanning uniforms and weapons in case the offender moves on to topical toxins."

"To be going to such great lengths...it *must* be a human," Rel remarked disdainfully. He paused, glancing at me. "You know, whenever I make a comment that could be construed as an insult to humans, I feel as though I should apologize to you. Yet..."

"Don't apologize for speaking the truth." I laughed. "Now, *why* does that information lead you to believe this person is human?"

"Because a Syldrari would have succeeded already," Ciheri offered quietly, looking deep in thought. "We're raised to never underestimate an opponent or target. Hunting or otherwise. If a Syldrari wanted to use poison to kill you and your team members, they would have used something that can take down either a Syldrari or one of our most difficult-to-hunt creatures."

"We're efficient," Rel mused.

"...*So*, if Jysel wanted me dead..."

"Yes, you would be already." Rel nodded, chuckling. "Humans have a saying… I believe it goes, 'His bark is bigger than his bite'? You frustrate my brother because you fall outside the parameters he is used to dealing with, and that rattles his resolve to an extent. You are very easily someone we could grow attached to, and as he has sworn off such attachments…"

"Okay, so I challenge his way of thinking just by existing. I get that. But, if he's so…*him*, why is it that he's so driven to save these captured queens?" This time Rel laughed outright.

"Because he still dreams of being the aloof hero who saves a queen who is *deserving* of her power. I would offer you some books of Syldrari fairytales so you could better understand his admittedly simple and honestly childish motivations; however, they haven't been translated into the human languages."

Aldiner grinned and leaned forward. "We could read them to her. I'm sure you could translate on the fly."

"I could, or I could preserve what little is left of Jysel's dignity for him to destroy himself," Rel suggested, his lips pulling into an amused smile. "Now then, why don't we find a more pleasant topic of discussion while we still have some time together? Perhaps I can show you some of our visual and aural arts while we wait—I have my data pad with me today."

"Oh! I think the capitol's virtual museum tour may be live now as well!" Ciheri spoke up excitedly. "Since we can't take her to see Syldra and its museums herself, that would be a good place to start!"

"Ah, yes… They have some new art exhibits opening, right?" Rel murmured as he pulled out a rather different-looking data pad, allowing it to hover in front of him. Next, he placed a half-sphere thing on the table. "There we are. New art exhibits, as well as additions to the archaeology district."

"…Did you just say archaeology *district*?" I stared at him in disbelief.

"Hmm? Yes, of course." He gave me a brief, puzzled glance, then a look of realization crossed his face. "Ah, being such an old species and liking our things to be a certain way…the 'museum' is a city adjacent to the capitol building. It is arguably the most well-defended place on Syldra. We take the arts rather seriously. The capital city would fall sooner than the museum would."

"That's…" I trailed off, trying to imagine such a thing. As if reading my mind, he tapped something on the data pad and the sphere projected what had to be the museum. I stared in disbelief at the incredibly beautiful, albeit alien, submerged city. "I…sure, let's start with the archaeology district."

"Oh?" His eyes brightened. "A connoisseur of the ancient?"

"When I was still holed up in my cell, the way I learned about humans was by consuming books about ancient humans and their myths," I offered, adjusting myself a little in my seat so I could lean forward to examine the projection. "I think learning about the past is important with any culture and especially with other species. We can learn from the past, and I'm sure different species erred in vastly different ways throughout their respective histories."

"Then we can save the art and music for some other time." He gave me a small smile. "I certainly can't argue with your observation, and I wouldn't dream of keeping you from learning more about our culture—past or present. I can only hope that I will be able to answer your other questions so candidly very soon."

CHAPTER TWENTY-EIGHT

I stared at my ceiling, utterly consumed by boredom. My new room was great, sure, but I was spending too much time in it, and I was starting to go stir crazy with barely anyone to talk to. After a moment, I pulled myself to my feet, got dressed and slipped on a pair of shoes, and left the room.

Okay, who do I try to pester? Zafir? I pocketed my keycard as I strolled down the hall.

The floor I was on contained rooms for me, my team, and Zafir. The central area had a kitchen, a large table for communal meals, a room with a large TV and plush seating, a reading area, and a gaming lounge. Across from our wing, rooms for a second team were still being finished, while above us by one level was a gym and a pool. Above that were conference and office rooms, above *that* was a dedicated lab for growing our own food in case of emergencies—

and then there was the top floor, which was essentially the team's armory, along with parking for our skybikes and access to a landing pad for any transport that needed to come or go.

Below our floor, it was similar layouts for Resonance Project staff and their families—from android and human janitors to the guards and staff, researchers, and even people whose roles I wasn't clear on. Every few floors there was another set of recreational floors to keep people happy—and so they wouldn't have to come up and mingle with the 'subjects.'

According to Zafir, it had taken a great deal of work to convince the government to construct such a building for the Resonance Project HQ, let alone keep it from being subterranean. Apparently, quite a few of our staff couldn't mentally cope with being underground for long periods of time. Since it caused their performance to suffer, he'd been able to convince the bosses that a more pleasant environment would make everyone happier and therefore both more efficient and productive.

I wasn't exactly going to complain about Zafir's manipulation tactics getting us better living conditions, even if I now had more space than I knew what to do with.

The underground hospital, science labs, and holding cells were still atrociously white, though. But at least the guards had rotating shifts throughout the building to keep from being stuck down there.

I stopped by Zafir's door and raised my hand to knock, only to find a note taped to his door. *'Making breakfast. Come to the lounge if you need me.'*

I raised an eyebrow at the note, then made my way back down the hall. *Huh. He's learning.*

Zafir was coming out of the kitchen as I walked into the TV area. He had a questionable amount of food on his plate and a *huge* thermos of coffee in his other hand. He gave me a tired smile when he spotted me, then motioned his head in the direction of the kitchen.

"There's a plate on the counter for you, and enough hot water to make coffee or tea."

I nodded. "Thanks, I'll join you in a moment, then."

When I returned and sat on the other end of the couch, he glanced toward me. "You aren't going to ask me how your team is doing?"

"If there had been any significant change one way or the other, you would have forgone breakfast in favor of charging into my room unannounced while I was half-dressed. Again." I shot him an amused smirk when he scoffed.

"The investigation seems to be going more quickly than expected, but hasn't produced any useful information," he added, and I shot him another glance. For someone who looked so tired, he sure was being talkative. "I have my suspicions regarding who is responsible for the attacks, but even if I'm right, we can't act. I propose we focus our attention on the Resonance Project for now. There are plenty of things you and I can test. Plus, there are the survivors who show no signs of cellular dissonance. They require taming and training."

"*Zafir.*"

He frowned. "Yes?"

"Are you okay? You're rambling *before* you've had your morning coffee." I pointed at his thermos.

"The silence is difficult for me to cope with." He sighed reluctantly. "I had grown used to everyone as background noise, perhaps."

"Then play music or ambient sounds while you work?" I suggested. "Don't get me wrong—I'm happy to chat. But I can't tag along every waking moment. And even if I did, I shouldn't distract you from your work."

He hesitated before speaking again. "There are a few other matters bothering me. The R'selkti queen remains in orbit, and there have been no more reports of break-ins at any military installations despite our knowledge that there are rogue Syldrari searching for something. And, on a related note, the brass have started suggesting that we should have you seduce your contacts for information. They're convinced you could use your body against the Syldrari in the same way you could against a human."

I tried to parse the onslaught of *what the fuck*. "Let me get this straight. The people who have been like, 'Oh no! Don't let

Subject Zero fuck anyone or anything' want me to…"

"I disagreed, of course, and explained that Syldrari are above such behavior."

"…Oh, really?" I peered at him.

Zafir let out an amused chuckle. "Yes, *really*. Syldrari are higher creatures. They would know precisely what you were doing before you even tried."

"That has implications I rather dislike." I grimaced. If Syldrari could so easily know someone was trying to seduce them, just how much of my intentions could they read the rest of the time? Had Rel already caught on to my frequently drifting thoughts?

Zafir gave me a mysterious smile before continuing his non-answer. "Yes, well, given that Syldrari emotions are such an open book, they learned effective methods for reading other species. As it is exceedingly difficult for Syldrari to lie to each other…"

"Right. So, they've found a way to accurately read other species. That, combined with a cultural—I'd imagine—disapproval of lying is why it's always better for me to be bluntly honest when dealing with them." I gave him an unamused look as he finally picked up his fork and knife.

"Indeed. Their ability to determine your…*innocence*, I'll call it, is likely why they've taken to you," he mused, before taking on a more serious demeanor. "We should discuss matters closer to home. Are you still eager to get back to your patrols?"

"Well, yes. I think we proved my extended absence hasn't gone unnoticed." I picked up my fork and stabbed at a piece of omelet. "I'd say waiting too much longer will make the military ties too obvious—or maybe the public will start thinking the government captured us."

"Yes, I agree," Zafir murmured. "You said Rel appeared quite distressed over your disappearance?"

"Yes. Even Aldiner was worried. Ciheri was too, though he was a little more focused on keeping the rave fish in check," I answered dryly, startling a snort of laughter out of Zafir.

"Rave fish?" a puzzled voice questioned. I turned in my chair to see General Crowe coming toward us. Before I could even pretend to be formal, he held up a hand. "At ease."

"One of her Syldrari acquaintances is rather like a party light, sir. They've been known to both consciously and subconsciously change their glow along to music if they're listening to any," Zafir offered, quickly composing himself. "I imagine he's been listening to Syldrari music via an implant most of the times she's seen him. Thus, the nickname."

A lopsided smile twitched at Crowe's mouth as he glanced at me. "Good to see you've managed to keep a sense of humor. I'm not sure I'd be able to maintain niceties with the Syldrari if I were in your situation."

"Well, sir, I believe it's important to recognize specifically *who* is responsible for such devastation. Blaming their species as a whole would make me an animal incapable of critical thinking skills," I answered as I proceeded to cut up my breakfast. Zafir turned a little pale, but I ignored his warning expression. "From what I understand, there are humans off-world who have done horrible things to the Empire as well—yet clearly we know not to blame the entirety of our own species.

"There's much we can learn from other species if we make them our allies. And given the reactions I've seen to the R'selkti queen's statements, I imagine there are Syldrari who would be willing to work with us. There's nothing that says we *have* to be at odds with other species, and we'd only grow stronger with good connections and alliances."

Crowe scratched his chin. "I've been digging. The R'selkti who caused the Resonance Incident are no more—a son killed the guilty father and had the weapon destroyed. The R'selkti queen has essentially disowned her late husband and the son who put a stop to him. We can't agree who to trust—though this 'queen' personally makes me sick. Can't imagine treating my kids the way she treats hers. Of course, in the grand scheme of our discussions, I have to keep personal feelings out of my arguments if I'm to make an impression on my peers."

"A good example of how centuries of social and cultural manipulation can be harmful," Zafir offered, leaning back in his seat. "Ah, but we shouldn't keep you with hypotheticals and debates. I'm sure you sought us out for a purpose?"

"Yes, we have had an odd development." Crowe nodded,

glancing back and forth from Zafir to me. "The brass voted to find a Syldrari opponent for Elara to train against. They're not happy with her results against human targets and machines. We can tell she's having to hold back, which means she's not making progress—which in turn is going to mean the others aren't making progress. If she's going to train the other teams, she needs to get better and more powerful."

"Finding someone to cooperate…" Zafir hesitated.

"Which is why they're pinning the task on her. They want her to prove her connections are real." Crowe rubbed his temples. "There are classified missions we want to send her on, but not until we've determined her current strength against an actual Syldrari."

"And where, exactly, am I supposed to spar with a Syldrari? The only real choices are here or outside the city." I sighed irritably, looking over at Crowe.

"My recommendation is you ask one of the three Syldrari who already know you live in this building. I know they're smart—they'll have realized this is a military installation." He shrugged and offered me a small box. "I've prepared a badge for you to give to whichever one agrees to be your training partner. It'll identify them as volunteer staff. Everyone working in this building has been advised to treat them as a member of the team—within reason, anyway. Conversations are to be held carefully."

I took the box, then gave him a hopeful look. "Uh, does this mean I'm finally allowed to go outside?"

"Indeed. Your patrols won't be resuming just yet, but you are free to go outside when you aren't on duty inside. My investigations have concluded, and now I'm on to the next phase. There's a note in there for whoever you pick as your sparring partner." Crowe turned away, looking mighty pleased with himself. "Zafir, instruct your people to continue scanning all food before consumption until we've caught the culprit. If you need more scanners, I'll pay for them. Invoice me."

"Yes, sir," Zafir murmured, nodding. "Regarding Elara's patrols, it would be wise to permit her to patrol as Lethe, at least. The public..."

"We'll be discussing the Lethe project at one of our next meetings. For now, no patrols." Crowe shook his head and began walking away, giving us a brief wave. "Call me if you need anything else, Zafir."

Once the general was gone, Zafir sighed irritably and sunk deeper into his seat.

I raised an eyebrow at him. "Going to pretend this wasn't part of your machinations?"

"*Here,* though? Why, I was trying to arrange for your duels to be outside the city." He shot me a sideways look, an amused smirk spreading across his lips as he studied me. "Which you don't believe in the slightest. I must admit, even I am surprised they agreed."

"Oh yes, your master plan is coming together famously, I'm sure." I rolled my eyes and took a large bite of my food. *Honestly. Bringing a Syldrari here? Will anyone even agree to that? Hell, who am I even supposed to ask?*

"I have some suggestions…" Zafir offered thoughtfully.

I peered at him in suspicion. "Are you telepathic?"

"Perhaps. Why?"

I narrowed my eyes further. "That wasn't convincing. You interrupted my internal monologue a little too perfectly for it to *not* be a direct response."

"A coincidence, I assure you. Humanity has made a great deal of progress, certainly, but we still haven't developed a method for telepathic abilities. The closest would be sending messages via implant—which, of course, requires that both parties make a conscious effort."

Rubbing my temples, I muttered, "*Fine*. Have it your way. What are your suggestions?"

"I'd recommend Rel for the task. The other two wouldn't have enough experience or self-control—they would either play too rough or too soft. Rel, I believe, will be more adaptive." He took a swig of his coffee before continuing. "Of course, he may want some manner of payment or exchange. I'll have to see if Crowe sent me the full briefing for what is and isn't acceptable."

"And you think he'll accept?" I raised an eyebrow.

Zafir smirked. "I think he will leap at the chance to make

certain your home environment is safe and comfortable."

"Uh huh…" I sighed and shot Zafir an unamused look. "When am I going? I need to stock up on ludrán, anyway."

"This afternoon, assuming it doesn't take me all day to read Crowe's briefing. I'll make a list of things I need you to pick up for me as well."

CHAPTER TWENTY-NINE

I grimaced at my reflection and fidgeted with my clothes, attempting to like them. Something about most human clothes just didn't seem right anymore after the outfits Xilen had put me in. Aside from my uniforms, all I really had were a few sets of pants, plus a couple pairs of shorts and leggings. My shirts were all tank tops or sweaters. It was too hot for sweaters, so I'd opted for a black tank top and shorts set, with a light jacket over it to hide the blue mark on my back.

While my outfit made sense, it irked me somehow. It was like the annoyance I felt if I put my right foot into a left shoe. Except for my whole body.

But I'm not getting anywhere like this, and it's already getting dark. I sighed heavily, giving myself one last glance in the mirror. *Does everything look and feel so wrong because...it is? If I'm actually*

Syldrari…

In all honesty, I wasn't fully sold on the idea. Not because it didn't make sense—it made too much goddamn sense, let's be real—but because I didn't like the questions that needed answering if I really was. Was I female? Statistically, it was unlikely. If I was female, was I a queen? Again, statistically unlikely, yet the way my acquaintances reacted to me made me wonder. Why was I on this planet? Had I been sold like Ciheri? Had my family been in hiding for some reason? Was I the only member of my family affected by the Resonance Incident after all?

There were dozens more questions I wanted answers to if I was indeed a Syldrari, and I had a feeling my acquaintances couldn't answer even a quarter of them. They were just as perplexed by my existence as I was.

"You look uncomfortable. Should we postpone your errands?" Zafir asked when I strode into the common area.

"Overactive brain and I don't like my clothes," I answered shortly. "I'm going. You have a list for me?"

Zafir frowned slightly as he stood, a sheet of paper in his hand. "I do. But what is wrong with your clothes?"

"Don't get me started. Let's just say I may find myself pestering Xilen for options. These just don't feel right." I sighed heavily. He'd gotten me started. I shook my head hard. "Never mind that. Give me your list before I decide to complain your ear off about things that don't matter in the grand scheme of things."

"If you need to vent, I will listen. Perhaps we can find an alternative…?" he offered, trailing off when I shook my head again.

He looked mildly hurt by my refusal, so I quickly added, "If I'm still stewing on it after my errands, sure. It's already getting dark, though, and I'd rather not find myself in a position where I need to change into Lethe while out and about. So for now, I'll leave it at human clothes feel wrong."

"You're sure?" he asked worriedly, and I nodded. "Very well, then, I won't keep you. Though you're off duty, be careful, please. And if you run into any trouble, call me. I can send a team and—"

"I'll be fine." I patted his arm as I walked by. "Assuming certain antagonistic… Hmmm, I need a nickname for him."

"Don't encourage him," Zafir muttered dryly. "I'll see you when you get back. There are some reports I'd like to show you."

"Mhm, sure." I nodded, disappearing into the elevator. *Such a worrier… I can't decide if it's infuriating or endearing.*

My communicator beeped a few seconds later, and I sighed and lifted it to my ear.

<One more thing, I almost forgot.> Zafir's voice came immediately. <Could you possibly bring food for me and your team?>

"For the team, too?" I murmured. "Aren't they still…"

<No. I just received a message that they've woken up and are undergoing additional tests to determine whether they are ready to

be let out of isolation,> he answered. In the background, I could hear him tapping away at his data pad. <There is something I would like to check—and I also have a craving for… Ah, I'll forward you a list to show Rel.>

"And I'm supposed to carry all of this how?" I placed a hand on my hip, my eyes flicking up to check how long it'd be until I reached the ground floor.

<Assuming Rel agrees to assist with your training, why don't you ask him to help you? It would do your team well to meet him,> he answered, and I pressed my fingers to my temples. <Trust me. He will be delighted to foist his food on more humans, and I doubt he will say no to you. After all, you have something Xilen does not.>

"Which is?" I asked dryly, wondering why he was now comparing me to Rel's childhood friend.

<You have a genuine respect for *lun'iri*.> Zafir's tone had me glancing sideways at the communicator. <Xilen rescues people from falling to cruel queens, that is true, but that she sees *lun'iri* as something to rescue is a problem itself.>

"I don't think that's a sign of her not respecting *lun'iri*, it just may be a different type of respect. It's colored by the lens of Syldrari cultural and societal norms, as well as a better grasp of what other queens are like.

"*I*, however, am just working with the information I have. Besides, Syldrari can take care of themselves. They don't need me *or* Xilen to babysit them—but if they're already in a stupendous amount of trouble, Xilen is more likely to be in a position to help them than I am. Now, I'm about to reach the ground floor. Anything else?"

Zafir chuckled. <Don't sell yourself short. You are very different from other *iri*—delightfully so—and it will draw *lun'iri* to you whether you like it or not. It's what you do with your ability that will define how you continue to be received. For example, let's say Rel attempts to kiss you—how would you stop him?>

"Uh, by saying I'm not ready for that yet...?" I frowned. It sounded like a stupid question, but Zafir's questions usually weren't stupid. *Where is he going with this, and when is he going to be comfortable having these conversations face-to-face instead of behind the safety of the comms?*

Another amused laugh, this time to the tune of 'I knew I was right.' <Elara, a reluctant queen would ask if he made a move because her power made him lose himself. Someone like Xilen would take the move at face value. The cruel queens would be the initiators, then likely make him feel like he was a bad person for anything happening.

<Then there's you. Your suggested reaction shows that you'd respect both his feelings and your own, without taking into account your draw—as it should be. We aren't slaves to an *iri* or queen's natural draw—but we can be. It's that risk that makes people like Jysel so defensive and antagonistic around you.>

"I see…" I murmured. The elevator shuddered to a stop, its doors sliding open. "Have to go. I'll keep what you said in mind—and don't forget to send me a list of the food you want."

<Erik should be waiting for you with civilian-style transport out front,> he offered. <I will go brief the building's staff. It wouldn't do for them to mistake Rel for Jysel.>

With that, he hung up, so I pocketed my communicator and headed for the front door. Spotting Erik, I gave him a little wave as I approached.

"I'll take you to the edge of the Syldrari sector and wait for you there, ma'am," he offered, holding the door open for me.

"Oh? You won't be joining me?" I asked, sliding into the back seat.

"Afraid not. I've been ordered to stay put." He closed the door, then hopped into the driver's seat. "Probably for the best. If they're as taken with you as I hear, I don't think they'd take kindly to you having a military escort when off duty. We'll be near my stomping grounds, so take your time. Just give me a call when you're on your way back to the car."

"Sure, that works for me if it works for you." I nodded and began to poke around as I examined the interior of the supposed civilian vehicle. It was a lot comfier than anything I'd ridden in thus far, with no sway, jitter, or bumpiness to its glide.

"First time in civ transport?" Erik asked amusedly, and I nodded. "They're built with everything they need to—

hopefully—keep people's kids placated during long trips. Got TV and games in the back, and there's a small fridge built in for snacks and drinks.

"Why we don't incorporate some of this stuff for military vehicles, I'll never understand. Get a group of soldiers stuck in the back of transport craft for a few hours and you'll *wish* you were haulin' kids instead."

It occurred to me that the closest thing to interacting with kids I'd done was walk past them at the mall attached to HQ. "So, no reading materials or anything to at least keep you occupied during transport?"

"Nope! We're expected to be alert in case of enemy attack. No distractions allowed." He snorted. "Here we are, ma'am. Know where you're going from this side?"

"Hmmm…" I peered around, looking for landmarks. "Yep. It'll take me a little longer than usual to get to my destination from this side, but that's fine. I haven't gotten a good look at the shops over on this side of the sector yet."

"Good. I'll park here, then." Erik turned the vehicle off and got out, then helped me to my feet as he motioned toward a set of buildings across the gap between the sectors. "I'll be doing some shopping of my own over there. You gonna be long enough that I should grab dinner, too?"

"Yeah, Zafir made my list longer, so I'll be a while—plus I'm picking up way too much food from Rel's." I nodded. "Oh, and in case Zafir forgot to mention it, we may be bringing Rel back with us. At the very least, he'll probably be helping me carry things. He's Jysel's twin brother. So—"

"Twin?" He shook his head. "Right. No shooting on sight. Got it. See you in a while."

We parted ways, and I strolled through the Syldrari sector at a leisurely pace. Since I was off duty, I decided to pay more attention to what manner of goods were being sold, both by the street vendors and in the stores themselves. There were things I'd expected, like street food vendors and drink stands, but what set the Syldrari's shops apart from the other sectors, in my opinion, was how many were selling things like art, books, instruments, and music. Those were much more common than shops with clothing or jewelry, though there was a healthy amount of that, too.

Perhaps one of the most amusing things I saw was a vendor selling actual human textbooks as a novelty item. I had a feeling the notion wasn't exactly inaccurate, but that some people might get a little upset about it. There were even a few Syldrari kids eyeing up the displays, with the same excitement I'd have expected from children looking for novels or comics.

"You must be that girl I've been hearing about from Rel and Xilen," an unfamiliar voice called. I glanced over to see a male Syldrari with soft pink skin and white hair waving to me. "I don't think I've seen you on this side of town before. My name is

Lynir."

"Am I that obvious?" I laughed, walking over to his storefront. "Name's Elara. Nice to meet you, Lynir."

"There aren't many humans around here." Lynir motioned around us, giving me a warm smile. "Xilen said something about you being an excellent model for Syldrari hybrid fashions. She's a frequent client of mine, and showed me some shots of you in my designs."

"Oh, those were your work?" I remarked curiously, taking a second glance around his shop. Sure enough, there were some similar pieces displayed in the windows.

"That they are! Care to take a look?" he offered, stepping aside. "Xilen already informed me of your little quirk that requires privacy. I can either take your measurements for custom pieces, or I can find you something ready-made. Perhaps both if you like my work enough."

"Maybe just a quick look. The sooner I can replace these damned human clothes, the better, honestly. They itch!" I relented happily and walked into a sea of vibrant colors and high-contrast pieces. There was even an entire wall dedicated to perfumes, though I couldn't for the life of me determine where the women's and men's sections were. *Maybe their clothing is more unisex than I realized?*

"Now then, what colors do you like?" Lynir walked a circle around me, then stopped and waved his hand in the direction of a display of colorful outfits with sheer cutouts.

"The only colors I don't like to wear are yellow and orange," I answered. "Though I have a feeling that may mean something different to Syldrari eyes. How about we look at it from this angle—what can I wear that won't offend any Syldrari *or* piss off my bosses?"

"Ah yes, the delicate balancing act of self-expression under an oppressive gaze…" Lynir pivoted gracefully and eyed the selection. "Perhaps we should peruse my military-inspired designs? Items with which you can express yourself subtly, maintain freedom of movement…yes, yes…"

He began murmuring to himself in Syldran as he sorted through various sets of displayed clothes, gravitating toward a pair of leggings with a subtle sheen. They looked almost like leather, but the way they moved when he stretched and folded them appeared closer to cloth.

He picked out nearly a dozen shirts—some colorful, others more subdued—and then set aside a few jackets and coats in a vaguely military style. Many of them had the flowy half-cape thing I'd noticed on the outfit Xilen had given me.

Finally, he set aside boots of varying lengths. With nearly fifteen separate outfits set aside, he glanced over at me. "Ah, before I get carried away—perhaps we can try some more traditional Syldrari attire as well? For more casual wear?"

"I can only afford so much," I remarked dryly, spotting a mind-numbingly high number on the price tag. "Let's see what fits, first?"

"Ah, worry not. Xilen insisted that, should I meet you, I outfit you fully and invoice her with the bill. I'm always more than happy to foist my prices on my sister." Lynir waved a hand dismissively as he made his way over to some more flowy, colorful attire. "I haven't heard her complain about 'human clothes' and a 'lack of wardrobe' so much in decades. Trust me—she will not take no for an answer. If you desire any control over what you will be wearing…"

Xilen was his sister? The poor bastard. If she teased her friends and acquaintances so much, I could only imagine how bad her siblings must have it.

I followed him over to a few of the more interesting pieces, nodding. "…I should cooperate and pick it out myself. I get it. Okay… Are there any styles or colors I should be wary of, so I don't offend anyone?"

"No, any taboo colors won't have made it into my designs," he answered with an amused smile. "You have free rein to pick whatever you please. Though I do hope you will allow me to design you some custom pieces as well. It would be excellent for business."

"Hmmm… I'm seeing a prevalence of spiral patterns." I picked up a black pendant with a brilliant multicolored spiral on it.

"Ah yes, I believe humans refer to it as a logarithmic spiral." Lynir nodded. "I take much of my inspiration from patterns and shapes occurring in nature—especially those found deeper than humans can venture. I'm also quite fond of asymmetry. Here we are—casual wear."

"I see Syldrari have better taste than humans in all categories," I remarked dryly. By human standards, even the casual clothing was formal. Syldrari clothes were generally just less shoddy, and by a significant margin. "How about a few dresses and some things I can exercise in?"

"Excellent choice!" He nodded, snatching several short dresses and a few long ones off the racks, then motioned me over to a section with pants and shorts of varying lengths. "Our exercise attire is made of the same material as our under-armor. You'll find the pieces there. I'd recommend grabbing a few sets so you won't get bored. From what I understand, you will be training frequently."

As he carried off an array of dresses to the pile of outfits he'd already picked out, I began going through the selection of clothing. After picking out a broad variety, I moved on to shirts. Exercise clothing, at least, was all similar enough for me to know what I liked. Though I tried to challenge myself to at least pick out things that weren't simply black, white, and beige.

"Now then, for shoes," he murmured as I approached with my cargo.

"Question—how am I going to carry everything?" I peered at him over the mountain of fabric in my arms.

"Ah, you don't have a wardrobe module? I will fix that as well, then," he remarked, motioning toward the back wall.

"Look through the jewelry back there and pick something you'd be able to wear at all times. I'll find shoes to go with your outfits."

Wardrobe module? I wondered absently, heading over to the jewelry display. As I did, though, the scent of one of the perfumes caught my attention and I wandered over to it instead. The bottle was made out of a dark, multicolored material that looked like abalone.

I held up the sample to my nose and gave it a tentative sniff. The fragrances weren't anything I had a name for, but the perfume smelled…sexy and powerful, was the best I could describe it. I glanced at the price tag and cringed internally, then picked up a sealed box and skimmed the back of it while I made my way over to the jewelry wall.

Each piece appeared to be unique, and made of a metal I couldn't quite determine the color of. It was like it was different each time I looked at it. There was an empty slot for a gem in each one, and a sign nearby in Syldran that I couldn't read. Rings were out since I used hand-to-hand combat. I didn't need to break a finger. Necklaces were also out since someone could try to choke me with one. Earrings were a no as well… My gaze drifted to the bracelets and armbands. A bracelet seemed a little risky…but I figured I could make do with an armband.

The prettiest ones had intricate pieces of metal and jewels hanging off them, but I knew that wouldn't be practical. Instead, I needed to go with something simple—a solid metal band. After a moment, I spotted one that was solid but not plain. A scene of abstract and geometric imagery was engraved deeply into the band the whole way around, giving it visual interest without too many moving bits. The geometric half met the abstract half and twisted around the jewel setting.

I picked up that one, then returned to Lynir with the armlet and perfume in hand. He smiled cheerfully when he spotted the latter.

"Ah, I was hoping something might catch your attention. That's an excellent choice." He took the box and set it on the counter, then accepted the armlet and examined it. "Now then, let's see…what manner of jewel shall we set in this? Follow me."

I'm starting to feel spoiled… I kept the thought to myself and followed the happy pink Syldrari over to another counter, from which he pulled out a hefty book.

"Now then, which colors would suit you best…" He flipped the book open to a page of multicolored gemstones as if he knew precisely where to open the book. "How about a more intriguing jewel to match your complexity? I wouldn't dream of assigning you some boring, one-dimensional gem."

I raised an eyebrow at that comment, decided to write it off as a Syldrari compliment, and studied the pages of the book. I immediately pointed to a gem that appeared to be black, blue, pale green, and deep purple all at once. "How about this one?"

"I'm glad to see you are an *iri* of excellent taste!" Lynir exclaimed excitedly. "I will set the jewel and return momentarily. Please, look around and see if there's anything else you would like."

He went off to a back room with so much excitement bubbling from him that I had to assume he was being genuine and not simply a good businessman. I didn't have much reason *not* to look around, so I did as he suggested.

Off in a back corner, I found a formfitting dress in an iridescent leather-like material. It had a high collar and long sleeves and went down to mid-thigh. The back was cutout with a sheer black material. Curving cutouts through the bodice and skirt were filled with the same sheer fabric, and it was paired with matching leggings and black ankle boots.

I already have a lot, but… I hesitated, then plucked the set from the rack and made my way back to the massive pile of garments. *Well, if Xilen's buying…and besides, I have what, three shirts that aren't part of my uniform?*

"Now then, should I assume you don't know what a wardrobe module is?" Lynir inquired, returning with a luxe-looking box. As he neared me, he opened it to reveal the completed armband. I had a feeling I didn't want to know what a jewel of that size cost.

I nodded. "Yeah. I have no idea what that is."

"How to explain it in human terms…" he murmured, before perking up. "Ah! It is a psylinked module connected to a virtual storage space for your attire. It can be programmed externally or internally with different outfits, and you can swap between them and what you are wearing at will.

"One of my services is predefining and programming your styling, as well as setting up your virtual space for you. This way, your clothing is with you wherever you go."

That sounds similar to my battle suit... I peered curiously at the armlet. "All I need to do is wear it?"

"Yes, the necessary components are all internal to the jewelry and the crystal itself will calibrate to you specifically once I run the program," Lynir answered with a pleasant smile and a nod. "Here, put it on and I'll run the setup from my computer. After, I'll tally everything up and invoice Xilen, and you can be on your way. I'm sure you have plenty more business to see to tonight."

"Yeah, thanks." I returned his smile and shrugged my jacket off on the side where my skin was unmarked so I could put on the armlet. "Does any skin show when I change between outfits?"

"Not at all. I believe that is one of the reasons Xilen planned to suggest you come to me," he answered with a low laugh. He tapped at his computer with one hand and tossed a small orb toward my mountain of clothes with the other. He turned a screen away from me as the orb scanned the tags on each of the clothing items, shooting me an amused look when he caught my expression. Instead, he motioned toward my arm. "You'll want to change now, I take it? Something about human clothes and their infernal itchiness?"

I nodded. "Yeah, I think I'd be a lot comfier if I changed."

"Good, that will be an excellent way to show you how this works." Lynir rose to his feet and held a different orb over the clothes. In an instant, the tags were all gone and a third, triangular device appeared in his palm. Suddenly, the clothes all burst into particles of prismatic light and flew into the gem on my armband.

He gave me a cheerful look. "I would explain the details of how it works, but I'm afraid we would be here all night and then some, as there are some Syldrari fields of study that you would first need a basic understanding of."

He strode over to me and placed the device into my hand, smiling. "This will scan any Syldrari-made clothing you acquire and store it in your virtual space. It will also stay in that same space until you require it. Try visualizing a closet—you should feel something akin to connecting to the internet in the back of your mind. Once you're successful, you should 'see' your outfit options in your mind's eye—as well as a storage slot for your scanner."

I did as he asked, and within seconds I felt the mental *click* he'd mentioned. In an instant, I knew every item stored there and the dozens of combinations Lynir had programmed for my convenience. After a moment, I picked out a bodysuit with geometric cutouts and the cropped jacket he'd paired with it. For shoes, it had high-heeled boots that fused with the leggings to create one long, sleek piece.

"Excellent, that was quick. You should have no issue." He

opened the perfume I'd chosen, offering it to me with a playful smile. "Do be careful—our perfumes are strong. Dab a tiny amount on up to two pulse points—it will last for hours. And I'm sure the scent you selected will be a *hit*."

I decided to ignore whatever he was insinuating and dabbed a tiny bit on my throat, and another on my wrist. Then Lynir instructed me on how to store my things—which led not only to me storing the perfume in the wardrobe module, but getting yet another entire outfit.

It struck me as a little strange how easily the process came to me. It was like sorting files or browsing the internet, but with a link to the physical realm. Not only that, it was more intuitive than any human programs I'd used at HQ.

"Wonderful! I do hope you will drop by again soon. Next time you are in the area, I should have some custom pieces for you to try!" Lynir remarked cheerfully. "And please, if anyone asks where you got such lovely clothing, tell them you acquired them at Therys-shyerr. I would adore more interesting customers."

"Of course." I smiled at him. "Thanks for everything—including your patience. If you speak to Xilen before I do, please relay my thanks to her as well."

I left the cheerful man's store and made my way through the Syldrari sector, this time at a slightly quicker pace. I'd lost a good chunk of time in Lynir's shop and still had a lot to get done. I was glad I didn't have to find a way to carry so many clothes, though. I kind of wanted to ask Xilen why she'd made such an arrangement.

Was my clothing before really so bad? Oh, who am I kidding. It was.

I decided to pick up everything on Zafir's list first, as none of it was perishable. By the time I made it to Ceyoh's candy stall, I was already draped in way too many damn bags—but I was going to get my candy, damn it.

"Elara! I was worried about you!" Ceyoh exclaimed when she spotted me. Then she seemed to notice just how much I was carrying, and looked off somewhere beyond my field of vision. "Oh my. Ciheri? Ciheri, are you still here? Elara could use some help."

The pale Syldrari peeked around a corner, immediately spotting me—and my outfit. He flushed a little blue as his glow turned a brief pale pink, but he quickly composed himself and joined us. "Wow, why are you carrying all that by yourself?"

"Because I'm here by myself?" I countered. Then it occurred to me that maybe even that was odd to Syldrari. Instead of commenting, I looked over at Ceyoh. "I think Rel put in an order for the ludrán I wanted, right?"

"Sure, but how are you going to carry…" She sighed, pressing her fingers to her temples. "Where are you going next?"

"Rel's café. I'm supposed to pick up dinner for a good, oh…seven? Eight? Nine? People." I shrugged and gave her a sheepish smile. "My escort is at the sector border; I figure I may end up taking a few trips depending on how Rel responds to my other business with him."

"Other business?" Ciheri peered at me, then held out a hand. "Give me some of your bags. I can help you carry them to Rel's, at least. Watching you teeter around in those shoes while carrying so much is giving me anxiety."

I blinked at him. "Are you sure?" My question seemed to take him aback. "If you want to help, I'll welcome it, but if you have other things to do—"

He pouted and wiggled his fingers. "*Give.*"

"And I'll bring your ludrán to Rel's after I close up shop in half an hour." Ceyoh patted my shoulder and smiled. "If he has to cook for that many people, it'll be a while before you can leave."

I gave her a half-smile. She had a point. "Thanks, both of you. See you in a bit then, Ceyoh. Shall we, Ciheri? Which bags would you like to carry?"

Ciheri promptly took all the bags from my left arm, so I redistributed the ones from my right to balance out my load. With that accomplished, we strolled off in the direction of Rel's café.

We walked in silence for a little bit, before Ciheri seemed to grow uncomfortable. He glanced at me hesitantly. "How…are your teammates doing?"

"Better, though I'm not sure I can talk about it here," I offered, glancing over at him. He looked a little nervous in my presence, though nowhere near as skittish as I'd seen him on other occasions. Though his skittishness had made him seem particularly young, he looked to easily be in the same age bracket as Aldiner or Rel. "How are you settling into your new home? You're staying in one of the apartments above Rel's café now, right?"

"Yes! And he isn't charging me rent, either. Instead, I just help out in the café. He's been very patient in teaching me how he likes things to be done." He latched onto the topic eagerly, giving me a bright smile. "Unlike the others, he doesn't pry unnecessarily. He's letting me find my own way and giving me support if I need it. Working at a café is quite different from what I'm used to, but there aren't many research opportunities here for a Syldrari who wants to lay low."

Right, he'd mentioned something about being from a clan who loved research. In which case, I had to imagine he was trying to lay low for a reason. After a moment of consideration, I replied, "Do you have access to useful reading material, at least? If not, I know some human universities with research papers and books that are open to the public. They're probably eons behind Syldrari advancements, but you might learn something interesting due to differing perspectives."

Ciheri tilted his head as if he needed a moment to process what I'd said. After a moment, his gaze refocused and he smiled brightly. "I see, understanding the perspectives of non-Syldrari individuals could lead to further advancements and a better understanding of how to interact with them?"

"Who knows, maybe you'll learn something too," I suggested with an amused smile, which broadened into a grin when he gave me a perplexed puppy look. "You know as little as I do about the humans, if not less, right? Well, you now have the chance to learn about humans and their civilizations from their own tellings. Inaccurate as they may or may not be."

"Hmmm…" He murmured something to himself in Syldran, then glanced over at me questioningly. "I'm always interested in more reading material. Do you have any suggestions?"

"Well, that depends on what you want to read. Do you like mythology?" I waited for him to nod. "Then you might find the mythology from one of humanity's dead planets interesting. The planet was given back to nature, from what I understand, but Imperial researchers were able to recover data from what remained of the previous civilizations. Their tales of ancient deiform entities and the like are quite interesting."

"Ah! Would this be one of the primitive worlds ravaged by wars?" Ciheri inquired excitedly, and I nodded. He smiled brightly. "Excellent! I've been wanting to study human emotions and motivations in order to better understand why they are so violent. I'm sure texts from one of the more primitive worlds will be most enlightening."

Our conversation came to a halt as we arrived at Rel's and

Ciheri opened the door for me. I hadn't really been paying attention to passersby on the way, but the moment I stepped into the café all eyes turned to me. It was a little unsettling, as I'd grown used to going mostly unnoticed. But I *had* chosen an interesting outfit and perfume. I should have expected some kind of reaction—especially considering my absence the past few weeks.

"Elara...?" Rel stared at me for a second, then glanced at the customers directly in front of him at the bar as they began to argue with each other in Syldran—and I was quite sure I heard my name a few times during the exchange.

"Oh dear..." Ciheri murmured, leaning over to whisper in my ear. "The one on the left is trying to free up 'your' seat."

"Oooh. No need for that." I walked over to the counter and gave Rel a pleasant smile. "We need to speak privately, and I have a rather large list of things to order, so I won't be sitting at the bar today."

"You smell..." Rel shook his head faintly, then narrowed his eyes at the two arguing Syldrari. "You heard her. Knock it off or I will throw you both out. Now then... *Aldiner!*"

"I didn't do it!" Aldiner exclaimed, skidding out of the back room. Then he noticed me, and his expression spread into a mischievous grin. "Oh-ho, Her Tastiness is back."

"If you start calling me that, I'm going to drop you from the capitol building and see how high you bounce." I pressed my fingers to my temples. "Honestly..."

"Oh, *please* try," Aldiner purred, leaning forward. "I'd be happy to give you any kind of romp you—"

"**Behave**." Rel, much to my surprise, shimmered briefly with cyan energy and sent Aldiner flying backward into a wall. He looked at me with sharp eyes. "I'll show you to one of the private rooms. Ciheri, bring her things, then go help Aldiner serve the customers."

"Aw… I wanted to talk more about mythology with her…" Ciheri deflated a little, and Rel's expression softened.

"You can talk to her later. It sounds as though she has important business to discuss with me—and only me. Is that right, Elara?" He looked my way again and I nodded. Returning his attention to Ciheri, he motioned us both forward. "Come along, then…and preferably before my customers decide they agree with Aldiner's sentiments."

Once we were in a smaller room on the next floor up, Ciheri gently deposited my bags for me and I set down my load as well. Disappointed, he quietly took his leave as Rel closed and locked the door behind him. Suddenly, I noticed a faint ripple of pale energy arc across the room.

"What was that?" I wondered, and Rel stiffened.

After a moment, he turned and narrowed his eyes at me. "You…saw that?"

"I saw pale blue energy arc across the ceiling, yes," I answered, pointing to the ceiling. I leaned toward him slightly. "Ah, is this another of those, 'you're seeing things you shouldn't see, so please pretend you saw nothing,' moments?"

"This isn't the first time?" He sighed heavily and rubbed his temples. I shrugged and took a seat at the table, waiting for him to sit across from me—which he finally did after a few moments of hesitation. "What exactly are you wearing?"

"Well, Xilen was apparently so offended by my lack of a wardrobe that she arranged for the issue to be fixed," I answered dryly, resting my elbow on the table so I could prop my chin in my hand. "I get the feeling that the total came to a price I really don't want to think about, but Lynir seemed happy to pawn the bill off on his sister. I have a wardrobe module now, at least."

"…And you can use it?" he asked carefully.

"It's much more intuitive than any of the human programs I've interfaced with, yes," I answered with a faint nod.

Rel glanced at my bags, then back at me. "Yet a shopping trip isn't why you were finally let out of that place, is it?"

"Oh, I'm not under house arrest anymore." I smiled, enjoying watching him squirm and try to pretend that it hadn't caused *any* reaction. "My patrols won't be resuming any time soon, but I'm free to go wherever I please when I'm not on duty inside HQ. That said, you're right that this isn't simply a pleasure visit."

Rel attempted to give me an unamused look, but the quirk at the corner of his mouth gave him away. "Must you use that phrasing?"

"What phrasing?" I gave him a sweet smile and continued before he could answer. "My bosses have decided they want me to have a

Syldrari training partner, because I have to be too careful with our people and in-house equipment. You've been volunteered for the role because they figure you've already worked out that HQ is HQ. If you don't accept, they intend for me to seduce Aldiner or Ciheri into cooperating. They seem to not realize I never actually agreed to seduce people…but I figure it's safer to let them think whatever they want right now."

"And *why* would I ever agree to help train someone whose purpose was originally going to be *hunting* Syldrari?" Rel sighed and raised his hand over his eyes, rubbing his temples.

"That's what *I* want to know." I leaned forward a little further to procure a box from inside one of my bags. "There's a letter inside for you, apparently. And the badge is for if you decide you want to cooperate."

"What aren't you telling me?" he inquired dangerously. As he leaned forward, the air around us grew…tight, for lack of a better word. I had a feeling that, if I gave him an answer he didn't like, I might end up a bloodstain on the wall. But that was fine.

"I believe Zafir arranged all of this, much like how he arranged for HQ to be moved to a less-defensible location." My amusement returned when I noticed his attention starting to drift. "Don't like my outfit?"

"What—" His eyes snapped back up to meet mine, startled, before narrowing again. "You've selected rather a distracting perfume and garments. Were you any other *iri*, I would have to question your motives."

"For what it's worth, as fun as it is to get a reaction out of you, seducing you is the last thing I intend to do," I offered after a moment of consideration. "I would prefer to keep however much trust it is you have in me. Even if you sometimes infuriate me with your non-answers, just like all the others."

"You know it's for your own well-being." He gave me a firm look, picking up the letter and opening it. "However, I wouldn't mind if you tried to seduce me—or if we tried to seduce each other. To be blunt, it's the intention that matters—not the act of seduction itself. It can be quite flattering, you know, if done correctly."

He shot me a sultry, triumphant smirk over the sheet of paper when I said nothing, clearly satisfied that he'd surprised me into silence. To keep my mind off the rather inviting thing he'd just told me, I started rummaging around in my bags for the list of food I was supposed to order.

"Hmmm...this does present an opportunity..." he murmured after a few minutes, and I finally glanced his way. "It isn't every day a Syldrari is given a legitimate reason to go inside a human government or military facility. Plus, if your abilities are growing as quickly as these scans suggest, you *are* going to need Syldrari assistance, in order that you don't harm anyone or yourself."

"Mm?" I frowned at him in confusion and he held up one of the sheets of paper—which, unfortunately, was meaningless to me.

Realizing this, he explained, "Your abilities are either growing or breaking free from some manner of suppression. At your current rate, I'd give it a month before you begin uncontrollably discharging elemental energy. You are essentially an overcharged battery as you are now, and lightning is a dangerous element. However, I'm seeing traces of other abilities here, too…"

"Is that a problem?" I asked, and he gave me an incredulous look. "The other abilities, I mean!"

"It depends what they are. The readings are still unclear, but…let's say you were a full-fledged adult Syldrari before the Incident—which I'm certain you were—you would have more than one ability at your disposal." He motioned with his hand as he spoke. "The longer we live, the more we learn. It is quite rare for a Syldrari to have merely *one* ability. It happens, of course, and when it does that individual must specialize in an appropriate field. But that may be too complicated of a topic for tonight. I believe you said something about needing to order a great deal of food?"

"That's right." I held up the list for him and he stared at it, aghast.

"*Ten* meals? Ah—your teammates have woken?" He gave me a smile. "That's wonderful news. I'm sure you must be relieved."

"Relieved? Hmmm… I suppose I hadn't really thought about it. They woke up as I was on my way to the Syldrari sector," I answered, frowning faintly. With him saying that, it occurred to me that yes, I should have been relieved. And perhaps I was, but it was like I couldn't fully focus on that feeling. Something else was gnawing at the back of my mind.

"Besides, we still have to catch whoever is doing this. The new building should lull any attackers into a false sense of security, I suppose, but…"

"Elara," he interjected in a soothing tone, causing me to fall silent and look toward him. "Relax. You are off duty, remember? You're going to give yourself a headache and then some if you don't give yourself a break."

"I suppose you're right." I sighed, watching as he stood up. "What about their proposal, though?"

"I'll have an answer for you by the time you leave here tonight," he answered with a mysterious smile. He took my list and made his way to the door, then stopped, giving me a questioning look. "Be honest—do you find me attractive?"

Where's that *coming from?* I wondered, examining him from head to toe before meeting his gaze. He looked awfully confident despite having asked such a question. "Yes, quite."

"Interesting…" he murmured, then rubbed his chin, his lips pulling into an amused smile. "I'll bring you a drink while you wait for us to cook your food. I would appreciate it if you remained here."

"Sure…" I tilted my head, confused, and watched as he left the room, shutting the door behind him.

Hmm, just what did I get myself into? Should I be concerned, or excited? And why did he ask that question if he already knew the answer? Then there were his customers... Why were they ready to brawl...oh.

I grimaced as it hit me. Zafir had *told* me that Syldrari got competitive and violent over queens and usually didn't even realize it at first. If my suspicions were right—which I really hoped they weren't—then whatever latent draw I had was beginning to affect the Syldrari sector. Given how sharp Rel obviously was, I had to assume he was separating me from his customers to reduce the chances of them realizing what was going on. After all, if they reported me to the R'selkti queen...

I sighed. *Just shut up and go along with it. He knows better than I do how to deal with these people. Plus, I suppose a little alone time wouldn't hurt.*

CHAPTER THIRTY

It hadn't been long since Rel had left to fetch the drinks, yet my mind was already whirring. I had already decided I wouldn't try to seduce him into cooperating. If I *was* going to seduce him, it would be on my own terms—not the military's. My motivations would be objectively more fun, too.

Which left me with the issues at hand: How to convince Rel to agree to train me, determine what was going on with me, and figure out how many of my problems were related to the Syldrari. Oh, and figure out why he had asked if I found him attractive.

And why was my answer interesting, anyway? He clearly knows he's attractive, so what else did he expect? Or was the answer expected—and it's interesting for some other reason? That could be trouble.

There was a faint knock before he opened the door. His gaze went briefly hazy, but clarity returned almost instantly and he shot an amused smile in my direction. Hell, the drinks on the tray he was carrying didn't even waver.

"You chose quite the daring fragrance, didn't you?" He glided across the room and placed a glowing white-to-orange drink in front of me, giving me a sultry smile. His fingers lingered just long enough to glide ever-so-briefly up the glass. "Or did you get dragged deeper into Xilen's machinations?"

"My choices were my own. I've been trying to get better about establishing my likes and dislikes." I reached for the drink, but he caught my wrist, shaking his head faintly as his thumb pressed into the underside of my wrist.

"Let it sit. There's one more addition. They'll both taste better after soaking." Rel dropped three skewers of different, but pretty, shiny-glowing things into my drink. Then, he sat across from me again, studying me intently. "Do you understand why I asked you to stay here instead of joining us on the main floor?"

I nodded. "You're concerned that I may be a queen, and that whatever it is that queens do is starting to affect the residents of the Syldrari sector. If they believe I'm a queen—or somehow manage to confirm it—they could report me to the R'selkti queen. Which would be…problematic."

"You're still in denial that you're Syldrari?" He raised an eyebrow and nudged my drink toward me.

"Denial? Not exactly. It's more accurate to say that I don't like either the implications or how few answers are left if it is true." I reached forward and grabbed the ice-cold drink, pulling it toward me. "Alcoholic?"

"You did say you were off duty," he answered with an amused smile. "And I did say we would have a drink together. Now, you were saying?"

"Let's say I *am* a queen…" I grimaced at the thought. "Then I must ask why I was on this planet, if I was in hiding, if I had anyone with me, or if I'd even been discovered yet. Then there's the matter of the Incident itself. It caused clear issues with me and my team— but why? It seems likely that either Clan R'selkti targeted us specifically—or someone from the Imperial government did something to manipulate the situation. Then there's the issue of getting my answers. Anyone who *could* give me answers is either dead, suffering amnesia just like I am, or an enemy that I'm going to—"

Rel chuckled and leaned forward. "*Elara.*"

"What?" I pouted, taking a tentative sip of my drink.

"I am beginning to understand why Zafir wants you to just play along and question as little as possible," he remarked, an amused smile spreading across his lips. "If you start getting answers, you might kick-start your progress irreversibly and he's afraid of what will happen. Or maybe he's simply concerned that his carefully laid plans will be ruined. Hmm…"

"He's mentioned leaving the planet *with* me if I have to take Xilen up on her offer to evacuate me," I offered, earning a sharp look. "What?"

"If you reach such a point, it would be safer for you to be with me or Jysel. Xilen is intelligent and manipulative, certainly, but hers is a clan of *merchants*. They are not equipped to defend more than one queen." Rel spoke dangerously, his eyes narrowing. "In a clan such as hers, all resources are directed toward protecting her. With the V'shir and whatever Jysel decides to name his new clan, our resources are free for us to do as we please. I have the V'shir Elders, including myself, well-protected. The remainder are spread throughout the sector or taking on various tasks in others.

"Then, of course, there's Jysel, who mobilized his entire force based on the information you delivered. At the moment he's too busy sulking over our mother's behavior to recognize the degree of freedom he now possesses, but thankfully, the residents of his city-ship intend to remain with him instead of leaving."

"He seems a lot more spoiled than you," I remarked dryly, but Rel shook his head. "Oh? Are you saying *you're* the spoiled one?"

"Hardly. Neither of us were spoiled—we're *lun'iri*." Rel downed nearly half his drink before continuing. "I adapted at a much earlier age to our situation—he craved attention and recognition for much longer. In fact, he was at one point willing to be groomed into the perfect marriage candidate our mother wanted us both to be.

"I grasped my independence firmly, but he struggled with his. By now, I imagine he's made just about every mistake any attention-starved boy would. Thankfully, he began to grow up when our father took him under his wing and began training him with the fleet. Of course, you're aware of how that ended."

"And so the puppy found himself alone again," I remarked with a grimace. "I take it the reason people apparently find you more difficult to get along with is because he seeks out attention and you're fine without it?"

"It would be simpler to leave it at that, yes," he answered with a mysterious smile. "However, I will add that I typically reject attention because I dislike what I get. You, at least, are respectful and interesting. Of course, you have your infuriating moments, but I believe disciplining you would be entertaining enough to balance it."

"And it's normal to be this open about things?"

"Of course. It's difficult for us to hide our feelings." Rel motioned at his arm, which was glowing a light, almost white, pink. "I don't know how Zafir does what he does. Even knowing that withholding information from you is what's best for your health, it goes against every instinct and everything I've learned as a Syldrari. Quite frankly, it feels like a betrayal—especially when you are so understanding of why we are holding back."

"It's logical to keep information from me if it will do more harm than good," I pointed out flatly. "That doesn't mean I like it, by any stretch. It often pisses me off, but yes, I understand. I've simply decided to wring answers out of one of you as soon as I can safely do so. Now then—"

Rel blurred into a streak for a moment before suddenly appearing to my right on the bench. I gave him a questioning look as he casually took another sip of his drink, feeling one of his arms slip behind my shoulders.

"The least I can do is be a good confidant, even if I can't give you all the information you desire," he suggested in that cool, calming tone of his. "And, yes, I fully expect you to hold me to telling you all I know. Which, at the rate matters are currently progressing, may be sooner than you think. Of course, it depends on what Jysel finds at the end of this lead he's following, but..."

"But?" I prompted, shifting toward him, not at all bothered that I was pressed up against his side. I sighed, deciding to rephrase just in case. "Let me guess—it may or may not be related to me, thus the 'but.' You don't want to get my hopes up."

"Your draw doesn't affect me as strongly as it does the others," he informed me with an amused smile, bringing his fingers up under my chin. "But I appreciate your thoughtfulness."

He leaned down...but then stopped, a positively *devious* smile spreading across his face. "I should go check on your food."

And just like that, he stood and left the room. With him gone, I suddenly realized I was holding my breath and my pulse was racing. I growled in frustration, picking up my drink and taking a healthy swig of the sweet-sour alcohol.

That goddamn tease. He knew exactly what he was doing. Is this what I get for my behavior? Hmph. Next time I'll just pin him to a wall myself… Wait, no, I won't. Tempting, but no, I don't think I have the guts for that.

I tapped my nails against the table as I considered methods of revenge—methods that all slipped my mind entirely when Rel returned with a full pitcher of the same alcohol, plus a tray of snacks. He gave me an odd look when he spotted me.

"Your eyes…" he murmured as he set his cargo down. I moved to reach for a snack, but he turned me away from the table and toward him, grasping my face in both hands as he studied me.

"What?" I asked, a little disgruntled by the face-smooshing.

"Hmm…" He gently turned my face at an angle. "We may need to ask Zafir or Jysel how they manage to hide their eyes. Your pupils are visible at certain angles—though they're inactive."

"Inactive?" I asked begrudgingly.

"Yes, such as… Look at mine," he offered. When I complied, all his pupils aside from the central one closed down to barely perceptible specks. "I would wager that your link to your additional pupils and retinae hasn't mended yet. Even so, your human skin is slipping."

"Are you going to let go of my face now?" I gave him an unamused look, but he remained fascinated. "What now?"

"You're not at all perturbed by my proximity—meaning the humans failed to reprogram you," he mused curiously, then leaned closer, smirking. "Do you still want me to kiss you?"

I felt heat rush to my cheeks and he released a delighted laugh, his devious expression turning bright.

"My, what a pretty shade of blue you've turned," he remarked as he finally released my face. Picking up his drink, he returned to his seat across the table in one graceful movement.

"I think, instead of indulging you, I will keep my distance so you can stabilize before returning to HQ. It wouldn't do for you to be so visibly inhuman when you return. And, no, I will not get you a mirror. Pout all you like—it's quite endearing."

"Hmph. Just keep racking up that karma..." I grumbled, picking up one of the snacks—some kind of savory skewered stack of...something. Meat? I was pretty sure it was meat.

"Karma? Ah—that human construct. I do not believe in karma," he informed me cheerfully as he reclined, his drink in one hand and the other lazily unbuttoning the top few buttons of his shirt.

For the love of... I groaned internally, feeling a few excited twitches run through my body at the glimpse of his throat and chest. Irritated, I narrowed my eyes at him. "Neither do I. That doesn't mean I can't make my own karma."

He spread his arms to his sides in a welcoming motion and gave me a confident look. "You are most welcome to try."

I huffed and downed the rest of my drink, then reached for the pitcher and poured myself a new glass. "I take it Ciheri and Aldiner are in charge of cooking? They won't burn anything down?"

"Indeed. I decided you require more supervision." His gaze drifted down my torso, then back up to my face. "What else did you acquire? I doubt Xilen or any of her clothiers would have allowed you to stop at just one outfit—especially Lynir. He can be just as demanding as his sister."

"I'm not giving you a fashion show."

"Perhaps I simply want to know how difficult you've made it to undress you?" he countered, his eyes narrowing as he continued to study me. "Convenient as a wardrobe module may be, there's something irreplaceable about removing a partner's attire by hand in the heat of the moment."

Before I could formulate a response, there was a knock at the door and Ciheri poked his head in. "Um, everything's ready. Should I help Elara carry her things?"

"No, I'll be escorting her." Rel knocked back the rest of his drink and handed both the pitcher *and* my glass to Ciheri. "Prepare our drinks to go and add a few thermoses of non-alcoholic beverages to her order."

"You're going to escort me?" I raised an eyebrow suspiciously when he offered me a hand, but against my better judgement, I took it.

"I am not letting you walk around at night by yourself looking and smelling the way you do." He pulled me to my feet, a little closer than was strictly necessary, then leaned down with a warning look. His voice took on a melodic, soothing quality. "And as much as it pains me to say it—*calm down*. There's nothing I can do to hide your flushed complexion."

"Oh, wonderful, you have the aural equivalent of a cold shower." I sighed in agitation. "You spend all this time pushing my buttons just to—"

"Of course, we can't have you being discovered," he answered innocently. "And now I know just how dangerous it is to toy with you, entertaining as it may be. Of course, further testing will have to wait for a safer environment. Now, hand me your bags."

Begrudgingly, I did as he asked and followed him downstairs. The temptation to give him a sharp smack across the ass was high, but I wasn't confident I'd miss his swishing tail and I had a sneaking suspicion that it'd hurt like hell if I clipped it.

"...How are we going to carry all this?" I stared at the mountain of food and drink waiting for us. Beside it, a good three dozen jars of ludrán waited, but Ceyoh was nowhere to be found.

"Quite easily." Rel set my bags down and stepped behind the

bar, where he fetched a ring and slid it on. Cyan light immediately emitted from the ring and scanned the foodstuffs, much in the same way that my wardrobe module functioned. "Ah, and I believe I left something upstairs. One moment."

Right, the badge, I thought, still not exactly clear on whether or not he was cooperating. When he returned, he made a show of sliding the box into his pocket and strolled past me with an amused smile. I resisted the urge to stick my tongue out at him and instead asked, "Are we ready, then? I'll take some of the bags—"

"No, you won't." He lifted the bags in both hands and walked off. "You may, however, get the door."

I opened the door, hurrying after him when he glided through it. "But I should at least take some—"

"No."

"But—"

"I said *no.* Now, accept my help and join me or I will carry you, too."

"You stubborn..." I grumbled as I fell into step with him. "You're not a manservant."

"No, I'm not. I'm a gentleman who wants to make certain his lady friend will be quite alright when walking in heels after indulging in hard liquor."

"That was hard liquor?" I asked skeptically. That might explain the fuzziness I was feeling, but I was a little surprised it wasn't worse, if that had been *hard* liquor.

He laughed. "Well, it was a mixed drink that I'm considering adding to the menu. What do you think—should it make the cut?"

"I think it could use a few tweaks; currently the sweetness is overpowering the sour. Unless you intended it to be more sweet than sour?" I murmured thoughtfully. "Or perhaps the idea is that people will buy more and more, chasing the sour notes?"

"Oh dear, she's caught on to my secrets!" he remarked dramatically. Laughing, he shook his head. "No, I want it to be sweet. Perhaps I can concoct a more sour drink for you—something with *syezei?*"

"Which one is that, again?"

He shot me an amused smile. "I believe you described it as citrus-y. More than half your ludrán jars are *syezei* flavor."

"Ohhh, yes, that could be good. If you kept this drink's level of sweetness and then pumped up the…" I trailed off, giving him a questioning look when he slowed to a stop. "What is it?"

"Uh, where are we going?" he asked, giving me a sheepish smile.

"Oh! Right, this way, down past Therys-shyerr. And, I need to call my driver-guard-man-thing, too." I pulled out my communicator and navigated through a few menus.

<That you, Elara?> Erik asked over the sound of loud dance music in the background.

"Yeah, my guest and I are on the way to the car now. We'll

wait for you there, Erik."

<Have you been drinking? You sound different.> He sounded amused.

"A little," I answered. "See you at the car."

Rel eyed me, his expression unreadable. "You have a driver now? Or a guard?"

"Hmm? Oh, I don't think he's mine, but he's driven me a few times," I offered with a shrug, glancing down at the bags. "Are you sure I can't—"

"The more you ask, the longer I will wait to indulge any of your more entertaining desires," he informed me with a cheerful smile. "Now, what else can you tell me before we get to your HQ?"

"Oh…well, all I really know is that everyone has been briefed on who you are so there's no mix-ups. And they've been told to treat you as a member of the staff. Most conversations should proceed normally, though they're supposed to be mindful of certain topics."

"Interesting…" he murmured. "All this to make certain you receive training?"

Why does it sound so naughty when he says it? I peered at him, noting the faint smirk he shot me. Maybe that was why. "Apparently, if they're going to keep me on past retirement, I need to be…better. They would be keeping me around to train the new blood, but apparently my performance isn't satisfactory. I'm holding back too much against my sparring partners and the equipment so I don't break anything permanently."

"Break them, hmmm…" he murmured, smirking, and I decided I really didn't want to know what he was thinking. "I will have to inspect the training area. Do you know how much I'll have access to?"

"All the aboveground floors aside from the top few, plus the first four basement levels, I think," I answered after a moment. "Most of the building is housing and recreational areas for everyone involved in the project, plus their families. We have some training areas up by my floor, but it's more likely we'll be using the ones underground; they're sturdier."

"Elara!" Erik waved a hand when he spotted us approaching, keeping his rifle pointed at the ground with the other. Then his gaze flicked to Rel and he let out a low whistle. "Damn. I understand the briefing now. Most people involved in the project are too young to quickly identify Syldrari differences. Rel, I take it? Nice to meet you."

"Likewise." Rel nodded, accepting the handshake Erik offered him.

"You weren't wearing that earlier," Erik remarked, glancing back to me.

"It's a long story. Let's summarize by saying that Queen Xilen decided to have me lavished with new luxuries." I shook my head, then opened one of the vehicle doors. "Shall we?"

"I'll open the trunk," Erik offered to Rel, casting a glance at the bags. "Thanks for not letting her take the load."

"Oh, come on," I groaned.

"Her stubbornness is nothing against mine." Rel laughed as he set the bags in the trunk. "Now then, where will I…?"

"In back with Elara—you're a guest and all," Erik answered, making his way to the driver's door. "Oh—what about the food? Do we need to make another trip?"

"No, I brought a module with me for delivering food; it would have been far too much to carry otherwise. You would have needed to come directly to my café." Rel climbed into the back with me and closed the door, curling his tail between us. Then he apparently decided to get comfortable and just let his tail flop over my thigh. "Given the circumstances, I added a few more meals to the order. I think it will be quite enjoyable to see how Elara's team takes to Syldrari food."

What is he up to now? I eyed him as his tail coiled around my knee, calf, and ankle. There was something vaguely sexual about the motion, but his glow remained a steady cyan.

If he was looking for a reaction, I wasn't going to give him one. Instead, I leaned forward slightly to address Erik. "Sorry I took so long, Erik. I wasn't expecting to get pulled into so much shopping."

"Not a problem. I'm surprised Zafir didn't go momma bear on us, though." Erik laughed. "Did he call you?"

"No, surprisingly. He must be buried in work again." I shook my head, then glanced toward Rel when I felt energy climbing up my thigh from his tail. "*Yes, Rel?*"

"Your drink," he offered innocently, summoning a cup in his outstretched hand.

"…Thanks." I peered at him suspiciously as I took it.

When we arrived at HQ, most of the lights were out and the night guards were on duty, their uniforms and helmets glowing with Imperial colors. Much to my surprise, Rel didn't even garner a second glance as we entered the building and made our way to the elevator. Erik got off a few floors below us, saying something about having work to do before he could take Rel back to the Syldrari sector.

When we'd reached my floor and left the elevator, Rel paused and grabbed my arm to stop me, his glow swirling between silver and cyan. "This is your floor?"

"Yes, why?" I gave him a puzzled look.

"It's…different. The Resonance survivors and Zafir live here?" He frowned, looking a little unnerved.

"Yes. The wing down that way isn't complete, but that's where the team that isn't showing cellular dissonance will be living," I offered, giving him a worried look. "What is it?"

"…You are right to be so concerned about what the answers to your questions may be," he muttered. His gaze sharpened, his glow returning to its usual steady cyan hue. "Lead the way."

CHAPTER THIRTY-ONE

I led Rel through my team's floor and toward the common area in the middle, as I'd picked an elevator that exited into a different section of the floor. As we walked down the hallway containing the individual apartments, I glanced at my contemplative companion and the bags he carried—which reminded me of my precious ludrán.

"Here, let's stop at my room so you can drop off the ludrán," I suggested, pulling my keycard out.

As I opened the door, Rel grimaced. "This is quite…bare. I'm beginning to see what you meant by attempting to define your likes and dislikes. Where would you like your things?"

"Anywhere is fine, I can stash them later." I leaned back against the doorframe and watched as the Syldrari glanced around the room. He seemed displeased. Amused, I asked, "Not to your taste?"

"It lacks flair." He stacked the jars of candy off to the side on top of a table. "I expected something colorful or perhaps high-contrast, given your personality."

"Nothing feels right," I murmured thoughtfully. "Much like how human clothes make me uncomfortable, so do most human furnishings when I consider placing them in my space."

"You could decorate with Syldrari furnishings," he pointed out as he exited back into the hall. "You seem uncomfortable, and not just because of the room."

"You're going to find Zafir infuriating," I remarked after a moment. "I thought it might be entertaining, but I've realized it won't stay that way for long."

"He can't be that bad," he countered doubtfully.

"Oh, yes, he certainly can." I leaned toward him. "And he will. At least it may give you some insight into why I can be so cranky about certain things."

"I'll hope you're wrong," he stated dryly. "Where to now?"

"The common area. If no one's there, I'll call them in for dinner." I moved ahead of Rel, leading him down the hallway.

"You didn't have a music system or player in your room."

"I don't know what I like, so I decided to forgo either for now."

"…What do you *do* while you're holed up here?"

"Read. Train."

"What else?"

"Sleep."

He sighed in exasperation. "Elara, that is hardly living. If you don't know what you like, then *experiment*. You'll find experimentation is key in many factors of life."

"Oh, I'm sure it is." I gave him a small smile. "But never mind. We can talk about it another time if I'm still in a sharing mood."

Something about Rel's expression made me think he knew precisely what I'd been about to divulge—that discovering what I liked was a frightening prospect, and that I was concerned that, if I were to ever recover my memories, I'd hate everything I thought I liked, and my current self would disappear.

"Elara…" he began carefully.

"It's fine, Rel. Truly." I shook my head.

"You do realize you are lying to a *Syldrari*, right?" He gave me a small smile when I glanced at him. "I'm of the opinion you don't need to worry that you'll become someone else. Your memories were fully erased; there is no regaining them. This is you now, and you deserve to have nice things and be treated like a *person* instead of a caged dog. That's all that room is in its current state—a cage."

"I doubt I can get Syldrari furnishings imported, though," I pointed out as we walked into the common area. There, to my surprise, I found most of my team plus Zafir on the sofas watching TV. "Oh, most of you are here already. Good. Everyone, this is—"

"S-Syldrari!" Aisu scampered backward on the sofa, nearly tipping it over. I sensed a change in her as her gaze became clouded.

"Of fucking course," I muttered as her suit manifested and she leapt toward Rel, her mind clearly gone. Instead of letting Rel handle the problem, I stepped forward and roundhoused her in the stomach before she could reach him, sending her skidding back several yards—and drawing her attention to me. She shifted, ready to launch herself at me again. "Aisu, sit down and de-suit. He's an ally, not a punching bag. If you attack him again, I'll let him put you in your place himself."

Aisu froze like a frightened deer, and everyone else in the room stiffened—including Rel. I glanced briefly at him, noting that his gaze was still entirely clear. He had reacted for some other reason, given the contemplative smile he was watching me with.

"But, Elara, the Syldrari—" Aisu cut herself off, shaking her head groggily as I walked toward her. "They're the ones who made us like this!"

Amused, I stopped in front of her and crouched down to her level. "Are they?"

"What do you—" Aisu stopped, staring at me, her suit fully disappearing. Her cheeks turned deep blue as she took in what I was wearing. "U-uh…"

"Something deeper is going on," I informed her, leaning forward slightly. "Now, apologize to Rel. Considering I know you've been chasing Brihl girl ass all over the city, it's obvious you're not xenophobic. Quite the opposite. So…"

"I don't require an apology from her," Rel remarked

dismissively. "I'm here to train *you*. If the others wish to be problematic—"

I shot him a glare over my shoulder, which resulted in a satisfied smirk. "*I* require an apology from her. We're supposed to protect the city and *all* its peoples. If she can't do that, she'll end up back in isolation. If she won't get herself under control, *I will*."

"I see Elara is in a fine mood," Zafir remarked, finally rising to his feet. He shot Rel a suspicious look. "What did you do?"

"Nothing." Rel smiled.

"…And I imagine that's half the problem." Zafir rubbed his temples. "And the clothes?"

Aisu stood, and so did I. She hesitated briefly before walking over to Rel and extending a hand. "I'm sorry. Don't know what came over me—I've been just fine 'round Syldrari before…"

That latter part seemed to grab Rel's attention, and he looked to me for confirmation. I nodded. "We ran into Jysel before his threat-to-humanity speech. She didn't like him much, sure, but nothing like this happened."

"I will forgive you this once, then, Aisu." Rel gave her what I could only describe as a powerful smile—one that certainly made Aisu squirm, and not from fear or discomfort. "Now then, where will we be eating?"

"*Well*, my room—" Aisu started, but Rel walked past her and in my direction.

He glanced back just long enough to respond, "The only such

invitation I would accept would have to come from Elara."

"Aww, really?" Diana peered over the back of the couch at Rel as we walked past them to the dining area. "There go my chances…"

Zafir sighed heavily as he joined us. "Please forgive them. The brass has forbidden sexual relations for all the survivors and banned access to tools—virtual or otherwise—that could assist with such matters."

"Do they all use Syldrari under-armor?" Rel asked, and Zafir gave him his best confused human researcher expression.

"Under-armor? I'm afraid I don't…"

Rel muttered something venomously in Syldran but Zafir didn't waver. I tried to bite back a snicker, and instead just patted Rel's arm as I picked a seat and made myself comfortable.

Crossing his arms, Rel snapped, "The suit that Aisu girl summoned is merely under-armor. It blocks weapons meant to cut or pierce, plus the brunt of blunt impact. It does nothing against elemental, energy, or harmonic weaponry, and only provides slight protection against concussive or shockwave-type attacks."

"Ah, I see… That could be problematic," Zafir murmured, rubbing his chin. "It's much stronger than any armor we have, so it didn't occur to us that it could be something else. I'm afraid it is our best equipment."

"So you haven't checked whether Elara or the others have an

armory module or at least a true battle suit tucked away anywhere." Rel massaged his temples, then glanced at me. "You were right."

"Unfortunately." I smiled back at him. "I take it an armory module is the combatant's equivalent of my wardrobe module?"

"Yes. Only Syldrari soldiers, queens, and royal guards are outfitted with them." Rel glanced briefly around the room, then summoned all the food from his ring to different seats.

Only... Well, no, I don't want to know. I sighed and propped my cheek against my fist. "So, by your standards, I've been doing battle in my underwear."

Both of them paused at that, giving me the impression that they may have been considering just what that would look like.

"Not quite..." Rel laughed. "But we need to determine whether you have proper armor. It will dictate the methods I use to train you. Zafir, if you're going to do nothing but smirk and mumble to yourself—go fetch the others for dinner."

"Ah, speaking of which," I remarked, glancing up at one of the cameras. "Amara, get in here. I know you're starving by now."

After making certain everything was in place, Rel strolled over and sat down beside me. He leaned down and spoke quietly into my ear. "Be careful with that little submission trick of yours. It's good you called your target by name, but in a more crowded setting it could still be problematic. Especially near other Syldrari."

"Is that why you were fine? Because I said her name instead of leaving it vague?" I inquired, reaching for my drink.

"I was not *fine*. Under any other circumstances I'd be challenging everyone in this damned building for the right to bend you over the nearest surface," he growled back, this time getting a *look* from me. "Be more careful. If anyone else attempts to attack me, let me handle it. Understood?"

"Mhm, loud and clear." I leaned toward him with an amused smile—clearly not the reaction he was expecting. "And even if you beat up every person in this building—that doesn't mean I'd fuck you. I'm not that simple, and I'm less likely to have some fun if I think the catalyst was something like my power."

"*Behave.*" Rel narrowed his eyes at me.

"I should be saying that to you—you're in my territory now." I smirked and gently pressed him away. "And unfortunately, Zafir was quite right about sexual…anything being forbidden."

"Yet they still wanted you to seduce us for information?" he muttered bitterly.

"Your guess is as good as mine on that one," I offered with a shrug. "If you really want to know, you could try asking Zafir."

"I think I will pass on that suggestion." He reached out and grabbed a thermos. "Finish your drink. This will pair better with your meal."

"Mmm?" I peered at him curiously, then knocked back the remainder of my drink and placed the empty cup between us. "What's this one?"

"Another mixed drink—and likely the last one I'm giving

you tonight," Rel replied dryly.

"Indeed, she should get some sleep once she's had her food. After all, I imagine you will likely be waking her up early for training," Zafir remarked as he joined us at the table. He placed a sheet of paper next to Rel. "This is Elara's schedule. After dinner, I'll give you a tour of our facilities."

"I'm not tired." I pouted.

"You will be." Rel nudged my drink closer to me with an amused smile. "Did you think I wouldn't notice you haven't been sleeping well? It's easy enough to fix."

"Thanks?" I asked, not entirely sure how to feel about his observation or apparent attempt to fix the problem.

"Now then, my superiors have asked that you give the team your opinion on the R'selkti queen, so they know just what they're dealing with should they encounter either her, her servants, or the other queens." Zafir flicked his data pad a few times, then showed Rel a message from General Crowe.

"She's still here?" Rel narrowed his eyes and glared at his drink for a moment while the others gathered around to listen. After a moment, he sighed. "I will admit, I don't particularly care what happens to the team—I am here to train Elara, and that is it. However, this information will be of use to her as well.

"Queen Citomy is the most controversial *jalan-ki*—that is the short form word for a queen who rules and oversees the Tower of Celestial Houses—that we've had in several thousand years. There are those who adore her and believe she has brought upon us a golden era of Syldrari culture and power—and then there are those who believe she destroyed it.

"A third, smaller group believes that this era can still be reclaimed and salvaged, but they are widely considered crazed fanatics because their beliefs are wrought from forbidden legends and self-proclaimed prophecies."

"Then those clans must be outlaws, right?" Diana murmured, earning a curt nod from Rel. "But what do the legends say?"

"Who knows? I may not approve of the current *jalan-ki*, but I don't associate with those dogs, either," Rel answered dismissively, waving his hand.

"What's this Tower of Celestial Houses?" I asked, and Rel gave me an odd side-glance.

"It is like… I'm honestly not sure if humans have a word for it. It is our system of government—each clan that hasn't been outcast has a representative within the tower. Usually, it is a queen. The V'shir have one of our founding members—an *iri* who is not a queen—to serve as our representative. Ours is the only such clan."

"So, it's a congress or parliament-type of body," Zafir murmured, continuing to take notes as if he didn't already know all this. "With Citomy as its head? Then what is her role?"

I felt Rel twitch beside me, but he answered levelly, "Her

word is final, and she can veto anything she pleases. Much like your Imperator, though significantly older and more conniving."

"So polarizing…" Aisu murmured. To her credit, she didn't flinch at the piercing glare Rel shot in her direction. "There's no way for us to know how someone feels about her beforehand, is there?"

Rel slowly shook his head. "No. And if any of you encounter her, it's unlikely you will be returning to HQ. Your cellular dissonance is quite obvious to Syldrari, visibly and audibly.

"Citomy and her entourage will identify that you are muddled between human and Syldrari, which has varying degrees of implications depending on which of the two species you originally were. You would be captured, studied, and either forced to serve her clan or be executed. She bounces between extremes with everyone and everything in her life."

"Well, in that case, it's in our best interests to be careful," Nikolai remarked, crossing his arms. "What about other Syldrari and other queens? Elara is the only one here who has interacted with any Syldrari other than Jysel."

Sighing, Rel shifted and crossed one leg over the other, looking surprisingly like a bored aristocrat. "Be honest and do not lie to Syldrari. Half-truths, such as those Elara has used, are acceptable when you're asked something you cannot answer. If the question you're asked is direct, you should simply say you cannot disclose that information.

"However, if it's something you can't say because the

information attached to it is sensitive, say… Well, Elara's misdirection when questioned about Lethe would be an excellent example. When asked questions about Lethe, Elara often referenced the fact that the Imperial forces weren't told much aside from being ordered to bring her in."

Nikolai nodded. "Which is true, because the Imperials *were* given that order, but also false depending on how you look at it."

"As for dealing with queens…you should hope you don't have to." Rel glanced over at me. "You are going to be getting an early start tomorrow—you should head to your room."

I wanna listen to him talk more, though… I considered it for a moment, then narrowed my eyes at him. "Or I could stay and learn what other information you have to disclose."

"*Or* you could make certain you're prepared for a real fight." Rel leaned toward me, his glow shifting to a deep silvery green. "Unlike Jysel, I am not going to go easy on you. Someone such as you needs to be prepared for the conflicts you will face. Nor will I coddle you as Zafir clearly has."

"I don't coddle—" Zafir started to protest, but he went silent at the look Rel gave him.

"I am going to escort Elara to her room. Afterward, Zafir, you and I have things to discuss—and I will require that tour you mentioned." He rose gracefully to his feet and pivoted to offer me a hand. "Please. Don't put on a brave face. You are tired and have had enough alcohol to knock a human out for the next eighteen hours. It would be irresponsible of me to let you return to your apartment alone in those heels."

"Okay," I grumbled, letting him pull me to my feet. I couldn't exactly argue with his logic, and I didn't want to insult his gentlemanliness, either. "They're not that high."

"Hush." He pulled me out of the dining area and down the hall. I studied his physique for a moment, then his expression. "You're staring."

"You're agitated," I pointed out.

"I wonder *why*." He grimaced, then gave me a sideways glance. "You're not even the slightest bit tipsy, are you?"

I held up one hand, spreading my thumb and forefinger barely apart. "A little bit tipsy."

"I will keep that in mind." Rel chuckled and shook his head, slowing to a stop outside my door. He turned and looked down at me, a questioning expression on his face. "Do you remember how to use your wardrobe module? It wouldn't do for you to sleep in that."

"I remember." I shot him an amused smirk. "Try not to strangle Zafir, alright?"

"I'm sure I can find other uses for him if he frustrates me too much," he remarked, rubbing his chin. "Though I doubt he would be quite as entertaining as you—and you are significantly higher on the endearment scale. Now. Behave and go to bed. I meant what I said about—"

"*Rel*," I interrupted, pressing him back against the wall. I wasn't tall enough to place my hand against the wall beside his head, but the situation seemed to have the desired effect anyway. "Zafir already took the mother hen role. If you start down that path too, me waking up on time will be the least of your concerns. I don't have to be a capable fighter to be a massive thorn in your side." I paused and leaned closer, smirking. "I'd prefer we maintained the playful, respectful rapport we've had up to this point. Even if it's a different kind of…frustrating."

He let out a low laugh and leaned down, smirking, a mischievous twinkle in his eyes. "Oh, you needn't worry about me mothering you. I'm here to *train* you–and I am keeping track of just how much work you will be for me."

Dammit, Elara, don't kiss him. You know there's surveillance everywhere, I told myself. *Kissing him to shut him up would just lead to other…things that'd only make it worse for us both. Behave. Behave, behave, behave!*

Rel gently extricated himself and ruffled my hair, an amused smile still playing on his lips. "Good night, Elara. Get some rest, perhaps work off some of that aforementioned frustration…"

He laughed outright at the look I shot him and let his tail brush against my legs as he strolled off, hands tucked into his pockets. I wasn't sure he could possibly look any more full of himself. Why was it so sexy?

Shaking my head, I unlocked my apartment and strolled in. *What was I doing here again…oh. Right. Shower, bed, rest up for whatever it is he has in store for me in the morning… It can't be that bad, right?*

CHAPTER THIRTY-TWO

Repeated knocking on my door pulled me out of whatever dream I'd been having and back to reality. I grumbled a few choice curses as I pulled myself out of bed, fully expecting to find Zafir outside my door with one bullshit request or another.

"What?" I demanded with a groan, yanking my door open. The sudden light made me squint, but after a moment my eyes adjusted to find Rel standing in the hallway. A surprised, bright pink Rel. "Rel? What are...oh. Right. Training?"

"...*Elara*." Rel raised his thumb and forefinger to his temples, obscuring most of his face. "Where are your clothes?"

"Hmm?" I glanced down at myself, then back to Rel. "I was sleeping. Why would I wear clothes in bed? That seems silly."

With that, I pivoted and teetered back into my room, listening as Rel released an aggravated sigh before following me. I opened my closet and peered at the contents, not quite sure what to grab.

"Underwear first, perhaps?" Rel suggested dryly. I glanced over my shoulder, only to find his gaze was focused partway down my back. "You know, many humans believe our coloration to be indicative of the clan we come from. They aren't entirely wrong, but it is more accurate to say our coloration is determined by region, depth, and manner of light source. It's become more muddled over the years, of course, as clans inter-wed. But I can't say I've ever seen someone quite that color before."

"Regional? Hmm…what does that make your region, then?" I murmured, more curious about him than I was about myself.

"Deep ocean caverns on Syldra—thus the increased number of…" He paused to point at the glowing section of his arm. "I don't think there's a word for it in the human language. If we're going to try to be scientific about it, let's call it luminescent epidermis."

"Mhm. So, deep ocean and caverns. Glowy bits. Following so far." I nodded.

"For once I find myself agreeing with Xilen…" Rel suddenly appeared beside me, hand on his hip. He peered into my wardrobe, then glanced down at me with an amused smile. "Shouldn't you be trying to cover yourself? Perhaps yelling at me to look away?"

"That seems childish." I blinked at him. "Do I come off that way?"

He laughed and placed a hand on the small of my back, nudging me in the direction of my dresser. "No, Elara. But that is how your average human would react. They are quite shy about their nudity and will try to cover themselves with their hands."

"That's just silly. They don't have enough hands for that." I pulled open my dresser and grabbed a black sports bra and matching panties. "What should I wear, shorts and tank? Or am I going to be using my suit? Oh, and breakfast?"

"No breakfast." His entire demeanor changed, tone deepening and eyes narrowing. "I'll save you the indignity of vomiting all over the floor. Once your session is complete, I will make you a recovery meal."

"Hmm?" I frowned slightly at him, wondering why he was suddenly so serious. "Vomit? I've never…"

"If you are hit hard enough in the stomach, you will," he answered quietly, closing the distance between us. Cupping my face in both hands, he rested his forehead against mine. In a soft, low voice I almost couldn't hear, he said, "I need you to trust me, Elara, and trust that I have your best interests in mind."

Oh, he smells really good… I swallowed and took a moment to steady my thoughts, steering them away from where they wanted to wander. "I trust you, and I prefer that you take this training seriously, anyway. I won't learn anything otherwise. Though I think I'm a pretty decent fighter…"

"You can be a decent fighter *and* totally helpless against the

Syldrari," he informed me, taking a step away. "I'm sure your current skill level is more than enough to deal with an average human—and maybe even some of those who are augmented.

"However, Syldrari…we don't require augments. Any augments we have are for convenience, aesthetics, to please a partner, or to please a queen. And even then, we prefer the permanence of using guided evolution instead of augmentation the human way."

"The human way?" I echoed. "Then what's the Syldrari way?"

"Syldrari augmentation is usually used to give existing Syldrari their clan's new evolutionary traits," he replied, after seeming to contemplate his word choice. "For example, if a queen deems it necessary for her clan to have armored tails, that new trait will only appear in new offspring—unless it is retroactively applied to existing clan members via augmentation methods. However, those armored tails would still be natural, as they would have been formed the same way—just at an accelerated rate."

"Whereas human augments are mechanical and tech-based. I get you." I adjusted my tank top, then moved closer to Rel. "In other words, Syldrari are the designer lifeforms that humans wish they could be. You have near complete control over who and what you are, both as a species and on an individual level."

"And yet we still find new frontiers to explore." He gave me a smug smile. "And of course humans wish to be like us. It's only natural, as they were designed in our image… poor imitations that they are."

"So, back to the regional coloration discussion?" I suggested amusedly, running my fingertips along his arm. The human military brass overhearing his comments was the last thing I needed. Much to my fascination, my fingertips left a trail of pink in their wake.

"Natural camouflage." Rel shook his head. "The R'selkti's region is comprised of rock and lit primarily by bioluminescent flora. The ceilings of the natural cave systems are reminiscent of the night sky.

"By comparison, Xilen's birth clan comes from one of the great reefs and a shallower depth. That is why she, Ceyoh, and Lynir are so colorful."

"And me…?" I trailed off, watching his lips tug into a slight frown.

"I would prefer to keep my hypothesis to myself for the moment, as you already dislike the implications of other topics," he answered after a moment. "However, I will say that your unusual color is another reason to keep your changing body hidden. You will face far too many questions if you don't."

"Implications I'll dislike?" I sighed heavily. "What else is new? Anyway, I suppose we should do this whole training thing. Which area did Zafir say we should use?"

"A subterranean one. He doesn't approve of my chosen method, but he also has no valid argument against it." Rel followed me out into the hallway and towards the elevator. "He doesn't want to check to see if you have full armor stashed away somewhere, either. You'll be using your suit, and I will be fulfilling the role of a full-fledged Syldrari soldier—with some rules in place, for now. I won't be using energy or elemental weapons yet, and I won't be using elemental abilities, either."

"We're working purely on my physical ability for now?" I questioned.

"Yes. After hearing that most of your training was done on your own based on books given to you by an individual whose motives are questionable at best..." He trailed off, clearly aware that he didn't need to expand any further on that line of thought. Instead, he shifted gears. "I wanted to work on reintegrating your...feral...before diving headlong into training, but I've been informed that isn't possible right now."

Not possible? More like Zafir has a reason to keep us fucked up. Wonderful. I made a sour face. "Yes, well, I'm just glad to know there's a chance. I think some of the others would be against it, since they're still scared of it, but it sounds to me like something that should be done."

"I wonder..." he murmured as we got on the elevator.

"What?" I turned to face him.

"Your team was found scattered around the site of the first Resonance Incident, and they all show signs of cellular dissonance. They also didn't question your assignment as leader… Have you met any of these other survivors?"

"One. Zafir's lucky I put her in her place instead of outright eviscerating her and hanging her from the top of our old HQ."

That seemed to break his concentration, and he stared at me in disbelief. "Pardon?"

"Just thinking about her makes me want to kill her. Can we talk about something else?" I crossed my arms and narrowed my eyes at him.

"Why?" He stopped and stared at me. "There must be a reason she makes you feel that way."

"Her presence is offensive." I scoffed and glanced away. "I can't put my finger on why. It's been a while since I met her. I was less…"

I heard footsteps from behind us, and a moment later Zafir spoke up. "Less *you*, which means your reaction was instinctual and lacking the ability to process specifics."

"Coming to observe?" Rel eyed Zafir. "I won't change my mind."

Zafir waved a hand dismissively. "I'm a researcher, of course I'm coming to observe—it's my job even if I disagree with your chosen method. Plus, someone should be there to render medical assistance if necessary.

"As for Elara's feelings regarding Sydney, we'll get to gauge them soon enough. She's being moved to the other wing of this floor. Her feral hasn't had any outbursts since her meeting with Elara."

Rel raised an eyebrow. "Is that so?"

"Elara picks up tricks from aggravating Syldrari she meets a little too quickly," Zafir answered sourly, giving Rel a 'you know precisely who I'm talking about' kind of glare. "If I didn't know better, I would think mimicry was one of her abilities."

We all piled into the elevator and Zafir swiped his keycard as I leaned back against the wall. Rel's demeanor remained…odd. I didn't quite have a word for the peaceful, threatening, yet still-relaxed way he was carrying himself. It was as if his state of being had completely changed—yet he clearly hadn't taken a moment to meditate.

"This arena should suffice." Zafir stepped out of the elevator and motioned off to his right. "I've instructed the others to stay upstairs so that you and Elara can freely unleash. In the event that Elara releases…certain traits, I would prefer her teammates remain unaffected."

"I don't want to use *that* power in a fight. That's cheating." I snorted, crossing my arms. *Like hell I'm going to use queenlike whatever-the-fuck in a fight. If I'm going to fight, I'm going to fight.*

"You may not have a choice in the matter." Rel motioned loosely as he breezed past me. "It's unlikely you have full control over your various abilities. There is very likely a point where that control will vanish. Which is what we are going to find out."

I don't like the sound of that… I kept quiet and followed Rel into the arena, then we waited for Zafir to get to his safe position of observation.

"Ah, and Zafir?" Rel glanced toward the viewing deck. "Elara requires a new alarm clock. She appears to have fried hers."

"I did?" I blinked at him, and he outright laughed. "What?"

"You didn't notice the smoking plastic box by your bedside?" He gave me a mischievous smile. "I'm glad to know you find me so much more important than your observational skills."

"Right…" If that *was* true, I didn't recall such an issue occurring previously. "So, I should suit up?"

"That would be best, yes. Otherwise this will be over rather quickly." As Rel spoke, his voice changed to something both more melodic and more mechanical-sounding as his armor slid into place. Much like with Jysel, it looked as though vines had burst from his back, covering him in strange armor. The color of his was different, however, being a dark blue-grey with a pale blue glow shining from within the crevices. "Now then—try to kill me."

"…What?" I raised an eyebrow.

"How else will I gauge your ability?" He spread his arms to either side. "Give me your all."

Fine… I summoned my suit and gauntlets, then took an offensive stance. After a moment, I launched at him and faked a punch, then shifted to knee him in the gut. Sensing motion to my upper left, I spun into an upper roundhouse kick and hit his forearm with the ridge of my foot.

He was holding a sword. Great.

I remained close and attempted to disarm him, not exactly keen to give him space to swing the weapon. Suddenly, a strike to my midsection sent me flying backward into the nearest wall. He didn't give me time to recover—instead he sped toward me, sword in hand, and sliced from my right shoulder down to my left hip.

The suit protected me from the sharp edge, but I still took the brunt of the force. *And it made me mad.* I shouldn't have been so slow. Launching myself at him again, I tried my damnedest to land a strike, but he easily blocked and dodged everything I threw at him—even going so far as to discard his sword.

Then he did what I wasn't quite expecting. He took the offensive, and at a far greater speed than I could even track. The first several hits shocked my feral awake. At first, it was only startled and frightened as to what was going on; then it tried to lash out. I shoved the damn beast back down and tried to block Rel's next attack, but I was too slow. His fist connected with my jaw and snapped my head back, causing me to stagger.

A cold feeling washed over me, my senses muddying. Before I quite knew what I was doing, I rushed him, lightning crackling in my wake. I leapt into the air and swung an ax kick down at his shoulder—and it landed. He looked up with a faint smirk, utterly unfazed by the kick, and the feral recoiled. I bared my teeth in a snarl and attempted another punch, but he grabbed my arm and tossed me into the air like I weighed nothing. His elbow connected with my stomach, and I felt something crack—

but he wasn't done.

Several more strikes and I collided with the wall again, this time crumpling to the ground. I coughed, trying to get up, and bright blue blood splattered from my mouth. My head spun as pain surged through multiple parts of my body. Some dark part of me wondered why he would *dare* strike his queen, but I buried that thought deep as I coughed again.

"Well, well," Rel remarked as he slowly walked toward me, his armored legs filling my field of vision. "As I thought. Human martial arts are useless." He paused and crouched beside me, placing a hand on my back. "Stop trying to get up. Now that we've established your weakness, I have much to teach you. The first of which is how to mend yourself."

I know exactly how to make him submit... The thought echoed blearily through my head. I threw a mental dagger at the damn thing. I *refused* to manipulate anyone with whatever queenlike powers I had.

"Good girls listen when someone is trying to help them." He gripped my jaw and made me look at him, and I finally registered that his armor was gone. "I didn't hit your head that hard. Focus. Breathe. You need to feel every little hurt if you're going to fix them. Oh, and take off your suit."

I hesitated before doing as he said and letting the suit disappear. He gave me a small smile and wiped some of the blood from my mouth.

"What now?" I asked bitterly, sounding a little rougher than I expected. Had he kicked me in the throat at some point? After a moment, I realized we were no longer against the wall where I'd crumpled. "Wait a minute—"

"Zafir will have the footage of your feral taking over if you want to see it." He placed his hand on my head, continuing in a quiet voice as if trying to avoid being heard. "Now, listen carefully. One of our greatest strengths is our ability to mend our own wounds in battle. With the correct resonance of internal sound, you can put yourself back together. Our skeletal structure is comprised of vastly different material from a human's. We are natural harmonic conductors, if you will. Listen and feel while I heal your broken rib. It won't be pleasant, unfortunately."

That was a fucking understatement. I screamed as bone-deep pain echoed through my entire body. My rib shifted, and I could have sworn I felt every single strand of bone reaching out and reknitting itself back into place.

When it was finally done, he waited a bit, letting me catch my breath. I rolled over and retched a few times from the pain, but nothing came up. After a moment, I groaned. "I think leaving it broken may've hurt less..."

Rel placed a hand on my back and stroked it softly, a low, soothing sound I could barely hear coming from him. It sounded somewhat akin to a song, but not quite. When my head finally stopped spinning, I plopped my ass down on the ground and gave him a begrudging pout.

"Did you manage to feel *how* I put you back together?" he asked with a small smile. How he could seem both concerned and unconcerned at the same time was beyond me.

"Think so…" I grimaced. "Did the feral do anything stupid?"

"Only in the sense that your feral lacks any form of organized fighting skill. It appears purely bestial." Rel chuckled. "Now, I want you to try healing your arm. It's not cracked or broken—just deep bruising. The same frequency will suffice."

"Uh, but how do I…" I made a face and pointed at my throat. "I get the impression you didn't make the sound from here."

"You heard it?" He narrowed his eyes, glancing over his shoulder. "Zafir?"

"News to me." Zafir shook his head as he came into view. "We need to hurry this up. I've got security asking if they need to come in, or if they need to bring in a med team. The imbeciles thought you'd killed her for a moment there."

Then I must really look like shit. I grimaced. "Well?"

"Hmm? Ah. The sound you heard wasn't vocal, no. As I said, we are harmonic conductors. If you stimulate your cells correctly, it causes a reverberation with your skeletal structure, which in turn hastens your cellular turnover. You can then focus that on your injuries to heal them. It is a mental ability, not a vocal one."

…Right. I thought for a moment as Rel placed a hand on my forearm. He briefly did the thing again, but stopped when he

seemed to think I'd gotten the idea.

Here goes nothing…

I concentrated on the feeling of the sound I'd heard, attempting to mentally mimic it the way I would normally try to match notes when singing along to a song. Suddenly, a sound akin to the resonance left by a struck chime echoed through my being. Instead of fading, however, it persisted, and I felt my entire body tingling in response. I could feel sharp pains and dull aches in dozens of places as I did my best to do as Rel had instructed.

"I said your *arm,* not your entire body, but well done." He patted me on the head and gave me an amused smile. "Well, that answers one of my questions. You most certainly knew—once— how to do that already. That sort of knowledge is more like muscle memory, or instinct, than anything else. I'm afraid the Syldran word doesn't translate."

So I didn't lose it with my memories? I wondered, stretching my arms tentatively. I shot Rel an odd glance. "I believe you said something about useless human martial arts?"

"Yes. I am going to begin your training from scratch." He rose to his feet, offering me a hand. "But first, we should shower and have breakfast. I anticipated that things could go like this, so I left the café to Ciheri today."

"Shower…oh." It finally registered that Rel had quite a few smears of my blood on him, and I could feel damp patches in a considerable number of places. "Just how badly…"

"…Did I beat you? Well, the humans weren't entirely unjustified in thinking I'd killed you. If you were a normal human…" He trailed off, giving me a pointed smile. "I do hope you understand this was for your benefit."

"And I hope *you* understand that half the battle wasn't even fighting you," I grumbled, stomping past him. Zafir grew a few shades paler when he got a good look at me. "Oh, don't you start too."

"Rel, you may use Elara's shower once she's finished. I'm afraid the public showers are currently occupied." Zafir's voice sounded thoughtful, and I considered pivoting to punch the fake human right in his damn mouth. "I'll compile the data I recorded and share it with the two of you while you eat breakfast."

With that, he peeled off and Rel fell into step with me.

"Well, shall we?" he offered, giving me an amused smile. "You will have to shower by yourself, of course. I know we can't both fit in that contraption."

…Right. Because that's what I'm so concerned about. I rubbed my temples. "You said Syldrari will heal themselves like that on the battlefield? How…"

"Our training involves repeatedly breaking and healing our bones so we can learn to cope with the pain of putting ourselves back together. We can effectively play dead while healing and then get back up when the enemy's back is turned," he offered as we stepped into the elevator. "Of course, this doesn't work in Syldrari-versus-Syldrari situations, as we can hear each other healing. Most other species aren't evolved enough."

"Huh." I grimaced as I processed the thought. "That sounds…horrible. Logical in a sense, but awful to go through."

"*Iri* rarely go through it—most are content to stay safe and pampered, whilst letting others fight," he stated dryly. "If you insist on remaining personally involved, you may need to go through that training yourself. I would rather not break you repeatedly; at least, not in that fashion, but if I deem it necessary to your survival I will."

"Right. Because I have a choice in how personally involved I actually get to be." I decided to ignore his inviting insinuation for the moment. "I assume you have a change of clothes?"

"Of course." He nodded, giving me an entertained smile. "Now, just how difficult was your internal struggle, I wonder? I felt like your thoughts weren't fully on our battle."

"Ugh… I don't want to talk about that."

His smile turned into a grin as he leaned down. "But you should. I intentionally put you in a situation where your survival instincts should have kicked in—yet all you did was 'go feral,' as the humans say. Meaning that the other battle you alluded to was with yourself."

I let out a bitter laugh. "Yes, well, apparently my survival instincts are to either go feral or go queen. I'm not particularly fond of either option."

"Ah…good," he murmured.

"*Good?* Which part?" I asked, dumbfounded.

"You controlled your urge to use that power. Consider, for a moment, the myriad problems you could face if you used that power on a battlefield." He motioned with one hand. "There are all manner of difficulties you would have to contend with if you unleashed that ability on an enemy and their army—and you would never be able to fully trust those new followers."

"No shit. That would be one of the most idiotic—" I fell silent as Rel turned and leaned over me, his grin broadening.

He spoke in an amused, yet somehow dangerous tone. "Why, yes, it would be. Yet most queens don't think deeply on it—if at all. They believe they are entitled to have the other sexes worship the ground they walk on—this is what my mother has taught them.

"Then there is you, whose brainwashing was either eradicated with the rest of your memories, or you were never discovered in the first place. I am leaning toward the latter, given what little I've learned, as you simply don't appear to exist in any known database."

"Is that a problem?" I challenged.

"Only in the same sense that a puzzle is," he murmured, drawing a finger up my throat and to my chin. Smiling, he stepped away just moments before the elevator *ding*ed and the doors slid open. "Ladies first."

"Honestly. Sometimes I can't tell *what* you think of *iri*." I shook my head as I led him out of the elevator and down the hall. It finally occurred to me that the shower happened to be directly adjacent to my bedroom, and I sighed. "I won't bother telling you not to peek. I suppose it means we can continue our conversation while I shower, at least…"

CHAPTER THIRTY-THREE

"What happened to indulging in conversation?" Rel queried as he stepped out of the shower. I was about to explain myself, until I noticed his unusual anatomy.

There was no dick hanging between his legs, yet the slit that *was* there wasn't feminine in the least. He noticed my confusion before I could articulate a question, and laughed.

"Ah yes, I imagine you're only familiar with the human species' terribly vulnerable masculine genitalia." He smirked as he grabbed a towel and proceeded to dry his hair, causing his body to stretch and curve in a rather enticing way. "I think we will forgo the personal demonstration today. Suffice to say, *Syldrari* masculine genitalia isn't at risk of being bitten off by random passer-fish or mauled in other settings."

"...Retractable?" I recalled that Jysel and Zafir had also seemed to dislike the fact that humans had outards instead of innards.

"Quite. I'm not certain why humans evolved the way they did and why our scientists didn't fix them." He shrugged and pulled on a pair of skintight black shorts, then rose to his full height and stretched his arms above his head. "And yet they were willing to carefully mold human women into—mostly—the image of an *iri*. A choice that has become more controversial in recent years as we grow to know humans as something other than objects of research. Especially since human women can't quite withstand relations with their own Syldrari species, let alone any of the others. At least, not without becoming a different person."

"Care to explain?" I raised an eyebrow.

"Well, humans are so easy to break with pleasure, and it appears to be mostly irreversible without expert help from outside the Empire. There have been multiple instances of a queen or one of her males having a human pet. The humans get so hooked on Syldrari that they became useless for anything other than a...pardon the term, but I believe the closest translation would be 'starter fuck.'"

"The sexual equivalent of an appetizer?" I laughed. "Alright then. Human women aren't mentally equipped to deal with what you're *physically* equipped with, got it."

Rel chuckled as he summoned black leather pants and a white, low cut tank top. "Yes, well, I believe we got a little off-track. You were about to explain the lack of during-shower conversation?"

"Oh…right. I was wondering just how much Zafir has told the staff about the cellular dissonance, and how many people in the building know. I find it a little odd that security was apparently watching but didn't come running in over the blue blood issue." I sighed and leaned back on the edge of the bed, resting my weight on my palms. "I have to assume that either they were already expecting my blood to be the wrong color, or perhaps a filter on the cameras…?"

"I'm inclined to blame—or perhaps I should say thank—Zafir." He offered me a hand, his expression one of mild concern as he pulled me to my feet. "How are you feeling? No lingering pain anywhere?"

"A little stiff, though perhaps that's due to the lack of a warmup." I shrugged.

"Or the awful bed." He waved dismissively at the bed before leading me toward the door. "Now then, let's get some food in you. Depending on how much Zafir decides to talk our – I mean, *regale* us, we will return to your training after."

"Since you said human martial arts are useless, I take it you mean to teach me a Syldrari discipline?" I inquired as I fell into step with him. "That will be awfully time consuming, won't it?"

"In a sense." He ran his fingers through his damp dark hair and glanced at me. "Of course, Syldrari arts are much more efficient than human. Even at a lower proficiency you'll find them more effective than their human equivalents. And they're easily adjusted with the addition of weaponry or elemental abilities. But for the moment, you should go play good little team leader."

He nudged me gently in the direction of the lounge area, where most of my team plus Zafir were all gathered. I reluctantly obeyed and joined the group. Zafir noticed me first and quickly pulled over an extra chair, motioning silently for me to take it.

"Why's everyone look so grumpy?" I sat down and glanced around the table.

"They are upset that you are all so inferior to a Syldrari." Zafir gestured loosely to the team. "Your loss gave everyone a dose of needed reality; they have been lucky thus far. If they wish to survive, they must stop relying on continued luck and instead make their own way."

"Uh huh… *Everyone.* So, just how many people saw what color I bleed, Zafir?" I narrowed my eyes, but he didn't even flinch.

Smiling, he answered, "Why, it was covered in my briefing regarding cellular dissonance, Elara. No one here cares what color or substance you bleed. Your continued results and contributions speak for themselves."

"Fuck, I hate it when you talk like that," I muttered irritably.

He leaned closer, dropping his voice to a whisper. "Oh, I'm *very* aware of how you'd like to hear both me and Rel speak. Yet you never quite push us…"

"What? Keep talking so I can decide how bad I need to kick your ass." I glared back at him, but his expression had changed entirely.

"Your change is hastening, isn't it?" he murmured worriedly. "That poses—"

A loud crash echoed from the kitchen, and I was immediately on my feet, followed by Diana. The others looked too nervous to join us in heading in the direction of the indistinct yelling.

As we reached the doors, I heard a familiar voice shout, "You almost killed her, you son of a bitch!"

I pushed the doors open to find a bored-looking Rel standing with his arms crossed while Erik shouted what sounded like curses into his face in various languages. Amongst the onslaught of verbal abuse, I caught snippets along the lines of, 'we don't care if she's not human' and 'she treats us more like people than anyone else does.' Zafir and I exchanged a glance, then I caught sight of Erik pulling a dagger.

"*That's enough*," I snapped, entering the room and approaching the two men. Rel's eyes glassed briefly but were back to normal in a blink. "Erik, what the fuck are you doing?"

"This bastard could have killed—" Erik took a step closer to Rel, shaking with rage—yet he didn't raise his weapon any further.

"He could have. He didn't. That isn't what he's here for. Rel is *here* to make me more difficult to kill." I crossed my arms as Diana peered around me at the two men.

"Seriously, just kiss, fuck, and make up already. But don't do it near the food," she remarked good-naturedly, earning a sharp look from Erik. "What? You kinda look like you wanna kiss him."

"I am not in the mood for a hate fuck right now," Rel stated flatly, taking a step toward the significantly shorter human male. "You are delaying Elara's access to a recovery meal. Do you or do you not care about her well-being?"

"Isn't hate a bit strong of a word?" Zafir sighed irritably, earning a side glance from Rel.

"Humans don't exactly have a good word for the kind of release I would require in this situation." Rel whirled so his back was toward us, reaching for a skillet. "*Now.* Are you going to leave me to my work, or shall I see if any of you have edible parts—aside from Elara, of course."

"Sorry to interrupt, but Elara will be needing her breakfast to go. She's got a mission." General Crowe appeared behind us, his formal tone causing Rel to shift to a more neutral demeanor. "Elder Rel of Clan V'shir, I take it. Thank you for agreeing to our request for training. I'm aware you intended to give her more instruction today, but she's received a summons we—and you—can't dismiss."

"A summons? From?" I frowned at Crowe when he grimaced.

"Queen Xilen has requested *Lethe's* presence aboard her city-ship, in the lounge she uses for entertaining human dignitaries. She said it's a party…and has instructed you to come dressed in 'acceptable' attire. I get the impression she dislikes our standard-issue." The general sighed. "We're sending you suited, but you should be prepared for questioning from the Syldrari. We're not quite sure what they want with you."

"That's an understatement, but yes—she doesn't like standard issue. My question is why you're bending the knee to her request." I turned to look at Crowe, who sighed heavily and shook his head. "And why you said she requested Lethe."

"We put it to a vote. The majority have decided that cooperating with the Syldrari is the best way to put their minds at ease about you and your origins." Crowe linked his hands behind his back. "They think meeting you in person will prove you're merely a modified human, and Xilen made it quite clear she's aware of who you are—and that any Syldrari who meets you in either guise will know too." He turned to address Rel next. "You're welcome to stay and draft more training details for Elara while she's gone, but I understand you're a busy man. Erik will drive you back to the Syldrari sector whenever you're ready. And, with that, I'll be going. I've got another meeting to attend."

We all watched him leave, and it wasn't until he'd been out of the room for several minutes—during which Erik also took his grumpy leave—that anyone looked away from the door. Zafir sighed and fidgeted with the sleeves of his dress shirt, while Diana tapped the toe of her right shoe against the floor.

To my surprise, Rel strode briskly over to me and took my face in his hands. "This isn't safe. You shouldn't go."

"It doesn't sound like I have much of a choice," I countered with a faint shake of my head.

"You don't understand—this is a party of *queens*. Xilen couldn't get permission for any of the V'shir Elders to attend. There's only so many reasons she would request your presence." He narrowed his eyes. "It likely wasn't her who asked at all. It was likely Citomy—"

"Rel. Those greedy women won't change me. They can't." I gave him a firm look. "What they *can* do is react violently to a 'mere human's' refusal and hurt my team or even civilians. Let's not push them."

To my complete surprise, he closed the distance and kissed me. I felt myself losing ground to his magnetism, and before I knew it, he had me pressed back against the edge of the island counter. Just as my thoughts drifted toward all the ways he could undress me, he pulled back, resting his forehand against mine.

"That is in case I never see '*you*' again..." he whispered, shutting his eyes. "They have a way of changing people..." Instead of letting me go, he kissed me again. This time, his long, nubbed tongue filled my mouth as his glow shifted to a bright reddish-pink with a blue aura. He pulled away, his mouth drifting to my neck just under my ear and whispered, "And *that* is a promise of reward if you manage to keep yourself whole…"

Under other circumstances I might have been utterly entranced by the surprisingly passionate kiss, or the way he'd begun tracing his thumb over my lower lip. Or hell, how close the absolutely delicious-smelling man was to the inferno of my body.

But despite my quickly rising lust, I was too surprised to act on it. It took me a few moments to steady myself before I murmured, "I…understood you, and you were not speaking in…"

"In which case, the odds of you protecting yourself while you're up there just increased, did they not?" He gave me a mysterious smile, his gaze drifting briefly down to my lips. Then his eyes met mine and his expression morphed into the serious one I was used to. "You should go get ready. I will prepare a meal you can eat on your way up to Xilen's ship."

"*What did you do?*" Zafir hissed, stepping in close to us. "I understand your concern—I am beside myself with worry as well— but she shouldn't be able to understand Syldran! This is a risk—"

Rel turned to give Zafir an amused smile, reaching out to grip the other man's jaw. "Ah yes, but she has a Syldran neurochip, does she not? Did it not occur to you that Syldran could be uploaded into it? Or, perhaps…you're concerned I awoke something dormant within her?"

"You—" Zafir growled

"I am concerned for her as well, but she needs tools to survive. Tools that I'll give her if you won't. Besides, why wouldn't the

Imperials *want* a soldier who can speak Syldran?" Rel smirked at Zafir, then turned away from us both and placed his hands on the edge of the stove. "Now, I suggest you go draft a briefing to explain to your bosses that your precious pet project had Syldran uploaded into her chip by a concerned citizen."

I hesitated, then followed Zafir and Diana out of the room. The latter turned to peer at me as she walked. "Sooo… Are you okay? Uploading a whole language into your head…"

"It was into her chip—not her head. The chip will translate in real time on its own processing power so that her brain is free to actively focus on other tasks and determine what to do with the information…" Zafir muttered, looking a tad lost. He looked at me with a pained expression. "I hate to admit it, but Rel is right. This is dangerous. Xilen is powerful, but she can't protect you from Citomy or the other high-ranking queens if they decide to…"

"To be blunt, I'd rather die than let bitches like them change me. I've had enough change to last a few damn centuries," I snapped irritably. Diana rejoined the others and immediately began whispering to them, while Zafir followed me down the hall. "I'm more concerned about what we're going to do about the footage from the kitchen."

"Nothing. The brass *want* you to grow closer to influential Syldrari. They'll see this as another notch on your obedience belt." He shook his head, his eyes narrowing. "Go change. I have something that may assist you—I will go fetch it from my office."

With that, we parted ways and I headed into my apartment, where I let out a groan of frustration and leaned against my desk. I was burning up, yet a glance in the mirror confirmed I wasn't even flushed. Rel's sweet, fresh taste lingered in my mouth, along with the sensation of his unusual tongue.

Fucking hell. How am I supposed to concentrate on the mission like this...

I stalked over to the bathroom and drenched my face in cold water. That was a little better. I smacked my damp cheeks a few times before bouncing back and forth on the balls of my feet, telling myself to *focus*.

When I'd finally started to calm down, I took a deep breath and called up the AR interface for my wardrobe module. Even if I was going suited up, I had a feeling I needed a backup plan. Otherwise, Xilen wouldn't have mentioned dressing 'appropriately.'

CHAPTER THIRTY-FOUR

I practiced breathing exercises as my shuttle ferried me to Xilen's city-ship, through the clouds and up to the orbital docking array. Much like the structures on the surface, the array had designated sections for ships by species, while the largest ships, such as the city-ships, waited further away. There was a brief stop on the array, long enough for me to board a second vessel more suited to system flight, and then I was on my way.

When I arrived at Xilen's ship, my transport docked at a different docking bay, one marked with symbols I didn't understand. *So I can understand the language when spoken but not read or speak it myself? Great...*

"Elara, darling." Xilen greeted me with a tired smile. "You must realize I didn't mean for you to come in your suit. Would this be your superiors' silliness?"

"You asked for Lethe, so they sent Lethe." I let the suit disappear as I walked toward her and the single guard accompanying her. Her smile broadened when she spotted the Syldrari-inspired pencil dress I'd chosen.

"Ahhh, Lynir mentioned that you have excellent taste." Xilen giggled, circling me briefly before stopping at my side. "I need you to act as neutral as you can muster."

"Because this is a party of *queens* you invited me to?" I shifted, watching her grimace.

"*Citomy* invited you. She heard rumors from somewhere regarding the Resonance Project—and rumors that you and your team's DNA was spliced with that of the humans' captive queens," she muttered bitterly. "I don't know what she's up to, but she's saying we need to embrace the 'synthetic queens.' And she's overly interested in what effect this splicing has had on the males of your team."

"So you think there's another mole," I murmured, rubbing my chin. *None of that sounds like the information Zafir has been giving Jysel. Hell, it sounds like the work of another researcher. Hmmm…*

"Be careful, dear." She gave me a firm look. "Now then, we should go, lest my guests grow suspicious."

I followed Xilen and her guard down the hallway leading away from the docking bay. The decoration was very human. Light walls, light stone tiled floors, and various *human* artwork and motion photography hanging from the walls.

"The Imperials are more comfortable talking in what they consider a homey environment," Xilen remarked, shooting me an amused smile. "One day I'll give you a proper tour of my ship. I think you'll find Syldrari aesthetics are much more to your taste."

"Quite likely," I agreed.

A pair of guards opened a set of double doors leading into a lounge area with deep red carpeting, leather and carved wood furniture, and nearly a dozen women—each accompanied by one or two guards. There was a bar at one end of the room, stocked high with glass bottles of both human and Syldrari liquors.

Not a single man here. I guess I shouldn't be surprised. Even all the guards and staff... I quickly spotted Citomy over by a pair of empty seats—which Xilen led me directly toward. *Great.*

"Ah! You didn't tell me she enjoys Syldrari fashions. I would have brought a different gift!" Citomy exclaimed, a bright smile spreading across her face as she examined me.

"A gift?" I kept my expression and tone neutral.

"Yes, I wish to personally thank you for your contributions protecting the Syldrari sector." Citomy rose gracefully to her feet and lifted a dark blue wooden box from her side table. She opened the box, revealing what appeared to be a dark, opalescent shell. Patterns were carved into the entire thing and lit from within using some kind of glowing substance that looked to be part of the shell.

"An early form of Syldrari art," she went on to explain. "The name translates to 'Hunter's Lantern' in your language. Syldrari warriors and hunters would carry these with them in the depths to light their camps and deter beasts—water flowing through the carvings creates a sound that disturbs the more dangerous cavern creatures."

"Thank you. It's beautiful." I accepted the box and visually traced the intricate patterns, then looked back to Citomy. "I apologize, I'm not quite sure of the proper way to address you."

"Citomy is quite fine." She continued to smile at me as she reclaimed her seat. "Syldrari don't have many formal titles—and the ones we do either don't translate well, or other species can't pronounce them."

Xilen sat as well, gesturing for me to do the same. Once I had, she turned to Citomy. "Elara has done much to help the Syldrari sector, but I must ask why you requested her presence here. Bringing a human to one of these get-togethers is unheard of."

"My sources tell me Elara's genetics were spliced with those of a queen—I wished to confirm that in an environment free of interference." Citomy focused her gaze on me. "It is quite unusual to encounter a human with a Syldran name."

"Your son, Rel, named me so that he wouldn't have to call me by a numerical designation like the humans did," I answered, drawing the attention of several other queens. "It was only within the past few months that the brass allowed us to take on names. For the past several years, we've all been referred to as 'Subject' followed by our assigned numbers."

"A *number*? How dreadful!" One of the other queens, a woman with deep brown skin and tri-toned neon pink, blue, and purple hair came to join us. "Humans. They treat all their subjects like they were grown in tubes..."

"For all I know, I was," I responded with a shrug. "My past was eradicated along with Grand Anldu. No one who may have known me is left. The same is true for the other survivors of the original Incident, of course."

"'The original?'" Citomy narrowed her eyes.

"You haven't heard?" I asked, and she shook her head. "Someone got their hands on either partially destroyed components of the resonance weapon, or perhaps fragments of the design. There have been eight more attacks that I'm aware of—with varying degrees of destruction. It appears that someone is using this planet for weapons testing."

Citomy's eyes widened. "You don't believe it's Jysel?"

"Hmm? Ah—the Syldrari who threatened the Creshe Empire?" I furrowed my brow and frowned, feigning brief confusion. "No. I hear he killed his own father in retribution for the Resonance Incident. It strikes me as illogical for someone who feels that strongly to turn around and use the same manner of weapon themselves. I'd sooner believe someone sold the damaged parts to another clan, or even the Imperial military.

"Besides, if his goal is the queens the Imperial military may be hiding, testing a weapon so recklessly would put those queens at risk. I would like to think Syldrari aren't anywhere near as stupid as humans."

Citomy just stared at me for a moment, while several of the other queens—Xilen included—attempted to hide amused laughter. "It's strange to think you're a mere soldier," she responded after a moment. "I thought the Imperials didn't allow their soldiers to think."

"I get that a lot." I smiled at her and crossed one leg over the other, leaning against my left arm rest. "I'm told I would have made a good researcher if the Incident hadn't changed the course of my life."

The queen with dark brown skin leaned on her armrest and smiled. "I see why Xilen likes you. My human name is Lilaek. It's a pleasure to meet you."

"It's good to meet you as well, Lilaek." I gave her a small smile. "Forgive my curiosity, but…human name?"

"Syldran names are long and difficult to say." She swirled her drink in her glass. "When we're born, we receive several names—a variant for each of the species we've encountered, as most Syldran names are only partially discernible to anyone else. In human terms, you could say that each Syldrari's name is a song.

"'Elara' translates to 'song of the depths' in your language because that is essentially what the full word is—a song about the deepest reaches of Syldra's oceans, and the mythical monsters and gods that dwell within it."

...Seriously? I wondered, aghast. *Does that mean that in Syldran, someone's full name is minutes long?*

"Rel did always enjoy the ancient legends and texts," Citomy murmured, an amused smile on her face. "He can be quite standoffish. There must be something about you that drew his attention immediately, for him to have named you after something so dear to him.

"Perhaps he should be another gift to you. As you aren't a queen, I'm sure he wouldn't mind terribly much. Would you like to have my son?"

Her offer took me by such surprise I could only stare at her for a moment. It was Xilen who spoke up first. "Citomy! You know Elara couldn't possibly afford his price—but *I can.*"

"Yes, yes, you're filthy rich—but yours is a clan of *merchants.* You're not warriors, you have no hope of capturing a R'selkti's interest beyond the money we can make when you hire us to guard your convoys.

"Elara is a human with a queen's genetic material, and a warrior in her own right. She's much better suited to keep my Rel. As for the price...well. I'm sure the Imperial government would be happy to pay."

What in the... My mind sped through the options at hand. If I said yes, that seemed like a surefire way to damage Rel's trust—and it would break my own moral code to boot. If I said no, then Citomy would continue attempting to sell Rel—and potentially succeed with a horrible buyer. Then there were the myriad other issues…

"I struggle to see how selling your offspring is an acceptable practice. However, putting that aside, I won't be alive for long even if I retire comfortably."

Citomy paused mid-reach for her communicator and gave me a strange look. "What is so unacceptable about it? And humans have plenty of technology to keep themselves alive forever. I'm sure you'll manage just fine, dear."

"I'm incompatible with their life extension technologies. All of them. I'm nearing the age where they typically replace a soldier's body, so they began running tests." I narrowed my eyes at her—an expression that made the others visibly nervous. "As for selling *people*… Humans from many planets have a storied history of human trafficking and enslaving both other races and species merely because they're different and therefore apparently inferior.

"As someone who is working for the military only because my other option was to be sold to the highest bidder—I can't condone such practices."

"They would sell someone with a queen's genetics?!" Lilaek demanded, turning to look at Citomy. "We can't let the humans—"

"You *do* want my son, though, don't you?" Citomy leaned forward, her expression unreadable as she peered at me.

"If I'm going to 'have' or 'keep' *any lun'iri*—or anyone *else*, now that I think about it—it will be because they give themselves to me willingly. Not because they were sold, or gifted, or anything else of the sort," I shot back, refusing to back down. "People shouldn't be sold. *That* is how you end up with dozens of species forced into an 'entertainment' club like the one I busted. The one, I should point out, that had Syldrari of every sex held drugged and captive.

"It's a slippery slope. Take a wrong step and suddenly even more of your species will be selling their own people to turn a profit or silence people."

"What do you mean, 'more of?'" Lilaek frowned, turning to face me fully. "As far as I'm aware—"

"Yes, Imperator Julien? I wish to discuss the potential sale of my first-born son to one of the women produced by the Resonance Project," Citomy drawled into her communicator, ignoring the rest of us. "Hm? Of course I know about the Resonance Project. I have eyes and ears everywhere, dear. Now then…"

"Elara, what were you talking about?" Lilaek nudged me worriedly. Noticing my questioning look, she explained, "I'm…well, think of me as the Minister of Defense, Justice, and Law."

"I see. At least one of the Syldrari was sold to the club by his queen, and it sounded like it's a fairly common practice. The other people I rescued, and the other Syldrari I've interacted with, were all unsurprised," I answered, watching as Lilaek's expression began to contort with anger, her gaze darting between the other queens. "Would it help if I explained what he looks like? From what I understand, Syldrari coloration is regional…"

"Yes. Please." Lilaek nodded firmly. "Selling Syldrari for profit is illegal, and this queen must face punishment."

"He's translucent white with blue and pink hair, and he appears to be from a clan dedicated to research," I offered, watching as Lilaek's eyes widened. "I would appreciate it if you didn't make too much commotion or drag him back into the mess unnecessarily. The poor boy is quite traumatized."

"What makes you think you can give *any* of us orders?" one of the other queens snapped, glowering at me.

"It was a request—not an order." I gave the woman a foul look. "And considering you aren't human, you shouldn't find me so threatening that you feel the need to start barking like a frightened dog."

"Would you like to take Jysel, too? My twins would be perfect for you," Citomy called, glancing in my direction before returning her attention to the communicator. "What do you *mean* that's more credits than your treasury would have even if your Empire had never spent any of it?"

"The Empire is less than a thousand years old. They can't

pay even a fraction of what you want for *one* of your children, let alone two of them..." Xilen rubbed her temples as Citomy shot her a blank look.

"What about that planet we were discussing? Give it to me, and I will give both Rel and Jysel to Elara," Citomy suggested. "There will be some terms, of course, to make certain you and your people don't dissect or study my sons overmuch, but you did say the project forerunners wish to see if breeding hybrids is a possibility, yes?" Citomy stood and began pacing in front of the window as she argued with the *fucking leader of the Creshe Empire* about selling her twins to me.

"Shhh. Have a ludrán." Xilen covered my mouth with her hand, shoving at least half a dozen candies into it. "Imperator Julien is a smart man. For a human, anyway. He won't give in. He, unlike Citomy, has a firm grasp on the known universe's economy..."

"How dare he!" Citomy threw her communicator across the room. Crossing her arms, she stalked over to the bar.

Xilen shrugged and gave me a small smile. "See?"

"I didn't see anything," I mumbled around my mouthful of candy.

"Smart girl," Lilaek remarked dryly. "Before I begin my investigation, I suppose I should calm Citomy down."

"Citomy, Elara's allotted time is up—she must return to the surface." Xilen's words earned a disgruntled pout from the other woman. "Come along, Elara."

I considered leaving behind my gift, but something told me not to. Instead, I picked up the box, thanked Citomy for her generosity, and left the room with Xilen.

Once we were out of the damn room, I glanced at Xilen. "Why did she seem so bitter about your wealth?"

She perked up, a bright smile coming to her face. "Ah! I'd be happy to explain Syldran trade to you! Traditionally, Syldrari use money for very few things. Throughout most of our history—and even now—necessities are provided communally and without charge. Luxuries are bought with *i'jahlti*, which is a leaf-shaped currency carved from shells like the one in that box you're carrying.

"Luxuries, to a Syldrari, are things that can't be traded for fairly or created yourself in the absence of trade. Usually, this means paying someone to play a part in the creation of an artistic work, such as hiring someone who plays an instrument you can't to improve your composition. These services are often traded as well, but there are also situations when they aren't. At any rate, exposure to other cultures made it necessary for us to understand and adopt a more direct currency system for trade with other species."

"I can't even begin to understand how Syldra even *has* an economy." I rubbed my temples.

"We're creators and scholars by nature, darling." Xilen smiled. "All most of us wish to do is create, research, and experiment in peace without other stresses distracting us.

"Citomy has come to feel that her clan is underpaid and has been slighted for millennia, as both her birth clan and the R'selkti are warriors who spend their lives fighting off the dangerous fauna of our world—plus other off-world threats. She expects the compensation to mirror the old trades. As I'm so rich that I could afford a living ship if I wanted one, Citomy is quite jealous of my wealth and the freedom it affords me outside Syldra."

I rolled my eyes. "She sells her children off and she still isn't rich enough? Oh, how my heart breaks for her…"

"Yes, well, she's awful with money and never listens to her financial advisor since he's one of her husbands." Xilen sighed in exasperation. "Granted, she didn't listen to any of her other advisors, either. She believes that if she wants something, she should take it. If she can't take it, she will buy it. She is very human in that regard."

"How did she manage to produce such emotionally mature sons, then?" I asked, aghast.

"Oh, the tried and true desire to not become like one's parents transcends even the boundaries of species," she mused. "A half-grilled steak would be observant enough to tell that Citomy's habits are almost all frowned upon." She paused for a moment, humming odd sounds under her breath. "Half-grilled steak, hmmm… That saying didn't translate quite as well as I'd hoped."

"Do I even *want* to know?" I grimaced.

"There's a delicacy I enjoy on another planet, but it's cooked alive. Well, 'alive' is a fairly loose term, all things considered, as no one can seem to agree whether it should be classified as a living creature or a vegetable…"

Yep. Didn't want to know. I shook my head. "Right. Anyway, this is my stop?"

"Yes… And I recommend you regale Rel with his mother's antics the moment you have a chance." Xilen narrowed her eyes at me. "It's best he hears it from you before she gets a chance to twist the tale. She's spiteful—it's likely she will try to ruin whatever relationship you have with both Rel *and* Jysel."

"Thanks for the advice." I nodded to her as she opened the door to the ship's bay, the waiting pilot bowing slightly when he spotted us.

I stopped, turning to look at Xilen, but she merely placed a finger over my lips and smiled. "Don't worry, Elara. I'll be fine, and I'll keep tabs on Lilaek's investigation. The sheer amount of wealth I can command makes the other queens *highly* inclined to stay on my good side."

"Still, be careful. There's things happening on the surface that I'm concerned about too, and they're not the kind money can save you from." I sighed and gave her a firm look. "You know who you can ask for details."

"Just for you, I'll be extra cautious." She giggled, gently nudging me toward the shuttle. "Go on, now. I'm sure Rel and Zafir are beside themselves with worry."

CHAPTER THIRTY-FIVE

When I returned to the surface, it was raining heavily, so I hurried indoors and stepped into the elevator that would take me to my team's common area. The room was empty, leaving me to wander around for a few minutes in search of Zafir—who I found sitting in his office with Rel. Both looked rather grumpy, though they perked up when I poked my head in.

Rel was first to his feet, striding over to me with concern in his eyes. "Elara, are you alright? You were gone longer than we anticipated."

"I'm fine, we can talk about it shortly." I nudged gently past him and placed my boxed present on Zafir's desk. "I assume we don't wish to outright trust a gift from Citomy?"

"A *gift* from…?" Rel joined me at the desk and reached past me, opening the lid. There was a brief flicker of emotion I didn't recognize before he too looked to Zafir. "Well?"

"One moment." Zafir reached into a drawer under his desk and pulled out a weird glove-thing with pinpricks of light all over its surface. He ran his hand over the outside of the box, the inside, then gently handled the object. "We appear to be clear. I suppose she didn't anticipate that there could already be animosity brewing."

"A gift… A shame she chose one that is actually an insult." Rel's murmured comment earned him a questioning glance from both me *and* Zafir. "This is one of the pieces I carved when I was much younger and had yet to leave Syldra. As such, Citomy is aware that it has no monetary value, as it wasn't created by a skilled artisan. Then, of course, there's the indication that she doesn't value any of my work enough to keep it for the sentimental reasons a mother normally would."

"Oh… Is it okay for me to keep it, then?" I asked, a tad concerned. I nibbled on one of my knuckles as I studied the intricate piece. Maybe he was being humble, or perhaps he was just being honest—I couldn't tell. All *I* knew was that I found it beautiful, and I was going to be disappointed if he said no—or worse, suggested we destroy it.

"Keep it?" He turned to face me fully, his eyes slightly widened. "I certainly won't complain if you wish to keep one of my pieces, but are you certain you wouldn't prefer something more professional?"

"But I like this one." I pointed at the lantern and stared back at him. "It's beautiful and you clearly spent an immense amount of time on it. Why wouldn't I want to keep it?"

"That's..." He floundered, clearly at a loss.

"He must have spent months on this," Zafir murmured, giving the lantern a thorough examination. "Ah—and this gash here on the underside—caused by a close call with your prey, I take it?"

"Yes. Like the other R'selkti *lun'iri* my age, I whittled and carved it when I was off duty," Rel answered, looking surprisingly embarrassed. "It served me well. When I was pulled from my duties permanently, I gave it to my mother like the naive boy I still was at the time."

"About your mother..." I crossed my arms and sighed. "Let's sit down. There a cup around here for me somewhere? I'd like some of that tea, too."

"Certainly," Zafir answered, carefully placing the lantern back in its box and closing the lid. Once he'd poured me a cup of tea, he sat back down. "What do you have to report?"

"Citomy tried to sell Rel to me, and insinuated she wanted me to take Jysel off her hands too," I stated bluntly.

"What... Why didn't you? You should have accepted. You, at least, are—" Rel fell silent when I reached over and put a finger to his lips to hush him.

"I didn't get a chance to answer her either way. She called Imperator Julien to try to get him to pay for you. She seems to think 'gifts' must still be bought. She was quickly informed the Empire doesn't have that kind of money.

"As for whether I should have accepted… Wouldn't that be breaking your trust? I'll admit I considered saying yes just to avoid her trying to sell you to some other awful queen, but I'm not sure my intentions really matter in such a situation."

"I would have *forgiven* you. It might take a few years, of course, but…" Rel fell silent for a moment at the look I gave him. "What?"

"I could be dead by the time you forgave me, at the rate things are going," I stated flatly, causing him to narrow his eyes. "We shouldn't forget the situation I'm in. Since I'm incompatible with the military's usual methods of prolonging a soldier's life, I'll be retired in the next year or two, maximum. My retirement will either consist of training the teams here, or a complete mind wipe and reprogramming so they can sell me to the highest bidder—either an individual or a brothel. Then, of course, there's the possibility I could die in combat."

"She may lack a certain amount of tact when discussing the various forms of death, but unfortunately she's quite correct," Zafir stated with a heavy sigh. "This will only become a bigger problem if the war council orders me to research a method of delaying her progressing cellular dissonance. There are some among the brass who want her to remain completely human."

"Purists," Rel muttered irritably. "We should be hastening

her return to Syldrari form, not delaying it. The longer her DNA remains mixed with human genetics, the more likely it is that one of those weaknesses will be exploited."

"To be quite blunt, I'm more concerned about why Citomy tried to sell you and Jysel to Elara." Zafir frowned and rested his forearms on the desk, his hands clasped together. "I've never heard of a queen trying to sell a child to someone she believes to be human."

"About that…" I hesitated, glancing around the room and then back to Zafir. "Is it safe to talk in here?"

"It is as of a few hours ago," Rel remarked with amusement, shooting Zafir a smug look. "Because one of us, at least, is more than happy to knock all offending devices offline."

"Okay, then I should report the entire experience on Xilen's ship." I nodded, proceeding to explain my discussions with the queens, including the strong indication that Zafir wasn't the only mole in the Resonance Project.

"Such a strange conclusion…their rank must not be very high…" Zafir murmured. "It's very clear that you were not spliced with foreign material to make you as you are now."

"Unless it happened before the Resonance Incident. Even so, I think it's clear the human material is the intruder." Rel tapped his fingers against the armrest. "We can't rule out the possibility that what Citomy said is in fact the truth, but merely flipped. She and her advisors often hide the truth in plain sight by simply switching, for example, the cause and effect of certain events in their reports.

"As for the mole, it would have to be someone either lower or higher-ranking than you—someone you haven't come into contact with. Otherwise you would have discovered them already."

"Unless the R'selkti have new stealth technology, yes," Zafir grumbled irritably. "Alas, we don't have any contacts who might be able to find out. At best, I could have other departments rotate through different sections of HQ, or perhaps spend some of my time personally overseeing certain tasks."

"Then you yourself would be discovered. No," I stated flatly. "We'd all be better off if you just told me what to look for."

"She's right. You shouldn't risk yourself." Rel shook his head faintly. "I will remain alert for suspicious individuals when I am here. However, I do not think Elara should go looking for them, either. Considering she is one of the few things keeping a modicum of peace between the humans and the Syldrari, it would be best if nothing bad happens to her."

"Hmm? Me?" I gave him an odd look. "I don't really do enough to be classified as the glue currently holding peace together."

"You do more than you know—simply by being you. Try not to think on it too much." Rel gave me a half-smile before turning his attention to Zafir. "You've gone quiet."

"A report came in…" Zafir murmured as he skimmed his data pad, a frown forming on his face. "I need to study this, if you will excuse—"

Both men paused, Rel's head turning in the direction of the door.

"What are they watching…" he muttered, rising to his feet. Zafir was right behind him, leaving me to hurry after the pair of concerned-looking males.

When we reached the lounge, I spotted my female teammates sitting on the couches, their knees pulled up to their chests as they watched TV. They looked utterly entranced by whatever was on the screen. I followed their gazes, finding a glitching, obscured image of a cloaked figure on the screen. The image appeared to be in greyscale, making it impossible to determine the individual's skin color. By the texture, however, I had a sinking feeling they were Syldrari.

The figure's long coat was adorned with a strong tentacle motif etched in metal, and while I couldn't tell if it was because of the glitching image or the greyscale, I could have sworn I saw some of the tentacles shift and move.

"…*You can make the R'selkti chase their tails, but those blessed by the Abyss Father will not be fooled. You will pay for what you have done to our people, for the twisted experiments you've performed and the devastating weapons you've stolen. Humans are merely overgrown children, and you* will *be shown your place.*"

The image glitched out again, then the screen went dark. Aisu smashed futilely at the buttons on the remote, while Sarah and

Diana both brought up data pads, trying to pull up any feed they could find. I peeked over their shoulders, but no video came up, not even static or noise. After a moment, Diana glanced back at me and shook her head.

"Nothin'," Aisu muttered irritably. "They cut their feed and looks like all systems are down."

"Go see if Amara can work her magic," I ordered, watching the three women rise to their feet. "We need to figure out who that was and, if possible, where they were broadcasting from."

"'Those blessed by the Abyss Father?'" Rel repeated quietly. "When did *they* get here? The last I heard, they were dozens of systems away from Syldra—and in the opposite direction of this planet, at that."

Sensing movement, I glanced over my shoulder to find an agitated General Crowe walking toward us. He promptly caught Rel's attention and asked, "Who are 'they'?"

"You could call them a religious cult, for simplicity's sake." Rel fell silent for a moment, seeming to consider something. "If I may go into slightly more detail…"

Crowe nodded. "Please. All our reports claim Syldrari aren't religious."

Rel sighed and crossed his arms loosely. "Syldrari do not worship deities. We venerate historical figures—our collective ancestors—who made great discoveries or advancements in their time.

"The 'Abyss Father' is a more controversial figure, as he is one of the few venerated *lun'iri*—men. It was thanks to his discoveries and developments that early Syldrari were able to master the depths of our home world. However, the many contradictory legends surrounding his person make most hesitant to acknowledge he ever actually lived.

"The deeper he fades into obscurity, the more fanatical groups rise around his mythos. Most of the groups are harmless, as they simply wish to preserve history. However, there are other sects who now consider him to be a deity...and they can be dangerous in their devotion."

"Do you have any idea what they're accusing us of?" Crowe frowned, glancing toward the blank screen. "It sounded personal."

"It could be as petty as someone mocking Syldrari culture, or as serious as believing that your government tortured and killed someone important to their cause. They're unstable and unpredictable." Rel glanced in my direction. "Of course, if the rumors Citomy told Elara are circulating through other Syldrari circles..."

"Rumors?" Crowe turned to look at me fully. "You and Zafir are coming to my office. I require a full report. You may rest after.

"Rel, I am having Erik drive you back to the Syldrari district for now. Zafir will notify you of any potential changes to Elara's schedule."

"...Very well." Rel glanced at me, hesitating briefly before making his way to the elevator and taking his leave.

As for me, I joined Crowe and Zafir so I could give a full report. Again.

CHAPTER THIRTY-SIX

I walked through the common area, carrying a stack of books back to my room. I had the floor to myself, as Sarah had taken the team out to get more acquainted with the city. She'd offered for me to join them, but I'd chosen to fetch the martial arts books Rel had sent instead. After a few days of stewing on my defeat, I figured I needed all the help I could get.

Watching TV had crossed my mind as an option, but every time I tried, it was all just news of murder victims, interspecies tensions, or reports of people finding torture victims. Most of it sounded like propaganda created to turn the human populace against their alien brethren. I could only stomach so much of that.

And so, I'd decided on more productive, happy activities.

"Elara, stop that!" Zafir hissed, grabbing my arm suddenly. I shot a puzzled look at his stern face. "My office. Now."

"Stop what?" I asked, baffled, as he pulled me into his office. He brushed his hand over an object by the door that I'd begun to think was how he signaled Amara to start tinkering with the surveillance. "Zafir?"

As if *another* measure of protection was needed, a sound I *felt* more than heard *ping*ed through the room. Finally, he turned to me, his eyes narrowing as his human disguise vanished. "If the wrong person heard what you were just doing, they would glass this planet and write the loss of Clan V'shir and any visiting delegates off as permissible losses."

"Uh…?" I frowned more deeply at him. "Ok…ay? But what was I doing? I was just carrying these books back to my room."

Zafir took off his glasses and rubbed the bridge of his nose. "You were *humming*."

I shot him a foul look over the stack of books I carried. "If you're about to tell me that *humming* is so culturally offensive that it'd warrant such an extreme response, I will slap you."

"It's *what* you were humming, Elara. Forbidden knowledge, locked-away histories, suspected clan erasures—many generations have done their damnedest to keep songs like what you were just humming sealed away. There isn't a single living queen who is privy to those secrets." He took a deep breath and then collapsed into a chair, leaning his head back. "And you didn't even *realize* you were humming… I'm going to have to prohibit you from humming or singing. Perhaps your chip can be modified…"

"Slow down. What do you mean, forbidden knowledge?" I sighed in exasperation as I moved to stand in front of him. Slowing down, I took a moment to consider how I felt before asking, "Was this what I was humming?"

Zafir tensed as he listened to the brief melody, his pupils closing so tight I could barely see them. "Yes. Yes, that. You need to stop doing that. If someone discovers you know even part of that song, we won't be able to protect you."

Confused, I stared back at him. Deep in my bones, I could feel that it was nothing so dangerous as he was implying. I often heard it in my mind when I was trying to go to sleep for the evening.

"Zafir. It's a lullaby. That's all. I know it deep in my bones. Why would—"

"How would you…? A lullaby? …Oh no." He was on his feet in an instant. Moving over to a bookcase, he pulled some kind of metal instrument from it. He laid it flat on the nearest surface and a 3D star map shimmered into view above it. None of the labels or other symbols were legible to me, leading me to believe it was a Syldran star map. Zafir continued to mutter to himself as he flicked through multiple parts of the known universe, his skin several shades lighter than usual.

"…Zafir?" I called.

"If you think it's a lullaby, then…" he mumbled, tracing a line from one planet down through a series of multiple galaxies and the many systems within them. "Then…hmmm, there's only so many clans who would fit the profile. If it was *them*…"

My shoulders slumped. I wasn't going to get a clear answer out of him anytime soon, and the books I was carrying were getting heavier by the moment. Finally, I set them down and took a seat across from where Zafir had been sitting. From there, I watched him continue to trace between more and more points in space. It was a good ten minutes later when he finally stopped on a planet I recognized—the one we were currently on.

"It is possible…" he murmured in Syldran, then glanced at me. "If I'm right, it would explain why I can't match your genetic data to any legal database. However…it means we must be careful. I can't tell you a single *word* of my hypothesis. At least, not regarding your specific clan ties. It's too dangerous. They might be willing to strike even if Citomy was still on the surface."

"And you're just going to leave me hanging after all that?" I narrowed my eyes. "Like I said, it's a—"

"The only clans who would use such a destructive song as a *lullaby* have been dead for four millennia or more—and queenless for longer!" he snapped back, his hands curling by his sides. "*Unless* I'm right. And if I am, the humans and Citomy are the least of our concerns right now."

I stared back at him in begrudging silence as he walked over and sat across from me.

After a moment, he leaned forward pleadingly. "Elara... I need you to trust me as I've trusted you. If you want to live—if you want any of the Syldrari you've met here to live—don't press me. Don't hum. Don't sing."

"You're asking me to act like you don't have a lead on my origins, and like I—"

"*Elara.* We have a saying: Syldrari create, all others destroy. Yet there are clans who see art in destruction – and they invariably go too far. Maybe not in their first generation, maybe not even in their six thousandth. But eventually.

"There are only so many crimes, clans, or people so depraved that we would be willing to glass a planet—and we would then spend the next several centuries bringing life back to that planet. Perhaps even less, given how far our technology has advanced since the last such occurrence...

"Then there are primal fears. Much like how early human explorers feared their oceans—the creatures, or where the waters flowed—the Syldrari once feared their seas too. Then, we had the entire universe to fear.

"For a time, the universe was believed to be flat—only as thick as the thickest body suspended within it – but gradually, we advanced. We came to understand that the universe is yet another ocean, one of indeterminate shape. It even has incredibly strange lifeforms living within it, beyond planetary confines.

"When you see something you initially believed to be an asteroid *breathe* or *bleed*, or chew through a ship like it's a midday snack, you begin to wonder what other fascinating horrors exist in the universe.

"And if the universe is just another ocean… Do you have to swim deeper to discover the *true* oddities and nightmares lurking there? How deeply into the abyss of the universe must you go—is it even measurable? Would you know when you've arrived…or whether you had piloted your ship directly into the stomach of one of those horrors you were searching for?"

I eyed the rather serious Syldrari. "And what does this have to do with—"

"A forgotten—or hidden—fact about many of those so-called crazed clans: They created destructive art because they believed they would need it where they were going." He folded his hands in his lap and leaned forward, locking eyes with me. "I will investigate during my free time. There should be evidence on this planet *somewhere* if early Syldrari explorers crashed, settled, or otherwise formed an outpost here. Once it's safe to do so, I will let you know what I find. In return, *you* will act like a good little ignorant human and lay low. No humming. No singing. I would rather not tinker with your chip, but if you can't control your need for song…"

I groaned and gave him a pout. "Seriously. I didn't realize I was humming until you said I was. If it's really that dangerous, then maybe… Look. I don't want to endanger you or the others.

But wouldn't it be suspicious if I'm put in a situation where I'm expected to sing and *can't?*"

"I'll leave your chip alone for the moment, but I should be able to program it to only allow you to sing or hum certain things." Zafir rubbed his chin, an odd sparkle in his eyes. "Though I must confess, dangers aside, I'm curious to know how you could still know such a song, with your memories so thoroughly gone… Perhaps gene memory? Or…"

I eyed him, unamused. "And why do *you* know it? If it's really so dangerous, I doubt it was broadcast with a 'don't sing this' warning."

He gave me a mysterious smile. "I worked in many interesting places after I graduated last."

"Graduated *last?*" I echoed, finding his phrasing odd.

"You don't live as long as we do and study only *one* field." He waved a hand dismissively and rose to his feet. That actually hadn't been the source of my confusion, but he continued on. "I should get to work on these new conundrums, and you have reading to do."

"It's supposed to be your day off…" I sighed, a wave of guilt briefly hitting me.

"And what better way to spend it than on a passion project? It's been a while since I last worked on something I found personally interesting. Let's see…" He wandered over to his desk, his human disguise reappearing.

I hesitated before deciding to take the hint and left with my books. What was I supposed to do with the information Zafir had given me? I wanted answers, and not on Syldrari time. No, I wanted them before my inevitable demise.

I paused outside my door. *Or…is he hinting that my aging and lifespan haven't been reduced to that of a human? In which case…he* wants *the Imperials to retire me. For what reason? Protection? What is his aim?*

Whatever it was, my gut said to trust him—so that's what I decided to do.

CHAPTER THIRTY-SEVEN

"Out of the question. Elara is meant to be distancing herself from the Syldrari sector to alleviate suspicions." Zafir's firm voice drifted down the hall, piquing my curiosity.

"And your decision has been overruled. I need her," a woman's voice said in calm, measured tones. I peeked around the corner to spot a human woman with dark skin and hair in many small, adorned braids. She wore a pantsuit and low heels, along with a few pieces of jewelry that looked more like tech than decoration.

I considered my options for a moment, then sighed, straightened, and stepped out from the hallway. "You need me? I'm right here, but I'm getting breakfast first."

The pair of them stared at me in surprise as I walked past, both seeming to register at the same time that I was wearing Syldran clothes.

"Elara, I know you have nothing else to wear, but—"

"See? She will make a perfect ambassador! She's adopting their aesthetics, learning about their culture and mannerisms—gaining their trust!" The woman rounded on Zafir. "All of which I've been unable to do! I can't set foot in the Syldrari sector without drawing suspicion—with or without an escort!"

"You say that like they weren't suspicious of me at first."

"You got through, so clearly they—"

"They were suspicious of me. I didn't care." I shook my head and kept moving toward the kitchen. "Being the typical frightened little human isn't how you get to know the Syldrari, Miss…uh…?"

"Ambassador Nomusa." The woman quickly hurried to follow me. "Just Nomusa. I cast off surnames ages ago. Never liked the practice."

"And what, exactly, is it that you need me for?" I asked as I rummaged around in the fridge for something easy to make.

"I've been trying to make connections in the Syldrari sector ever since I took over as Ambassador," Nomusa began eagerly. "Clan V'shir's relationship with my predecessor fell apart a few years before I replaced him. Since then, the Empire's understanding of the Syldrari has waned, while their fear has risen. I want to close that gap before the Empire does something stupid."

"Crowe briefed her on our suspicions regarding purists

within the Imperator's inner circle causing problems," Zafir offered as he leaned against the doorway. "This accelerated her timeline, she believes."

"I know the Empire, professor." Nomusa turned to glare at Zafir. "The moment they convince the Imperator the Syldrari are a threat, they'll fire their strongest weapons at the Syldrari sector and all orbiting Syldrari ships. It's my *job* to keep it from coming to that."

"So you want me to take you into the Syldrari sector and introduce you to people?" I sighed. "Like that's going to be enough."

"No, I want you to work with me directly on this project. I want you to introduce me to the V'shir, certainly, but it's going to take hard work on both our parts to mend the wounds my predecessor left." Nomusa stared back at me with fiery eyes. "I won't stand idle and let countless Syldrari lives be lost!"

I glanced over her shoulder at Zafir, who appeared lost in contemplation. After a moment, he nodded and I let out a small sigh. "Fine—we can see how it goes. *After* I eat—"

"You'll just be going to Rel's anyway. Pick up breakfast there," Zafir interrupted, an amused smile spreading across his face. "If Ambassador Nomusa is serious, she will have to learn to enjoy—or at least tolerate—Syldrari cuisine and its scents."

"Uh…?" Nomusa glanced between us questioningly.

"Most humans consider it an acquired taste." I shut the fridge and rummaged around in my pockets. "Syldrari taste things differently…hmmm. Here, have a ludrán. It's a Syldrari candy."

I offered Nomusa a bright red ludrán, which she carefully unwrapped before giving it a tentative sniff. As she hesitated, I preemptively poured a glass of milk for her.

"It doesn't taste that—" Nomusa cut herself off with a sound of pain and strangulation, then began fanning her mouth. I handed her the glass of milk, which she knocked back like it was a damn shot.

"Sweet and fruity, to a Syldrari." I informed her, walking past. "I'll try to convince Rel to go easy on you, but he enjoys testing his food on non-Syldrari. He finds their various reactions fascinating."

"Sweet…that…*how?*" Nomusa chased after me, faint beads of sweat on her forehead. "Even my mother's cooking isn't that hot!"

"Well, there's lots of reasons. Uh…" I eyed her. "Perhaps I should explain on our way there? Do you have a driver?"

"Erik will take you," Zafir called as he strode past us. "I instructed him to meet you in the lobby, and to join you in the sector for once. If you aren't gone too long, bring back some food for the rest of us. I'll be in my office."

Nomusa peered at us. "…You all *enjoy* Syldrari food?"

"Look. I'm sure you know that food is a great vehicle for learning about different cultures among humans, right? It's the same with aliens, too—but don't call them that." I pressed my fingers to my temples. "The Syldrari are artists in all they do.

You want to understand them, learn more about their culture? Then start by experiencing their food. Or, well, trying to. They can be quite chatty with people who show interest."

"Artists…" Nomusa murmured the word to herself a few times as we descended in the elevator, then her expression lit up. "Artists! That's it! Artists wish for their work to be recognized and appreciated, and as such they must be eager to talk about their art. This 'Rel' person must be an artist of the culinary variety, yes?"

"It's one of his many talents, to be sure." I nodded, noticing the sly look she gave me. "What?"

"What *other* talents do you know about? Hmmm? I hear they're very…*giving*." She waggled her eyebrows at me.

"No idea. Subjects in the Resonance Project are forbidden from engaging in intimate or pleasurable acts with anyone—inside of the facility or out." I shrugged and linked my hands behind my back. "You're more likely to find out than I am. Between the two of us, you're the free *iri*."

"*Iri?*" Nomusa inquired, chasing after me yet again when the elevator opened.

"I see I need to give you a briefing on the way there." I sighed and looked to Erik as he approached us. "Morning, Erik. You mind taking a longer route? It looks like I need to give Ambassador Nomusa a crash course on our way to the Syldrari sector."

"Sure." He nodded, tossing me a packaged bar, then grinned at my questioning look. "You're gonna need a snack if we're taking the long route."

I smirked at him. "Thanks."

Erik and Nomusa followed me down one of the Syldrari sector's main streets, just barely managing to keep up with my brisk pace. Erik looked a tad uncomfortable, but not for the reason I'd have expected. More than a few particularly androgynous Syldrari appeared to recognize him, either calling to him by name or waving flirtatiously at him.

I was starting to get a mental picture of why there had always been dance music in the background whenever I called him to pick me up. But I wasn't going to tease or question him about it. The Syldrari clearly *liked* him quite a lot—and I wasn't entirely sure I wanted to know why.

Nomusa, on the other hand, was a tad harder to keep in line. She wanted to look at everything and everyone. Her obvious fascination seemed to be making the Syldrari a bit uncomfortable, but they were tolerating her...for the moment, anyway. I just hoped I hadn't appeared so obnoxiously curious when I'd first come to the sector.

"Come on. I'm hungry." I pulled Nomusa away from the Syldrari she'd been inching closer to. "And *you* need to get ahold of yourself. These are people. Not a circus for you to gawk at."

"I— Sorry. It's just…they're so pretty. *Everything* is so pretty!" She glanced around, then pointed to a mural on the side of a building. "See? In the rest of the city, no matter how beautiful the piece, it would just be mocked as graffiti and removed. Here, it's left on display!"

"Elara *did* tell you they're an artistic bunch." Erik shrugged, his hands in his pockets.

"Mhm. Artistic." I shot him an amused side glance. "Which you clearly know more about than I thought."

"Er…" He cleared his throat. "Let's get moving."

"I don't mean to offend anyone…" Nomusa murmured. "It's just so rare to see any Syldrari since they usually stay in this sector."

"You've never personally met any of them?" I sighed in disbelief. "Well, come on. We can fix that, at least."

With some difficulty, we got Nomusa moving and made our way to Rel's café without too many more interruptions. Erik held the door open for us, though he hesitated before following us in. An amused smile came to my face when Casair whipped around at the bar and raised a weapon—which he clearly forgot completely when he spotted me.

"Uh… Elara…" The rifle drifted downward, his gaze running down my body.

"Put that away, won't you?" I walked over and patted his arm, giving him a charming smile before I flicked my eyes back the way I'd come. "I would appreciate it if no one here frightened

Ambassador Nomusa. She's already a bit overwhelmed by all the sights, sounds, and smells she's never experienced before."

"Ambassador…" Casair looked past me, then lowered his rifle and glanced away bashfully. "Apologies, ma'am. Everyone's on edge with all that's been goin' on as of late…"

"What is all the—" Rel appeared from the back room, pausing as he rolled up his cuffs. He tilted his head faintly when he spotted Nomusa and Erik, then turned his attention in my direction. "Elara, should I be preparing a private room?"

"Rel, this is Ambassador Nomusa," I informed him, shaking my head no. "She wants my help learning more about Syldrari people, culture, and customs. Considering I'm still learning myself… Well, you like trying your food out on new humans, right?"

Rel gave me an odd look, then eyed Nomusa. His expression grew stern when he looked at her—a fact that didn't go unnoticed by Casair, who stroked his chin thoughtfully.

"Nomusa, is it? You're aware that there's bad blood with the former ambassador?" He finished rolling up his sleeves and fastened them in place, then gracefully glided along the bar, his fingers trailing over the polished surface. Suddenly he stopped and narrowed his eyes at me. "Elara, I can hear your stomach from here. Take a seat." He paused to glance briefly at Erik. "I suppose you may find a seat as well, though you and Ambassador Nomusa will likely be taking a booth."

I perched on the remaining free seat beside Casair and leaned forward with amusement. "Her palate is a bit delicate. Don't be too mean."

"...Delicate?" he asked wryly.

I held up one of the red ludrán. "*This* flavor is too spicy for her. She mentioned something about her family cooking spicy things, but..."

"Elara, there are a dozen flavors in that color. Be more specific—" he started, so I promptly unwrapped the candy and pressed it into his mouth. I gave him a sweet smile in response to the half-flustered, half-aggravated look he shot me as he begrudgingly chewed the candy. After a moment, he raised an eyebrow. "...That is spicy to humans?"

"Mhm." I nodded, settling back in my seat. "I'm pretty sure she's genuine about wanting to learn, but if you want to question her and her motives, be my guest."

"What—?" Nomusa started nervously when Rel gave her a sharp look.

"Syldrari know when someone is lying," I informed her sweetly. "So, if your intentions aren't as pure and innocent as you claim..."

"...Then you're in a room full of people who can make you disappear, and escorted by two people who will help," Erik finished, crossing his arms over his chest. "The Syldrari are some of the nicest, most hospitable people I've ever known—but only if you're worthy of their trust."

"I suppose I should handle the questions..." Rel hesitated, glancing my way again, then released a reluctant sigh. "Aldiner, Ciheri—come keep Elara entertained. Show her how you've improved your cooking abilities while you're at it."

"Hey, I can entertain her just fine myself." Casair shot Rel a disgruntled glare.

"You can. But can you feed her? No? I thought not." Rel made a dismissive motion as he moved toward Nomusa and Erik. "Now then, I believe we should speak privately. Once I've determined your intentions, we can return here and I will prepare a meal for you—assuming your intentions are favorable."

He led the pair of them somewhere upstairs, leaving me with the intrigued-looking Aldiner and Ciheri and the clearly uncomfortable Casair.

"Elara, last time I saw you, you mentioned potentially not being around for much longer..." Casair started quietly, causing Aldiner and Ciheri to give us simultaneous odd looks. "You aren't thinking of doing something foolish, are you?"

"Hmm?" I blinked at him for a moment, before it hit me what he was implying. "Oh! No. I was speaking in relative terms, Casair. I've been led to believe my lifespan is that of a non-augmented, untouched human. I could be gone in fifty years or I could be gone in five. Hell, with luck I could make it into my nineties or lower hundreds. But seeing as I'm a soldier and tensions are high..."

"I see. That is a relief." He sighed heavily and reached for his drink.

"'Led to believe' is an interesting phrase..." Ciheri murmured, his expression inquisitive.

"Well, I don't know for certain because I haven't been outright told. I just know the Imperials want to retire me in the next few years." I gave him an amused smile. "There's a few ways I can interpret it, sure, but without more information..."

"More information you *can't get*," Casair corrected me bitterly. "Sorry, Elara. I really wish we could say more, but we prefer you alive."

"It'd be kinda weird if we didn't," Aldiner pointed out, placing his hands on his hips. "Besides, Rel, Ciheri, and I know even less since no one wants to keep us in the loop."

"Sorry, it's just..." Casair muttered, deflating a little. "Why's this planet gotta be so damned complicated?"

"I know better than to blame you," I informed him, giving him a pat on the arm. Raising an eyebrow, I looked to Aldiner and Ciheri. "So, about breakfast..."

"Right!" Ciheri smiled brightly. "We aren't as good as Rel yet, but we're getting there. It won't be long until we can help out more regularly around the café!"

"But it'd be better if you could do what you wanted..." Casair grumbled, propping his cheek in his hand. Ciheri gave him a puzzled look. "You'd rather be researching and cataloging, right?

Yet the humans are in the way, and no one can make 'em see reason."

"Yes, but they, statistically, will not remain in the way. I can be patient." Ciheri hummed cheerfully to himself as he turned and began preparing ingredients.

Aldiner shrugged. "He's right, though. We've got, what, another century at most before this human empire is as advanced as the last one that destroyed itself. If the theories are right and that is humanity's apex, this planet will fall within the next hundred years."

"Why am I not surprised Syldrari have statistics for these things?" I remarked dryly.

"Survival and efficiency." Ciheri gave me a puzzled glance. "Why waste time, money, and lives on wars—or other people's wars—when they're due to destroy themselves soon with or without our intervention?"

"Statistics help us to know when and how to act," Casair offered with a half-smile. "There are more whimsical Syldrari too, of course. You can't have an artistic culture such as ours without a healthy amount of whimsy. But it's balanced by people like Ciheri here."

"Because he can separate whimsy and logic as needed?" I asked, earning a nod in response. I looked over to the pale Syldrari in question. "In which case...which arts do you like?"

"Um..." he murmured, blue creeping into his cheeks and the

tips of his ears. "I'm sorry, could…could you be more specific? There's so many things, I just…"

"You don't need to apologize. It *was* a bit broad of a question." I smiled at him. "I was thinking along the lines of what you like to indulge in for relaxation purposes. Something you enjoy but don't take on as, say, a career."

"Mmm…" He hummed quietly to himself before answering. "I like listening to music while I design… I'm not sure what the human word would be. The closest might be…patterns?"

Casair said something to Ciheri, which my chip also translated as 'patterns.' He shrugged. "To humans they'd look merely decorative, but they serve technological and aetherological functions. Most clans aim to have their own unique patterns, but they have to be functional as well."

"I design and freelance them to clans who don't have anyone who can," Ciheri murmured, flushing a deeper blue. "I like research too, of course, but it is more mentally draining than design. Drawing can be quite relaxing."

Why is he so embarrassed? I wondered, propping my cheek against my fist. "Now I'm curious. Maybe you could show me sometime— or, if you're not comfortable with that, you could share the kind of music you listen to with me."

"I can share some great music with you, too!" Aldiner quickly jumped in, grinning as he leaned against the counter. "And before you ask—dance. All kinds of dancing. Even some of the human dances are fun."

"What about you, Elara?" Ciheri murmured, even though asking appeared to make him even less comfortable.

"Hmmm… I'm still figuring out what I like. I do a lot of reading, but none of it is for pleasure. It's to learn. I have been listening to music while I do it, but human music is just…missing something." I considered for a moment. "It's like my brain expects three dozen more instruments and sounds to be in effect, yet there's only four."

"Human music usually lacks a certain depth." Ciheri turned to nudge Aldiner out of his way, placing a glowing, pale pink drink in front of me. "There are some genius composers and lyricists among humans. I think if they worked with Syldrari musicians they could bridge the gap."

"That's always the problem, isn't it? Bridging the gap," Casair remarked. He released a small sigh, glancing down at me. "You know, Syldrari, human, or anything else—it's odd to hear an *iri* who is genuinely interested in what mere *sol'iri* and *lun'iri* enjoy."

"Really…?" I swiveled in my seat and leaned toward him. "What about you, then?"

"Me? Uh…" He looked taken aback by the question. "Don't laugh. I'm at home in a forge and craftsman's shop. Metal, wood, shell, stone, some materials you won't recognize—I'll work with it all. Weapons, decorations, dinnerware… I make whatever strikes my fancy."

"In other words, he's good with his hands," Aldiner suggested slyly, waggling his eyebrows. "Whereas I am good with my *entire body* and Ciheri is good with his mind."

"I'm a soldier—I'm damn good with my body too," Casair snapped.

Riiight… I glanced between the three men. After a moment, I decided not to play Aldiner's little game and instead picked up my drink. *Let's see…new topic?*

"Now that I think about it, what does Rel even like aside from cooking?" Aldiner asked, looking over at Ciheri. "Like, what does he *do* when he locks himself in his apartment at the end of the day?"

"I study ancient history and lost knowledge," Rel answered from somewhere behind me. I glanced back at him, while Casair stiffened.

"Don't start." He shot me a side-eye.

"Oh, lovely. Is that why you're here? To keep an eye on me?" I shot Casair an irritated look. "To make sure poor Elara doesn't start poking around the forbidden knowledge?"

"Only half of it," he grunted.

"Care to explain?" Rel placed a hand on his shoulder and all the color drained from Casair's face. "Come with me. You are not leaving me out of the loop again."

"Mmm?" Ciheri looked between the two. "This sounds interesting! Can I—"

"No. Finish feeding Elara," Rel stated flatly, pushing Casair in the direction of the stairs. He paused suddenly, motioning off behind me somewhere. "Inform Erik and Nomusa of their breakfast options and take their orders."

"Fine…" Ciheri slumped.

"*Tch.*" I guzzled the remaining half my drink in irritation and pouted at Ciheri and Aldiner. "Another, please."

"What was all that about?" Erik stopped next to my seat.

"Just like I can't ask, I can't say." I shot him an agitated glare.

"Right…" He grimaced, then glanced over his shoulder at Nomusa. "Shall we?"

"Yes, a booth will do." Nomusa nodded, following him across the room.

"Hey, can the two of you send me a list of music to listen to?" I eyed Aldiner and Ciheri.

Aldiner grinned. "I'll do you one better—give me a moment." He conjured an unfamiliar device in one hand and scanned it by the side of his head, then did the same with Ciheri. With a smile, he held it out to me. "May I?"

"Sure?" I watched him quizzically, not quite sure what I was agreeing to. He waved the thing by the side of my head and I felt a faint magnetic pull. Then I sensed—for lack of a better term—*thousands* of songs.

"There, now you have all the music we listen to." Aldiner grinned broadly.

"Thanks, both of you." I gave them both a smile. *So, what, I just access it like AR or the internet? Hmmm… Maybe I'll wait 'til I'm back at HQ…*

CHAPTER THIRTY-EIGHT

Rel watched as the last of the day's customers trailed out, then proceeded to lock up behind them. After carefully adjusting the curtains at the front of the building, the usually patient Syldrari turned, fastening his sharp, threatening gaze on Casair.

"You are going to take me to Jysel," he informed him in an eerily calm tone.

"…Yes, sir…" Casair's shoulders drooped.

Several minutes later, Rel strode into his brother's temporary headquarters as if he owned the place. He passed confused and wary soldiers without a second glance as he made his way to Jysel's office, Casair following reluctantly behind. Upon arrival, Rel sheared the door clean off its hinges and stormed straight across the fallen contraption.

Sal'aphel let out a forlorn whine as he scented the air, but he made no move to stop his other owner. Rel paused long enough to scratch Sal'aphel's head, then continued his march toward his brother. Jysel sighed as his twin leaned over the desk, his irritation tingeing more than just his physiological glow. Even Rel's 'aura,' as humans might call it, was alight with myriad hues of irritation and anger.

"What now? I have queens to rescue."

"You will keep me informed of developments in your work from here on out—*especially* those pertaining to Elara," Rel informed his twin stonily, the room beginning to vibrate as he glowered at Jysel.

"It's safer for you to remain uninvolved—"

Rel bared his fangs. "Uninvolved? I was hired to train her how to fight—training she desperately needs. I'm already involved!"

Jysel rubbed his temples as he slumped back in his seat. "My mission remains to save the majority of the queens trapped on this planet. I can't afford for things to become solely about her."

"You may not wish to focus on her, but that doesn't mean I can't or won't. Brief me." Rel straightened to his full height and crossed his arms, but Jysel still hesitated.

"Should I call Zafir in?" Casair asked.

"I… Yes." Jysel grimaced. "He can explain the situation and his hypothesis to Rel himself. I simply don't have the time to go over it again. Then, Rel, you can decide for yourself if you truly want to be involved with my mission…or with her."

"*What*…?" Rel started, narrowing his eyes, but Casair quietly placed a hand on his shoulder and shook his head. He looked back to Jysel, but he had already buried his attention back in his pile of documents.

"I'll find you a room and call Zafir in. He should be free at this time of night." Casair kept his voice low as he led Rel down a hallway. "Listen… Jysel has Elara's best interests in mind and so does Zafir. If the good professor is right, Elara poses a serious threat. It's on you to decide if you think she's worth that risk. Jysel is still struggling with that himself—among other things.

"And that damned cult is only making our job harder. They've started trying to beat us to rescuing the queens—claim they need to prepare a spouse for their reincarnated Abyss Father. It's getting out of hand, and the last thing we need is them catching wind of Elara's…quirks."

"Quirks?" Rel questioned, eyeing Casair suspiciously.

Casair raised his hands, attempting to placate his friend. "Zafir will give you the whole story. But the short version is, she was humming something that gives us reason to believe she may've come from a clan of Depthwalkers – or worse. Most likely worse, if I'm bein' honest. She may not have even been aware of it before the Incident, but if she was…"

"Depthwalkers? *Here?* This planet hasn't been a frontier for centuries!" Rel countered in disbelief. "And she has none of their characteristics. She's hardly cold or crazed, and that blue she's begun to turn… It's inconsistent with that of any clan I've heard of."

"She's not catalogued in any database—legal or otherwise—that we know of, either," Casair offered. "Jysel's got a small team of people he trusts searching for hints of a Syldrari crash site or outpost here, but most of us agree with your assessment.

"Personally, I'm inclined to think she was raised not knowing any of it. If they believed they were stranded on this planet with humans, they would've bided their time here by blending in with the locals."

"Fetch Zafir and tell him he will divulge everything he knows—or I will wring it out of him myself." Rel narrowed his eyes at Casair. "Jysel may be concerned about his mission, but *I* am prepared to undock the entire Syldrari sector and take Elara somewhere the humans will never reach her. Give me a reason not to."

Casair swallowed hard. He wanted to voice his agreement with Rel's method, but he knew that would only serve to encourage the other man. There was a bigger picture to look at—especially if they wanted to keep what little of Elara's trust they still had.

"I'll get Zafir, but Rel, you need to *listen* to what he has to say. We've all gotta be careful with how we choose to move forward—you included." He picked up a communicator, pressing a series of buttons that released reverberating *ping*s in different tones.

"Zafir, get your ass down here and brief Rel before he does something stupid. Yes, I *am* holding you responsible for stopping him. You're the only one with the full picture here."

Rel shot Casair a disgruntled look, then settled into a seat to wait. "I won't be kept in the dark any longer, Casair."

"You know that isn't my decision," Casair reminded the other man. "I'm worried about her too, but give Zafir's information time to sink in before you decide how to act, alright?"

"Of course. When is the universe ever black and white, or even black, white, and grey?" Rel gave Casair a small smile. "Jysel is worried about Elara as well?"

"I'm pretty damn sure convincing you to stand down is gonna be easier than convincing him was," Casair answered with a snort. "He may bluster about staying on-mission, but we had to physically hold him down so Zafir could talk sense into him. At this point he's just trying to convince himself it's the right thing to do."

Rel stared at Casair in disbelief. "What could cause him..."

"Maybe we should restrain Rel too, just to be certain?" Zafir asked irritably as he stepped out of a portal. "Before you ask, yes, Elara got home just fine. She's already fallen asleep to the music your two scoundrels sent her home with.

"Now then, let's get to your briefing. I have work to do on this very subject and I am not pleased that you are taking up my time."

CHAPTER THIRTY-NINE

"I want to preface with the following," Zafir began, taking a seat across from Rel and motioning for the guards to shut the door. "Unlike Jysel, Casair and I are prepared to put Elara's safety before that of the other queens, depending on what information is uncovered. Jysel is focusing too heavily on saving many instead of one."

"Then why do you force her to continue this nonsense with the humans?" Rel narrowed his eyes. "Not only is she a queen, but if she is a Depthwalker as they suggested—"

"Let me explain from the beginning." Zafir made a dismissive motion. "The other night, I caught Elara humming to herself as she wandered the building—she had just returned from fetching the books you sent her.

"I recognized the song as one of the forbidden arts and pulled her aside to stop her. She is utterly convinced it's merely a lullaby, when in fact she was singing one of the *lethal* songs. You study our past during your leisure time, yes?"

"Few known clans would have sung such songs as a lullaby," Rel answered quietly, frowning. "However, Citomy and her predecessor supposedly extinguished those clans."

"But those clans didn't *create* the forbidden songs." Zafir pulled out his data pad. He tapped it a few times then handed it to Rel. "During interrogation they spoke of powerful clans that had removed themselves from both Syldra and its politics in favor of free exploration—of both space and the arts."

Rel skimmed the document warily, a pit forming in his stomach. "This...implies that not only was the Abyss Father actually alive, but that he led rogue clans into space. Are you certain these aren't the ravings of a madman? I've seen his tomb, he—"

"We've seen the outside of his tomb. Never its interior." Zafir shook his head quickly. "I charted several possible courses from Syldra with exploration in mind. The Abyss Father and his followers were always searching for darker, more dangerous 'depths' to explore. His Final Verse spoke of sifting through the deepest reaches of the universe—most believe he went to the Fringes."

"But our long-distance scans say there isn't anything out there..." Rel stared at Zafir for a moment, then back to the data pad, flipping through the files until he found the star charts. "You believe one of the clans may have crashed on this planet?"

"Or, depending on how their culture has changed, she could have been exiled because of her powers as a queen." Zafir hesitated, then let out a small sigh. "What I am about to tell you doesn't leave this room. Understood?"

Rel narrowed his eyes but nodded.

Zafir let out a reluctant sigh. "Elara's team…they are her guards, Rel. Their memories are partially intact—they remember the Resonance Incident and they recall making some kind of pledge to defend her, but the rest appears to be missing. They're just barely managing to pretend they're human."

"Yet they have no clan marks… What of their bloodlines?" Rel prompted.

"Much like Elara, they don't exist in any of the databases I've tried."

Casair stepped forward. "Hold on a minute. There's a detail about the Abyss Father you skipped over."

"Which is?" Rel demanded.

"It isn't just that Zafir thinks the Abyss Father went to the Fringes, he thinks he's still heading for them…unless he finds a reason to come back." Casair crossed his arms over his chest.

"And if he lost contact with his people here…" Zafir shook his head abruptly. "We're getting ahead of ourselves. The primary issue is Elara—at best, she's a queen whose mind was wiped before she was dumped on this planet. At worst, she has some connection to one of the Abyss Father's clans."

"If she belongs to one of his clans, wouldn't that make her valuable to them? None of those clans ever produced a queen." Rel frowned deeply. "And with the Abyss Father's rumored ability, he wouldn't need to fear her power."

"She would be a threat to the others," Zafir pointed out. "Yet still she was given guards. Someone wanted her to survive."

"Survival becomes less and less likely the longer she remains with the humans." Rel narrowed his eyes.

"Which is why we need to be cautious in our attempts to draw out anyone with connections to her," Zafir stated flatly. "We need more allies. Even if Clan V'shir and Jysel's still-unnamed clan team up, we have nowhere near enough resources."

"You want to use her as *bait* for whichever clan she belongs to?" Rel exclaimed. "Are you out of your mind? What of all the other bites you will get in the process? They'll eat her alive."

"Not quite..." Zafir hesitated a moment, then glanced to Casair. "Do you still have that report?"

"Ugh, this is a mistake." Casair stalked over to a wall and pressed a panel, revealing a stack of stored documents. He plucked a sheet of black paper from the top and offered it to Rel.

He pored over the chart several times before looking to Zafir. "This can't be right."

"I've checked several times. It is."

Rel hesitated and studied it again. "I've sparred with her several times, now that I'm training her. You've been there. Not once has she shown this kind of power or potential."

"She could change things," Casair stated bluntly. "Sure, she may not forgive us if we prioritize her over the seeming majority. But…saving her *is* saving the majority. If we help her survive—"

"She could replace Citomy…" Rel breathed, his voice a mere whisper. "You would let that kind of power rest in human hands? I cannot condone—"

"Sir, if I may…" One of the guards spoke up, looking nervous, before Casair motioned for him to speak. "Shouldn't we be finding a way to win her over as our queen? With her leadership, the other clans would respect us again!"

"No, they would hunt you down quicker, believing she's a rogue queen." A smile slowly spread across Rel's lips. "For the V'shir, however…"

"*We* discovered her." Zafir narrowed his eyes at Rel.

"Please. Which of us is hiding in foreign caverns, and which of us can move freely?" Rel smirked and steepled his fingers. "Besides, you know as well as I do what my connection is to Jysel and this clan. My queen is his queen."

Zafir narrowed his eyes at Rel. "Even if she's a Depthwalker or Abysstouched?"

"This is Elara we're talking about. When does she ever let others or events define who she is?" Rel leaned forward, lacing his fingers together in his lap. "Now, explain to me why I shouldn't just lure her to the Syldrari sector and undock the first chance I get?"

"That's..." Zafir sighed heavily and pinched the bridge of his nose. "The humans have been keeping the resonance weapon trained on the sector for a few weeks now. There are individuals within Imperator Julien's inner circle who are pushing for it to be fired immediately—they want to start a war to wipe out all non-human life and believe the weapon to be so perfect that their success is guaranteed.

"If you undock while their attention is on you, not only will your clan and Elara perish, but so will everyone and everything on this planet—including your brother, plus anything that could give us a clue to Elara's identity or origins."

"You've been spending too much time with humans. You should have simply said that from the start." Rel gave Zafir a thoroughly unamused glare. "If whisking her away isn't an option, then what?"

"We bide our time and collect information so we *can* extract her from this awful planet." Zafir nodded once. "You know as well as I do that taking her to Syldra, even if the gate were fixed, is out of the question. We can't let the other queens sink their hooks into her."

The door swung open and an exhausted-looking Jysel

walked in. "I found another military installation linked to the missing queens. We have a problem."

Rel frowned at his haggard twin. "What is it?"

"It's in the same region as the first Resonance Incident." Jysel rubbed his jaw. "Close. It would have suffered some of the weapon's effects, but the facility is still running."

"You think Elara may have been experimented on there?" Zafir murmured with displeasure.

"I had my men study the samples you asked for help with," Jysel began, hands rummaging in his pockets. "You were right to find it odd that Elara...how did you put it...?"

"She reacted poorly and venomously to one of the survivors outside her team," Zafir answered. When Jysel handed him a folded piece of paper, he went pale. "Sydney has some of Elara's cells? That..."

"I wouldn't be surprised if the rest of her team has also had data stolen and infused into other humans," Jysel stated flatly, his eyes narrowing dangerously. "They're still attempting to create artificial super soldiers. You need to be careful of this 'Sydney' creature. If she's inherited any of Elara's abilities—especially those of a queen— you're in great danger."

"You don't think she's already claimed us by accident?" Rel inquired dryly, earning a warning look from his brother. "Was that not your concern the last time we spoke?"

"But you were right...she hasn't taken us over," Jysel answered begrudgingly.

"But she is struggling more and more to contain her power," Zafir murmured, drawing the attention of everyone in the room. "She doesn't know how to control it. Instead, she takes care with her phrasing. But that will only last so long, and I am not qualified to teach her."

"Only another queen would be, and I don't believe it's safe to expose her to them any further." Jysel crossed his arms over his chest.

"Xilen—" Rel started.

"—has wanted you for centuries," Jysel interjected flatly. "She is still a queen, born and raised on Syldra. We can't trust she won't begin to see Elara as a threat."

"What did you say...?" Zafir murmured distractedly. "Born and raised..."

"What now?" Casair sighed.

"She isn't in our databases because she wasn't born on Syldra or any of the planets whose databases have been connected," Zafir answered, quickly navigating through his data pad. "But explorers would use localized databases off the grid, leaving them as caches they could return to or for us to find whenever we caught up. If this planet—"

"There should be a cache here. Right." Jysel touched a device encircling his wrist. "All hands assigned to data retrieval: Be advised we believe there to be a Syldrari information cache somewhere on this planet. *Start looking for it.*"

"Mmm, my scans when I brought Clan V'shir here didn't detect anything," Rel remarked, propping his cheek against his hand. "Granted, that was with old technology…"

"Shouldn't you be getting back?" Jysel gave his twin an unamused glance.

Rel shot the look right back at him. "Perhaps, but our discussion isn't over. You *will* draft a plan to extract Elara and her team—and you will not be leaving me out of it."

Zafir spoke up before the brothers could begin arguing. "You both need to be prepared for the possibility that she may become your queen—and not by choice. Yours *or* hers. Citomy is still pressuring anyone she can."

"You think she's after something on this planet?" Casair asked as the twins fell silent. "Well, apart from the usual."

"We're certain she has someone on the inside at Resonance Project HQ." Zafir sighed and nestled back in his seat. "Plus, knowing her reach, I wouldn't be surprised if she is already aware that Depthwalkers or Abysstouched have been to this planet. She may believe that we've already found the cache and is trying to bind Rel and Jysel to a queen so they can be forced to disclose the information."

"She hasn't learned of Elara's potential yet?" Rel murmured, frowning.

"No. I doubt HQ would still be standing if she had." Zafir rose to his feet, his eyes still on his data pad. "If you'll excuse me, I have work to attend to."

"What work?" Jysel shot Zafir an expectant look.

"Information on the eighth, most recent, Resonance Incident. I've had someone digging for footage."

CHAPTER FORTY

A few weeks later, I found myself scouring one of the human residential areas in Lucdra.

The disturbance was reported around here, right? I tiptoed silently through the back alleys, keeping my senses tuned for any sign of movement. I'd been dispatched in response to reports of suspicious figures wandering around and causing trouble, but so far, I'd found nothing. Hell, most of the residences had their lights off by now.

I didn't see any signs of disturbances, either. Sure, there was trash piled in the alleys, but that was hardly unusual. The sound of melodic murmuring caught my attention, and I peered around a corner to find a group of Syldrari in rather distinctive attire—but unfortunately, they spotted me first. I started to cautiously back away, though they didn't make any move to reach for their weapons.

The central figure turned my direction, his face obscured down to his mouth by his hooded trench coat. Iridescent metal carvings adorned the coat with upward-flowing tentacles, and the bodice and shoulders were armored in the same distinct, sharply layered material.

Isn't that… I stared at the group. Those clothes were an exact match for the person who had recently threatened the Creshe Empire.

"It's *true*," the man breathed in awe, his voice a clear match for the one I'd heard on TV. "The so-called vigilante is a *queen*! Please, you must—"

Run. Something echoed deep within me, and I immediately turned and ran.

"Wait! We just want to talk!" their leader called after me. "Dammit! Catch her and calm her down before someone else finds her!"

Shit. I reached up, pressing a button on my visor as I picked up the pace, and Zafir's image fuzzed into view. I didn't bother to let him say anything. "I need an extraction. *Now*."

<An…> His eyes widened as he listened, likely hearing the yelling Syldrari behind me. He disappeared from the inside of my visor, but I could hear him typing rapidly. <Head toward the station at the head of the community you're in—east from your current location. There's enough ground clearance there for us to land a craft. Are they armed?>

"Unknown," I stated.

<Did they threaten you?>

"No."

<Strange... Do they know what you may be?>

"Yes."

<Elara, I need you to calm down. You're discharging energy.> Zafir spoke in a calming tone. <Keep running for the extraction point while you rein your nerves in. You might hurt yourself if you don't stop sending currents of electricity everywhere.>

I did my best to do as instructed, but the looming presence behind me, though it wasn't particularly menacing, was not helping. Even when I skidded onto the main thoroughfare, the cult continued to follow me—but finally I spotted my transport descending from the skies.

I sensed someone preparing to attack, so I pivoted and mustered my strength, envisioning a barrier forming between me and my pursuers. In an instant, a writhing mass of dark energy crackling with blue-white lightning emerged from the ground, hovering over the pursuers like a half-melted mass that was considering eating them.

Their confused shouts and warnings to each other bought me just enough time to close the distance between me and the blacked-out military craft.

I pulled myself onto the ledge, feeling a presence behind me. The waiting soldiers' faces drained of color and they raised their rifles to aim behind me.

"Don't let them change you."

I looked over my shoulder to find the hooded Syldrari mere inches behind me, his hands in the pockets of his coat and an amused smile on his mouth. The human soldiers fired, but the bullets *curved* around the man and then just…stopped. He turned and sneered at the hovering bullets before pulling his left hand out of his pocket. The ammo trembled, then *liquefied*, flowing through the air to form a carved-looking sphere in his hand—which he tossed casually into my transport as we flew away, not even looking where he was aiming.

"Don't touch that," I stated flatly, walking over to snatch the orb off the floor. "We'll have the boss inspect it."

"Ma'am…" One of the soldiers nodded hesitantly before sliding the door shut. "Move out!" he called to the pilot.

What the fuck was that about? I turned the orb of metal over in my fingers, eyeing the wave-like patterns curving around its surface. If I hadn't seen what he'd done with my own eyes, I would never have guessed it was made from fired bullets.

"Fuckin' bogey appeared outta nowhere…" one of the soldiers muttered in disbelief.

"Could've snatched her right off the damn ship before we saw he was there—why didn't he?" another asked, plopping down on a seat.

I frowned at them. "You're not more curious about how he deflected your shots?"

The soldiers present exchanged looks. "Ma'am, that's the

norm when facing trained Syldrari. Sometimes we'll get lucky and a single shot will get through, but that's rare—and for the shot to matter, that's even rarer."

Then humans really are fucked when the Syldrari finally tire of their shit. I eyed the soldiers briefly, then returned my gaze to the metal orb. Maybe stopping bullets was normal, but liquefying them without heat and turning them into a work of art? I doubted that was common.

When the ship landed on the roof of HQ, I had barely taken a single step off it before a worried Zafir filled my field of view. The poor bastard looked like he wanted to hug me – and like he was having a particularly hard time not doing so.

"Elara, are you alright?" he asked worriedly as I started to walk past him. He looked to the soldiers and nodded to them briefly. "Thank you. I've arranged a nice dinner for you—speak with Erik when your shift is over."

"We need to talk." I led him inside at a brisk pace, my suit melting away to reveal the shorts and tank top I'd been wearing before I was called to duty.

"Then..." Zafir narrowed his eyes when he spotted the orb in my hand. "Understood. My office, then, and keep that out of sight."

That, at least, was as simple as closing my fist.

Once we'd arrived on our floor, Zafir stopped by the kitchen to grab us both bottled drinks, then went through the process of disabling anything troublesome in his office. He held out a hand to me expectantly. "Let me examine it while you brief me."

I sat down with my drink and told him everything that had happened during the brief chase, along with the very clear show of power. The more I thought about it, the more curious I was as to why he hadn't just snatched me right off the ship.

"You found no signs of the reported disturbance, either..." Zafir muttered, his eyes flicking rapidly over the surface of the sphere as he examined it. "We should operate under the assumption that they were specifically trying to draw you or your teammates out. They must have been looking for information, but..." His mouth pulled into a frown as he turned the orb over again. "You said his coat had a tentacle motif?"

"Yeah." I nodded.

"Then...are we dealing with Clan Drah-emh?" he murmured, then shook his head. "No, this behavior is inconsistent with their MO. Clan Kal'ild is currently in a different galaxy, and..."

He continued to list off clans as he pulled up the footage from my visor cam on his data pad. He watched the brief encounter several times, looking more confused by the moment.

"What is it?" I probed.

"None of them have clan imprints, which is highly inconsistent with all known Abyss Father admirers." He glanced down at the orb again. "Controlling metal in such a way isn't exactly a common talent. And, setting aside the waves, the rest of the 'carvings' are consistent with those of the clans who live in the very deepest reaches of Syldra's oceans.

"I will have to speak with the rest of my contacts to see if they recognize this work—or if they can think of anyone who would be so cocky."

"Cocky is the wrong word." I grimaced at him. "That was the behavior of someone who knows every little thing he's capable of. He has utter confidence in his abilities; I'm only here because he let me get away."

"Yet you don't believe he just wanted to talk," Zafir pointed out.

"No. Something made my instincts scream to run away, so that's what I did." I sighed and took a sip of my drink, then looked over to Zafir again. "I can't put my finger on it, but I don't like how they reacted to my presence, how they immediately *knew*. It's a little unnerving when someone acts like they can clearly see something I can't."

"See something you can't..." he echoed, his eyes widening. "Clan Naylor-radyrr, or perhaps a descendant? If a descendant went rogue, perhaps there will be records..."

"Elara, you're off duty for the rest of the night. I want you to get some rest. If you can't sleep, then see to the reading Rel or I gave you. If I discover something you can safely know, I'll inform you immediately."

"Well, that's more promising than usual, at least." I gave him an amused smile as I stood up. "Don't stay up too late."

"I… Thank you for your concern," he grumbled, the tips of his ears turning a little bluer. "Good night."

"Good night." I nodded and left him to the strange sphere and his studies.

CHAPTER FORTY-ONE

Despite Zafir's concerns regarding the Abyss Father's worshippers, the next month and a half passed without incident. My team and I continued with our duties throughout the city, arresting or snuffing out various criminals depending upon the severity of their crimes. Rel continued to train me in Syldrari martial arts, though my patrols in the Syldrari sector had been suspended so I could work in significantly more boring areas.

In addition to having my patrols shifted to another sector, Zafir had effectively uninstalled Syldran from my chip—to my dismay and Rel's fury. However, after a conversation I couldn't understand, he had finally agreed – albeit begrudgingly – with Zafir's reasoning.

Aside from that, everything seemed mostly normal, even if every now and then I caught Rel watching me with an odd look on his face. Half the time I could almost guess what he was thinking, but the rest of the time I had no idea. It was as if Syldrari had a broader range of emotions, with expressions and mannerisms to match. I suspected that was precisely the case.

The ones I could guess at, though… Conflict and admiration vied equally for dominance. I was curious as to why either feeling was on the table, but I wasn't sure I really wanted to know, either. And I was fairly certain I wouldn't get an answer even if I did ask.

Everyone had been more tight-lipped since my encounter with the cult. They were all on high alert, yet everyone was always telling me to relax. Take a breather. Enjoy my 'me time.' Yet I hadn't been allowed to go to the Syldrari sector at all. Rel had taken it upon himself to fetch ludrán for me, but had pronounced my consumption level far too high—so now I had to ration out my treats.

To top it all off, I hadn't heard a peep about attacks on government facilities from anyone. Jysel, Citomy, and the cult were all utterly silent. No more threats, no talk or even rumors of movement. Nothing. The citizens throughout the city had already forgotten there had been any threats in the first place.

I glanced sullenly at my door when I heard a faint knock. "Come in."

Zafir walked in with a folder under one arm and a platter balanced on his other hand. On the platter was an arrangement of snacks I liked, both human and Syldran, as well as a pot of tea and two cups.

"I figured a peace offering was in order since the topic I've come to discuss isn't exactly one you've been wanting me to touch on." He took a seat on a chair nearby.

"Peace offering? I'm not *that* bad—but snacks are good." I put my book aside and leaned over to snatch one up. "So, what nonsense has landed in our laps this time?"

"Progress—with the murder attempts." He opened the folder and showed me what looked like photo taken of a slide via microscope. *So* helpful. "The suspects have been narrowed down, but Crowe's hit a wall. He can't directly question people within Imperator Julien's inner circle without risking his own position.

"The person responsible is one of the purists in the Imperator's inner circle, which leaves us at something of an impasse on the investigation. Unless they do something that goes directly against the Imperator's wishes—and is *also* caught doing so—we can't press that route any further."

"What are we going to focus on instead?" I frowned at him.

"Much. Crowe wants you to look over the aftermath of the— highly classified—attacks on the military facilities and determine which group is responsible." Zafir placed five folders beside me. "He isn't willing to send you to the sites themselves because they're hazardous; however, he seems to think you'll be able to discern the attackers just from the images here."

"You disagree?" I challenged him, watching as his eyes widened and he recoiled slightly.

"I…think you are intelligent, Elara, but you are still quite ignorant about…ah…" He hesitated, looking like he expected some manner of retaliation.

I let out a soft sigh. "Zafir, that isn't what I meant. You're right that I'm ignorant regarding many things, especially when it comes to Syldran culture.

"I was trying to imply that I think the different groups we're dealing with would each have rather distinct styles. Jysel, for example, I'm sure he performs one of two ways: Either he tries his damnedest to distinguish himself from Citomy, or he tries to copy her exactly in order to make it easier to frame her. Citomy, I'm guessing, does nothing herself and instead sends her husbands to do the dirty work. The cult…well, they're the wild card. I know the least about them, and I'd rather not think they're comparable to a human cult."

"It's been a long day." Zafir slumped in his seat and shook his head faintly.

"You *have* seemed rather busy lately, even with the lull in activity," I remarked, leaning forward to peer at him. "Are you doing alright?"

"I cannot disclose—" He stopped and gave me an odd look. "Did you just ask whether I'm alright?"

"Is that so strange?" I murmured, frowning.

"Ah…yes. For someone in your position, it is quite odd," he

answered, making a show of shaking off his woes and sinking into his usual facade. "As the doctor here, *I* should be asking *you* if—"

"And who takes care of the doctors?" I interrupted, flapping a hand at him. Though I did get the point. He didn't expect someone with a queen's ability to actually care. "Look, I'm a person too and I can empathize. Working too much will make the quality of said work—and you—suffer. I'm just saying, don't make yourself sick. You *normal* humans are so prone to stress-induced illnesses..."

"When you put it like that..." He smiled, adjusting his glasses. "I will try to rest more. After all, I have you...all, relying on me."

"Mhm. So, let me worry about this for now, while you go take a break. Maybe get some tea and a snack, or something."

I drummed my fingers against my hip, debating whether ordering him to pay more attention to self-care would be edging over a line I shouldn't cross. After all, I was trying *not* to use my queen power. But I also wanted him to stop pushing himself so hard.

"Make sure you follow your own advice." He shot me a small smile as he passed me. "I will let you know if any new work comes up for you."

I watched him leave my room, then turned my attention to the stack of documents I needed to look through—and my snacks. When I opened the first folder, I frowned. The installation looked desolate; there were no signs of a struggle, battle, or...anything. It looked as though it had been abandoned for at least a few years.

Setting my drink aside, I worked through each folder, my

confusion growing. Finally, I hopped off the bed, dressed myself in Syldran leggings and a cropped shirt, and left my room in search of Zafir.

"Already?" he questioned when I swung the door to his office open.

"You sure these are the right pictures?" I asked, receiving a perplexed look in response. "There's no sign that there's been activity in any of these places for years, let alone an invasion or conflict."

I handed the files to Zafir who, after a moment, called for Amara to join us. After a few minutes, she arrived and started looking over the pictures as well, her face contorting into a small frown.

"This is not what the facilities look like. These aren't even the right era architecture," she stated after a moment. "Someone gave you the wrong pictures, Zafir."

"Who compiled these reports for Crowe?" I looked over at Zafir, watching as he frowned and shook his head. "Amara, can you spot anything that would tell us which facilities these images came from?"

"They're all from the same one," she muttered, laying out each image. She took a moment to arrange them as she liked before speaking again. "Database says these are from an abandoned facility at the location of the first Resonance Incident..."

"And?" Zafir prompted, suddenly looking much more interested.

"Uh…it's all classified, but the facility is supposedly still running." Amara frowned more deeply. "I'm gonna go out on a limb and say whoever gave these to Crowe is a problem. Someone could be trying to lay a trap for Elara and her team by showing you this place. Everything is still powered and running, but it looks like no personnel have been there since just after the Incident."

"In that case, investigation is off-limits." Zafir shot me a warning glance, then looked back down at the images. "Elara, you're to forget you saw these. We will handle investigations into where these came from. For now—"

His communicator chimed and he let out an aggravated sigh before picking it up and assuming his usual facade when talking with his superiors, the one that made me want to slap him. He shot me a knowing glance and then turned his back to us as he listened to whoever was on the end. When he was done, his shoulders slumped and he turned to look at me.

"There's been a disturbance reported in the Syldrari sector, right by Rel's café. You're to go investigate as Lethe. I will send Calder and Nikolai with you; I think Maelor will be too tactless, and Aisu and Diana are busy."

I stared at him in disbelief. "Wait, but it's daytime. I thought we were still being—"

"Our superiors have spoken," he muttered bitterly. "If you must reveal your connection to the military, you have my leave to. It's only a matter of time before the cult begins spreading word of just *how* you managed to escape them."

"But if I go as Lethe—"

"You know I can't countermand your orders." He glanced away in discomfort. "Please. Just go, before this disturbance gets out of hand."

"This isn't going to go over well," Calder remarked, leaning back against the wall of our transport.

"Where exactly do we enter from in this situation?" Nikolai frowned. "No skybikes, just a small transport? We're too obviously military like this."

"I think that's the point. Right, Elara?" Erik spoke from the pilot's seat. "You were given leave to reveal the military connection so you took it. Right?"

"We're going to barge in the front door, so to speak," I stated flatly. "We received no information as to what this disturbance is, aside from 'deal with it.' So, we're going to walk right in and do our damn job in the open for once."

"Which the Syldrari will appreciate, even if they dislike the military, because you're being openly honest. Right?" Erik nodded, keeping his eyes on the skies. "I'll set you down by the main thoroughfare, just a few minutes' walk from the café. Holler if you need extraction."

The moment we stepped foot off the transport, a Syldrari woman approached me, concern on her face. "This...this isn't a good time. The Abyss Father worshippers—"

"Then this is the perfect time to stop any altercations from getting out of hand. Where did they go?"

She hesitated before pointing in the direction of Rel's café and mumbling something about being careful. I led Calder and Nikolai down the street, keeping my head held high and my spine straight as we passed the worried Syldrari.

The closer we got to Rel's, the more commotion I could hear. By the time we were in view, a familiar Syldrari man in a long trench coat was sent flying out of the establishment by what I could only describe as a pulse of power. The sound reverberated low throughout all the metal nearby, making the earth tremble slightly.

The man in the tentacle coat slid across the ground on his back, coming to a stop several feet from me. Calder and Nikolai tensed as I continued moving toward the man, eyeing him apprehensively. Yet...something seemed off about his height. He appeared shorter.

The hood of his coat had fallen back to reveal a handsome face with skin the color of chocolate. His hair was black and cut at an asymmetrical angle, and he had similarly asymmetrical horns—the left was longer than the right.

He coughed a few times as if trying to regain his breath before opening startlingly green eyes—which were focused directly upon Rel's establishment. "My king, I meant no offense! I—"

"Syldrari have kings now?" I asked, watching as the cultist froze. He leaned his head back, his lips parting slightly and his eyes going wide when he spotted me. I sighed and placed a hand on my hip. "You just had to go and make a scene during broad daylight."

"What... *Lethe*, get away from him," Rel ordered as he came storming out of the café, his sleeves rolled up and a murderous glint in his eyes. "This *utter imbecile*—"

"It's true, then, that you've given yourself to the humans?" The cultist looked like he was about to *cry* as he gazed at me. "A queen such as yourself would turn your back on—"

"Did he just say a queen...?" Whispers rippled through the onlookers.

"Whether I have had queen genetics grafted into my cellular structure remains to be seen," I stated flatly, taking another step toward the surprisingly upset – but still very pretty – Syldrari. "However, I am *tired* of people questioning my decision to live. Would it have been better if I had been sold to brothels or for spare parts instead? Perhaps you would prefer that I'd been turned into a mindless slave, instead of finding my own path through this nightmare of a planet? Or perhaps—"

Dark, gooey vines suddenly erupted from the Syldrari and I retaliated with my lightning, bursting each one into a shower of ooze before summoning my own well of dark, glowing sludge around him. Unfortunately, *fear* was not the response I got.

"You're—" He was interrupted when a shockwave of energy emanated from Rel, a streak of light piercing the cultist's skull. He fell to the ground at my feet as Rel stalked over, stopping beside me.

When he finally spoke, his voice was a low hiss. "What are they thinking, sending you here like this?"

"Yes, well, lack of options and all that," I muttered bitterly. "I should take him in—"

"This is Clan V'shir's jurisdiction and a Syldrari matter—*I* will handle this." Rel gave me a warning look, then glanced toward the still-murmuring civilians making their way toward us. He let out a small sigh. "What are your orders?"

"We're to guard your café for the remainder of the evening in case more bogeys show up, sir," Calder answered formally, earning an odd look from Rel. In response, he motioned to the visor he wore and continued, "HQ is worried more will arrive, and want us to lend our expertise, as it were. They won't take no for an answer."

"I tried," Nikolai offered, motioning to his data pad.

"Stealing the freedom of...a queen and..." the cultist mumbled groggily, already beginning to wake up. Rel's heel connected firmly with the side of the muttering Syldrari's head, knocking him back out. Then he reached down and pulled the other man's arm over one shoulder, hauling him upright.

"Come inside," was all he said before turning and dragging his captive back into the café. Aldiner and Ciheri closed the doors behind us and shut the curtains, then proceeded to help restrain the cultist.

"Why did he call you 'my king'?" Nikolai asked flatly.

"Old legends of *lun'iri* with the power of queens—they would translate to 'prince' or 'king' in your language," Rel muttered bitterly. "He's convinced that Jysel and I are such individuals because we haven't been 'defeated' by Lethe—he wishes for us to join him rather than be culled if anyone finds out."

"What do you mean *culled*?" I demanded sharply, turning to face Rel. He looked taken aback by my tone and started to raise his hands, as if to placate me. "Rel, what the hell is going on?"

"People like him believe *lun'iri* throughout the ages have been killed the moment their power was discovered, or that they were enslaved by a queen through some other method," Rel answered, running his fingers through his hair. "There are rumors that this is why the Abyss Father and a few other clans left Syldran society behind. 'Princes' were still weaker than queens, but more powerful than everyone else. Queens saw them as competition and threats instead of allies or protection. As such—"

"Why are you...telling a queen this..." the cultist muttered.

"Look." I grabbed the cultist by his chin and made him look at me. "I don't want to be a queen. Having power over people isn't something I want, but if I'm stuck with it, then I'll do my damnedest to not use it unless I must, or unless it can save someone. I don't have a choice what power I was born with or given, and I don't have a choice who I serve. All I can do is try not to become the same sort of *utter cunt* Citomy and the other queens are." I paused and glanced toward Rel. "No offense."

"None taken. Your words are less harsh than the Syldran ones I would have used," he stated, amused, before turning his gaze to the cultist. "Must you dirty your hands touching this trash?"

"Rel, he's still one of you. He may have pissed me off, but there's a reason he's on this planet and stirring up trouble. I want to know why." I studied the cultist's face, unable to read his expression until it turned fiery.

"Then compel me to speak," he challenged, straining against his restraints.

"No." I let go of his face and straightened. "Listen to me or don't, I don't care. This isn't my jurisdiction and you aren't my problem. I have plenty of other shit to worry about."

"…She is serious?" he muttered under his breath.

"You know as well as I do that she is." Rel grabbed the back of the cultist's chair and dragged it toward an adjacent room. "Having no training to control her power and using it to manipulate others are two vastly different things.

"Ciheri, get them a drink while they wait. Aldiner, go inform the other Elders what is going on, and that I want this kept quiet."

"I'm not done talking to Subject Zero yet," the cultist snapped. I narrowed my eyes behind my visor and stalked over to the pair. "Treating Syldrari like lab rats...the *nerve*. Capturing queens, and..."

"Subject Zero?" Rel inquired, glancing my way and noticing the set of my mouth. "I take it he isn't wrong. This means...you were the first?"

"*That*, I wouldn't know. That's just what they called me when I woke up after the Resonance Incident." I shrugged in response. "They implied I was the only one who didn't succumb to my feral and become trapped in the state of *kuhir-dal*. That said, I've effectively been a prisoner for the past five years or so. They kept me in isolation. Books were my company, but they always chose what I was allowed to read."

"Elara, you should bind him," Rel stated flatly. "We won't get any information from him otherwise."

"What? Absolutely not." I stared at him in disbelief. "I am not binding *anyone* to me. Like him or dislike him, I refuse to use my power to get my way. My curiosity can be satisfied later in a healthier manner."

"He'll never comply," Rel argued, narrowing his eyes. "The worst that could happen is that his clan submits to you, and you have a trove of forbidden knowledge at your fingertips. At best, you can leverage your possession of them to buy yourself safety on Syldra and extraction from this planet."

"No." I crossed my arms, watching as the bound man flinched. Suddenly, his expression loosened, his eyes ticking back and forth as if he was trying to comprehend something. "The only way I would ever bind someone is by accident, or if it's the only way to save someone, or if I'm forced to."

"She…" the cultist murmured, astounded.

"Do you believe her now?" Rel smirked, but it was quickly replaced with a frown when he noticed just *how* stunned the cultist seemed.

"She is not from Syldra, is she?" the cultist murmured. "Subject Zero's file…let's see…"

He seems to know more than he should about me, like my original designation, and likely the Resonance Project, too… I wonder.

"You're responsible for the pictures we received of the abandoned installation near the first Incident site," I realized, narrowing my eyes at the cultist. He looked up, surprised, and his whole appearance *glitched* briefly.

"You received our message? Then why are you still…" His voice seemed to split, a much deeper one reverberating beneath the younger one. A voice that made Rel freeze, his skin going pale and his glow shifting to a dim grey.

"There was no message. Only pictures." I narrowed my eyes when the cultist slumped, his expression becoming sorrowful. "Who am I speaking to?"

The deep voice took over again, as did the rich brown-skinned appearance. "A vessel. Eager to prove himself...but a touch too emotional for this manner of work. Return him to me."

"How about you say *please*?" I pressed my fingers to my temples. "The lack of manners with people as of late..."

"I am disinclined to say please to a traitorous queen. Shouldn't you be working to free yourself and the other captured queens?" The voice maintained a calm tone, and he smirked when I twitched.

"I try to operate on a baseline of respect and interpersonal *decency*." I motioned with my hands as I spoke. "You are quickly dropping below that threshold."

"Lethe *can't* act if she wants to survive. She may not be in a physical cage anymore but she is just as trapped as the other queens!" Rel snarled, grabbing the other *lun'iri* by the front of his coat. An icy calm came over him. "If you want your vessel back, you will make a deal with me."

"I will entertain the idea."

"The humans have reconstructed a resonance weapon out of damaged and incorrect parts," Rel began. His captive went a shade paler and began listening intently. "If they fire it, every living being on this planet and in orbit will die. The humans, however, are confident they have built it properly. They are keeping it trained on the Syldrari sector so they may fire it at the slightest sign of danger—or to send a message to my mother, Citomy.

"Neither you nor Jysel can free more queens from this planet while the humans are watching. Lethe can't be freed and returned to whomever her people are. This planet has become a dangerous place for any Syldrari to be—and we cannot leave."

"…Unless something is done about that weapon, you're saying, and it is in quite literally everyone's interests to do so." The cultist released a sigh, then looked to me. "The humans haven't realized what you are yet?"

"As far as any of us are aware, the Resonance Incident caused human and Syldrari genetic material to fuse together, and…" I stopped talking and motioned loosely with my hands in a shrug.

"That is the version you've been fed?" He sighed and shook his head, eyeing at me with a piercing stare—one that didn't quite match the emotional vessel we'd been talking to. No, *that* stare was more akin to the *lun'iri* I'd run into weeks ago. "I apologize for this vessel's accusations and my suspicions. You, too, are a victim of human greed…yet I sense there is more to it. Rel?"

"I do not have the full picture either, nor do I answer to you." Rel crossed his arms over his chest. "My concern is the safety of Clan V'shir, and of Lethe. Either you agree to my terms for your vessel's release, or you do not."

"If we can do something about the weapon, we will. Otherwise, as you said, saving the captives will not be possible." The cultist shot Rel a bored look. "You are a smart *lun*. I suggest you concoct your own escape plans for when the weapon is destroyed—and I recommend you *don't* simply go crying to your mother."

"*'Lun'*?" I murmured curiously, watching the now-fuming Rel.

"*Lun'iri* means 'man,' therefore *lun*…" He smiled innocently at Rel. "Ah, I see. You are that *creature's* firstborn, my mistake. So you are not that young. I had heard you and your brother were working to escape her tyranny, but you didn't make it far."

"Yes, well, considering she thinks she has the right to sell them even now…" I trailed off into a scoff. Just thinking about that woman made me want to hit things.

"You should have accepted," Rel muttered as he worked to untie the cultist. "With you, at least, we would be able to maintain our freedom."

"You have that much faith in Elara's character?" the cultist remarked, earning a sharp look from Rel. "Please. We have just as many plants inside the Empire as anyone else—perhaps more. Did you think calling her by her code name would be sufficient?"

"Ugh… Yes. I trust Elara and thus far have been given no reason not to. She may not have come from Syldra, but she has proven herself to be a better and more trustworthy ally than most people I've met." Rel took a step back and crossed his arms once he had finished freeing the cultist.

"You aren't going to arrest this vessel?" The cultist shifted to look at me.

"This isn't my jurisdiction. So long as you don't do anything to harm the people here or start conflict…" In lieu of glaring, I let my words hang in the air for a moment. "My job is to keep the peace. That's it. Whether that requires inaction, an arrest, or removal of your head is up to you."

"She is very like us in her punishments," Rel added amusedly. "I suggest you look into the rapists who were put on display in another sector."

"That was your work?" The cultist eyed me for a moment. "I will not promise that we aren't your enemy. We will free the trapped and the enslaved…but we desire no part of the queens' machinations."

"Then don't give them a reason to stay?" I rolled my eyes behind my visor. "*I* don't want to deal with them either, unless it involves…" I felt the feral stir, and dark blue-black liquid with faintly glowing flecks started to ooze between the floorboards around me. "You know what, never mind. I should be returning to guard duty."

The cultist asked something in Syldran as I moved past them, receiving a short answer from Rel. There was a shaky intake of breath, and I found myself cursing Zafir's decision to uninstall Syldran from my chip.

"Uh…" Nikolai inched back from me when I leaned back against the bar. "I'll…go post up at the door."

"Me too." Calder promptly knocked back the remainder of his drink and followed Nikolai outside.

That obvious, huh… I let out a small sigh, glancing to my right in surprise when I felt two arms around my shoulders and a cheek against my head.

"It's okay to be frustrated." Ciheri gave me a light squeeze and rubbed my upper arm. "I think, were I in your shoes, I'd have torn down most of the Empire looking for answers by now. I admire your patience."

"Is it patience?" I let out a small sigh as he released me to perch on a seat beside me.

"In a sense. You're biding your time, waiting for the right time to act. That *is* a form of patience." He shot me a calming smile. "Besides, patience is more likely to get you your answers. Right?"

He had a point there, but I remained silent, watching as Rel escorted the cultist back into the room and toward the front door.

"You can see me, can't you?" He stopped, turning his head slightly, though I couldn't quite make out his expression. "The master behind the puppet."

"Perhaps? What do you see, Ciheri?" I looked to my right at him, watching as he frowned.

"Monochromatic *noise*. Unless, he *is* actually white, black, and grey?" he murmured, and Rel nodded his agreement. Ciheri motioned toward a TV that was currently off. "It's like looking at someone who stepped out of one of those old black and white films the humans have in their museums, yet the edges are...wrong, somehow."

I stared at them in disbelief. "What? No. When he isn't flickering between appearances, he has black hair, skin the color of…chocolate, I suppose? Sort of. His eyes are the brightest peridot green I think I've ever seen. And—"

"Enough," Rel interjected. "We see him as he wishes us to see him. Nothing more. Such are the forbidden arts. Don't dwell on it."

The cultist's mouth pulled into an amused smile and he shot me one last glance before leaving the café. Once he was gone, Rel walked over to me, a serious expression on his face.

"What?" I asked tiredly. "You're not going to answer any of my questions, so why bother looking at me like that?"

Rel's hand lifted up to my face, cupping it as he leaned down to press his forehead against mine. His eyes fluttered shut and he simply stood there like that for a moment, his glow shifting from a rich, pale pink to vibrant sapphire blue. "Thank you, for being *you*."

"Um?" I gave him a perplexed look, then remembered he couldn't actually see any of my expression aside from my mouth. "What—?"

Ciheri cleared his throat, his translucent white skin tinged blue. "Rel, what are we going to do about business for the rest of the day? Since that imbecile let it slip that Lethe is a queen…"

Rel took a step back and opened his eyes, releasing a small sigh before looking to Ciheri. "We will play along with her theory that she may have been grafted with foreign genetics. After all, it is technically true. Just not in the way she wishes it were, perhaps."

"Yes, well, I'm not supposed to be asking questions or dwelling on implications, and thinking I'm a queen-turned-human will do nothing but *make* me dwell on things and ask endless questions." I pushed away from the counter and started to head toward the front door. "I should get started on the whole guard duty thing."

"No." Rel caught me by the arm and pulled me aside. "You're staying inside where we can keep an eye on you and quell any questioning parties."

"That's…" I hesitated, but relented after studying his firm-yet-pleading expression. "Alright. But it's probably best I don't talk, since everyone in this sector can hear through the modulator…"

"We can *see* who you are, as well." Rel ran a hand through his hair. "But my clan will understand the reason for your lack of speech. Let us handle any visitors who may not be so understanding. Alright?"

"Mhm…okay." I nodded and allowed Rel to lead me to a section of the room where he thought I should play guard.

Once I'd leaned back against a wall, Ciheri inched over to me again. "He didn't really want you to bind that *lun'iri*, you know. He was trying to prove that you're trustworthy. I think that's why he thanked you for being you."

"That person's reaction to me is what's bothering me…" I thought back to the encounter from several weeks ago. "It wasn't the same person. The one with the deep voice *sounded* right, but the vessel…"

"One of the forbidden arts allows a stronger individual to superimpose themselves over a willing vessel," Rel informed me as he walked over, a drink in his hand—which he offered to me. "However, what you see or hear is still whatever identity they want you to think they have. While it's possible you saw his true face, it is very unlikely. Such cults are too cautious for that."

"A cult, hmm…" Ciheri glanced at Rel. "Are we sure that's what they are?"

"If you have suspicions, do some digging," Rel suggested, motioning toward the stairs leading to their apartments. "You can use the computer in my room to access the Syldran network and research known cults—past and present. I haven't had the time."

"Will that help?" Ciheri asked, looking between me and Rel.

"Ciheri, if it's what you want to do…" I paused, struggling to find a way to word what I wanted to say.

Rel chuckled and looked at the puzzled Ciheri. "She wants to know but doesn't want to accidentally compel you into doing something you'd rather not do. Follow your instincts, Ciheri. If you wish to assist, then do so in whichever way you see fit—unless it would put you in danger."

"Yeah, no infiltration crap!" Aldiner declared as he returned, pointing his finger at Ciheri. "I'll help Rel with the café today, don't worry about it."

True face, or a mask? Does it matter? I wondered absentmindedly. I glanced in Rel's direction as he walked off toward the bar. *He looked so unnerved by my description of the man. Maybe I should do some digging of my own. Historical and prominent figures related to the Abyss Father, perhaps?*

CHAPTER FORTY-TWO

Another day, another patrol. I paced through one of the sectors bordering the Syldrari sector, alert for the first sign of trouble. I wasn't even an hour into my shift before I caught the sound of screaming. Awful, panicked, *pained* screaming unlike anything I'd ever heard before.

Rushing in the direction of the sounds, I found myself running down a series of alleyways until I found a Syldrari in a corner, barely clothed, with a nude woman under him.

That's blood... It took a moment for me to process what I was seeing, nausea rising in my throat. My pulse raced, an inferno of anger consuming me. I had to force it back down as another scream broke me out of my horror. I couldn't prevent what was happening to the human woman—but I could stop it from going further.

A sudden feeling of calm engulfed me as I stepped forward.

"Stop."

The Syldrari man stopped instantly, then turned to kneel, his eyes hazy and his expression enraptured. "My queen! Never did I think someone such as you—"

I barely heard him, internally recoiling. *Damn it! I didn't mean to use that power, my voice. I...*

My thoughts trailed off, my gaze following the man's movements in horror. He murmured something about being thankful to receive my blessing for his behavior. Of how Citomy had imprisoned him. How she didn't understand him.

Suddenly, I registered that the woman's arm was not actually connected to her shoulder, and the Syldrari's mouth was covered in human blood. Teeth marks covered more than just the removed limb.

He...is he... No!

I wasn't sure which one of us screamed. My senses distorted, righteous fury searing through me. The assault was bad enough. But *that?* How? Why? What sort of monster would do such a thing? It didn't matter that they were different species. That wasn't...

"W-why..." he stuttered, his voice hoarse. I refocused, registering that there was a charred hole through the man's chest. "I thought... My queen, why...have you betrayed me? Did I not please... Ah! Are you jealous? I-I can still..."

The hole in his chest began to close over, the healing hum

emanating from him. Behind him, the human woman was limp and silent, her expression frozen in terror. Her skin was singed over her heart, branching wounds from the lightning strike clear on her skin.

It was mercy, I convinced myself. She likely would have died from her wounds anyway. Keeping her alive hadn't been an option. Not after such an experience.

My attention snapped back to the Syldrari man when I heard him rise to his feet. Clearly, I'd missed his heart. He was muttering nearly incoherently now, but I had to do something. I couldn't be next.

"If you desire my—"

Fire. White hot. Anger and disgust. Darkness, then sizzling. When I regained my senses, the scent of scorched flesh drew my hesitant eye to the criminal. He lay in chunks on the ground, his blood splattered everywhere and mixing with the woman's.

Did...did I... Nausea threatened to overwhelm me. *My feral...no. I...executed...*

I staggered back, feeling as though I'd been hit by a freighter. Exhaustion threatened to claim me, but I couldn't stop here. Before I'd consciously decided to move, my feet had already begun tracking a path away from the horrifying scene.

I staggered down a narrow street, blue blood dripping from my suit, my hair, my visor…everything. My pulse raced, my head spun, I didn't know where I was going—just that I had to get away from the corpses I'd left behind.

"What in the—" I heard weapons raise, a sharp intake of breath, and then a familiar voice ordered, "Stand down!"

A hand clamped down on my shoulder, stopping me in my tracks. "Elara? By the ancestors! What happened? Are you injured—"

"Not…mine…" I barely managed to get the words out. Fingers grasped my visor, pulling it off, and I found myself standing face-to-face with Jysel, of all people. Yet…he looked concerned. Not angry.

"Casair, take a group of men and go find out where she came from," he ordered, then turned to address someone else. "Bring me something to clean her off with. We can't let her wander around like this."

I remained silent as Jysel checked me over for injuries, a low humming coming from him as he worked.

"Sir…" Casair spoke from behind me, but continued in Syldran. Had he really been gone long enough? Or had I not been walking for as long as I'd thought?

"Elara, calm down. Focus." Jysel carefully took my face in his hands, his expression firm as he stared at me. "What happened?"

"I was on patrol," I answered quietly. "Heard screaming. Found that bastard…" I clenched my fist, the feral threatening to rise with my anger. "I got angry and ordered him to stop. He...stopped, knelt, and I'm not sure what I did. He asked why I betrayed him. Then..."

I felt nausea welling up, but as if he could sense it, Jysel hummed...*something* and it vanished.

"You accidentally bound him before you killed him... Then what?" He spoke in soft, soothing tones.

"He said...that this planet is a warzone and whatever they want is for the taking." I shook my head. "He said they—"

"Who is 'they,' Elara?" Jysel prompted gently. "The cult? The humans?"

"No... Citomy. She released the contents of her prison ship onto the planet." I shivered and shook my head again. "She...they..."

"Why did you kill the victim too, Elara?" Casair asked, sounding concerned but significantly less gentle. I glanced at him, then at the ground. This time, I was sure Jysel wouldn't be able to keep me from being sick.

"You should move..." I put a hand against Jysel's chest and pushed him back. "I killed her because that bastard was eating—"

I couldn't make it through my sentence before I turned and dry heaved. There wasn't anything left for me to vomit, but that sure didn't mean my body wasn't going to try. My head swam as a hand came to rest on my back.

"We need to get you somewhere safe. Elara, do you— Elara? Hey! Stay with..."

Concerned whining and the smell of something vaguely coffee-like woke me enough to detect arguing voices nearby. I cracked an eye open to find Sal'aphel's snout mere inches from my nose as he pouted on the edge of the bed I was lying on.

I glanced around the dim room, unable to recognize anything. I was laying on the most comfortable bed I'd ever experienced, sure, and I could guess the purpose of the other pieces in the room…but not the style or materials. Even the floors, walls, and ceiling were foreign.

"We can't keep her here! The humans will be looking for her soon; even Zafir doesn't know she's here," a voice hissed angrily. "We should take her to Rel's, at least, as they trust him with her. If Citomy dumped her prisoners here, then we need to get moving—"

"We can't just leave her after such an awful experience. I know I've had my problems with her, but she needs support."

"Let me up, Sal'aphel," I grumbled, my voice cracking from dryness. I looked down at the feeling of soft material sliding across my skin, realizing that I was completely nude.

I sensed movement behind me, then heard a faint sigh. "Your suit disappeared when you fainted. If you need clothes, we can find something for you."

"Where am I?" I asked, keeping my voice low so it wouldn't

crack again. Standing up, I hesitated for a moment and looked around for clothes. Then I glanced down at the armlet I still wore. Right—wardrobe module. I summoned one of the warmer Syldran clothing sets, then turned to look at Jysel.

"Our hideout, which you've seen before. Casair didn't think it would be safe to bring you to our ship." Jysel glanced at his pet as Sal'aphel moved to follow me, a faint smile coming to his face. He said something to the creature in Syldran, then noticed my questioning look. "I told him he can accompany us only if he doesn't try to scare *or* chew on my soldiers."

"See? He's a good boy." I scratched Sal'aphel's cheek since I didn't quite feel up to reaching higher.

"Elara, about…the *lun'iri* you executed," Jysel started carefully. "I believe you should be grateful that you accidentally bound him."

I grimaced before looking over to the uneasy man, doing my best to keep from snapping. He *sounded* serious and had the look of someone who was expecting to get hit for stating their opinion. "I hope you're going to tell me *why* instead of leaving it at that."

"Let's get you a drink first." He offered me a hand, then hesitated, glancing away.

I placed my hand in his, half to ease his concerns and half because I wasn't confident in my steadiness while walking. Jysel looked at my hand as if it were some unknown object, then to my face.

"You…" He hesitated, though I had a sneaking suspicion he

thought I'd confused him for his brother.

"Jysel, what happened after I passed out?" I asked calmly, watching his eyes widen slightly. He glanced away like a shy puppy, a hint of blue creeping into the tips of his ears.

"Ah… We took the aggressor's body and put him on a suitable display for his crimes," he murmured, rubbing his chin. "Sending a message to the other loose prisoners may help intimidate them. The woman… I've sent one of my insiders to deal with claiming what remains of her, so that the correct story is told to the human media.

"Your visor wasn't functioning and your suit disappeared when you lost consciousness, so I've no idea if Zafir is aware of what happened. I made the decision to bring you here, though we have yet to agree whether we should send for Rel and Zafir…"

"We should," Casair stated flatly as he joined us. "The Imperials won't take kindly to *us* being the ones to give her back, and it would add fuel to their claim that we don't care about all queens. They'll work together with Citomy to further damage our image."

"We *shouldn't* send her back." Jysel nudged me ahead of him and through an archway, into what looked vaguely like a lounge area. "I'll contact Rel. We can discuss where to go from here with him."

"*Fine.*" Casair sighed irritably, pointing to a seat and giving me a look. "Sit down before you fall down. I'll get you a drink. Think you can stomach food?"

I started say no, but my stomach rumbled and Casair took that as his cue to grab some food, too.

"I'm not sure I can—" I grumbled as he set the drink and a bowl in front of me.

"It's something light," he offered. He took a seat across from me and glanced at Sal'aphel, whose head was on my armrest and nearly in my lap. "That's *Elara's*."

Sal'aphel whined but stayed put—at least, until the door swung open and both twins walked into the room. Rel must have either been getting ready for bed or just gotten up, because all he wore was a set of pants and a robe. He didn't even have shoes on.

"Okay, are you going to explain things to me now, Jysel?" I asked as they drew closer.

"Explain…ah, yes, I'll do that first." He nodded and took a seat off to my left, leaving Rel sit a little way off to my right since Sal'aphel wouldn't budge. "Syldrari are already quite dangerous, as you know. That man had been drugged, and was already a violent criminal. He was a serial…ah…rapist, murderer, and…cannibalist? Among other things I'd rather not touch on. But is 'cannibalist' the right word? He didn't merely eat other Syldrari. Anyone was food. Um…"

"What he's trying to say is, you would have been next if you hadn't bound and executed him. He eluded capture for centuries."

Rel leaned over his armrest and nudged Sal'aphel over. "We will need to hack into the ship's manifest, but it is likely that the other freed prisoners are of similar… skillsets."

"What was that woman thinking?" Jysel muttered bitterly.

Rel glanced at the table in front of me, noting the untouched bowl of food. He coaxed Sal'aphel out of his way, picked up the bowl, and perched on the armrest to my right, his expression firm.

"Elara, you need to regain your strength. You should be able to keep this down, as it is designed for soldiers who have just seen their first kill." He spoke calmly but firmly, lifting the spoon in his fingers. "Of course, I'm aware you are experienced…but not with *that*. Tonight you saw something no one should ever have to see."

"Fine," I grumbled, reaching for the spoon. Rel, however, insisted on feeding me himself. Something about my hands being too shaky to hold the spoon.

"Jysel, you know Zafir is probably sick with worry after losing contact with her," Casair began, receiving a short grunt in response. "We need to tell him she's fine, and he has to know what Citomy has done. Elara and the rest of her team are all in danger."

"Yes…and perhaps that is precisely Citomy's aim," Rel murmured, glancing down at me. His expression softened. "Where is your room? You need more rest. Allow us to handle

Zafir."

"We shouldn't send her back." Jysel rubbed his temples, looking conflicted. "Not to that city. If a relocation could be arranged…"

"That isn't enough. Not with such filth on the loose." Rel got to his feet and glanced toward the kitchens. "Give me some time. I'll make you something warm."

I glanced at the bowl in his hand, finally registering that it was empty, though I didn't recall eating more than a spoonful or two.

Jysel, noticing my confusion, stood and walked over. Before I could say anything, he lifted me fully out of my seat and called back to Rel, "Casair'll show you to her room when you're done. I'm taking her back; she was focusing better there. I don't think she is going to do well in open spaces, for a time."

"Open…?" Rel hesitated, then turned to look at Casair. "How about you fill me in fully while I prepare a meal for her."

"Sure…right." Casair grimaced and scratched his head.

"Is it really necessary to carry me?" I grumbled quietly as Jysel carried me down the hallway.

"You can barely focus on a conversation; do you think you can focus on walking?" he countered, his face expressionless.

"I don't want to be coddled," I pointed out.

"It isn't coddling. You've had a traumatic experience, and you need to recover both mentally and physically." He carefully sat me on the edge of the bed in my room, catching me by the shoulders when I swayed. "Listen to me. You didn't simply expel the contents of your stomach when you saw what that criminal was doing. You expended most of your energy when you bound and subsequently executed him. You were still discharging electrical currents when you stumbled upon us.

"We're lucky you're conscious at all, to be honest. The food Rel is preparing will help replenish what you've lost, but you also need *rest*. And I need to determine if there is a way to keep from having to send you back to the humans. Sending you or your team members to deal with the released criminals would essentially be sending you to die." He paused, a frown forming on his otherwise blank face. "What were you *doing* in that sector, anyway?"

"Why, did I interrupt Syldrari business?" I snorted.

Jysel tilted his head. "Would it make you feel better if I said yes?"

That managed to earn a short laugh from me. "No, I've had enough of having to repeatedly explain my situation to everyone I meet."

"Then…?" he prompted.

"It was just a routine patrol. We've been rotating our patrols to cover different sectors for several weeks. They're mostly keeping me out of the Syldrari sector because they don't want to raise more suspicion that I'm Lethe." I leaned back on one hand, watching as Jysel moved over to a chair and sat down, crossing one leg over the other. "We haven't had many team excursions or directed missions, for some reason, and we've been receiving hardly any intel. I think it's been over a month now since we last heard about a military facility being attacked by you or the cultists."

"Mmm…" Jysel's gaze averted, his eyes unfocusing as he seemed to consider something. "There must be a reason that so many forces have converged on this planet in particular. It has no rare resources to speak of, it's owned by one of the weakest species in the known universe…" He shook his head as if to dismiss that train of thought. "You're certain it was a routine patrol?"

"Yeah, it's been on my schedule for over a week," I answered, tapping my foot against the air. "Which isn't to say this couldn't have been orchestrated somehow. We know Citomy and the cultists both have moles inside HQ. Citomy's don't appear to have particularly high clearance, but I'm assuming the Empire's databases and network systems are fairly easy for Syldrari to hack."

"And you're still bothered by how that criminal reacted to being bound?" Jysel asked hesitantly. "Forgive me, but as it is what saved your life, I struggle to understand why you are reacting in such a way."

I took a moment to consider how I wanted to word my answer to such a complex question. "Disregarding the obvious part of the equation for a moment, it's…the immediate one-eighty he did. He went from…uh…*dining* to practically vowing his eternal servitude to me—and his feeling of betrayal was completely genuine. He mistook me binding him as a blessing to continue what he'd been doing.

"I'm bothered that binding someone means such mindless devotion and obedience. The thing I *like* about people is that they're their own, with their own hopes, dreams, aspirations, and ambitions. If binding someone completely negates that, how is it any better than the reprogramming the Empire does?"

"And this," he released a soft sigh, giving me a tired smile, "is why it's imperative that queens receive training in how to control their abilities. In this case, it was for the best that you took him over so completely. Had you not, he would have killed you – or worse."

"We should find someone to train her." Rel entered the room carrying a tray of food, Casair following behind with a pitcher and four glasses. "We can't ignore the fact that, as your cellular dissonance progresses, your powers grow stronger. I will have Ciheri do some research and see if we can refrain from involving another queen, such as Xilen."

"I thought you trusted Xilen?" I asked, puzzled.

"I trust Xilen's ambitions. But under the right circumstances, she would be our enemy rather than our ally." Rel hesitated, eyeing me and his twin in turn. "You are different from other queens and we would prefer you stayed that way. *Right, Jysel?*"

"Yes…" Jysel muttered begrudgingly.

"Sit back." Rel looked pointedly at me and then the head of the bed. "You can't balance the tray on your lap as you are."

"What are we gonna do about Zafir?" Casair asked as Rel carefully placed the tray onto my lap.

"We have to figure out what we are doing about Elara first," Rel stated. He caught my questioning look and returned it with a firm one. "You need to rest, preferably somewhere you feel safe. I would imagine that means here, with guards and Sal'aphel to make certain you aren't disturbed. Or do you really feel safe at HQ?"

"We both know HQ isn't safe," I answered dryly. "But waiting too long may make it even *less* safe. Either the moles or the Imperials, if not both, will know something has gone wrong soon."

"Unfortunately, it may be for the best if we call for Zafir." Jysel spoke up after a moment, earning an odd look from Casair. "What? I've had time to think. He's our man on the inside for a reason—he is able to navigate complex situations with ease. Of the four of us, he is the most likely to know, and quickly, how we should proceed."

"We can wait to call him until *after* Elara eats and settles down to rest," Rel stated in a tone that left no room for argument. He sat on the edge of my bed and gave me a gentle look. "Do you need help, or are you feeling less shaky?"

I wanted to say I didn't need help, but then I remembered how easily the three of them would see through that. Sighing, I glanced away in embarrassment and grumbled, "Still a little shaky."

"Elara, there is no need to be embarrassed. What you are feeling is completely natural," Rel informed me, his voice reverberating faintly with calming tones. "Any one of us would have been horrified to come across what you saw."

"You aren't the only one who got sick," Casair offered, nodding his agreement. "That kind of brutality…you don't see it much with most species. Not to mention the other issues."

"It's very different from killing in self-defense or in battle," Jysel murmured absentmindedly, his eyes still unfocused. "Most of my men struggled to stomach it. You shouldn't feel ashamed or embarrassed for having such a strong reaction. If it helps, be thankful for the confirmation that you're a *person*, not a monster."

"Here." Rel quietly picked up a piece of bread and tore off a small piece. "Let's get you fed so you can rest. Alright?"

"Mhm…" I hesitated, then let him feed me. Casair poured us all a drink, through Jysel barely touched his while he did…whatever it was he was doing in the corner. After a few bites, I asked, "Where is Sal'aphel?"

"Outside. I'll let him in when you're done eating," Rel informed me with a small smile. "Otherwise, he will try to eat it all—tray included."

Casair suddenly stopped mid-sip as if listening to something, turning his head slightly. A frown touched his lips and he glanced between the twins. "One of our men says he's got an urgent report for me. If I may…"

"Go." Jysel nodded. "Rel and I can handle finding suitable guards for this room."

"Guards, huh?" I glanced at Jysel.

"I may be…rash, at times." Jysel shot his twin a foul look when he scoffed. "But I know when to exercise caution. No one goes in or out of this room without permission from me or Rel."

"So you *can* be reasonable," Rel remarked. "I'm so proud of you, Jysel. You're growing."

"Oh yes, I'm sure you're so thrilled," Jysel muttered as he continued to focus. "You want to stage an escape from this planet just as much as I do. Tell me, is Clan V'shir even prepared?"

"Of course. Everyone is prepared to man their stations and set a course for uncharted space at a moment's notice," Rel answered with a dangerous smile. "The real question is whether *you're* prepared to follow us."

"Do I want to know what you two are on about—and *why?*" I looked between the pair.

"Not yet," they answered in unison, and immediately returned to their individual tasks.

While I ate, I noticed that they periodically glanced or nodded at each other as if they were having a conversation, yet I heard nothing. I wasn't sure if they were communicating via neurochip, or if they had some ability I wasn't aware of. Not quite in the mood to interrupt and ask, I remained silent and let Rel care for me.

Once they were satisfied that I'd been properly fed and hydrated, they let Sal'aphel into the room and he promptly curled up on the bed with me. Well, as much of him as would fit on it, anyway. Then the twins shut off the lights and took their leave. I had just started to wonder how I could possibly sleep after the night I'd had when a melody reverberated through me and I felt my body go limp, my mind drifting into darkness.

CHAPTER FORTY-THREE

I stared at the ceiling, listening as voices argued in Syldran. This time, I was fairly sure I was in Rel's apartment, but several other voices had joined the argument since I'd fallen asleep. Grimacing, I gingerly sat up and waited to see if my head spun. When it didn't, I carefully got to my feet, summoned clothes, and hastily finger-combed my hair before making my way out of the room.

Most of them failed to notice me coming toward them, though Ciheri immediately began trying to turn their attention my way. I shot him a small smile, then walked straight up to Rel and declared, "I'm hungry. What's for breakfast?"

My sudden appearance left Jysel and Zafir struggling for words, but Rel, Casair, and Aldiner were quicker to react.

"You shouldn't be on your feet yet," Casair stated, taking a step toward me.

"Maybe she needs entertainment?" Aldiner suggested slyly, striking an alluring pose. "Maybe I—"

"She said she is hungry. It's simple as that." Rel shot Aldiner an annoyed glance. "Learn some tact."

"Your arguing woke her up," Ciheri murmured quietly, slinking closer to me when Zafir and Jysel both gave him foul glares. He didn't stop until he was hiding behind me, the sleeve of my robe clutched in one hand. "Glare all you want, it's true. You're *loud* when you're upset…"

Rel motioned for me to follow him. "Here, come sit—"

"Now that she's awake, we won't be staying," Zafir interrupted, his voice harsh. "I can't keep our superiors off us for much longer. It's for the best that she—"

"For the *best*?" Jysel snapped. "It's merely a means to an end—and an unreliable one at best."

"What *is* reliable is what the humans will do if we try to take Elara off-world," Ciheri snapped in exasperation. "Until someone cripples the resonance weapon, and Citomy's interests move elsewhere, we are just as stuck as Elara."

"*Tch*, to think a *cult* would be freer to act than us…" Jysel muttered bitterly.

Casair crossed his arms over his chest. "Zafir, you can tell she's not recovered enough to give a report. Stop pushing."

"The humans don't understand the *delicacies* of the mind," Zafir argued, turning to challenge Casair. "Nor do they believe in giving a mind time to recover. I wish we could take a measured pace as well, but we simply cannot. They expect her to begin working again tonight. Unless, and I quote, 'the Syldrari have done something to her.'"

"'Tonight' is in four hours!" Rel exclaimed. "Are they *trying* to get her killed?!"

"We know at least one person in the Imperator's circle wants this project ended. Who is to say there aren't others?" Zafir rubbed his temples. "You have people with the know-how to shadow her. If you're so worried, give them orders to keep her safe. Meanwhile, *I* will continue to do what I must to keep her safe from the humans."

"While I appreciate the concern, shouldn't the focus be on saving the other queens?" I asked, watching as most expressions in the room turned to discomfort. "They're easier to save than me. It'd be more productive—"

"That isn't your decision," Rel stated. He turned to look at me, his expression unreadable. "Furthermore, we have enough hands to focus on saving both."

I stared at him for a moment, then glanced to Jysel, who was fidgeting and appeared a little lost. "And you have sufficient protection from the queens you have been saving?"

"...No." Jysel hesitated, then seemed to resolve to give me an answer. "I've lost several men to the queens we've rescued already. We had hoped more of them would be reasonable, but we have had to tranquilize most of them to protect ourselves. Their behavior is largely the reason we have handed them over to our contacts on Syldra."

I released a small sigh and crossed my arms. "In that case, I can sort of understand why you'd prefer to focus on me, but…"

"Don't tell me not to." Jysel turned his back to me and promptly left the room.

Casair groaned, his shoulders slumping. "I'm sorry 'bout him, Elara. I'll see if I can talk some sense into him."

Zafir opened his mouth to say something to Rel, but before he could speak, he was met with a firm, "No. She is having breakfast first—I already prepared something, as I knew *you* and the humans would be unreasonable."

"Mmm… Do they have a tracking device on her, though?" Aldiner came and leaned against my left side, peering at me curiously. "We could just hide her somewhere."

"I believe trying to hide her is what led to her being caught in the Resonance Incident. So, no." Zafir took several steps toward us, his mien dark as he glared at Aldiner. Then he looked to me, his expression softening. "Elara, how are you feeling?"

"Like I have a pod of Syldrari fighting to make my decisions for me," I answered sarcastically, shooting him a sharp look. "But really. If I have trustworthy people shadowing me, I'll be fine. I don't want to have to use my queenly powers to subdue someone for execution again. I can deal with combat killing just fine, but that…and his victim…"

Ciheri's grip on my arm tightened as he leaned into me. "You did the right thing! And…and is it executing that sub-Syldrari that upset you…"

"…Or his victim?" Zafir sighed and pressed his fingers to his temples, his expression conflicted. "That was something no one should ever have to see, let alone experience. You did the right thing."

"Even though people's limbs and bodies are replaceable?" I muttered irritably.

"She was not wealthy enough for replacements, and the Empire's mental healthcare system isn't equipped to help someone work through the trauma of *being eaten*," Zafir snapped, momentarily losing his cool before his shoulders slumped. "Honestly, where does Citomy *find* such horrendous…"

While Zafir was muttering to himself, Aldiner and Ciheri took the opportunity to lead me into Rel's personal kitchen and over to a table, where they sat themselves down on either side of me.

"You're sure about this, Elara?" Rel asked softly as he plated some sweet-smelling food.

I considered my answer for a moment. He didn't sound as though he was questioning my decision, more like he was concerned whether I was okay with having no choice in the matter. In which case, he deserved a proper answer. "Considering that the repercussions for disobedience would harm more than just me, yes. I have to consider the safety of my team and Zafir, too."

"Is that so?" Rel glanced back at me.

"Mmm... Aliens and hybrids aren't the only people they'll reprogram and enslave," I answered after a moment. "Zafir is in danger of being reprogrammed into a sex slave and sold off, too—they've no doubt realized he's pretty, and he's alluded that he's at risk. If he's removed, the project may be shut down. If it isn't, there's still the concern of who would take his place.

"I'm not sure if the others are aware of how important Zafir's safety is to ours, but I think I at least have a decent grasp on it."

Rel bristled, shifting to look back at me. "They'll do this to *everyone*? That's..."

"There were human prisoners and slaves where Elara rescued me from, too," Ciheri interjected softly. "They just care about power and control over others. If they find you attractive, they'll sell you to brothels or similar to provide 'services and entertainment.' If you're too troublesome, resistant to their drugs or have the wrong reaction to them, they'll force you into fighting rings or find some other way to use you."

Rel sighed as he carried some sort of cold porridge over to me. "I'll find people to follow you. Those *animals* Citomy freed shouldn't be underestimated."

"Hey." I caught the dejected man by his wrist when he started to turn away. "I'm confident that, if saving me is what you want to do, you'll all figure out a way to do it. So, for now..."

"For now, let you and Zafir do what it takes to keep you, *you.*

Right?" Rel sighed quietly, his glow shifting between grey, pink, and blue before finally settling on cyan. "We're here if you need support."

With that, Rel wandered off, leaving me with Aldiner and Ciheri. After a moment, Zafir joined us and sat down across from me at the kitchen table. He looked exhausted, but still tried to crack a small smile when he finally looked at me.

"I tried to convince our superiors to wait..." he murmured quietly. "They are not well-informed on matters of the mind. They believe you should be fine, and you may have to pretend you are. When humans sense what they believe to be weakness—"

"I know, Zafir. There's only so much that can be done when you're dealing with them, and they've been wearing you down." I gave him a small smile. "Let's focus on what we *can* do, instead of what we can't. Something has to give if we're going to deal with what Citomy's done—and we need to figure out why she did it. And..."

"What is it?" Ciheri asked worriedly when I fell silent, my eyes narrowing.

"What do we know about Citomy's current motives?" I asked slowly. "We know she tried to sell Rel and Jysel to me, and we know she appears to be trying to gain leverage over the Imperials for some reason—putting them into debt by selling her sons to me might have done just that.

"But that plan fell through. How else could she make the Imperator indebted to her? By 'saving' them from an outbreak of

Syldrari criminal activity, of course. When my team continues to fail at stopping these animals, the project will be in danger and so will the Empire."

"I…I have to make a call!" Zafir shot to his feet, pulled out his communicator, and dashed out of the room.

Aldiner sighed heavily, resting one elbow on the table and propping his cheek against his hand. He watched me for a moment, then pointed at my food with his free hand. "If you're not gonna eat that—I will. Or do you require being hand-fed now, *Your Majesty?*"

"*Mine.*" I pouted, pulling my bowl away protectively. "And I don't need to be fed. I can take care of myself! …Mostly."

"Maybe we should entertain you, then?" Aldiner grinned devilishly at me. "I'm a great dancer, you know. We could take a break from all this serious talk, and—"

"Maybe she *prefers* the serious talk?" Ciheri countered, leaning forward in his chair. "Elara is very inquisitive and intelligent! I'm sure—"

"She is. But that doesn't mean she doesn't need a break now and then." Aldiner glanced over to Ciheri, then back at me. "Being in work mode all the time isn't gonna get anything done quicker. You should take a breather 'til it's time for you to go to work. Clear your head, center yourself, and all that."

"I don't exactly know *how* to…uh…" I leaned back a little when Aldiner leaned forward to peer at me. "What?"

"Your eyes. For a second, they…" He frowned and stood up. "I saw your eyes—your real eyes—for a moment. I'm going to go get Zafir."

"Uh…" I blinked after him, then looked to Ciheri when he tugged on my sleeve.

"If it's happening more, we'll have to ask Jysel and Zafir how they hide their appearance from the humans, because you may have to start doing the same." He paused and leaned closer, his expression filled with worry as he examined me. "Are you sure you're okay? If you need to talk, I don't mind."

"I just… It's hard to quantify the kind of behavior I witnessed," I answered after a moment. "It's… Subhuman? Sub-Syldran? I'm not quite sure what to call it, but it's so incredibly opposite to what I've come to expect from Syldrari, that I just don't…"

I grimaced, feeling a twinge of nausea.

"Mmm… Just like with humans, Syldrari can be ill in the head," Ciheri began carefully, his expression contemplative. "Usually, the environments we're raised in help avert such problems—but there are always people who, no matter their upbringing, are just…wrong.

"And I haven't seen the report, but some of our worst criminals are people who were kept or raised by certain queens. That man could have been made that way by a queen. Some of them… Some of them have a twisted idea of how to exert control over their clan. I've heard rumors, but…"

"Yet queens remain revered…" I muttered bitterly. "Why?

Because Syldra is a utopia compared to other species' homes? Or is it merely because of the natural power they hold?"

"It isn't all bad!" Ciheri exclaimed quickly. He clung to my arm, his expression one of immense worry. "It's a small minority of queens who are bad people. Really! It's just they've risen to the top because of how much power they have, and their willingness to abuse it. Someone like you... Someone like you would be able to defeat them easily with more training. Your potential—"

"Is that so?" I raised an eyebrow as Ciheri clamped his hands over his mouth, flushing deep blue.

"Please forget I said that," he whispered between his fingers. "They...they don't want too much knowledge to hurt you. U-um..."

"Ciheri, it's okay," I reassured him with a smile. "Even with that kind of information, I can't actually do anything with it."

"At least someone is being reasonable today," Zafir remarked with a sigh as he and Aldiner reentered the room. He gave Ciheri a tired smile when he started to apologize again. "It is fine. Just be more careful in the future. We don't need Elara getting any ideas she won't come back from.

"Elara, have you finished eating? If what Aldiner said is correct, I need to give you a quick examination to determine whether a more powerful disguise is in order."

"Yeah. If I eat any more, I'll puke because I've had too

much," I answered with a nod. "You think the dissonance might have accelerated again?"

"It is possible that the stress sped it up by several stages—I won't know until I check, but I should be able to determine if the rate is still increased, or if it has returned to a slower pace," Zafir answered, conjuring a large black trunk and beginning to rummage around inside of it.

While Zafir worked to find his instruments, Rel returned, looking a little more relaxed.

"I've given orders to my best people to tail Elara, and have advised many more to keep an eye on her team as well. We've also increased our own patrols, as the loose criminals are more likely to prey on the Syldrari sector and its borders." Rel gave Zafir a questioning glance as he moved past, but continued talking. "Depending on how deeply Citomy is behind this nonsense, the criminals may have been told to make it appear that our sector is to blame."

"Would they obey even if they weren't bound?" I frowned at him.

"It depends what they were offered in return for their obedience, and how well they were persuaded. A queen of her power doesn't have to claim someone to control them." Rel shook his head, disgust briefly washing over his face. "It is a shame that her mentor instilled such poor values in her, and that she is continuing the custom..."

"Speaking of mentors, I'll get to work with my research." Ciheri wrapped me in a quick hug before rising to his feet, giving me a bright smile. "I'll find everything I can about how to control and harness your power, Elara. Then you won't need to worry!"

I watched him dart off, then turned my attention to Zafir and Rel. "Why do you all seem to have such faith in me?"

"Because actions speak louder than words, and because we can tell your disgust with the status quo is genuine," Zafir answered, pulling a glowing disc out of his trunk.

"And you treat all the sexes with the same amount of respect," Rel added, giving me an amused smile. "Though you do clearly have your preferences, seeing as you've befriended mostly *lun'iri* and *sol'iri* thus far."

"I'm still a little fuzzy on…" I tilted my head quizzically when he laughed and grinned at me.

"It's good to know you aren't picking and choosing based on what you find visually or physically appealing." He gave me a mysterious smile, then turned his back to us as he busied himself in one of the cupboards.

"Yes, well, if we start counting our blessings now, we'll never stop, and Elara will miss her duties," Zafir interjected dryly as he approached me with various devices, including a pair of strange gloves with glowing bits along the palms and fingers. "You can remain as you are, Elara. This will not take long."

CHAPTER FORTY-FOUR

<I have good news and bad news.> Zafir's voice came over the comms as I made my rounds. <The bad news is that a fleet of war-capable ships have entered the system and appear to be on their way here. We do not know if this planet is their target, or merely a stopover. The good news is that the Empire has aimed the resonance weapon to the skies in case they need it.>

Let me guess. The other bad news is that it will still destroy a huge chunk of this planet if it's fired... I grimaced, but remained silent. With so many species having set up patrols in the city, we'd agreed it was safest if I didn't talk. There weren't many Syldrari patrolling, but they weren't the only ones who might be able to hear through the modulation.

It seemed like Zafir had taken it upon himself to talk my ear off, though. I was getting the impression he thought it was necessary to keep me company for some reason.

<Indeed. We're all still in danger. I'm receiving reports that the Abyss Father cult has taken its leave, but I'm not sure how reliable that is.> There was a sound of rustling papers, then he continued. <Next... Ah. We were right to suspect Citomy's motives. She is offering 'removal services' at a premium price and has given Imperator Julien several options. One, outright payment to kill or capture the rogue criminals. Two, buy Rel and Jysel for you so that you can order their clans to do the work. Three, pledge loyalty to Syldra and be adopted as a...pet planet, if you will. The proper term does not translate well. Talks are currently on hold while the Empire and Citomy work to determine whether the incoming fleet is a threat. From what I understand, they aren't entirely sure what species the fleet belongs to, as the models are 'mass market,' if you will.>

I stopped by the mouth of an alley and frowned, listening to the voices coming from it. That was the direction I was supposed to go, but I was fairly certain those voices belonged to Jysel and Casair. I pursed my lips, trying to recall a different route I could take. They'd been very helpful after my ordeal, but I wasn't supposed to talk and I didn't know how to convey that – or the reason for it – to them. Furthermore, I wasn't confident that Jysel would still be in nice mode.

Unfortunately, if there was another route, I didn't know it. I started walking down the alley and soon came across the Syldrari pair. They had a handful of soldiers with them and were splashed head to toe with blue blood. Jysel had a nasty gash down one arm, which one of his men was cleaning and bandaging.

"And where do you think you're going?" he asked as I attempted to sneak by. When I flinched and turned to look at him, he frowned. "Are you alright?"

"…" I almost spoke reflexively, but managed to cut it off into a frustrated sound. After a moment of thought, I pointed at myself and made a motion like I was zipping my lips.

"…Do you have any idea what that meant?" Jysel looked to Casair.

"She's got orders not to speak. Right?" Casair made a sour face when I nodded. "*Tch*, of course. Who'd need to speak on duty?!"

I tried to move past them again, but this time Jysel blocked me physically. "Lethe, you shouldn't go that way. It's a mess."

Twitching, I crossed my arms at him.

"Think she *has* to go that way," Casair remarked. "We've established she doesn't actively try to piss you off, yeah?"

Jysel sighed and gave me an unreadable look, though it somehow made me feel smaller. "You're required to go that way on your route? Then I'm escorting you part of the way in case more show up."

Hesitating, I pointed at his bandaged wound, but he promptly called his sword to one hand and let his Syldrari battle suit appear.

"I will remain in the shadows. Walk." His entire form wavered and then vanished, leaving me more irritated than before.

"He's fine, it's not a serious wound—just a ragged one," Casair offered with a smile. "Go on then, don't let us keep you. Though I'm sure that'd make him happy— Ow!"

Jysel's form briefly appeared when he whacked Casair upside the head, then disappeared again. Without much in the way of options, I made my way down the alley, walking through the trail of blood. I grimaced as it oozed up around my feet.

[Some of the criminals have banded together to increase their odds,] Jysel remarked, his voice reverberating around and through me and causing a physical reaction I wasn't quite prepared for. I moved to brush at my arms and legs as if he'd physically touched me but stopped when he let out a low laugh. [Ah, you aren't familiar with this method of communication? Don't worry. No one can hear me but you.]

I shivered involuntarily. His voice both sounded and *felt* far too intimate. Like fingertips trailing over my bare skin.

[You will learn this method eventually, as it involves your neurochip,] he continued conversationally. [As for all the blood... We are in the process of removing the corpses and cleaning up the aftermath. Are you sure you want to go this way?]

I nodded faintly.

[Do you want to know their crime?]

Again, I nodded.

[They were arranging a hunt, with humans and other aliens

on this planet as their prey.] By his tone, Jysel could have been giving a report. [My mother… Citomy is easily won over by vicious, bloodthirsty individuals. She prizes her ability to capture, woo, and subdue them.]

Like dangerous pets… I thought, then glanced down as I realized the blood was up to my ankles now that we'd descended deeper into the alley.

[Precisely. Like dangerous… Ahem.] He attempted to backpedal. [The criminals most likely believe they can win favor and a pardon if they perform well enough, as most of Citomy's spouses are vicious criminals, former system lords, or powerful warriors.]

Well, thanks for confirming that you and Rel can hear my damn thoughts. I pulled myself up onto a ledge as the blood grew deeper. *I suppose this works. To answer your earlier question, I'm under orders to remain silent because of the high probability that species who can filter out the modulator will overhear me. The military still wants to keep 'Elara' and 'Lethe' separate.*

[Are you…feeling better?] he asked quietly, reappearing in front of me without his battle suit's hooded helm-thing on. He had a hesitant, lost look in his eyes that I wasn't sure how to interpret.

Better, yes. Recovered, no, I answered, deciding to leave it at that. The sight of someone being eaten alive was going to haunt me for a long time, for one—and then there had been the *sounds.* But also…I hadn't quite grasped the gravity of a queen's power before. Now, I wasn't sure how to talk to the males in my life. Even being playful seemed like a risk.

[Can I do anything to help?] Jysel asked, surprising me into returning my focus to him. [Ah…if you would prefer Rel—]

As much as I would like to answer your question, I'm not sure how to do so without causing problems. So, if you don't mind, I'm just going to continue my patrol. I went to move around him, but he caught me gently by the arm and averted his gaze. For the life of me, I couldn't tell if he was struggling to look at the visor, or if he was simply that uncomfortable or shy.

[I think you misunderstand. Both our clans are prepared to become yours if necessary. Queenless clans don't survive for long, especially not when Citomy turns her eye to them.] Jysel spoke quietly, his expression firm even if he hesitated to meet my gaze. [Were we not her sons, our clans would have been absorbed into hers by now. As we are related by blood, she has to find someone else to take us. Her fixation on you is suspicious at best, but beneficial to us.

[You've proved to us that you're not like the other queens. We believe you would be fair in your handling of us, that you wouldn't strip us either of our sense of self or our power.]

I still struggle to accept that I'm a queen. I released a small sigh, shaking my head. *Regardless, we know I can't control most of my abilities very well. I appreciate the faith you both seem to have in me, even if I don't understand it. To be honest, I'm just relieved you don't hate me. Given how most of our meetings have gone—*

[Wait.] Jysel turned, the rest of his suit appearing as he adjusted his grip on his sword and looked upward. A group of skybikes whizzed overhead, and he let out a small sigh. [Perhaps we shouldn't linger here. Let's move.]

I started walking again, then decided to ask a question that had been bugging me. *So…does my power sway you to answer me every time I ask a question?*

[No. It depends on how demandingly you word it, and how commanding your tone is,] he answered, shaking his head. [Your power surfaces less often than you think it does. It is intimately tied with how you, as an individual, think and believe. That said, someone whose senses are often dampened—such as Zafir—is at risk regardless of how you word something. The same can be said for Syldrari who are new to adulthood. With Rel and I, you should be able to be at least mostly candid.]

Okay. How many of you can hear my thoughts? I asked, a little concerned by what the answer might be. But I needed to know.

[Rel and I, for certain. I'm not sure if any of the others are trained to hear thoughts,] he answered firmly. [And it is an ability that is usually kept off. It can be too distracting with how much we already perceive visually and audibly.]

How much risk is there of you being bound when you're retrieving queens? I asked, watching as he slowed to a stop, clenching one fist.

[It is a struggle. While there are ways we can protect ourselves, they can be worn down. Even when tranquilizing them, we must be careful. It is best if we don't alert them to our presence at all.] He sounded incredibly uncomfortable, and soon he released a long sigh. [I will be straightforward. There are those among my men who are pushing for you to become our queen before we free anyone else. We are quickly nearing a point where the only person who doesn't want you to be our queen is you.

[Of course, I intend to respect that decision to the best of my ability. But you should know, if it becomes a matter of survival… I will not beg, nor will I ask nicely. The survival of my clan is of the utmost importance to me. Rel feels similarly, though he is less likely to admit it unless directly prompted.]

You would take away my *freedom in order to survive?* I grimaced, and Jysel whirled with an utterly perplexed stare. *What? How am I supposed to find a nice guy to settle down with if I have clans bound to me? It seems like it'd wreck my nearly non-existent chances at finding a boyfriend or anything else.*

[I don't understand. Why would you only want *one* mate?] he asked, sounding even more baffled than before. [And binding someone doesn't mean that they will be your mate. There are numerous arrangements made solely for protective services.]

…Oh. Oh. That isn't at all what I thought… Why didn't anyone explain this to me? I brought a hand up over my face, then paused, tilting my head. *What do you mean by, 'why would I only want one?'*

[You have been around humans too long if you do not find

monogamy to be the unusual practice,] Jysel answered flatly. [Syldrari have taken multiple partners since ancient times. With *iri* being rare and valuable, they often took on multiple spouses for protection—if one died, there would be others who survived to continue protecting her. Taking only one mate or spouse would be like taking only one soldier to fight an army.]

Isn't Syldra mostly safe now? Why... I trailed off, feeling just as baffled as he looked.

[It is, but that simply means it has become acceptable for more than *iri* to become...] He struggled for a moment, murmuring several Syldran words. [Household leaders, if you will? *We* call them *trikar!xi*—a literal translation would be 'they whom others gather around.' Any of the sexes can become a *trikar!xi*, and their spouses or partners can be of any sex—even *iri*—though a queen will always be the *trikar!xi* of any family unit.]

I think I follow, but...if those bound to a queen don't have to be her mate, then why plural relationships? I struggled to grasp even the concept, let alone the odd clicking noise he made near the end of the word. *That's a lot of people to give attention to and make sure they're cared for, and conflicts would be difficult to navigate—especially if they were between different partners.*

[I... Why *wouldn't* you want to have a meaningful relationship with everyone you care for?] Jysel stared at me as if I had too many heads. [Furthermore, it isn't merely the *trikar!xi* who... For example, let us say you were our *trikar!xi*. I would be your wife, but

I would also be Zafir's— What? Is it so strange?]

It took me a moment to stop laughing and catch my breath. Once I'd managed to rein myself in, I answered, *Unless you're incredibly good at hiding the fact you're an* iri… *Wife was the wrong word. You were looking for* husband.

[Ah…] He cracked an embarrassed smile, a brief chuckle escaping before he pulled himself back to stoic seriousness. [Ahem. As I was saying. In most Syldrari relationships, all individuals involved must agree to the other individuals' presence. They are essentially…group dating, if you will. Or, 'group life partners' might be more accurate. The exception to this, as you can imagine, are queens. What they have is more akin to the concept of human harems or concubines.]

I kind of get it…but you also need to take into consideration that I have no idea if I've ever actually gone on a date before. I rubbed my chin in thought. *I have no idea what sort of shenanigans I might have gotten up to before the Incident.*

[That is fair. Then, suffice to say, Rel and I both fully expect that you would form a group of people you care about. Not simply pick one and leave the others to wallow in despair.] He shook his head slightly.

Wait…group dating. But what does that mean for your sexual preferences? I asked, receiving a blank stare in response. *There must be* some *limit. You…*

[I don't understand. What do you mean by sexual

preferences? Are you referring to activities in bed? That is another reason multiple partners is common. Not everyone shares the same tastes.] Jysel frowned when I shook my head. [Then I'm afraid I've no idea what you mean.]

Uh... Some humans like everyone, some are romantically but not physically attracted to other people—they're asexual. But the majority seem to only prefer men or women, and not both... I mean, some do, but...maybe I'm not the best person to speak on this? I did my best to word things with only my own limited knowledge on the subject.

[Ah... I am familiar with people who do not feel physical attraction and don't desire sex,] Jysel remarked, crossing his arms as his face twisted in thought. [I can't say I'm familiar with preferring a certain sex. It isn't uncommon to visually prefer those who present what humans consider male or female, but any grown Syldrari cares more about who the person *is*. Not how they look. That said, queens tend to be physically attracted to those they can produce offspring with, but even then, they usually have other romantic partners... None of this is making sense to you, is it?]

It's like you're trying to tell me that, this whole time, the sky has been yellow and not blue. I put my hand on my hip and sighed. *You've given me a lot to think about. I didn't realize Syldrari relationships were so complicated.*

[...I find *human* relationships to be more complicated.] Jysel looked aghast. [How is anyone ever emotionally fulfilled or physically satisfied with only *one* partner? How do they find one right one out of potential dozens? It doesn't make sense!]

Uh…whereas I'd ask you how someone finds more than one 'right one.' I frowned. *It's difficult enough to find one person to mesh with, let alone multiple.*

[We will be here all night and then some if we continue this conversation,] he murmured, flushing deep blue as he glanced away from me. [And you're supposed to be on patrol. We should continue onward.]

Oh, so you're just going to drop that information on me and change the subject? I don't think so. I quickly moved around him, blocking his way. Again, he averted his gaze, his glow shifting to deep yellow. *The way I see it, if you're potentially going to force me into a position where I have to become your clan's queen, the least you can do is have this discussion with me. Help me understand.*

Jysel hesitated. [What do you want to ask?]

You've told me what the social norm is, but not how individuals feel about it, I pointed out. *I get that it's a thing, but how do* lun'iri *like yourself* feel *about it?*

[Uh…] He looked utterly perplexed and took a moment to think, rubbing his chin. [Have you ever been in a situation where what someone else believes is so insanely illogical that you can't fathom living their way?]

Have you met *any humans?* I asked, earning a grin and laughter in response. *I live their way because I have to, not because I want to. Most of what they do seems illogical.*

[That is how most of us feel about monogamy,] Jysel offered with a small smile. [There are cases where someone wishes to be another's one and only, but it rarely comes from a healthy place. We are not, I believe the human idiom would be *wired*, to exist that way. We are communal in nearly everything we do, as that is what it took to survive on Syldra, and what is required to survive throughout most of the universe.]

When you put it that way...

[Consider this, as well: The *trikar!xi* isn't the only one who needs fulfillment in a relationship,] he offered. [As an *iri*, you can only offer certain manners of support and ah...*pleasure*, to your partners. There are some forms of emotional support and understanding that, say, a *lun'iri* may only be able to receive from another *lun'iri*.

[An example... Ah. Perhaps this will help your understanding. My late father was queen-obsessed, but despite this, he chose to...cheat? on their relationship group with a *lun'iri* soldier under his command.]

Why was 'cheat' a question? I leaned toward him slightly.

[I... That *is* the human term, isn't it?] He crossed his arms, his gaze drifting out of focus. Then his attention sharpened again. [Yes. 'Cheating.' A betrayal of a romantic partner. Or, in our case, a romantic group.

[As I was saying... He did this because he was not fulfilled in the group, yet he was simultaneously too immature and fanatical to discuss his needs. He took matters into his own hands, and when he was discovered, he was assigned to this area of space as a form of isolation punishment.]

So, fidelity is to the group rather than a single person...? I mulled it over, forgetting for a moment that he could hear me—until he nodded his confirmation, that is.

[The soldier he pursued is still quite traumatized by the experience. My father, with his obsessive nature, refused to allow the soldier to have any other relationships—romantic or otherwise. This is common in the Syldrari who seek out monogamous relationships. Unhealthy, maddening obsession that doesn't account for how the other person feels. If you were to speak of monogamy to most other Syldrari...] He trailed off, letting his words hang in the air, then glanced away in discomfort. [I suppose what I am trying to tell you is to be cautious. You may give others the wrong idea about your personality, or unintentionally upset those around you.]

Mmm... You've given me a lot to think about, I remarked, glancing up when I felt wetness hit my cheek. I let out a soft sigh and shot Jysel a small smile. *Thank you for being patient with me. I can make my own way from here; you're still a wanted man, and—*

Jysel arched an eyebrow and crossed his arms over his chest. [We're not even *to* the corpses yet. I am not going anywhere. Furthermore, you're meant to patrol in a storm without protection? Do they treat all their soldiers so poorly?]

I shrugged, then turned to start walking. *No idea. I don't have much contact with people outside of HQ and the Syldrari sector. Who we're allowed to interact with, and how, is inconsistent at best and suspicious at worst.*

Jysel fell into step with me, his expression pensive, before he finally seemed to remember his original intent to keep himself hidden. His hooded helmet returned and he vanished from the visible spectrum, though he continued speaking in the same uncomfortably intimate method. [Will you at least consider what I've said? Both about queenhood, and our people's preference for plural relationships? I, personally, would rather not experience what might happen if you chose only a single *lun'iri*—especially when Rel and I are involved. Worse still if you were to choose between us. With how attached to you Rel has become, I...]

I'll think about the queen issue, I informed him, taking a firm tone. *As for relationships... To be blunt, I'm not looking for* any *manner of relationship. Not until I'm free of the Empire—if I ever am. Romance is the last thing on my mind...but I will try to understand Syldrari customs, at least. It sounds as though I must keep it in mind, if I'm also to consider becoming a queen.*

[That is reasonable,] Jysel remarked quietly. He went to say something else, but fell silent when we came upon a pile of Syldrari bodies, along with their various parts, stuffed into the corner of the alley.

They were mostly male, but there appeared to be at least two women among the dead as well. They all wore ragged clothes and bore numerous scars made from primitive weapons. Additionally, they each had a brand on their upper arm with symbols I didn't recognize.

[Please do not linger.] Jysel's hand rested on my shoulder, though he didn't reappear. [Simply know they deserved to die for both the crimes they had already committed and those they were planning. We confirmed that Citomy's prison ship was full of…quite awful people. I would rather not repeat their deeds.]

Tch, *she's like an overgrown child throwing a tantrum. She isn't much better than these people.* I stalked past the dead Syldrari, doing my best to hold my breath until we were far away. Thankfully, the path angled upward again just around the corner.

[Only because she isn't trying,] he muttered venomously. I sensed him pause, then after a moment he asked, [Zafir says you have information to relay to me?]

I do? I asked blankly, wracking my mind for whatever the hell Zafir could have been going on about. Furthermore, why had he been so quiet on my end? Not a damn peep since I'd come across Jysel.

Does he mean… Oh! He must want me to tell you about the incoming fleet, and the Empire's response.

[The *what?*] he exclaimed. [You didn't think to say— sorry. I'm sorry. I know. Orders, keeping up appearances… *Nnnghh.*]

Yeaaah. I decided to let that one slide. *Anyway, there is a combat-capable fleet in the system, apparently on their way to this planet. We don't know who they are, whether they mean to start a fight, or if they're merely passing through. The humans have aimed the resonance weapon to the skies in preparation.*

[Then my timeline has been shifted.] Jysel halted, reappearing in front of me without his suit. He turned to face me, his expression one of determination. [I hate to ask this of you when it was I who insisted on escorting you, but will you be alright continuing on your own? The weapons platform *must* be disabled, and such a fleet could arrive in a matter of hours.]

I'll be fine. My shift is almost over. If necessary…hmmm, this is near Rel's, right? I asked, taking a quick look at my surroundings.

[Yes—he, Aldiner, and Ciheri can help you if you need it.] He nodded firmly and started to move past me, but hesitated once he was in line with me. [I apologize for leaving you like this. And for my behavior in the past. I am *trying* to be more understanding.]

We're both trying. I'd say that's progress. I gave him a small smile. *Really, I'll be fine. Seeing to the weapons platform is more important than escorting one* iri *in circles around the sector. If that weapon is fired, you won't* have *anything left to worry about.*

[You are certainly right about that.] He vanished again. [Take care, Elara. Don't linger longer than you must.]

With him gone, I started walking again and referenced the time on the inside of my visor. Once I finished the route, it would be time for me to head back to HQ. I wasn't keen on going back there, especially with tensions rising and the pressure Citomy was placing on the Empire – but it was better than what would potentially happen to the Syldrari if I tried to stay with any of them. For whatever reason, Zafir seemed content to remain utterly silent. I figured he must have been overseeing things for one of my teammates.

I glanced down at myself, noting the blood clinging to my feet and lower legs. *Ugh, I can't go to the main thoroughfare like this.*

I moved far enough away from the gore that there was no more blood around my feet, then summoned a sphere of water between my hands and did my best to rinse off. As I worked, I caught the sound of slow, measured footsteps growing closer. Glancing to my left, I spotted the cultist strolling toward me with an intrigued smile on his lips, his arms crossed as he studied me. He wore the same long coat as before, but this time his hood was down.

I don't have time for this… I sighed, debating how to convey that to him. It wasn't like I had a sign to draw on, and I didn't want to assume he had the same ability as Jysel. My instincts told me to run, and I frowned. I hadn't felt that way about the one at Rel's café. But the first one… I eyed him warily, letting the water splash to the ground as I rose to my feet.

Same one…? No, I don't think so. Something is different.

Height? Yes, but also…ah. He moves *differently. Less gracefully.*

"I'm not here for you," he remarked, stopping a few yards away. "A shame, that. Your abilities seem quite intriguing. Elara, was it? An interesting choice of moniker…"

Seriously, what is Zafir— I re-focused on my visor, releasing an agitated sigh. Of course it was disabled. Why wouldn't it be?

"Oh, don't worry. I'm aware what your orders are. I know you can't respond." He chuckled, taking a few more steps toward me. "All you need to do is listen. Ah—but you were told we had left this planet, weren't you? I doubt you believed that."

I crossed my arms irritably, hoping he would get to the point.

He turned, fixing his bright green eyes on the cloudy sky. "The R'selkti, rogue clans, *my* clan, and so many other species… It draws everyone in, but why? This planet is unremarkable at best, now that the humans have swarmed over it like the plague they are.

"The explanation is the queens. So much power all on one planet draws attention from any species. Syldrari have always been valued as trading partners and allies…but the human empire is so young. How long have they been capturing queens and using them for experiments?

"Too long, most would say. *I* wanted a more accurate answer."

When he paused, I did the best *And?* motion I could.

"This planet once belonged to the Abyss Father. Someone took it from him, and gave it to the humans," he breathed, his eyes still on the sky. "We found the remains of Syldrari structures buried deep beneath the ice caps, and a few more by the equator. After some investigation, we discovered that the humans banned archaeological work on this planet centuries ago. Before there were fifty-three captive queens…we believe there was *one*.

"*You* do not make *sense*."

I sighed and shrugged. It wasn't like I had any answers, even if I wanted them. In a motion faster than I could follow, the cultist closed the distance and snatched off my visor. "Your *suit* is ancient! Syldrari haven't used this model for thousands of years! I wager the inside of your visor…" His eyes widened as he turned it over in his hands.

I held out a hand expectantly. "I need that back."

"*You* may not be ancient, but your suit…" He looked from my visor to me and back. "A survivor, perhaps? Or…"

He grew pale, his eyes widening and his mouth twisting in rage. "Did they…a queen… They wouldn't *dare*…"

"My visor. Please?" I reiterated, as the horrified man finally looked from my hand to my face.

Much like the others who had seen me without my visor while suited, the cultist looked astounded by whatever it was he saw. It was almost as if he was looking *into* me, not *at* me. He was so stunned that his control over his servant flickered several times.

Finally, he spoke in a measured, neutral tone. "Your files say that your memory was destroyed by the Resonance Incident.

That isn't true, is it?"

"Ah…" I sighed heavily and pressed my fingers to my temples. Considering I'd already spoken, and I was beginning to *hate* misinformation, I decided to answer him. "It's true that I don't remember anything prior to the Incident. However, the manner in which my memories were removed requires technology the humans would have had to steal, borrow, or buy. There is simply *nothing* where my memories should be. No chance for retrieval. Does that answer your question?"

"That would imply…" he whispered, taken aback. After a moment, he offered me my visor back. "I thank you for answering this vessel. This information changes matters, drastically. The R'selkti twins would not have been responsible, meaning they are not our target. We are back to where we began…but that is preferable to eliminating those who are not involved with this planet's injustices."

"Perhaps, instead of wildly chasing loose ends, you should focus on the actual looming threats," I suggested icily. "There are too many rumors of war hanging over this planet, and if the humans act—"

"Why do you care what we do?"

"Do you honestly think I want to see all life on this planet *and* in its orbit erased?"

He smiled slightly. "Point taken. The flora and fauna are beautiful…even if the self-proclaimed natives are not most of the time.

"We will advise our operatives to avoid incurring your wrath. We find *iri* like you are more reasonable when the natural world isn't in danger." He paused, clasping his hands behind his back. "One piece of advice. Train. Your elemental and more…*unique* abilities are leaking."

My…? Oh. After he'd vanished in a streak of neon green light, I looked around myself. Tiny electrical currents arced through the water pooling around me, and dark ooze shifted in the shadows. I let out a small sigh as I put my visor back on. *I guess it's well past time I utilized the amulet Rel gave me, isn't it? I can't be losing control during times like these.*

Lights shone above me, and I looked up to find a skycar drifting down into the alley. Acheron and Styx—Aisu and Maelor, respectively— dropped out of it in their suits and walked over warily. Aisu was the first to speak. "Zafir sent us to pick you up. Somethin' about losing contact?"

I released a small sigh. "Yeah. Let's go. I should make a report."

"Bring it down, Erik!" Maelor called, waving his arm.

The soldier obliged, and three of the doors swung upward. The others climbed in the back, while I took the seat next to Erik. He shot me an odd look, then pressed a button to close the doors and began to drive.

"Yeah, Zafir, we got her. Why?" Maelor asked aloud. "Uh…

One sec. Hey, Elara, can you check your visor? Zafir says it won't reconnect."

"Mmm?" I reached up and lightly tapped at the sides. When nothing changed, I pulled it off and eyed the interior, pausing when I spotted a tiny disc tucked into the blind spot. On its case was a single symbol I didn't recognize. I did my best to remove it without anyone noticing, then tried again. "Nope. Nothing."

Erik gave me the side eye. "Want to stop by Rel's real quick and let him know you're alright?"

I studied Erik's knowing expression, then turned my attention forward. "Sure, we can make a quick stop."

I tucked the case into the hem of one of my gloves and put my visor back on. Erik pulled up in front of Rel's closed café, but Rel was already on his way out when we landed.

"Be quick," Erik called as I got out.

"Right. Will do. Thanks." I nodded as I turned to meet Rel at the bottom of the outside stairs.

"Quickly and privately?" Rel inquired before I could open my mouth. He gave me a comforting smile. "I can see that you're rushed, concerned, and nervous. Come upstairs."

When we got into his apartment, I didn't waste any time. I took of my visor and set it aside, then pulled the disc out of my glove. "I came across another cultist…disciple, during my patrol. He slipped this into my visor after stealing it."

"Did he hurt you?" Rel narrowed his eyes, reexamining me.

"Nothing except my brain. Too much information on top of my conversation with Jysel." I shook my head, watching as Rel instead focused his attention on my visor.

"You saw Jysel? And had an actual *conversation?*" Rel glanced at me, surprised. "Well, that is an improvement. If only it hadn't taken such extreme circumstances to make him behave kindly. *Honestly.* He would do well to…"

He trailed off when he finally turned his attention to the disc, his gaze landing on the symbol I didn't recognize.

"What is it?" I asked, a little alarmed by Rel's reaction. He looked *livid*, his glow a deep red that looked almost black. I half-expected him to crush the object in his hand and be done with it.

"Does Zafir know about this?" he inquired quietly.

"No, my visor is busted. It won't reconnect to HQ." I frowned and moved over to Rel, grasping his arm. "What's wrong?"

"That will depend on the contents of this disc…" he hesitated, glancing down at me. "You can't stay?"

"I'm afraid not."

He released a long sigh, his gaze drifting away from me and to the floor. "I will look into the contents, but I won't promise to divulge them to you when next we meet."

"Can you at least tell me what the symbol is?" I asked with a small frown.

"I can tell you that it is either a word or a crest," he answered hesitantly. "Until I know more, and for certain, I will say nothing else on the matter; save that I believe he *intended* for you to bring this to either me or Jysel."

"And nothing else?" I sighed and gave him a tired smile. "I'm too tired to pout, especially when I'm certain you have my best interests in mind. Just do me a favor and don't forget about *your* best interests."

"Go get some sleep." He adopted a soothing tone, running his fingers through my damp hair. "Or at least a hot meal. You are *drenched*."

"Too tired to notice." I grimaced. Rel just shook his head and escorted me toward the door, though he hesitated to open it. "What is it, Rel?"

"I can't help but question whether letting you return to that place is the right move. How many times can you return there before you're changed into a new person?" He inhaled deeply and visibly steeled himself, his eyes focusing sharply. "I *will* find a solution, even if it requires that I go over Jysel and Zafir's heads."

"Hey, don't do anything foolish with these grandiose aims of yours," I countered, grabbing the front of his shirt and tugging to make him look down at me. "I want you in one piece—and alive, and sane, and *you*."

"And I simply want the same for you. We will find a way." He leaned down and kissed my forehead briefly. "Go. I shouldn't keep you…*yet.*"

With a smirk, he shooed me out the door and closed it firmly behind me. I grumbled under my breath, feeling heat rising in my cheeks at his insinuation.

"Ready?" Erik asked as I got back into the skycar.

"No. Let's go," I grumbled.

"Heh. Yes, ma'am."

CHAPTER FORTY-FIVE

I wandered into the common area, not quite paying attention as I went. Syldrari music played in my head via the chip—I'd chosen calming, slightly eerie music that made me think of some lurking, beautiful monstrosity. It wasn't until the sound of bratty bitching overpowered my music that I focused on my surroundings.

Zafir was approaching briskly, while my team sat on the sofas, looking ready to murder someone. On the far side of the room, I spotted a vaguely familiar human woman. After wracking my brain for a moment, I looked to Zafir. "Didn't I tell her to drink bleach? She disobeyed me? I'm disappointed."

"Come with me. Now." He steered me back in the direction of his office. Once there, he pinned me against the door and I noticed he seemed winded. His eyes were having trouble focusing, and his skin seemed to have grown damp—or reverted to its Syldrari texture. I couldn't quite tell which. "Elara…what do you think you're doing? Every Syldrari in the city is going to…"

"Hmmm? What? What? I'm not doing anything!" I exclaimed, alarmed as his head drifted downward, his expression hazy. "I just woke up and was listening to music while I try to calm down. I didn't sleep well, you know…nightmares. Um…what?"

Zafir stopped with his mouth by my neck and released a distressed groan. "*Elara… Order me to focus on professionalism for the next five hours. That…should buy us time to…*"

"To what?" I prompted as Zafir's disguise flickered briefly, revealing a neon pink glow. "Zafir? Answer me."

His gaze regained some clarity and he focused on my face. "Team B's leader is moving to this floor today. She is legitimately a human with modified genetics. We can't trust her, but she is Imperator Julien's daughter. We must tolerate her."

"I…" His gaze went cloudy again, his human disguise melting away completely. He dropped to one knee and bowed his head. When he spoke again, he sounded fully Syldrari—even his accent had returned. "How may I serve you?"

What in the… I stared at him, utterly taken aback. His plea for me to order him to focus on professionalism suddenly made sense. "Zafir, you're to focus on working professionally for the next five hours of this planet's time. You have work to attend to, and we need to find a way to stop…whatever I'm doing."

The lights came on all at once, his glow abruptly going from bright pink to a deep yellow. He rocketed to his feet and glanced away in discomfort before disguising himself again.

"Can you explain to me what I'm doing, so I can try to stop?" I asked gently, placing a hand on his arm.

"You are…ah…" He struggled with his words for a moment. "It seems that you are effectively broadcasting your availability and status. Accidents such as this are how we usually discover queens. They lose control for one reason or another and… You said you were having nightmares?"

"Mhm. About…well, that woman who was eaten. Sights, sounds, smells. I can't get it out of my head, and the nightmares make it worse."

"…And you are reliving the binding of that criminal as well?"

I stared at him in realization. "Oh. I see where you're going with this. Yes."

"Try to…do the opposite of that. Considering you mimicked one of Jysel's powers, perhaps you can work out how to reverse your own," he suggested eagerly. "There is no telling how far you projected yourself. Every Syldrari in the system could have felt it, for all we know. You need to stop, and quickly, before someone manages to trace it specifically to you."

I did as he said, envisioning pulling everything 'me' inward, much as I did when I tried to stop any electrical discharge. I glanced to him questioningly.

"Thank the Abyss Father…" He sighed heavily, tilting his head. "Mmm…that doesn't quite have the right sound to it now."

"So, what does *super* bright pink mean?" I inquired curiously, eliciting a flinch from Zafir as he leaned away from me.

"…*Must* I answer that question? Had I been more composed, I would never have shown such a taboo—"

"I wouldn't say you *must*, but I would appreciate it since that color keeps coming up." I placed a hand on my hip and eyed him as he hesitated. "You don't *have* to, but forewarned is forearmed. Right?"

"Ah…yes…" he grumbled, flushing and turning his head away. "It…pardon my rather blunt phrasing, but I believe it would translate to 'wanting to fuck someone blind.' It is pure, unfiltered, all-consuming lust. It is considered incredibly rude to show such a color. I must apolo—"

"Nope. No apologizing. I should be the one apologizing for putting you in an uncomfortable situation with my powers," I interjected firmly. "But we should get back to work before people get suspicious. Have I withdrawn whatever I was doing well enough?"

"Yes…you did so quite well," he murmured thoughtfully. "I would like to study it further, but you are right. We should deal with Sydney."

I followed Zafir out of his office and back to the common

area, where the woman in question had turned her attention to my team members. She seemed to be trying to make them do things for her, but no one was having it.

"They're my team, not yours. Sit down and be quiet," I snapped as we approached. Several guards visibly stifled their amusement, while the researcher who had accompanied Sydney shot us a tired smile.

"How dare you! I am the Imperator's daughter. You should be thankful I haven't had you sent to the brothels for your treatment of me!" Sydney snapped back, her arms crossed.

"The Imperator's daughter, you say?" I gave her a cold smile. "I see. Then I will have to have your bones fashioned into dinnerware. I'm sure he'd be happy to see you finally making yourself useful."

"Please, ladies," a familiar voice interjected. I glanced over my shoulder to see General Crowe and another group of guards approaching us. "Sydney, this is Elara. You will be learning from her. If you want to learn to survive, you'll want to listen to her."

Sydney smirked. "Ohhh, so this is the bitch I'll be replacing after she retires?"

"Elara," Crowe began tiredly when my eyes narrowed, "that is *not* what she is here to do. Her team will be separate from yours and requires training. Aisu will be taking over your team when you *do* retire.

"If Sydney doesn't make herself useful, you have the authority to send her to be reprogrammed with a better attitude, or processed for the reproduction program."

"Hah! As if that will happen!" She dismissed the notion with a shake of her head. "That punishment is reserved for worms who are so incredibly useless that—"

Ignoring her ramblings, I raised an eyebrow at Crowe. "Even though she's the Imperator's daughter?"

That didn't sound right. Not at all. I almost felt sorry for her.

"Imperator Julien hopes that military service will correct her personality," Crowe answered, keeping his tone neutral. "If she is too problematic, she is to be treated just the same as any other soldier requiring disciplinary action. Understood? She is not to be coddled."

"Oh yeah? And where's my permission to send *her* to the— eek!" Sydney ducked behind a couch when I directed a mass of dark, glimmering ooze along the floor in her direction. She clutched the back of the sofa frantically as she tried to keep from being sucked into the floor.

While she struggled, I addressed the general in a calm voice. "I understand my orders, sir. Am I to train her as I do my team?"

"Yes. Treat her just as fiercely. We have no use for soft soldiers." Crowe cracked a smile, then looked to Zafir. "Furthermore, I have orders for both of you. Your office, Professor?"

"Certainly," Zafir answered, fidgeting with his glasses. "Elara..."

"She'll be fine. For now." I looked over at my snickering teammates. "See to it she learns some etiquette. If she continues to be a bitch, throw her in virtual for a while. She's going to need exposure training."

"Exposure training? What— Get back here. I'm talking to you!" Sydney snarled.

I inclined my head in Crowe's direction. "Sir, permission to—"

"Oh, how I wish. But no. We have orders to keep her alive." Crowe shook his head and linked his hands behind his back. "Even individuals such as her have their uses. We know the Syldrari won't take her in exchange for Rel or Jysel, so unfortunately we are stuck with her."

I frowned, a little unsettled by Crowe's comments. "Sir?"

"Bah, the Empire is fighting itself on the question of whether to annihilate the Syldrari ships or work with them," Crowe answered with a grimace.

"If I may... What is your opinion, sir?" I inquired curiously.

"Mine? We should be working with the ancient races toward the betterment of humankind," he remarked earnestly. "Our species and our Empire, they are young. There is too much knowledge just out of our reach because of imbeciles who think progress should be wrought solely by human minds and hands."

As we entered Zafir's office, he turned and nodded to Crowe.

"You mentioned orders, sir?" he inquired.

"Yes—we would like Elara to go keep an eye on this 'Rel'

person's café today. There are rumors circulating that there might be an attack on the Syldrari sector, and his establishment specifically, today." He glanced my way. "You're to keep him inside no matter what. If that means seducing him and using him for entertainment for a few hours—you've got my permission. Indefinitely."

"Uh…" I stared at him in disbelief.

"As for you, Zafir, I've got some samples for you to look into from off-world," he continued, looking to Zafir, then back at me. "Elara, you're dismissed."

"Yes, sir…?" I left as asked, completely baffled. Was it an attack on the Syldrari sector in general or Rel specifically? And I was *allowed* to fuck his brains out to keep him indoors? I grimaced when I felt a twinge between my legs.

Let's just…not think about that part. Nope. Not after the way today has already been going.

When I entered Rel's café, I found myself faced with Aldiner, Ciheri, and a pole that looked as though it didn't belong in the room. The two Syldrari were dressed in skintight body suits with translucent cutouts, the feet of which ended in heels that caused them to absolutely *tower* over me.

"What are you two wearing? What are you *doing*?" I stared

at them in disbelief. Aldiner abruptly stopped speaking in Syldran to Ciheri, whose hands were on the pole. The two of them smiled deviously, then grabbed me by the arms and led me over to a seat.

"You can watch me teach Ciheri how to dance!" Aldiner exclaimed excitedly. "Having an audience always helps."

"Mm. With the city so cramped, and my general disinclination to leave this building, Aldiner suggested I turn to dance for exercise," Ciheri added, giving me a cheerful smile. "I hear it can be quite entertaining! Plus, it strengthens the entire body."

"And the clothes?" I asked.

"What about them?" He blinked, then looked down at himself. "You don't like it?"

"Ohhh, right, Elara doesn't know," Aldiner remarked, clicking his tongue. He twirled gracefully around the pole in an impressive acrobatic maneuver. When he landed, he was facing me with his back against the pole and his arms crossed. "Syldrari clothing isn't gendered like human clothing. The six sexes all wear similar things—there's the general concept of feminine and masculine, of course, but that is so the consumer can decide what they find aesthetically appealing."

"Uh... so... You know what, I'm not going to question it." I rubbed my temples and shook my head. "You look good and you're comfortable—that's what it boils down to, right?"

"Human clothes are gendered?" Ciheri looked quizzically to Aldiner. "Is that why I get weird looks when we go to human stores?"

"Yes, it is," Aldiner stated dryly. "Humans struggle with self-expression. Don't worry about it too much.

"Now then! Let's start with the— Oh. Wait. Elara, why are you here? Did no one at HQ satisfy you?"

"*I'm on duty*," I growled defensively. "Dammit. That bullshit reached all the way *here*?"

"Hey, it's one of your gifts! Don't be mean to you!" Ciheri protested. He leaned forward, his expression distressed. "It was an accident, right? I'm sure there was a good reason. Why don't you just relax and watch us dance? That'll help calm you down and bring you peace, right?"

"I don't know about that… I'm on duty, and this type of dancing—" I started slowly.

"Aldiner, Ciheri, I'm going to go find Elar…" Rel spoke from somewhere behind me. There was a sharp intake of breath, and the room seemed to shudder. "We have discussed this! *No pole dancing in my café*! This is not a nightclub—take it upstairs!"

"Elara too?" Aldiner asked slyly, slinging his arms around my shoulders. "Or maybe the four of us—"

"Elara is remaining here with me. *Do not make me tell you twice.*" His dangerous tone did the trick. The pair quickly packed up their things and fled upstairs.

Rel placed a hand on the back of my chair, tilting it so that my feet were no longer on the ground and he could look down at me. "What are you doing here, Elara?"

"Duty calls, and all that," I answered with a smile – but something about my expression seemed to displease him. "What is it?"

"You look exhausted. Let me take a guess," he began in a grouchy voice, lifting me right out of the chair, "you barely slept because of nightmares, and the contents of those nightmares led to this morning's incident. After regaining control, you found yourself with orders to come here for whatever reason."

He deposited me in a seat at the bar, then locked the front door and closed the curtains. He even switched his sign from 'open' to 'closed.'

"Yeah...you're right on the money so far. I had no idea I was even doing it until Zafir—"

"Did he hurt you?" Rel demanded, his expression and tone equally fierce.

"No?" I stared back at him, baffled by his leap to conclusions. "He didn't *do* anything other than kneel and ask how he could serve me. Well, before that, he asked me to order him to be professional since he knew what was happening. I didn't do it until after he knelt, though—that was how I realized what was going on."

"I doubt any Syldrari on the planet missed that..." he muttered, leaning his elbows on the counter and covering his face with one hand. "The queens may have missed it, as they aren't susceptible to other queens. But..."

"I'm sure that's all important, but we should focus on the reason I'm here," I interjected pointedly. "There are rumors circulating that there will be an attack on the Syldrari sector—and specifically this café—today. I'm to keep you inside at all costs, quote, 'Even if it means using you for entertainment for a few hours.' Their words, not mine."

"An attack…" His eyes widened. "Forgive me, but taking you to bed is not on my list of priorities if my clan is in danger. I need to contact the other Elders and our soldiers."

"No offense taken. I figured you would be reasonable," I answered amusedly. "Can you contact them without going outside?"

"Who is to say this isn't a ploy to take us both out at once?" he countered with a low growl.

"Mmm… I have a hunch it's a misdirection. When did you last speak to Jysel?" I glanced toward the clock, then back to Rel—whose expression had grown defensive the moment I'd mentioned his twin.

"Not since you last saw us together."

I nodded, mostly to myself. "Thought so… I hate to impose, but could I ask for a drink while I explain what happened last night? You need the information too, and it will explain his whereabouts. Plus, I'm fairly sure it's the reason you and I are here right now."

"Impose?" He arched an eyebrow and glanced to either side,

then back to me. "You wouldn't be troubling me. Ah, you're still a tad rattled by your power, aren't you? Perhaps a drink with soothing qualities…yes, that might work."

He turned his back to me and busied himself with making the drinks, while I proceeded to explain the incoming fleet, the repositioning of the resonance weapon, and Jysel's decision to act.

"Is the fleet's identity still unknown?" he inquired, placing a glass of pale green liquid in front of me.

"Uh, let me check…" I pulled out my communicator and swiped quickly through the various apps until I reached the one specifically dedicated to HQ.

"Is there a reason you do it that way?" Rel wondered, his head cocked like a curious dog. "I mean no offense, it's just…odd."

"Odd?" I looked blankly from the communicator to him and back. "I don't know. It's just how I do it? Is there another…oh. *Right*. I forgot I can use the chip for that, um…"

Rel's mouth pulled into an amused smile as he leaned against the counter so his eyes were closer to my level. "Do what makes you comfortable. I was merely curious."

"Uh huh…" I grumbled, embarrassed, as I finished pulling up the list of new notifications. "It says here that they've been identified, but it's classified. They're not currently seen as a threat, as their course appears to be set for uncharted space, not this planet as we originally thought. However, they're still tracking the fleet with the resonance weapon until it's out of the system. Let's see…"

I felt something against my lips and flicked my attention to Rel. He had lifted my glass so that the straw was by my mouth, an amused, oddly dreamy expression on his face.

Noting he had my attention, he chuckled. "You did say you wanted a drink. Don't go getting too distracted to enjoy it."

"Thanks," I murmured, taking a brief slurp. "Anyway, I think we've been assigned the role of distraction. Sort of, anyway. The response doesn't really seem right for a suspected attack, and I wasn't given any details as to what sort of threat it might be."

"Well, one of us is likely right, and it would be best if it were you," he remarked, setting my glass down and giving me a contemplative look. "Hmmm, how to pass the time… And no, I am not reopening the café for the day."

"And I'm sure you can't tell me any of the things I actually want to know," I added thoughtfully. "In which case, I should probably focus on practicing with the medallion you gave me. I've been losing control of my powers a lot lately, and I get the impression Ciheri hasn't made much progress with his investigation into queen abilities."

"Yes, you do seem rather charged up of late…" Rel drew his fingertips briefly across the bar as he strolled along the length, then rounded the corner and finished up to my left. "Lightning, water, and…hmmm. It would be easier to advise you if I knew the extent to which Zafir has investigated your abilities."

"Didn't I say I don't want to impose?" I raised an eyebrow.

"Training you is reward enough," he answered slyly, a suggestive smile pulling at his lips. "Or were you thinking that your superiors' suggestion was more appealing?"

"Um…" I faltered. It wasn't exactly like I could say *no*. "What I was *thinking* is that I should probably learn to control my lightning, so I don't accidentally electrocute anyone I want to keep in one piece."

"I wouldn't complain if you…" He sighed heavily and looked toward the nearby stairs. A few moments later, I heard footsteps. "What is it, Ciheri?"

Ciheri peered shyly around the corner. "Um… About Elara's abilities, I did discover a few things…"

"Come here, then," Rel stated with a sigh. "You needn't lurk."

"Ah, I didn't want to intrude…" Ciheri flushed, his glow turning silver even as he darted over to us.

Rel sighed again and put an arm around Ciheri's shoulders. "It's fine, Ciheri. One of our highest priorities should be helping Elara learn to control her powers, considering this morning's accident."

"Mm, but if she's lived around humans, ah…" Ciheri flushed darker and glanced away from me.

I had an idea what he was implying, though I wasn't sure how best to broach the subject. After a second, I slowly spoke. "Sooo, I had an interesting conversation with Jysel last night?"

"About something actually meaningful? Impressive," Rel

remarked sarcastically.

"Mhm, well, we were so utterly confused by each other's statements that I'm not surprised," I answered, shooting him an amused look. "You see, I had some misconceptions and thought *everyone* bound to a queen was technically in a relationship with her. Which then resulted in a conversation about human-versus-Syldrari relationship customs…"

"He was *patient* with you?" Rel inquired, clearly astounded. "When it comes to the illogical nature of monogamy, he gets quite defensive because of…" He paused, his eyes widening, when I gave him a knowing look. "…He *told* you about our father's illness? By the… If he desires to be so open with you…hmmm, it is no wonder the imbecile once feared you had already claimed us. Such openness is very unlike him."

"I'm…not sure I follow?" Ciheri looked a little distressed.

Rel proceeded to explain what had happened with their father and his 'quirks,' then I gave them the short version of what I'd discussed with Jysel. Eventually, Rel drifted behind the counter and started making some sort of dough while he absorbed the information.

"Humans are *weird*," Ciheri remarked with a heavy sigh.

"Is that the scientific term?" I teased with a small smile.

"Ah! No—" He spotted my playful expression and gave me a sheepish grin. "I don't think the humans would particularly like any of our terms for them. They're proving to be quite accurate, though."

"Humans have a saying: The truth hurts," Rel stated dryly. "All you need to know about them, Ciheri, can be extrapolated from that statement."

"Huh?" Ciheri stared at Rel in disbelief. "But lies and other forms of falsehoods are destructive! Humans may be...ill-equipped...to handle the truth, but that is something that can be fixed by adjusting their culture and bolstering their understanding of mental health. They—"

"They aren't your responsibility to fix," I remarked, stretching in my seat and letting out a long sigh. "Anyway—"

My communicator started buzzing with a frantic tone I didn't recognize and, confused, I pulled it out and looked at the screen. The caller was Zafir, and there were little exclamation points all over the screen.

After glancing in bewilderment at my two companions, I answered it. "Hello—"

<Is there any chance at all you could go into hiding?> Zafir asked sharply, causing both Rel and Ciheri to drop everything as they squeezed close to listen in.

"Doubtful, Zafir. I'm not a magician." I raised an eyebrow when he released a shaky sigh.

<You're at Rel's? Go up to the second floor and look to the northeast.>

Ciheri and Rel followed me upstairs, where I managed to catch a glimpse of smoke on the far side of the city.

"Is that…?" I murmured.

<The weapons platform was attacked overnight.> Zafir hesitated, his voice strained. <You have orders to do a sweep of the building and search for survivors. Your team has been assigned various basement levels, and you the top floors of the structure, where the control and access rooms are. It's…>

I glanced at Rel when I felt his hand on my shoulder, his grip tight. Grimacing, I addressed Zafir. "If my team is going, then I should too. I don't want to abandon them to whatever fate they may find there. However…if we're investigating the building, where is the smoke coming from?"

<The surrounding complex. We believe the main building was left relatively untouched. All scans show that the structure is intact, no fires or weak life signs. It seems that only the surrounding buildings were destroyed, and we can't determine whether the weapon was too.> He hesitated, his voice dropping low. <I need to go. One of Citomy's delegates recognized the weapon and demanded all our data on it. If we don't comply…>

"I get it. Is someone on the way to pick me up?"

<Erik will be there soon.> He sighed nervously. <Be careful, Elara. I…I hope you don't find a truly Syldrari mess on your hands.>

When I lowered the communicator, Rel offered, "And by that, he means he's concerned that Jysel truly let his hunters loose. It may have been a bloodbath."

"It's one thing after another..." Ciheri grumbled, throwing both arms around me and pressing his cheek against mine. "Be careful! We want you back in one piece. Cuddles are best that way!"

Uh...what's a cuddle? I wondered, then caught Rel's expression. He'd *clearly* heard that. *Oh, don't try to pretend you didn't hear that, Rel. Your brother already screwed up on that. I know you can both hear my thoughts if you want to.*

He looked briefly taken aback, then gave me a wry smile and placed a hand on top of my head. "I agree with Ciheri, of course. Be careful. The building likely isn't as safe as the human instruments would have you believe."

"I will." I nodded, then side-eyed the sulking Ciheri, who was still squeezing me. "Ciheri? Can you give us the short version of what you've learned about queens while you two walk me to my transport?"

That seemed to perk him up a little, and he immediately began talking. "So, I found out that it's only recently that most queens are forced to practice on *people*—it's theorized that this is to trick young queens into quickly building disorganized, eclectic clans that can never truly focus on anything.

"Before that was the common practice, however, queens learned to control their power by learning to control their other abilities; in your case, lightning, water, and whatever else you might have. Syldrari abilities all have similar structures, meaning that learning to control water or lightning naturally increases your control over whichever one troubles you."

"Similar, but not identical?" I asked with a slight frown.

Ciheri nodded excitedly. "Yes, the structure for elemental abilities varies if you're using a solid, a liquid, a gas, and so on. Think of it like…every power has its ideal container, and its ideal accelerant. The structure contains both."

"And we will be here for months if we give Elara a basic course on aetherology, natural and synthetic structures, or any of the related topics," Rel interjected gently, turning to face me. "In short, practice with what I gave you. I can work additional exercises into your martial arts training."

"You're sweet and all, but we have to go." Erik spoke firmly as he came over to us, his rifle aimed at the ground. He glanced around, then locked eyes with Rel. "You good here, or should I send for a few guards?"

"We will be fine," Rel answered with an amused smile. He looked meaningfully at me. "Hunt wisely."

CHAPTER FORTY-SIX

This doesn't seem right. I grimaced as I strode through the area surrounding the weapon's compound. There was human blood everywhere, along with signs of fighting with various forms of weaponry – yet there were no bodies anywhere. Instead, I could see drag marks and occasional scorches on the ground from a craft's recent comings and goings.

I doubt they took prisoners. In which case…who moved the bodies?

I sniffed the air hesitantly. From what I'd read, burning human flesh smelled akin to pork. However, all I could smell was burning buildings, chemicals, and something vaguely rubber-like. Nothing like meat or hair.

<We have a problem.> Zafir spoke quickly in my ear. <Our bosses are having me route the feed from your visor to all major news outlets. They're saying something about the possibility of you doling

out a public execution. Elara, I think…I think they may still be in there. You need to be careful. This is the last time during the mission I will be able to speak freely—I'm about to set up the feed now.>

"Fuck. Seriously?" I hissed. "Do what you have to do. I'll figure something out."

Of fucking course they were hoping for bloodshed. I felt anger writhe inside my chest like a caged animal, clawing at my ribcage. Steadying my breath, I stuffed it back down and sharpened my senses. This was the *worst* possible time for me to go feral—to enter the state of *kuhir-dal*? Whatever the proper term was.

Upon entering the main building, I scanned the area for signs of movement and stepped quietly across the bloodied floor. While there were no corpses yet, the blood spatter on the walls and the smears on the floor made it obvious the Syldrari hadn't been wasting time. If anyone had tried to fight, they died.

I swept two floors before I came across signs of recent conflict. Several human corpses littered the floor, blood slowly leaking from wounds to their throats or heads. Simple, lethal elegance. One or two strikes at most. Efficient.

In one of the last rooms, I found a man who clearly wasn't a soldier sitting in the corner, huddled into a ball. His eyes were wide, blood covering his arms and hands. He squeaked out a pathetic whimper upon spotting me.

"Are they still here?" I asked pointedly. "Soldiers will be coming to extract you soon."

"H-here, yes...up...up..." He raised a shaking hand and pointed at the ceiling, unable to say anything else but 'up.'

"Sit tight." I moved out of the room, stowing any form of emotion – such as sympathy – away for when the mission was over. Until then, I needed to focus. *Still here...? Then the attack wasn't overnight at all. What happened to the corpses outside? Was it Jysel's group, or...?*

I forced my mind into silence for the moment. If it *hadn't* been Jysel's group, I didn't need some unknown Syldrari hearing my conscious thoughts. Until I knew what I was dealing with, both my mind and body needed to be silent.

The next several floors were littered with the corpses of both guards and other staff. A severed artery here, a shot through the skull there, a few decapitated heads... Rather than the brutal, emotion-filled killings I'd half-expected, these were cold and businesslike. The people clearly hadn't been the target—but they had gotten in the way. Jysel's team was focused on efficiency.

It wasn't until I was three floors from the roof that I heard sounds of life. Syldrari life. By now, I understood enough of Syldran tones to determine that orders were being given to a smaller force. Orders that came, undoubtedly, from Jysel. My heart sank—I knew I wasn't a match for him, and he'd likely be furious over my slip-up with my powers. Compound that with my visor being hooked up to a news feed…

I decided reaching out first was the smartest thing I could do. Walking straight in would have been stupid, but I didn't have much time before my superiors began ordering me to move in.

Jysel, I need you to listen carefully. I have orders to stop your group and rescue any survivors. The fucking imbeciles at HQ forced Zafir to route my visor's feed to every news channel on the planet.

I can't back down, and you need to finish this job. We're going to have to give them a believable show.

There was no response at first, but I heard him continuing to give his men orders. When he finally answered via my chip, he said, [I understand. My men have been briefed. I recommend you play good little Imperial soldier if we are going to make this believable.]

I steadied myself before kicking down the door and calling lightning around my fists, taking an offensive stance. "By order of the Imperator, you are to stand down and cease hostilities at once!"

Jysel paused mid-speech to his men and half-turned to look at me, a downright *evil* smile on his lips. He held up a hand when one of his men raised a rifle and said something to him in Syldran before addressing me. "The humans would stop us saving their planet from this patchwork toy they call a weapon?"

"Sir, there's reinforcements on the way. We should hurry,"

Casair reported in the human language, taking a step forward and narrowing his eyes at me. "Let me take care of the human."

"No… No, you take the men. Finish the mission. I *will* have my rematch." Jysel let his suit disappear and began tugging off his gloves. As he did, he took graceful, predatory strides toward me.

<Lethe, stop his men!> Crowe barked in my ear.

In response, I launched forward, prepared to summon a wall to block them. Jysel was beside me in the blink of an eye, catching my arm and spinning me right out of the room. I crashed back-first into a wall, though he hadn't actually thrown me very hard. I recovered quickly, but his men had already disappeared.

"Now that I have you to myself…" Jysel rubbed his chin as he examined me, making a show of suggestively running his long, glowing blue tongue over his lips. "Why don't you tell me why the humans want to destroy themselves so badly?"

<What is he talking about? That weapon is our strongest defense! We can't let them disable it.> Voices I didn't recognize started arguing in my ear.

Suddenly, Citomy's voice cut through them. <Someone get me the blueprints for this weapon. My son is foolish but he isn't an imbecile.>

<Still, we can't let this villain get away with attacking—>

"You want a villain?" Jysel inquired, a devious sparkle in his eyes. "*Fine.* I will show you a villain. Killing your so-called 'protector of the peace' should suffice, yes? But first…I think I'll have some fun with her."

<Lethe, get out of— What in the heavens is that noise?>

I narrowed my eyes within my visor and raised my fists, sensing Jysel coiling to attack. His first strike missed, flying straight past my face. I twisted into a kick, but he caught my ankle in one hand and grabbed me around the throat with the other.

"Say goodbye to your precious heroine," he stated in a calm, powerful tone, his voice causing the air to practically vibrate.

[Uppercut me with your right hand. When I try to take your visor again, try to dodge—but fail. We need to remove that particular annoyance and let their imaginations run wild. ...And I apologize, but this little sparring session is going to hurt.]

Fine.

He feigned being taken off-guard as I did as he asked, then I pursued him with kicks and electrically-charged hand strikes, all of which he easily dodged. Distressed murmuring filled my ears as whichever superiors were watching realized that Jysel was wearing what amounted to a dress uniform, while they believed me to be fully armored.

<We should have her pull out, Imperator. Without better weapons—>

Jysel blurred, appearing inches away from my chest. His fingers grasped my visor and pulled it off, throwing it straight through the window and breaking the glass. He pinned me against the wall, a devious smile spreading across his lips as he studied my face.

When he spoke again, it was aloud. "Was that convincing enough for you, *salaith-daiyr?*"

"You know that won't be enou—" I went silent when he gripped me firmly by the jaw, his gaze blazing with some emotion I couldn't identify. His glow swirled with black, garnet, and navy.

"Are Zafir and Rel alright?" he asked calmly, his voice a stark contrast to the intensity of the emotion running through him.

"They are. Zafir helped me regain control of myself this morning," I answered calmly, bringing a hand up and lightly gripping his wrist. "My nightmares are getting out of hand, but this isn't the time or place to discuss that. Do you really think you can just let me go like this without drawing suspicion from the government?"

He sighed, cocking his head to the side as he studied me. "What, you don't want to kill me for all the humans we executed here today? I was expecting at least some degree of righteous fury."

"They got in the way of your mission, so they had to die. If your mission is halted, billions will die instead of a few hundred. It's logical." I gave him a puzzled look. "Sacrifice the few for the many and all that. But you and I—"

"—need to fight?" he finished, his eyes drifting to my lips and throat before he studied my bodysuit. "Fine. You want to be convincing? Then show me what you've learned from Rel. There is something I've been wanting to test, anyway."

"What's that?" I asked warily as Jysel strode into the more open room I had originally found him in.

"I want to know how much it takes to make you fall into *kuhir-dal*."

CHAPTER FORTY-SEVEN

I blocked a kick with my forearms, shoving his leg out of my way and shifting to side-kick him in the ribs with my booted foot. The impact was like kicking a concrete post. I'd definitely landed a solid strike, but it didn't do jack shit.

The amused Syldrari gracefully flipped his grip on his sword and punched me in the gut with that same hand, the sword's pommel thankfully missing my ribs. Even so, I crumpled to the ground, struggling for air, as he contemplated what to attempt next.

We had returned to our more private communication methods as the cameras inside the facility had recently reconnected—something he could apparently either hear or see.

[Mmm... You are certainly more resilient now, *salaith-daiyr*,] Jysel remarked, crouching down to my level. [I do dislike hurting someone when they're down, but if this is to be convincing...]

I told you to go all out, so go all out, I retorted bitterly.

His foot connected with my stomach, lifting me into the air and sending me tumbling. I struggled, trying to get up, when a piercing sound rang through my skull, making my vision go momentarily black.

When I recovered, it took my eyes a moment to fully focus on what I was seeing. I was lying several yards away from where I'd lost my sight, my body aching with several new wounds. Cursing internally, I tried to shove the struggling feral back into its cage.

Jysel stood over me, the tip of his sword pressed over my heart, his expression utterly emotionless. [I could kill you right now. Why have you not fallen?]

I won't let kuhir-dal *control me, it isn't...* I winced as the weapon dug against my chest, stopped only by the incredible resistance of the suit.

[Then I will make the *kuhir-dal* truly come out to play. If you are going to survive...] He trailed off, seemingly unwilling to state what he was planning. Instead, he raised his sword, his expression still frozen in that eerie, emotionless mask.

He swung down with full force toward my throat. A fount of overwhelming rage erupted within me, and everything inside my head went blank.

CHAPTER FORTY-EIGHT

"Don't start with me. She'll live." Jysel stalked past his fuming twin and the TV, though he hesitated upon spotting Elara's bloodied body being raised on a stretcher.

"'Don't start'?! She looks *dead*! Every station is talking about the color of her blood and theorizing about what the government's intentions are!" Rel grabbed his twin by the front of his uniform and slammed him back against the wall, pausing when he saw the amount of blood covering his brother. Blood that didn't smell like Elara's. "What—"

"*Kuhir-dal.* Hers—" Jysel erupted into pained curses in multiple languages as Rel peeled back the strips of his uniform, revealing deep, bestial wounds, singe marks, and punctures.

"By the Abyss Father, *what*—" Rel exclaimed. He immediately pulled Jysel's arm over his shoulders, helping him to walk upstairs. "Your wounds need to be cleaned before we can heal them. What happened?"

"I succeeded in forcing Elara to fall into *kuhir-dal*." Jysel groaned, shaking his head loosely. "She is…much more dangerous if allowed to enter that state. It took nearly killing her to stop her. She will be fine, but she's a monstrous warrior. Healing her wounds while still fighting, it's… I don't think she feels anything when she's like that. Her mind was a void of silence."

"Ciheri, go find something to replenish Jysel's strength," Rel ordered as he passed the still-stunned man. "And tell Aldiner to find Casair. We'll need to relocate Jysel to his hideout the moment we can."

Rel helped his twin into the apartment and sat him down on the couch before hurrying to gather the supplies needed to clean his injuries. As he worked, he asked, "You're telling me this was really necessary?"

"If you didn't want one or both of us to die…" Jysel left it at that.

"Did you finish the mission, at least?" Rel sighed irritably. He *didn't* want either of them to die, and he hadn't exactly been there for either the fight or their conversation, so he chose to trust Jysel's judgement.

Jysel nodded, teeth gritted, as he tried not to shy away from the liquid Rel was currently pouring over his wounds.

When he had a moment's reprieve, he stated, "The weapon has been destroyed—there will be no salvaging parts this time. Most of the humans involved with its construction and maintenance are dead; unless they receive new bodies from their government, of course. I'm sure they were being backed up regularly."

"Why didn't you return with Casair, you utter—" Rel jammed a cloth against one of Jysel's injuries hard enough to make him yowl in pain. "Well?"

"Their orders were to get out the moment they were finished!" Jysel answered, shying away from his angry twin. "Enough! It was painful enough to fight a queen we actually *appreciate!*"

"And your dark insinuations, the ones they aired on television?" Rel inquired dangerously, leaning toward Jysel.

"She asked me to make our conflict convincing, so I spoke in a language the humans would understand. We didn't do anything other than fight!" Jysel snapped back viciously.

Rel studied Jysel intently, then released a soft sigh. "'Convincing' is an understatement. I can only hope Zafir can use his medical knowledge to dispel the rumors that are circling. Even our mother has stepped in and is trying to insist you would not do such things."

"Yes, I'm sure she's terribly concerned as to how such rumors might affect her ability to sell us," Jysel hissed through gritted teeth, his glow shifting to deep red.

Rel sighed softly and placed a hand against his brother's chest, closing his eyes and emanating a melodic, resonating hum. Jysel groaned in pain as his cracked bones began to knit back together, bruises mending and gashes filling with new skin. A particularly nasty *pop* as something moved back into place caught him off guard, and he nearly choked on his own saliva.

Rel stepped aside, his work done, and watched as Jysel gasped for air, blood splattering the floor. Shaking his head, he walked a few feet away to wash his hands. "You will clean up the mess you've made—once you shower. Did you leave your wardrobe module behind, or…?"

"You're going to make *me* clean up—" Jysel cut himself off with an agitated growl. "…The shower is back there, right?"

"Indeed. I'll dispose of your clothes. Put them in the metal box." Rel nodded, side-eyeing his twin as he dried his hands on a plush towel. "Once Casair arrives, the three of us are going to discuss where to go from here. Understand?"

"Yes. Now we can focus on retrieving the important queen…" Jysel mused, a mischievous smile spreading across his face. He glanced over his shoulder at Rel. "We like her?"

Rel nodded. "We do."

"Then this poses opportunities…" Jysel murmured, mostly to himself, as he headed into the bathroom for a shower. "Many opportunities indeed."

Also: Please take a moment to leave a review!

Reviews are the lifeblood of any indie author and can make or break the success of a book. It doesn't need to be long, it could be a few words saying what you liked or five things you think could have been done better. Even a sentence or two would mean the world to me and would help me continue to write books in the future.

CONTINUE READING FOR HOW TO CONNECT WITH ME AND THE ILLUSTRATOR!

ABOUT THE AUTHOR

Bonnie L. Price was born in 1990 and has lived in four different states. At the age of twelve, while living in rural Upstate New York, she turned to writing as a way to entertain herself. Without internet or TV, there was little else to do during the long, cold winters.

What started as a way to amuse herself soon became a passion, and she's been writing ever since.

Want to connect with Bonnie?

PATREON: HTTPS://WWW.PATREON.COM/BONNIELPRICE

FAN GROUP: FACEBOOK.COM/GROUPS/BLP.DEMONDEN

DISCORD: HTTPS://DISCORD.GG/5UWSSC2

AUTHOR PAGE: FACEBOOK.COM/BONNIELPRICEOFFICIAL

TWITTER: HTTPS://TWITTER.COM/BONNIE_L_PRICE

ILLUSTRATION

In love with the cover illustration? Want to see more from the artist? Check out the link below for how to follow them!

https://www.artstation.com/rashedjrs